AN UNEXPECTED PROPOSAL

"I'm not looking for charity, Mr. McClain." The brown paper wrapping the garments rustled in Jessie's hand. "Besides, I won't be staying that long."

His broad back stiffened. "Yes, well . . . about that." He didn't face her, instead stared out the small window. "I have a matter to discuss. Vicky and my father had a conniption fit about you living here with me. Made me see how inappropriate it is and all."

Was he saying he'd made a mistake, that he didn't want her after all? Or perhaps he'd discovered the truth about her while in town?

"If you're having second thoughts—"

"Not entirely." He turned, but his gaze stayed glued to the spot on the floor. "Ma'am . . . Jessie . . . seeing as how you don't have a husband . . . and I don't have a . . . anyone . . . I think we should wed."

meet hers. "Not that I

own reputation, but to

ned from the room and

ng . . ."

KNIGHT ON THE TEXAS PLAINS

LINDA BRODAY

LEISURE BOOKS NEW YORK CITY

A LEISURE BOOK®

October 2002

Published by

Dorchester Publishing Co., Inc.
276 Fifth Avenue
New York, NY 10001

ISBN 0-8439-5120-6

Printed in the United States of America.

For my own knight, Clint,
who taught me that dreams are possible to obtain.

I don't have room enough here to devote to everyone who made this book possible. So many family members and friends believed in me and because of their faith I didn't give up. Special thanks to the beautiful ladies in my life: my mom, mother-in-law, and aunt.

I wish to express sincere gratitude to Helen Myers—I only hope one day to write as well. To my critique partner, Karen Kelley, you've given me unconditional friendship and love. To all the Red River Romance Writers who helped in immeasurable ways. I'm so glad to belong to this family of writers.

To Gigi and Lee for creating the first Marley Rose.

And in beloved memory of family and friends who have left this life. I salute you all. Sleep well.

Knight on the Texas Plains

Chapter One

Texas, 1880

The journey between yesterday and tomorrow dragged slowly, sometimes taking Duel McClain places he'd just as soon avoid. Like now. What the hell kind of place was Cactus Springs?

"Another card, mister?" The poker dealer's curt tone interrupted Duel's concentrated study of the amber contents in his whiskey glass.

The gurgle of a baby breached his self-induced haze. Bleary eyes focused on the child seated in the sawdust. Disgust rippled through him. Saloons were no place for nurslings.

Lazily, he put down the drink and pushed back his hat with a forefinger. He knew his unhurried attitude irritated the men seated around the table. Their state of mind didn't matter much to him. Time was a commodity he had plenty of.

"You come here to play poker or tiddledywinks?" the dealer prodded, prompting chuckles from the group.

Without glancing at the cards in his hand, Duel tossed three of the five onto the table. He figured it didn't make much difference. He merely breathed and took up space. Didn't have a reason to live or care about it—not anymore.

"Three."

Across the table, Duel caught a stranger's stare, watched his beady eyes narrow.

"Not much of a card player," the shifty man muttered.

Ignoring sarcasm came with the territory. No need to easily rise to the bait. Duel had learned to pick his battles. Yet something about this adversary turned his stomach more than some. Smelled worse than ripe horse manure—and that didn't pertain to his filthy clothes. The stench came from deep inside, from pure meanness. With sudden cursing, the poor excuse for humanity jerked the baby who strayed from his chair, smacking it hard before dropping it back to the sawdust floor.

Duel's jaw tightened. "Voicing an opinion without being asked will likely get a man a piece of lead for his trouble." His slow drawl carried the weight of the Smith and Wesson Schofield strapped to his leg. The threat earned him a small measure of satisfaction when the stranger dropped his gaze and fiddled with his cards.

If he was doing more himself than taking up space, he'd delight in teaching this jackass a thing or two. Truth to tell, Duel had become nothing more than a shell of a man. Too much losing and too little caring made his heart a bare slate like words on a tombstone wiped smooth by the harsh elements. This father, if that's what he was, and his kid weren't Duel's problem.

He lifted the whiskey glass and let the fiery elixir slide down his throat. The burning path brought an odd sort of relief, momentarily dulling the permanent ache that lodged in his belly.

With a noncommittal grunt, the dealer slapped three cards in front of Duel, who took his time picking them up. The baby, whimpering at the men's feet, unraveled the tightly knit threads of his composure. How could he concentrate with that sound?

A glance at the first card revealed an ace of spades. He stuck it between the eight of hearts and the two of clubs in his hand. Then he turned over an eight of diamonds. A pair might take the hefty pot in the middle of the table if he could bluff his way through it. That is, if he cared enough to try. One more card lay face down. Shielding it from the curious eyes of his opponents, he lifted it slowly. An ace of clubs.

His blood turned to ice.

Aces and eights—the deadman's hand. The unlikely draw struck dread in the hearts of all gamblers from Mississippi to Alaska ever since a sidewinder by the name of McCall shot Hickock in the back while he held that very array of cards.

A resigned calm welled up. If lady luck rode with Duel tonight, he'd not be taking up space much longer—except on Boothill.

Something brushed the leg of his buckskins. An animal must have sneaked under the swinging batwing doors and beneath the table. The baby's soft sniffling grew louder, and he hoped the dog or cat didn't harm the child. Whatever had motivated the father to bring a babe into the saloon? All sorts of harm could befall the infant.

Tiny hands gripping his buckskins got his attention. What in blue blazes? He leaned down. The baby had crawled to him and now tugged, trying to pull itself upright.

Thin and dirty, the child stared up at him and he fought against the protective urges that rose at the sight of tears glistening in the kid's big brown eyes.

"Up the bet, mister, or fold."

The dealer broke his trance. Duel pitched two bits onto the pile. He just wanted to get this over with and leave. One by one each opponent around the table tossed down their cards in defeat until it came to him again. Just two remained in the game—him and the stranger.

The baby played with the fringe running the length of Duel's leg, gurgling and trying to stick a piece in its mouth.

He shifted in his seat, feeling as if a gang of horse thieves had staked him out in a red-ant bed. If he had a lick of sense he'd fold and get the hell out of here. Deadman's hand be damned.

A smug expression drifted across the face of the babe's father when Duel closed up his cards, intending to lay them down.

Pure revulsion made Duel ache to smash the stranger's jaw. Instead he reached into his pocket for six bits, the amount of the bet plus a little extra—all that he possessed. He hesitated for only a split second, glancing down at the filthy child who deserved more out of life than the sorry-assed father it had gotten. Then he shifted his gaze, savoring the look of surprise on his opponent's face when he placed his bet.

The sour-faced weasel had been ready to reach for the pot, sure he'd won. His face colored. He was reduced to turning each of his pockets inside out for more coins. None came to light.

"Whatcha' gonna do, Will? Either come up with more or Duel here wins." The dealer's impatience grew.

"Just hold your horses." The man called Will leaned down. "Gal, where'd you go? Git your useless hide over here to your pa. Don't know why I didn't drown you when you was born."

So, the child was female. Didn't have much of a start in life. Duel reached down and drew her up. "Looking for this?"

The weasel snatched the girl by one fragile arm. "Tryin' to steal my daughter?"

Ignoring the question and the loud wails that came from the child, Duel leaned forward to scoop up his winnings.

"Not so fast, mister." Will sat the baby in the middle of the table. "I'm puttin' up this here brat. She's worth six bits I reckon. You win an' you got yourself a youngun."

"I won't gamble with a man's flesh and blood," Duel said. "You been eating locoweed?"

The dealer frowned. "The bet's proper, I say. Let's get on with it. Show your cards, Will."

Tears running down the face of the baby girl left white trails amid the filth. For a split second, Duel wished he held more than the lousy two pair. He wished could alter the hands of fate. But he'd never been able to change it before. What made him think he could now? He'd spent a lifetime making choices, and most had turned out wrong.

"Quit your sniveling, you brat," Will snapped at the child as he flipped his cards face up.

Two pair also. Kings and deuces.

Quiet calm washed over Duel. He gave the group a wintry smile and revealed his hand.

"Aces n' eights. Beats your pair, Will. Done in by the dead-man's hand." The dealer straightened his silk vest and poured himself a generous drink.

Duel stuffed the coins from the pot into his pockets. What on God's green earth did a man like him do with a babe? The girl had stuck a thumb in her mouth and sucked noisily on it between whimpers. He'd sooner grow wings and fly than take on the responsibility of another human being. Maybe he could just saunter out the door.

"Ain't you forgettin' something, mister?" Will's nasty snarl whipped the stale air like a thin, razor-sharp piece of leather.

Much as he sympathized with the small girl's lot, he couldn't accept his prize. "Take her home to her maw. Don't have any need for a kid."

Will grabbed his daughter's sparse hair and pulled her small face next to his own. Ignoring her sharp cries, he yelled, "Ain't got no maw. See there, Marley Rose. Ain't no one wants you. You're about as worthless as one of them Confederate greenbacks. Ain't never goin' to be any good for nothin'. Any o' you cowpokes wanna buy a snot-nosed brat? Sell her cheap."

Spurred by anger, Duel found himself reaching for the scared, helpless babe. "Changed my mind. Believe I'll take what I won."

Small hands clung tightly to the neck of his collarless shirt as he strode for the door before he could backtrack.

The last thing on earth he needed was another mouth to

feed. He must have lost what fool mind he had left. Maybe when the sun rose he'd find this had all been nothing more than a dream. Yet the girl's face snuggled against his chest told him reality had come home to roost.

Out on the sidewalk he took stock of the situation while he tried to untangle the girl's small fist from the tender tuft of hair that grew just below the hollow of his throat. But the little thing held her grip, refusing to release him. How tiny fingers no longer than a matchstick could cause so much pain he didn't know. The agony made his eyes water until, finally, he pried her hand loose.

Twinkling stars above shed little light on his predicament. His glance swept the length and breadth of Cactus Springs' main street. A few saloons and bordellos lined each side. Nothing suitable for a child.

Marley Rose sniffled loudly through the last of her tears. He glanced down. The liquid brown eyes staring curiously up at him brought a lump the size of a silver dollar to block his windpipe. He didn't blame her for being scared. Yet despite that, something else shone from those saucer eyes—trust. That was the part that did him in.

"Lord help us. Looks like it's just you and me, kid. Don't know if you're any better off than you were, but I sure as hell won't sell you. I promise you that."

A crooked smile curved her rosebud lips as Marley Rose examined his nose and mouth with probing fingers. He made darn sure they strayed no lower than his chin.

"Don't look at me that way. I'm dead serious. Haven't had a roof over my head in so long I can't remember, and I'm sorely in need of a bath. All I can offer you is hope for a better tomorrow. Thunderation! We don't even have a place to sleep unless you're counting the ground beneath our feet."

Marley Rose gurgled back contentedly, even though there wasn't a damn thing to be pleased with.

"Just wonder if you've got good sense, girl. Taking up with the likes of me at the drop of a hat. Don't know a dad-burned thing about babies. Guess we'll have to find you some milk before you start yammering again."

Tied to the hitching post, Preacher neighed and tossed his head. The movement sent moonlight dancing over the horse's black coat. Before Duel could take more than two steps toward him, a warm surge of wetness soaked his shirt.

"Of all the. . . ." Disgusted, he held Marley Rose at arm's length while a steady drip splatted the dusty street.

"Now you've done it! What the hell am I supposed to do now? I don't have a supply of dry . . . whatever they call those things you're wearing."

While he was contemplating his next move, a saloon girl swung from the establishment's doors, her heels tapping loudly on the wooden walk. She gave him a quizzical stare, then turned her attention to the babe and her puppetlike legs dangling from his grip.

"Trouble, mister?"

"Know where I can find baby needs this time of night?"

"Appears you could use some female savvy. I have a friend who has what you need. She'll be happy to lend a helping hand."

"Much obliged, ma'am." Duel breathed a sigh of relief when she took the child. He quickly grabbed Preacher's reins and fell into step beside her.

"Don't get much o' that around here." The woman's husky voice blended with the mysterious darkness.

"What's that?"

"Ma'am. Folks here in Cactus Springs ain't overly generous when it comes to showin' respect."

"Everyone deserves some dignity. I was raised to show good manners even if I don't have much else." Of late his belongings didn't include so much as a pot to piss in or a window to throw it out of.

Her tired gaze showed sympathy. "Name's Ellie." She jostled Marley Rose to her left arm and offered her hand. "Do you answer to anything besides mister?"

"Duel McClain."

"You're a good man, Duel McClain. I saw what happened in the saloon. That man oughta be horsewhipped."

"That's why I couldn't leave her behind, ma'am. Never cottoned to anyone who doesn't care spit for his own blood."

Near midnight, Duel sat by the campfire twirling an empty coffee cup in his hand. He watched the babe sleeping on the pallet he'd made with his only bedroll.

Despite draining her bottle dry, she held onto it for dear life. Each time he reached to pull the nipple out, she whimpered and began sucking feverishly. He guessed it wouldn't hurt to leave it.

She was a heart-tugger. And cute as a shiny new button to boot. He set the cup on the ground and reached to cover a leg that peeked from beneath the blanket. How in the name of all that's holy would she be able to survive under his wing?

A flock of magpies couldn't make more noise than the advice swarming in his head. Remembering it all would take a whole lot more brains than he had available.

Thank goodness the ladies in Cactus Springs had taken pity on a greenhorn. Without Mrs. Patrick's help he doubted he'd have survived the last few hours. Her healthy brood of eight inspired total confidence in the woman. She'd provided him with a bottle, and with squares of bunting that he had learned to fold in triangles. That was the easy part. She and Ellie just smiled knowingly when he attempted to pin the damn thing on. It was worse than trying to saddle a wild bronc. He was darn near tempted to sit on the kid's legs. And he stuck his finger at least a half a dozen times. Yep, they'd witnessed his true lack of know-how in child rearing. Okay, he'd give them that, but the two ladies had the gall to snicker behind their hands when he asked a simple question. How was he to know a baby could squirt pee that far?

Ever willing to assist in his education, Mrs. Patrick pointed him in the direction of a Mexican goat farmer, where Duel managed to buy a nanny with some of the poker winnings. Not that he'd ever milked one of the pesky animals before today. It would all come in its own time, he supposed . . . but having responsibilities sure changed a man's life.

He settled his hat low and leaned against a big rock for some serious thinking. Now he had another human being looking to him for food and shelter. And dry bunting, which alone seemed to consume a whole lot of time. He couldn't wander around the country footloose and fancy free. Bad as he hated the thought, he had obligations.

Duel let his eyes drift shut. Haunting images and sounds at once closed the space separating pain and reality—cries of desperation, blood-soaked bedsheets, the gray, fragile babe. A bare mound of dirt marking the grave also marked forever a desolate place in his heart.

Though it didn't do to dwell on what he'd lost, it didn't hurt on occasion to remind himself of the things that had ended his life and made him a drifter.

There was only one thing to do, he concluded. Go back to Tranquility. He'd try to persuade his sister to adopt Marley Rose. Victoria had two younguns, maybe more by now. Could be she'd see her way clear to taking on one more. That is if Roy, her husband, didn't throw a kink or two in his plan.

It would take some fast talking, and first he'd have to get the child there. But it would be best for the small, homeless girl. What kind of life could he provide?

He rubbed his unshaven jaw, the rough stubble scraping against his fingers. It must've been nigh on a month of Sundays since he'd had a decent bath and a shave. He'd become a slacker. Once prideful, he now cared less for his appearance than he did the direction of his wandering feet.

"Beats me what those little brown eyes saw in me," he muttered.

Marley Rose rolled onto her stomach, stretching out her arms on each side. Duel reached for the bottle that finally fell out of her mouth, and set it to the side.

Father material he wasn't—never would be. That piece of him had died when he shoveled dirt over the ones he loved. Nothing could ever give that back, not aces and eights, and not a helpless little baby whom no one wanted. His heart would remain in tatters along with the fragments of the past.

Preacher nickered softly and perked his ears. The horse warned of an intruder. Duel slipped his six-shooter from the holster and ducked for the shadows. Safety lay away from the light of the campfire.

Hidden in the obscurity of the night, he watched. Then his eyes lit on Marley Rose. He'd left that defenseless little one in danger!

Fine protector he made. Not a single night had passed and at the first sign of trouble he'd already forgotten her existence. Lord help him.

Duel started for her when movement caught his eye. Too late.

Time passed slowly. He held his breath until his lungs hurt, afraid for what the next seconds would bring.

Finally, after what seemed an eternity, a lone horse and rider walked within the circle of light. The rider slid from the saddle and crumpled to the ground in a heap.

Still cautious, Duel approached with his weapon drawn. It could be a trick of some sort. As he drew near he took in petticoats and a skirt—a woman.

Quickly, he holstered his six-shooter and knelt over the slight frame. When he reached out to touch her, his hand encountered something he'd never forget if he lived to be a hundred—the sickening stickiness of blood.

The woman roused, murmuring words he couldn't make out. He leaned closer and lifted her head.

"What happened, ma'am? You wounded?"

"Please." The word came softly from between swollen lips. Her lids fluttered, then opened, and she stared up at him. "Help me."

Chapter Two

Jessie Foltry struggled to align her vision. A stranger, whose features remained shrouded, knelt over her. She couldn't stop the panic that raced through her veins. The last time a man's hands moved this familiarly over her, pain had followed.

Instinct born from years of survival made her recoil from his touch. Such a crouch had saved her on numerous occasions.

"Don't!"

"Beggin' your pardon, ma'am. I'm not gonna hurt you. Maybe you can't remember, but you asked for my help."

She didn't feel guilty for her sharpness. Well, maybe a tad for the way he jumped back, because his low tone offered genuine concern—something she hadn't heard in a long time. Not quite so long that she'd forgotten how warm and safe it made her feel. And almost so nice her guard slipped for a moment before she sternly lectured herself. Nice could get a woman killed.

"Where am I?"

"About two miles from Cactus Springs. I camped here for the night . . . me an' the babe." The man waved his arm loosely toward a sleeping child curled on a bedroll. "Name's McClain. Duel McClain."

Jessie tipped her head slightly to acknowledge she heard. Strength to do more had seeped out hours ago on the trail behind her. Gauging the intentions of this stranger before she lost consciousness again commanded priority at the moment. Though the night obscured many of his features, light from the flickering fire enabled a clear view of his face. The lived-in look he wore told more than words—of days spent wandering and nights lost in the sleepless land of the damned. Somehow, the pain in his eyes matched the agony deep in her soul.

Kindred sorrow tempted her to trust him. Almost. That is, if she hadn't forgotten how to do that, too. She inched her tongue past her swollen lips, the simple action sending a sharp onslaught of needles to her brain. The unmistakable taste of blood rewarded her efforts.

Suppressing a moan, she managed, "Where's your woman?"

An expression she read as guilt dropped a shadow over Duel's sharp gaze.

"Don't have one. The babe, Marley Rose, is a long story."

Jessie tensed. Had her instinct to trust him been wrong? The man clearly hid something. Perhaps they had more in common than she thought. Could be they were both running from the law. A flesh trader? She'd heard tell of such men, and the pistol in her saddlebag wouldn't do her much good where she lay.

"You steal her?"

"No. Won her in a poker game tonight. You have a name?"

Jessie stared down at her trembling hands. She wished she could still the telltale tremors.

Duel rose from his squatted position and hooked both thumbs in his low-slung gun belt. His tall frame looming over her only served to increase her unease. "Guess not."

"Jessie." She didn't offer a surname. It didn't pay to give a man more than he needed to know.

"Wearing a lot of blood on you, Miss Jessie. You wounded?"

A vivid scene flashed before her eyes. Two, no three figures throwing her back and forth, then suddenly merging into one. A man laughing at her confusion. Pain, horrible pain as fists rained blow upon blow to her body.

Jeremiah.

She shut her eyes tightly to block out the images. But when she opened them again she still saw the revolver and the orange flame shooting from the barrel.

"No." Her voice sounded faint in her ears. "The blood's not mine."

"Want to tell me whose it is?" From beneath the brim of his hat, his dark gaze pierced her thin armor.

Jessie crossed her arms protectively over her chest.

"Suit yourself." He shrugged his shoulders. "Can't say it's any of my affair. Just wanted to make sure you weren't gonna die on me. Have enough trouble of my own without borrowing a heap from someone else."

Duel reached down. All she saw was his arm coming toward her. She reacted out of habit, swinging her head aside to dodge the blow.

"I won't hurt you," he said. "Rest beside the child. I'll care for your horse. Tomorrow's soon enough to sort things out."

After what seemed like a lifetime, Jessie finally placed her hand in his. She let him pull her up but kept her face averted, refusing to meet his confused look.

Her battered body couldn't resist the notion of sleep. Even if she wanted to ride back out, her head wouldn't let her. Curious thing how the ground kept spinning round and round.

The slight bundle huddling beneath a blanket drew her attention. She couldn't offer the child anything except warmth.

* * *

Duel watched her stumble to the bedroll and collapse. Lord only knew what had befallen the woman. She couldn't have tangled with a wild mountain lion and come out any worse.

After seeing to her horse, he returned to the fire. Jessie lay on one side, her arms around Marley Rose, hugging her close. Two misfits whom it seemed no one wanted. A fine mist clouded his vision. He blinked hard and settled down, leaning back against a night-cooled rock.

The woman's eyes were open, staring into the darkness surrounding them. Curiosity made him speak. He needed to know what he was up against if nothing else.

"Any reason why I shouldn't keep watch, ma'am?" he asked softly.

Silence stretched to a full minute. He had given up hope for an answer when she said at last, "Only if you don't care about living to see the sunrise, mister."

So much for hoping. "Go to sleep. Anyone gets you they have to go over me first and that's a promise."

Aunt Bessie's garter! Duel thought in the next instant. Had someone sneaked locoweed into his food? He'd just spent the better part of the evening deciding he didn't need the responsibility of one small baby. Now, he'd gone and added a desperate woman to the list, and who knew what low-down varmints were on her trail.

Damn!

He sighed and rose to throw more wood on the fire. It wasn't a good idea to advertise their position, but the baby girl needed heat against the coolness. It wouldn't do to get her sick. He reckoned a fight with a few mean polecats would be worth the risk. Right now he ached to ram his fist into the jaw of the no-good who'd turned Jessie's face into something resembling a belly-up armadillo.

Preacher nickered softly as if agreeing and nuzzled Duel's outstretched hand.

"It's been just you and me, boy, for the last year and a half. We haven't needed anyone else. Still don't." He let his hand inch down the mustang's muscled neck and bit back a sudden overwhelming urge to give in to his despair.

"God, how I miss Annie!"

Burying his face in Preacher's long mane, he succumbed to the rush of memories. His beloved's golden hair, her sweet smile that made everything seem right as rain even if it wasn't, and the way she looked at him when he entered a room like she'd just spied a rainbow for the first time. Those were the things he missed. Those and a few hundred other little incidentals.

"Don't do a man any good to recall what was. . . ." he squeezed his eyes tight to block the pain. "Can't ever be that way again, so there's no use dwellin' on it. It's over an' done with. Just felt I owed you an explanation, boy." Duel straightened and leaned back, putting himself on an eye level with Preacher. He must be getting maudlin, treating the horse as if he could understand. But Lord, it felt good to speak the thoughts aloud.

"Like I said, it's just you and me. Except now, for a little while, till I can get this mess sorted out, we have to take good care of that baby girl over there. She's never done a single hurtful thing to anyone, and she sure as hell doesn't deserve the rotten hand she's been dealt. Marley Rose needs us and we're gonna see that she gets a good home." The rasp of his fingers against a month's worth of stubble sounded loud in the quietness. "If I can figure out where home is."

Unconcerned, the mustang dipped his head to snip some sweet grass.

"I ain't done yet so don't start ignoring me. The other little lady who busted in on us is not our account. Most likely she'll vamoose come first light. Fine by me. The woman's way past grown."

Moonlight reflected off Preacher's black coat, casting it a shimmering blue. "The thing I'm trying to say is . . . this is only a temporary arrangement. Then, it'll be you and me again. We're a pair of aces."

But as Duel moved to the deep shadows out of firelight, he knew he'd uttered a lie.

He cared.

Something in him refused to let him do otherwise. Didn't help that he'd always had a warm spot for poor, defenseless creatures, big or small. He knew if Jessie wanted his help he'd not turn her down.

Movement from the sleeping forms on the bedroll arrested his gaze. The woman changed position but still kept her arms around the child as if to protect her. After all Jessie had been through and sorely in need of her own protector, she still tried to shield Marley Rose from unseen danger. The thought sent goose bumps shimmying up his spine.

His eyes lingered a second longer than necessary on the soft, womanly curve of Jessie's hip before moving onward over the length of her form. Sharp pangs of guilt knotted in his belly. Although he hadn't so much as laid a hand on Jessie, he felt as though he'd just committed some crime. A man didn't examine a woman's body uninvited as he just had. No gentleman for sure, not that he laid claim as one.

That brought his thoughts back to whoever had found pleasure in using her face for a battering ram. How did a man justify trying to destroy all that pretty softness?

A rock crunched beneath the heel of his boot as he settled down to wait for the dawn. Ah, the pleasure it would give him to crush Jessie's attacker beneath his thick heel, and add to that, Marley Rose's sorry-assed father.

No sign of that happening yet. Except for the occasional coyotes howling in the distance and the hoot of some night owls, the vast Plains held its secrets. If others followed Jessie, they were dragging their feet.

Without knowing why or stopping to wonder, he suddenly felt more alive, more aware of the sound of his own heartbeat than he had in a long time. A slow smile curved his lips. For someone who fought judiciously against adding the encumbrance of others to his life, he sure seemed to be losing the battle.

He tilted his Stetson and glanced up at the changing sky.

It'd be daylight soon. He might as well get more wood for the fire and scare up a rabbit or two for breakfast.

Panic set in when Duel returned to camp less than an hour later to find the bedroll empty. Blood pounded in his temples as he scanned the area for Jessie and Marley Rose. Then he heard the faint sound of a child's happy gurgle.

The creek.

He suddenly developed four left feet in his haste to find the missing pair. A mesquite branch grabbed his shirt, tearing a long gash. It didn't matter. Nothing did except finding his baby girl and making sure nothing happened to her. Only one thing stopped him dead in his tracks—the metallic click of a cocked hammer and a cold warning.

"Stop where you are or you're a dead man, mister."

She certainly sounded serious. He mentally kicked himself for not searching for a weapon when Jessie busted in on their camp last evening. The thought of running his hands over those soft curves looking for cold metal increased his sudden need for air.

With some effort, he pulled his thoughts back to the situation at hand. Was the pistol loaded or did she merely hope to bluff? Unfortunately, he had only one way of knowing.

"Ma'am? Miss Jessie? It's me, Duel." He inched forward.

"You come a step closer and I'll blow your head clean off your shoulders."

"I'm not gonna hurt you. Just want to make sure Marley Rose is all right." Heedless of the warning, he continued to steal forward, trying to glimpse them through a copse of cottonwood saplings and tangle of brush that grew beside the winding creek.

"She's here."

"I'd feel better if I took her back to camp. . . ." He used his most gentle tone—the one he might use to cajole a wild, scared mustang.

"Hang on to your nightshirt." She sounded a tad riled.

The time to dance was when the music was playing. With

a careful hand, he pushed aside the branches of a sapling to create a small opening. Then he saw them. A half-dressed Jessie sat on a rock holding a six-shooter pointed directly at him, while Marley Rose played happily at her feet.

Lucky for him the brush still hid him from her view or she'd have him doing the hot-water jig.

Early morning sunlight caught the woman's hair, sending shots of fire through the warm cinnamon curls. Duel held his breath, unable to move at the sight. Though marred by dark bruises, creamy skin peeked from a thin undergarment that dipped low across her bosom. He'd not seen such a vision since Annie died, and the sight stirred a longing in him.

Cautiously, Jessie laid the weapon on the ground and vainly looked for something to cover herself with. Finding nothing, she hauled her wet dress from the creek. He surmised she'd been washing blood from herself and the garment, blood that belonged to someone else, or so she claimed.

Holding the water-soaked clothing to her with one hand and picking up the gun with the other, she directed, "Come and get your baby, mister. But, I'm warning you. Touch me and so help me God I'll shoot you."

The crack in her flinty voice struck a cord. Duel ached to take her in his arms and hold her until all the hurt was gone. Until the fear of men had left. Until she could walk confidently in this wild Texas land. He wanted to make her smile again.

Taking care not to startle the woman, he eased his big frame forward with both hands in the air.

"There you are, Marley Rose." He spoke gently as he scooped the baby into his arms. "I'll bet you're ready for some vittles if I can only coax some milk from that ornery goat."

He stole a quick glance at Jessie. Up close and in the light of day, the severity of the dark bruises made his stomach lurch uncomfortably. Instead of a belly-up armadillo, her face resembled something that had been drug behind a horse—through a cactus patch. His anger bubbled.

The need to speak some words of comfort tied his tongue in knots. What could a man say that would change anything? Sorry that any fellow human could do that to another wouldn't suffice. Besides, blue fire in the eye that wasn't swelled shut told him what he could do with any pity he might feel.

"Coffee's brewing, Miss Jessie ma'am. I've got us some rabbits for breakfast when you're done here. Hope you're hungry."

Maybe she didn't expect kindness from anyone, or perhaps she didn't trust herself to speak, for she only nodded.

Marley Rose stuck two fingers in his mouth, finding his teeth of interest. He lowered his gaze and swung on his heels.

Call it curiosity or just plain nosiness, something made him turn for one last look. With her back to him, Jessie had knelt to resume her task.

That's when he saw it. The bitter taste of bile rose to his throat.

Burned into the smooth whiteness of her left shoulder sat the blackened outline of a diamond with the letter "J" set clearly in the middle.

A cattle brand!

Chapter Three

A whoosh of air left Duel's mouth.

What the hell kind of man would do this to a woman?

Such depth of savagery. Try as he might, he couldn't help but imagine Jessie's screams as the heated metal touched her skin. His stomach roiling, he hugged Marley Rose tighter.

"Gaga gooo." Marley wriggled, pulling on his bottom lip. Then the chubby fingers sneaked beneath his collarless shirt.

"Oh no you don't, little darlin'." With a painful tug he broke her hold and sat her on the bedroll. "For a little tadpole you sure know how to torture a man."

The tiny girl puckered up to cry.

"Aw now, please don't bawl." He rifled through his saddle bags for the rag doll Mrs. Patrick had thrust on him. Marley greedily reached for it, sticking tufts of yarn doll hair in her mouth. "Play with that while I milk the goat. And stay where I put you. Hear?"

He lifted a well-used pail and eyed the nanny. "I'd rather kiss a rattler than do this."

The goat bleated and eyed him with disdain when he untied the rope.

"All right, I hear you. But we've got a baby girl to feed." The animal balked when he tried to direct her to a tree stump. "We can do this easy or I can break your ornery neck, you good-for-nothing varmint."

Heavy breathing and a few choice expletives ended the scuffle and Duel finally secured the nanny to a sturdy branch. Worn out, he plopped down on the stump and placed the pail strategically under the swollen udders. After several tries, a thin stream of milk landed in the container.

"This ain't so difficult. Mind over matter." Movement from the vicinity of the bedroll captured his attention and the next squirt landed across the toes of his boots.

"Marley Rose, play with your doll, honey. Stay on the. . . . Don't put that in your mouth!"

Panic brought him to his feet. She had something brown and gooey clutched in her hand, which was halfway to her mouth. The pail went flying as he scrambled. Round chocolate eyes stared innocently at him when he grabbed for the offending goo. He gagged at the smell. Horse manure.

"I swear, child. The good Lord didn't give you much sense when he put you on this earth." Keeping her hand outstretched, he lunged for the creek before he remembered Jessie was there, most likely bare as a newborn babe.

A quick detour took him to the basin of water he'd drawn earlier. By the time he managed to pry Marley's fist open, she'd smeared the excrement up and down his shirt sleeve.

Ignoring her angry squalls, he washed her hands thoroughly. "Some things are just downright putrid, Marley Rose. That's why I'm here, I suppose, to teach you the difference between vittles an' horse shit."

"Pa pa. Pa pa. Pa pa."

Duel felt some of the tightness in his chest melt away under the brilliance of her smile. He mustn't lend too much weight to the child's babbling. Still, it sounded an awful lot like "papa." His heart jerked painfully.

"No, darlin', I'm not your papa. Don't ever call me that." He couldn't allow anyone to refer to him that way.

He gave her an extra hug before he plopped her little bottom back on the pallet. Keeping one eye on her, he pulled off his shirt. He'd wash it later at the creek, but for now he'd have to go without.

Not trusting the child to stay put, and not knowing what to do with her, he bent to pick her up. Just at that moment something rammed him from behind and he went flying. Duel spit dirt. Rolling over, he found the goat calmly chewing above him. Gleeful giggles filled the morning air.

"Damn your hide, you mangy critter. For two cents I'd set you loose." He gave Marley Rose a stern glare. "And you quit laughing, little lady. I think you're in cahoots with that blasted nanny."

Holding Marley firmly in one arm, he led the goat back to the tree and tied it with a triple knot. "There. See if you get loose from that."

Wasted milk soaked into the soil, bringing a new frown to his brow. *Aunt Bessie's garter!*

What gave him the notion he could raise this child? He must have gotten a snoot full of peyote. Couldn't even handle one stupid goat. A string of curses followed as he righted the overturned pail and resumed his seat on the stump.

With Marley astride one knee, he soothed the animal with a few words of encouragement before wrapping a hand around a teat. Not enough hand motion. He shifted the child's position and tried again. The white liquid went everywhere but the pail. Intent on his chore, he didn't hear Jessie approach until she stood beside him.

Until that moment, he hadn't given much thought to his bare torso. It had seemed as natural as breathing. Now, he became uncomfortably aware that he wore no shirt, and the urge to hide his nakedness with crossed arms was an overpowering one.

"My shirt . . . Marley Rose." At the moment he would have considered the unsavory piece of clothing a godsend. "It smelled. I had to take it off," he finished lamely.

Without a word, Jessie raised the hem of her very damp skirt. What in blazes? He wasn't sure he had the stomach for another brand.

Unsure of her intentions, he watched her rip a flounce from her petticoat. Using the torn fabric, she fashioned a sling which she looped over his shoulder and under one arm.

Her hands brushed lightly against him as she arranged the contraption and tied it. Sweat dampened his chest hairs. Duel felt as if he'd chomped down on a handful of hot chili peppers.

When she reached for Marley Rose, he realized she had designed a crude papoose wrap such as an Indian woman might have used.

"Now, why didn't I think of this?" Wonderment washed over him as Jessie settled the tiny girl on his back. "You seem to have a knack for little ones. Have any of your own?"

Jessie reacted as if he'd slapped her. He didn't miss the wet mist that quickly filled her eyes or the way she kept pushing the mass of curls off her face, tucking them behind her ear.

"No." Her voice was barely audible. She turned away as if ashamed she hadn't. The sadness, clearly evident, made him regret the question.

"I'm worse than a tenderfoot in the child-rearing department." He tried to ignore the smarting pain that shot through him when the tiny girl twisted her fingers in his thick hair and yanked. "I'm certain of one thing, though. Next time you rig this contraption, turn Marley Rose to face the other way. She deals out more misery than a bloodthirsty savage."

Jessie's back stiffened. She stared vacantly into the distance, lost in thought. Another place, another time. White knuckles clenched by her side told the depth of her anguish.

You stupid jackass, McClain! Someone beat the woman within an inch of her life and you have to talk about blood-

thirsty savages. Of all the dunderheaded things to do. No way to treat a lady. Show a little decency.

"Sorry, ma'am. Didn't mean to say anything uncalled for."

Jessie turned and he noticed the color of her eyes for the first time. The one that wasn't swelled perfectly matched the flowers on his mother's prized china. Lily McClain, God rest her soul, had declared them Wedgwood blue.

Did she have a husband? Was he responsible for her condition? Duel speculated on the possibility as he continued to direct the stream of milk into the pail.

"Don't mean to pry and if it's none of my business, just say so. This man who'd be looking for you, is he your husband?" He shot her a cursory glance while he wrested both ears from Marley Rose's steel grip. They were the latest part of his anatomy to capture the child's fascination. Besides, he didn't want anything to interfere with hearing Jessie's answer.

Her chin quivered an instant before she forced her head high. "No. The ones who come want justice."

For the second time since he'd met her he wanted to pull her against him and hold her safe. His throat clogged with a thick huskiness. "The only justice they'll find if they come is a piece of hot lead."

The goat lifted a back leg. Duel grabbed the half-full pail, dodging the kick aimed his way. "Oh no you don't."

His boots crunched on the hard ground when he stood. Jessie seemed oblivious to him as he strode to retrieve the child's bottle from the bedroll. The mysterious woman was once again lost somewhere inside herself. Lost and so alone.

"I'm taking Marley Rose home to Tranquility." He tugged the nipple off the bottle. It released with a plop and the smell of curdled milk reached his nose. "Phew. Girl, didn't know you'd be so darn much trouble."

Marley giggled excitedly, riding piggyback to the creek to rinse out the container. Jessie had moved to the campfire when he returned. The forlorn look etched shadows across her face as she stared into the flames.

"You're welcome to join us if you've a mind. Lord knows

I need help with this youngun." Something wet ran down his back. He could hazard a pretty good guess what it was. This baby business was no bed of roses.

Luckily, he managed to fill the bottle after missing the opening only a few times. Pulling the rubber nipple over the top proved the biggest challenge. It appeared to have shrunk when he took it off, because he didn't see any way in hell of getting it to fit.

"Let me."

Jessie had crept beside him again. The ghostly way she moved gave him the willies. Their hands touched when she took the two items, making her jerk back in alarm. Sheer terror contorted her features into a mask.

"You all right?" He'd never felt so helpless. What could a man say to ease the torment of a woman who'd suffered what she had? It would take more comforting words than he knew.

She didn't reply, just ran her tongue cautiously across her bottom lip. Then, before he could blink, she melded nipple and bottle together, once again proving herself to be capable and efficient, important things in raising a child.

"Much obliged." Duel accepted the fully assembled bottle.

Light fingertips brushed his bare skin when she lifted Marley Rose from her perch. He reasoned it was the heat of the sun's rays that caused the beads of perspiration dotting his forehead. Had to be.

He ducked his head, hoping she couldn't read his thoughts. He must have lost every lick of sense he had. The last thing on earth he needed was a woman. And, the way she recoiled from him clearly expressed her view of men.

Relieved of the babe, he dove into his saddlebags for the extra shirt he carried. Pulling it on, he could hardly button it fast enough. Covering his upper body made him feel a whole lot better. Not much he could do about his wet buckskins, though. The wind would have to dry them.

His growling stomach reminded him of the rabbits he'd killed. That blasted goat had taken too much time. Better get a move on or the sun would be overhead before he knew it.

"I could sure use your help, ma'am. That is, if you want to come along." Now that he was fully clothed he could glance at her directly.

Jessie had found a seat on the large rock he'd propped against during the night. She cradled Marley in her arms as if she was a precious treasure. The girl's noisy sucking on the fresh goat milk blended with the animal's protesting bleats.

The woman's attention appeared to rest solely on Marley Rose. She caressed the dark curls. "What would you want in return?"

Given what she'd gone through, her suspicion was expected, right down to the stony grit in her tone.

"Only your kindness with the babe, nothing more." When she swung her head his direction, he matched her intent gaze with honesty. "Make you a deal. I swear on the McClain family Bible I'll never lay a hand on you. I offer you safekeeping. When we get to Tranquility, I'll see you get any place you want to go."

"You promise?" Jessie's voice broke.

Duel didn't make deals lightly. "The word of a McClain has stood the test of war, famine, flood, and pestilence. I come from a long line of promise-makers. Heck, my grandfather once parted the Colorado River with his cane because he gave his word."

That brought a hint of a smile to Jessie's lips.

"You've got yourself a deal, mister."

At that, Marley Rose raised her head and grinned as if to say she was relieved to have someone along with good horse sense.

"Drop the "mister." Name's Duel." He threw it out offhand, trying to sound nonchalant as he bent to the task of gutting and skinning the rabbits.

"Don't think I can do that, Mr. McClain." Her manner stiffened again, shattering the small headway he'd made.

"Suit yourself." Duel lifted the cleaned rabbits by the feet and marched off to wash them in the creek.

After he speared them with sharpened sticks and propped

them over the low fire, he led the horses to the water to drink. He didn't remember his soiled shirt until he squatted on his heels to splash water on his face. He'd wash it before they broke camp.

A prideful woman, the mysterious Miss Jessie. Her refusal to call him by his name demonstrated her will to keep him at arm's length. Gaining her trust would take a lot longer than what they had. One thing for certain, she'd be mighty upset if she knew he'd seen the brand on her shoulder.

He smoothed the long neck of Jessie's sorrel. Now in the light of day he sized up the pretty mare. Good horseflesh if he ever saw any. He ran his hand down each leg, checking for signs of lameness. Better to know now than a mile or two down the trail. Then he came to the flank and his hand froze.

The animal carried a Diamond J brand—the same that marked Jessie.

Suddenly, bits and pieces of things he'd heard crashed together. The Diamond J ranch sprawled over fifty thousand acres down along the Rio Grande, or so the barkeep in the border town of El Paso had told him. Duel couldn't recall who owned the spread. Damn! Too much rotgut and too many nights of forgetting.

Preacher nickered and roughly nudged his arm.

"Jealous of the sorrel, huh?" He chuckled and gave the mustang his undivided attention. "Or just reminding me you're still around?"

Light footsteps sounded from behind and he turned.

"Beautiful horse, Mr. McClain." Jessie held up his shirt. "The babe fell asleep. I saw your shirt lying there. Thought I'd wash it for you."

"I can't ask you to—"

"I'm offering. I want to repay you for sharing your campfire last night." She knelt, dunked the shirt in the water, and began to scrub.

"You don't owe me anything, ma'am." It was a heck of a thing to see a woman touching his clothing so intimate-like.

"I intend to keep it that way."

Chapter Four

Jessie's sorrel danced in place as she looked down at the sleepy little town nestled in the valley. Cinnabar's skittish mood matched her own.

Duel's promise drifted from the back of her mind. *When we get to Tranquility, I'll see you get any place you want to go.*

In the week it had taken to cross the Texas Plains, he'd kept his word about everything else. The man had not laid a hand on her or questioned her further about the circumstances that led her to his campfire.

He'd not renege on this pledge either. Only where would she go? Not back. A rope awaited her there. Indecision swirled like a black cloud overhead. Her thoughts twisted and turned in the wind. How would Duel's sister and father accept her? Though some of the bruises had faded, no doubt she would still draw attention. If decent folks knew who she was, what she'd done, they'd have nothing but contempt for her.

And Duel McClain? She savored the name she could not bring to her lips.

She watched him mount his horse through a mist-filled gaze. He was careful not to disturb the dozing child tied on his back. Time spent in the Texan's company had shown her a compassionate, honorable man. His gentleness with her and Marley Rose created a warm place in her heart. Still, if he knew her secret, would he deem her unfit to associate with the child or his family?

The mist in her eyes grew, blurring the tall man's figure. Both he and the homeless bundle he carried had given her more peace and fulfillment than she'd known in the last eight years.

Leaving them would heap more pain on her already burdened soul. Yet she had no choice. Did she? To stay would invite trouble when someone came for her. It seemed no way to repay a man's kindness.

"Ready, ma'am?" The amber streaks in his clear hazel eyes softened his chiseled features. Add a colorful headband to his deeply tanned skin and he'd do more than look the part of a warrior.

Jessie inhaled sharply to still the wild quickening of her pulse. "Might as well get to it, Mr. McClain."

She urged Cinnabar down the bluff with a heaviness in her chest. Doubts nibbled away at any hope that she'd ever find the tranquility the town's name suggested. Soon she'd have to leave. An ache from the thought of never seeing Marley Rose or Duel again made it hard to breathe.

"Jessie, this is my sister, Victoria Austin." Duel introduced the lovely auburn-haired woman who stood a good six inches shorter than him. "She answers best to Vicky."

Vicky squeezed her hand. "A friend of Duel's is a friend of mine. Jessie . . . ?"

A hot flush rose as the woman searched for a last name. Jessie hadn't given any thought to this moment.

Duel winked at her and answered instead. "Just Jessie, Sis. Now, where are those younguns? They've got to meet the newest member of the McClain family."

Jessie breathed a sigh of relief when Marley Rose captured Vicky's attention. How gallant for the gentle Texan to come to her rescue once more—her knight of the Texas plains.

"Oh, my stars! Is this baby really yours, brother? Where? How? Is Jessie your wife? And where have you been?"

Her cheeks must have turned a bright shade of red as Vicky turned excitedly to her. How would he explain the new additions to his life? Her heart stopped for a full moment as she met what appeared to be a question in his hazel eyes. Surely he wouldn't.... Someone had stolen all the air from the room.

"Hold on to your pantaloons, sis. One thing at a time. This is Marley Rose, the prettiest little gal in the whole state. Yes, she's mine. And no, Jessie's not my wife. I haven't gotten myself hitched."

For a second, slow disappointment curled around her heart like charred edges of a love letter. Until she reminded herself a fine man like him deserved someone respectable, not someone who didn't know what the next sunrise would bring.

"Now, where are my nephews?" he continued. "Where are George and Henry?"

A big smile lit up Marley's face as Vicky tugged her from Duel's arms.

"Duel, this is the most precious child!" The woman hugged the chubby bundle tight. "Let's move to the parlor and get comfortable. Speaking of the kids, I have a surprise for you myself. You have nieces as well as nephews."

"Do tell. How many do you have to keep up with now, Vicky?"

"Only four. The twins, Betsy and Becky, came about a year after you left. Roy and Papa offered to give me a break today. They took them to see if the fish are biting."

"Pop?" Duel propped the Stetson on the back of his head and sank into a cross-stitched chair. "How's he doing?"

"Broke his leg trying to take care of the farm when you lit out of here for God knows where. Papa wanted to keep it up in case you had a notion to remember your roots. Finally gave up. He's moved in with us now." Though Victoria evidently loved her brother, her sharp rebuke seemed to hit a sore spot.

From the worn velvet sofa, Jessie watched Duel's jaw clench and suspected he struggled with strong guilt. She wondered what would make a man leave everything behind and disappear? Only something so awful that it took a body's reason for living. She knew all too well about that. The thought popped into her mind that he might take off again after she left. How stable was he? The likelihood that he might leave poor little Marley here with Vicky brought a bitter taste to her mouth. The child had already been abandoned once. Twice could leave deep emotional scars. Besides, a man should raise his own children, whether he fathered them or not.

A few nights ago by the light of the campfire, Duel had explained about Marley's true father and the poker game. She couldn't imagine anyone selling their flesh and blood, and that Duel would care for Marley as his own had touched a tender chord within her. In her opinion nothing could be more satisfying than holding your babe in your arms.

She'd almost had that pleasure—until Jeremiah snatched it from her grasp. Now her arms and her belly would remain forever empty.

"Jessie, can I get you something? I can make hot tea, some coffee maybe, or food if you've not eaten."

Vicky's question pulled her back to the present, yet she was unable to shed the heavy sorrow that also accompanied her memories. A real family, that's what made living worthwhile. Though it was too late for her, she prayed Marley Rose would have the chance.

The smell of fresh-baked bread filled every nook and cranny in the house. Ignoring the growls from her stomach took exceptional concentration. Despite her watering mouth, she considered her manners. "A cup of hot tea would be nice."

While the teapot boiled, Jessie accepted Vicky's generous

offer to use her bedroom to wash off a little of the grime collected on the trail. When she returned, she caught the woman's angry hiss and hesitated outside the kitchen.

"Are you responsible for Jessie's condition? Surely—"

"Have you ever known me to lay a hand to any woman, Vicky?" Wounded hurt seeped through Duel's angry denial.

Guilt told her to step into view, yet the scene would be awkward, and she couldn't face the pity she knew would be there. She couldn't bear that.

"How do I know what kind of man you've turned into in the four years you've been gone? Why did you leave without a word?"

"When I buried Annie, something inside died right along with her. You're right, I'm not the same man I was. I've done things. Even so, I'm no monster."

"Then who? Who would do such a horrible thing to that sweet girl?"

"If I ever find out there'll be hell to pay! She's a fine woman, Vicky. Too good for—" His voice froze when she stepped around the partition.

Shock rippled through her veins. That this amber-eyed Samaritan held her in high esteem stunned her. He thought her too good? For what? For the tongue lashing she'd gotten for not moving quickly enough to suit Jeremiah? For the whipping he'd given her? Or too good for the rope they'd tie around her neck?

No, she wasn't fine or good. And she'd suffer for that.

"There you are, dear." Blushing, Vicky fussed over the teapot.

Here came the awkwardness she'd tried to avoid. She kept her gaze fastened on Marley Rose, not meeting Duel's uneasy stare and the pity she was sure to see there.

"Did you find everything you needed, Jessie? The fancy soap Roy bought me in Austin was right beside the washstand. The wrapper promised the tantalizing scent of dew-kissed rose petals, but I swear it smells more like morning glories to me. You just never get what you pay for. However, I have nothing against morning—"

"Vicky, for God's sake shut up."

Jessie covered her mouth to smother a grin. "Yes, thank you, I found everything. The soap smelled wonderful."

They settled around the kitchen table, Duel with coffee and she with hot tea. Although Vicky tried to keep her curiosity veiled, Jessie caught her stealing glances.

"Now, brother, where did you meet up with Marley Rose and Jessie? I can smell a good story a mile away." Vicky bounced Marley up and down on one knee. The child's happy squeals were the only noise in the otherwise quiet room.

Jessie couldn't miss the tic or the stubborn set in Duel's square jaw that signaled his irritation. In closed-mouth fashion he was being protective of her and Marley. He was a special kind of man, capable of deep compassion. Then why did he judge himself so harshly, and what had been his relationship with the woman he called Annie? A wife?

"You know, Vicky, this is exactly why I hesitated in coming back. I wasn't ready to face all these confounded questions."

Tension stretched for a long minute between brother and sister. Both had private family matters to discuss.

"I think Marley Rose and I need to check on the horses." Jessie's chair scraped on the hardwood floor, bringing both combatants to their feet.

"You'll do no such thing! You're my guest." Vicky put a hand on her arm to stop her.

Duel's angry glare softened when he turned to her. "I'll go. You need to rest. Vicky, see that she does. The last few days have been rough on her and Marley Rose."

Before he could move from the spot the kitchen door burst open.

"Mama, Mama, a goat's outside pullin' your clean clothes off'n the line. It's eatin' my shirt." The excited boy looked no older than six or seven. Another smaller youngster, evidently his brother, followed close behind.

"Damn that blasted goat!" Three long strides carried Duel to the back door.

"Boys, that's your Uncle Duel I keep telling you about." The banging door interrupted Vicky's hurried introduction.

The two boys clipped at his heels. "Oh boy! Uncle Duel, wait for us!"

"I've got to see this. Come on." Vicky grabbed Jessie's hand and they joined the parade.

As they watched Duel wrestle with the stubborn animal, two men, one wearing a leg splint, approached from the barn. Each man toted a little girl on his shoulders.

"Duel?" The elderly man held up his hand to block the sun. "I'll be a horned toad!"

Walt McClain wobbled in his hurry to reach his son, his crooked gait impeding the speed of his progress.

Duel stopped in mid-tussle with the goat. At the sight of his father, his chin jutted forward.

Jessie watched his expression for signs of relenting. Whatever had happened had torn him and his family apart. She ached for the man who'd fed her soul as well as her stomach.

"Pop." They stood before each other in silence.

"Son!" With no hesitation, Walt embraced his son. "Welcome home."

A broad smile lit Duel's face. Jessie relaxed. Things were not as bad as he'd feared. Healing would come.

"Marley Rose, no baby, don't put that in your mouth." Jessie grabbed a dead bug from the small one's grasp and scooped her from the floor.

The meeting with Duel's family a few hours earlier had gone much better than she'd anticipated. Of course there were polite stares, but deep kindness lay beneath their interest. They even refrained from the million questions she knew they died to ask. She couldn't have wished for more. Now, Duel had brought Marley and her to the farm he'd abandoned. She felt his pain from the moment they rode onto the property. It'd taken a minute before he brought himself to step inside the door, and his face had been quiet and still when he walked the rooms he'd shared with Annie.

From Vicky, she learned that Annie had died in childbirth. "It broke my heart to watch him lay her in that coffin. He folded her lifeless arms around their infant son and nailed on the lid."

The grave stood on the rise she saw from the window. She moved closer and wiped away the grime with her fingers. Despite the grief that surrounded the farm like the barbed wire Jeremiah had used to mark his domain, there was beauty here. The winter cold had given way to early spring rains and produced a bumper crop of bluebonnets, Indian paintbrush, and prickly poppy. They carpeted the hills, creating a canvas with rich hues.

In the midst of all the color, the tall figure of Duel stood alone, facing the haunting demons that almost had destroyed his will to live. Head bowed, he knelt, then sat cross-legged amid the wildflowers that blanketed the grave. Not strong enough yet, she sensed, to slay the demons. Instead he sized them up in the true fashion of a gunfighter who eyed his enemies before a duel.

Maybe someday her brave knight would fight that battle—and win. For Marley Rose's sake she prayed that day would come soon.

"He'll love you like a daughter, little one," she murmured against Marley's soft black curls. "I know he will even though his heart still aches with pain."

"Pa pa." The child's serious expression suggested understanding despite the impossibility of it as she gently patted the window pane.

Jessie kissed her chubby cheek. "Yes, he's your papa now, my darling. It's up to you to fill the emptiness in his life." Because she couldn't linger, any more than she could hope to offer Duel the comfort he needed.

Marley threw both arms around Jessie's neck and clung as if sensing coming sadness. A bullet couldn't have done a better job of shattering her control. She held the child tight and forced back hot tears. Marley Rose could have been the baby she'd never have—the one she lost. Shimmering wetness blurred the figure who sat alone by his beloved's grave. Duel McClain could have taught her what it was like to live without constant fear, without hate eating at her soul.

Jessie forced a deep breath. Yes, it was time for her to go . . . before it became even more painful. Tomorrow at first light would be soon enough to slip away. For today she'd savor every second spent in her dear ones' company.

Duel lifted his head. He thought he heard singing, the sweet notes only an angel could produce. Then he realized the music came from the frame structure he and Annie had once called home. Curious, he rose and ambled toward it.

Just outside the door he paused and listened.

" 'Hush little baby, don't say a word, Mama's gonna buy you a mockingbird.' "

The steady creak of a rocking chair, the one he'd ordered all the way from St. Louis, added a harmonious rhythm to the tune Jessie sung to Marley Rose. That should be Annie in there rocking their son. Anger sparked an urge to reduce the chair to kindling. His hand froze on the doorknob.

" 'If that mockingbird don't sing, Papa's gonna buy you a diamond ring.' "

The woman's voice broke and overwhelming sadness enveloped the lyrics, telling more than he wanted to know. In the space it took to draw breath, he shoved his own problems back into the dark corners where they belonged. He'd lived with them four years, but Jessie's pain was fresh. Lord knows her plate heaped to overflowing in that department. He cringed, thinking again of the Diamond J burned into her shoulder. Her physical wounds would eventually heal. What of the damage inside? No amount of time would erase that. The muscle in his jaw tensed.

" 'If that diamond ring turns brass, Mama's gonna buy you a lookin' glass.' " The song drifted through the cracks.

He had no doubts she cared for Marley Rose. Her tone, her

tender touch, the growing shine in her eyes all told of how deep the nurturing ran. It went beyond mere fascination or a woman's duty. No, this was different. The bond between Jessie and the little darling seemed forged from some mighty strong iron.

Heaven forbid, that in the mad dash from her circumstances, could she have left a child behind somewhere? That might explain her deep concern for Marley Rose. He knew one thing for certain. If she had, it could only have been against her will.

His question addressing whether she had a husband had evoked sudden tears she stubbornly held back despite her quivering chin. She vowed there was no one. He wasn't entirely convinced.

A lump settled in the middle of his gut. Whatever happened, she didn't trust him enough to tell her story. Trust wouldn't come easy to Jessie.

Duel meant to honor his word to see her anyplace she wished to go. But how much trouble would he be borrowing if he asked her to stay? Just for a little while? Just until he got the hang of this baby business.

He had to ask—for both his and Marley Rose's sake.

Chapter Five

" 'If that lookin' glass gets broke, Papa's gonna buy you a billy goat.' " The nursery rhyme took Jessie back to when she was a child. She'd snuggled in her mother's lap, listening to the same song. Worries were an unknown commodity back then. Funny, it seemed only yesterday. Mama and Papa loved her. She had never displeased them, only Jeremiah.

"Will a nanny goat do?"

She stiffened. Duel's slow drawl startled her. Lost in her own thoughts, she hadn't heard him enter.

"Did I spook you?" His gentle tone calmed her fear, reminding her he was nothing like Jeremiah. Respect and compassion oozed from this tall Texan.

She shifted Marley Rose from her shoulder, laying the limp form in her lap. "What was it you asked? Something about a goat?"

Her gaze followed him as he removed his Stetson and hung it on a nail beside the door. The hat seemed a natural part of him, as much as the Smith and Wesson Schofield strapped around his slim waist. Most likely, he'd hung it there a hundred times before. And a woman named Annie would run to greet him with a smile . . . and a kiss. Jessie swallowed, relegating the vision to a scrap heap along with all the others.

"The song. I wanted to know if a nanny would do? Already got her one of those."

The image of him fighting to pull nephew George's shirt from the animal's mouth earlier in the day brought the barest hint of a smile to her lips. The tug of war had ended with Duel, his pride along with his rear, in the dirt.

"It's a fine gift for Marley."

He ran his fingers through his thick, dark brown hair in exasperation, then growled. "Thing is, I'm not her papa. Never will be."

"You're the only one the poor little thing's got."

Feathery black lashes fanned against Marley Rose's cheeks. The child's beautiful face reflected her quiet inner spirit. She was so precious. Jessie's chest ached. How could anyone wager their own flesh and blood as easily as they would a horse or an unwanted pair of boots?

Green-tinged bruises peeked from where Jessie's sleeve had ridden up, reminding her she'd known such a cruel one. Jeremiah had taken perverse pleasure in destroying a person's will, instilling mortal fear, then putting his mark on all he owned. She quickly pushed the fabric to cover the distinct fingerprints.

"That may well be, but I'm only a man who opened his arms, not his heart to the child. She'll call me Duel."

The firm closing of the door behind him squashed any rebuttal she might have made. Dark sorrow fell as she watched his proud carriage disappear. She knew he had uttered the words rashly. He couldn't mean them.

"Give him time, my darling." She brushed a gentle kiss across the sleeping child's forehead.

Duel shifted his weight from one foot to another. "Jessie, ma'am, I've got something to say and I want you to hear me out." He hated the instant distrust that leaped into the space between them. Maybe this wasn't a good idea. "Don't get me wrong, I still intend to keep my bargain."

At the word bargain, she grew still.

"But?" The word shot from stiff lips.

"Problem is Marley Rose here." He ruffled the child's soft curls, her infectious grin reinforcing his plan. The little darlin' needed a mother, and he couldn't have found one more suited for the job than if he'd handpicked her himself. If he could only convince the lady of that.

Therein lay a big problem. Jessie cringed each time he stepped too close. Could he live with that? With the reminder of what another had done? Although *he* would never lay a hand to her, he felt as if he shouldered the blame simply because he was a man. Each time he shut his eyes the memory of what he'd seen made his insides crawl.

He took a deep breath. The welfare of the little one had to come first. "The girl needs a woman's touch. I hate like hell to ask this being as you're in a hurry to leave and all." Not knowing what to do with his hands, he hooked his thumbs in his gunbelt. "What I want to ask is, could you see your way clear to staying on a few more days?"

Her blue eyes clouded and he hurried on, the words spilling out like marbles from a broken jar. "Just till . . . for Marley Rose's sake."

"Stay? Live here with you? On this farm?"

Heat rushed to his face as he realized how it sounded. Damn! He could stare into a killer's eyes at twenty paces and not feel this rattled.

"Purely a business proposition, Miss Jessie, nothing more. For Marley."

He watched Jessie wet the healing cut on her lip with her tongue and wished he knew the direction her mind took. On second thought, maybe he didn't want to know. Women were a mystery to him despite the fact he once was married to one. The toes of his boots suddenly gained interest.

". . . guess my plans could wait a few days." He looked up

in time to see the wrinkle that had creased her brow smoothed. "For Marley's sake."

The air he released resembled the noise his grandpa's still had made just before it blew to smithereens.

"But I'll hold you to your promise."

"You did what? Why, you should be shot!" Victoria blasted Duel upon hearing his news that Jessie would stay on with him at the farm. "Furthermore, I won't let you do it. Such a scandal. What would people say?"

"I don't care a fig about town gossip." He didn't understand what all the fuss was about.

"It's not you I'm worried about. It's that young lady. Papa, talk some sense into this mule-headed son of yours."

Walt McClain calmly looked up from his whittling. He blew the shavings off the wood. "She's right, son. Ain't right to fiddle with a woman's reputation. An' it appears that might be all the poor soul's got left. Your ma would turn over in her grave."

Exasperated, Duel ran his fingers through his hair. "It'll only be for a while. It's not like she's staying for good. Besides, Jessie didn't seem to object."

Victoria turned to her husband. "Roy, honey, tell this brother of mine what happened with Jane Sims last year."

"If Duel wants to end up the same as Jane and Charlie Maxfield, then we should keep our nose out of his affairs." Mirth twinkled in Roy Austin's eyes.

"What are you two blathering about?" He smelled a dead rat.

Roy lifted one of the twins, Duel had no idea which one because they looked identical, onto his knee. "Jane was riding into town in her buggy and her horse turned lame. Just so happened the rig stopped in front of Charlie Maxfield's house so she went to ask for his help. Now, this is all perfectly innocent, mind you."

"Oh goody, a faewy tale. Cindewella, Papa?" the daughter on Roy's lap interrupted, clapping her hands.

"Hush, Becky, you'll make me lose my train of thought. Anyway, Charlie found the horse in a bad way. Put it in his barn and rubbed it down with liniment. Before Jane could get around to borrowing an animal from Charlie, a lightning storm blew in, stranding her."

"Honey, I love you dearly, but you sure know how to drag out a story." Victoria took the reins. "To make a long story short, folks brought out the tar and feathers and ran Jane out of town because she spent one night unchaperoned in Charlie's house."

"That's the craziest story I've ever heard. Sounds kinda far-fetched if you ask me." Duel wondered what they were up to. If he remembered the same Jane Sims, she chased after anything in britches who wasn't spoken for. And maybe some who were.

"You didn't let me get to the best part, darlin'." Roy affectionately patted his wife's knee. "Charlie felt real bad for Jane so he went after her. He brought her back and married her. Now, Jane's in the family way."

"Anyone comes to tar and feather Jessie, they'll have to go through me to do it." The thought didn't set well. The brand on her back was still fresh in his memory.

"Uncle Duel, would you shoot 'em?" George's eyes grew big.

"Right between the eyes. No one'd better dare." He ruffled the boy's hair.

"Tarnation, son. A man shouldn't let it come to that. Think of the little lady, for God's sake." Walt folded his knife and dropped it in the pocket of his overalls.

"Pop, what would you have me do? Vicky an' Roy don't have room to put her up here. And it wouldn't do me a lick of good if they could. What I need is a woman to take care of Marley."

Walt eyeballed his son intently. "You plannin' on doin' some farming, try to make a go of the place?"

"Sure am."

"Whoee! That's the best news I've heard in a coon's age."

Victoria tapped her foot impatiently. "You two quit changin' the subject. What about Jessie?"

"She's stayin' and that's that, Vicky!" Duel jerked on his Stetson and stood, signaling an end to the discussion.

"Not so fast, brother. I'll not have the McClain or Austin name bandied about Tranquility like a rubber ball."

"What does bandied mean, Mama?" young Henry asked.

"Dummard, it means folks talkin' about somethin' they don't know beans about." George wore a serious expression.

"Only one thing to do, son." Walt rose slowly and hitched up the bib of his overalls. "An' that's the right thing."

The soft whinny of Preacher relayed the news that Duel had returned. Jessie quickly finished wiping dust from the last of the furniture. With no one occupying the dwelling, filth had accumulated atop everything. She'd even opened the windows and given it a thorough airing out.

Now, she straightened a lace doily on an oak credenza and gave the room a once-over. The furnishings fairly gleamed with her efforts. Clean as a whistle, if she did say so herself.

Marley Rose crawled over the spotless floor, investigating every nook and cranny. The child seemed perfectly at home. But then, she'd adapted just as easily to life on the trail. In return for her good nature, Marley asked very little, only someone to love her. Jessie swallowed hard and blinked. It was such a small thing to ask really. It wasn't something she could hope for herself, but surely it couldn't be asking that much for a small baby?

Jessie ran her fingertips along the back of the handsome rocking chair. While simple and sturdy described the contents of the room, this was an exception. A curved back and ornate carving told her the purchaser had placed the item in high regard. It spoke of the great love with which Duel and his wife had faced their firstborn's arrival.

A swift glance out the window at the grave on the hill, then back to the small child who sat playing contentedly, brought an ache to her heart. The gentle breeze made her shiver.

The ease Duel portrayed in handling the Schofield told her farming hadn't always been his chosen profession. Yet she admired a man who sought gentler ways.

She couldn't think of anything more honest than a man who tilled the soil. Something solid and lasting. At least she hoped it would be, for Marley Rose's sake.

Grabbing the broom, she hurried to put it away. A little out of breath, she turned as the front door swung open.

Duel's arms were full of staples, evidently from the general store in town. He kicked the door, banging it against the wall as he came through. Jessie hurried to help relieve his load.

"Aunt Bessie's garter!" His approval at her hard work shone in his eyes. "Give you a little water and a broom and you transform a shack into a castle."

The compliment came out of the blue and she ducked her head, hiding her quick blush. She'd enjoyed the task and taken pride in making the house a home once more, but she hadn't done it for his praise.

"I'm not the only one to make changes," she said shyly. "You've shaved."

He looked different without the stubble. His chiseled features were more defined. Not handsome in the strictest sense of the word, but striking. And wonderful.

"Thought I'd better. Past time for a bath an' shave." He set one of the boxes full of goods on the kitchen table and began rummaging through it. "Brought you an' Marley something."

It pleased her that he'd thought of the babe, but for him to buy her anything . . . ?

"I don't think I can accept. Not proper you bringing me a present." Especially when she had nothing to give in return. And that was one thing she wanted to avoid—being beholden to any man again.

"It's only a clean dress. Something you an' Marley Rose are sorely in need of." Duel found the twine-bound package at last.

She couldn't argue about the sad shape of her clothing. Though she'd managed to rinse out much of the blood that had covered her, brown spots remained where the stains had set. That, and rips in the sleeve and skirt, convinced her of the necessity of fresh apparel. Still, pride made her hesitate to accept the parcel he held out.

"Take it." His determined gaze gentled and entreated. "Consider it payment if you must, for cleaning the house and looking after Marley Rose."

At last she accepted the offering with downcast eyes. The man's generosity touched her and the warmth of his nearness made her regret her decision to stay. His large frame engulfed the room—and her. Perhaps it wasn't too late to change her mind.

"When she gets a chance, Vicky will get the twins' hand-me-downs from the attic for Marley." He started putting the food away and said over his shoulder, "She also mentioned she probably has a few things you can wear."

"I'm not looking for charity, Mr. McClain." The brown paper wrapping the garments rustled in her hand. "Besides, I won't be staying that long."

His broad back stiffened. "Yes, well . . . about that." He didn't face her, instead stared out the small window. "I have a matter to discuss. Vicky and my father had a conniption fit about you living here with me. Made me see how inappropriate it is and all."

Was he saying he'd made a mistake, that he didn't want her after all? Or perhaps he'd discovered the truth about her while in town?

"If you're having second thoughts—"

"Not entirely." He turned but his gaze stayed glued to a spot on the floor. "Ma'am . . . Jessie . . . seeing as how you don't have a husband . . . and I don't have a . . . anyone . . . I think we should wed."

At last he raised his eyes to meet hers. "Not that I give a tinker's damn about my own reputation, but to protect you."

All the air suddenly swooshed from the room and left her gasping. "You're asking . . . ?"

"Jessie, will you marry me?"

Chapter Six

The tightness of his tone told Jessie everything she needed to know. Duel loathed the idea of marrying her. The plot on the hill owned his heart. And, she suspected, he wasn't asking for the motherless little girl. That left one clear reason. He pitied her. Somehow he'd figured out she had no place to go. The man offered her a home and his name for all the wrong reasons.

"Don't you think marriage is a drastic step?" she began slowly. "A little more than a week ago you weren't even aware I existed."

"You care for Marley Rose and that's all that concerns me."

Old pain sprang forth. Duel saw her as property, the same as Jeremiah had.

"Seems to me a man and a woman should feel something for each other to take vows. They should have some reason besides a child to bind them together." Much as the thought of wedded bliss with this noble Texan tempted her, she would never allow it. Not with bloodstains on her hands.

"Look at it as purely a business arrangement," he insisted. "When—"

"No! I can't!" The strangled sound coming from her mouth wasn't due to hands around her throat, as had more often been the case. It came from a sense of honor—and from fickle fingers that threatened to pluck her heart from her chest.

Stumbling from the farmhouse, she clawed her way up one hill, then another until she found herself alone, staring down at the raging water of the mighty Colorado.

"Son, was that Jessie I saw runnin' up the hill like a banshee was chasin' her?" Walt rubbed his chin whiskers.

"Pop, do me a favor? Watch Marley till I get back." Duel didn't wait for an answer. His long stride had already taken him to the door.

"What's goin' on? I only came to talk about plantin' time."

"Later, Pop. Mind the child for me. Please."

He lunged in the direction where he saw the flash of skirts disappear. Questions turned and twisted in his mind while he chastised himself for springing Vicky's lame-brained idea on Jessie so suddenly. The least he could have done was prepare her a little. No wonder the woman bolted from the house like an unbroken stallion.

"An idiot," he muttered to himself, "a full-fledged dunce. I should've taken Jessie's delicate state into account."

He thrashed through the tangle of brush, searching for signs of Jessie, heedless of breaking limbs that fell to the ground in his wake.

Just when he had lost hope, a fragment of blue waved from the thorny branch of a mesquite. The snippet must have torn from Jessie's skirt.

So intent was he on the fabric he didn't see the low branch in time to duck. The whack sent his hat flying. Shaking off the pain, he picked up his hat and tore up the hill. He could hear the roar of the river and knew a dead end lay at the top.

If Jessie went this way, she had gotten herself trapped.

By the time he reached the bluff he was huffing and puffing. Then the crushing hooves of wild horses stampeded in his chest when he saw her.

Jessie turned, then took another step toward the edge of the cliff.

"Wait!" Duel stretched both hands in the air, palms up, to indicate he wanted only to talk. His blood raced as he took a tentative step.

"Go back. This is the best way." Tears left a trail down her cheeks. She wiped them angrily away and his breath stopped when she poised to jump.

"Please." He prayed for the right words that would keep her from plunging to her death. "Jessie, don't."

"There's no other way."

The sob in her throat released waves of panic. She meant to end her life for whatever reason. He had to stop her. Not because he felt it his duty and not for his need to provide Marley Rose with a caretaker. Deep down, he realized he couldn't bear to lose one more soul. And if he wanted the honest truth, she'd become a balm for his ache. Loneliness hadn't inflicted its breath-stealing grip on him quite so tightly. The chill inside had almost begun to thaw.

"There are always other choices. A person just has to find them, that's all. I'll help you."

"You don't know what I've done. I won't bring my worries to your doorstep. I can't."

He watched her stare into the water below. Resolute commitment that had shown so clearly on her face a second ago now wavered with last minute indecision. Taking hope, Duel forced himself to remain calm.

"Let me be the judge of that. I'm sure you can make amends for whatever it is you believe you did."

Jessie met his gaze. "Why? Why would you worry about what happens to me? I'll only bring trouble."

"Because the three of us—you, Marley Rose, me . . . we're broken. But together we somehow work." He inched forward.

"Do you really think so?"

He took advantage of the opening. "And Marley Rose needs you. You can't deprive that child of the love I know you're capable of giving. You can't snatch away the little bit of kindness Marley's known."

"Better she learns early the cruel facts of life." She turned back to the violent view below her.

The shuffling of her feet sent pebbles rushing down into the water. Duel had to move or the next instant would send her hurtling over the edge. Conversation had bought him precious minutes to creep closer. He lunged.

"I won't let you die!" His arms shook as he held her tightly. He'd almost missed her.

"I'm already dead. The only difference between now and when they put me six feet under is I'm still breathing. An inconvenience I could've remedied if you hadn't meddled."

He wasn't sure what he expected, but her deep anger caught him by surprise.

"I couldn't let you die." He struggled to change her focus. "I never had a woman kill herself just because I asked her to marry me. Wouldn't set well."

A startled expression swept her face. Then she rewarded his humorous efforts with a wan smile. "You're something, Mr. McClain. Making light at a time like this."

He couldn't answer in that instant because holding her this close, seeing the softness in her blue eyes made his legs shake. Tenderly, he lifted and carried her a safe distance from the precipice.

"Wasn't joking," he mumbled, all humor gone.

She dropped wearily onto a log tinged black by lightning. "Any woman would give her eyeteeth to wed you. Even if she knew it was nothing more than a business arrangement . . . if she was of the marrying kind."

He lifted his hat and ran his fingers through his hair. Unsure of the ground on which he tread, he twirled his hat in his hands. "Truth is, I merely wanted to protect you." He berated himself for listening to Vicky and Roy. "I'm sure I can find another way. A lady fine as you deserves a better man. I don't blame you for spurning a broken-down sodbuster like me."

Jessie's head snapped up to stare at him, her face becoming a cold mask. "How little you know of what I deserve."

"I'm sure as shootin' you didn't do anything wrong and certainly nothing that would merit the treatment you've suffered." He watched the blood slowly drain from her face, leaving it chalky white.

"You have no idea what you're talking about." Her words were razor sharp.

"I saw the brand you wear."

Her lips compressed in a thin, tight line. Her resolute control brought an overpowering urge to take her in his arms if only to give her a moment's peace. The kind she'd given him by allowing him to watch her with the babe.

"I killed my husband."

She delivered the calm statement as if she'd just announced she had a tangle in her hair or a piece of food stuck in her teeth.

"If . . . if he's the one responsible for your condition," Duel began slowly adjusting to the shock. "I'd say you had a mighty good reason."

"I broke the law." Her voice cracked and the rest of her confession became barely audible. "I'm a wanted murderer."

What could he say that would ease her agony? He stuffed his hat back on his head and lowered himself to the log beside her. With a shoulder touching hers, he offered her his handkerchief.

"Was he the one who hurt you?"

A trembling chin betrayed her as she nodded.

"Well, I can't imagine wasting sympathy on a wife-beater." Anger and hate left an acrid taste in his mouth. "From what little I can see, you were more than justified."

"Lord knows Jeremiah was the most mean-spirited human ever put on this earth. It still didn't give me the right." She blew her nose and straightened.

"I imagine you'd had enough that night you wandered into

my camp." Her delicate hand rested in her lap. Wanting merely to comfort, Duel took it in his. He was relieved when she let him.

"It didn't start off that way. When Jeremiah Foltry and I exchanged vows, I believe he truly loved me. Our first married year had its ups and downs, but we dealt with them. Then he changed. Drank too much, hung around with the wrong men, became obsessed with his possessions—the ranch, his land, which at fifty thousand acres was never enough—and me. The next seven years became a living hell."

Jessie Foltry. At last Duel knew her name.

He looked down at the long fingers nestled in his palm. Despite their condition from harsh travel and work, they were as dainty and fine as the heart of the woman they belonged to. He had to battle the temptation to bring her hand to his lips. Jeremiah Foltry had to be the worst kind of fool to have tried to destroy the bounty he'd had in his grasp.

"I'm sorry. If you'd rather not talk about it anymore. . . ."

"It actually feels good to tell someone after all these years. I've kept it inside far too long." When she shifted her gaze to meet his, a little of the pain had left. The brilliance of her honesty shone like a beacon in the midst of a great storm.

"Your husband owns—owned—the Diamond J ranch?"

"He was so obsessed with that damn land he strung that newfangled barbed wire around every inch of it and put his brand on everything that walked inside it."

"Including you."

Worry clouded the blue orbs. "I wish you hadn't seen that. I didn't mean for anyone ever to see the mark my insolence earned."

"I haven't been able to get it out of my mind."

"Have you ever been so scared, you think the next second is going to be your last? You're looking in the face of the devil and wondering how on earth you can keep him from taking your soul? Have you been that scared?"

Annie's cold, lifeless body flashed across his mind's eye.

He'd placed her in that wooden coffin. He'd folded her stiff arms around their son. He'd thrown dirt over the two most precious beings he'd ever known. Then he'd ridden off, knowing he'd be alone for the rest of his days.

"Yeah, I've been there." The hand he'd cradled in his palm dropped onto her lap.

Suddenly Jessie turned. "Marley Rose! You have to get back."

"Don't worry. Pop's getting acquainted with his new granddaughter."

"I shouldn't have run out like that, but I didn't know what else to do. And I meant what I said. I won't bring you and the girl trouble." Jessie twisted the handkerchief into a knot. "You know they'll come for me sooner or later."

"That's one more good reason for taking my name. They won't be looking for a married woman with a child. I can protect you if you'll let me."

"Think what that would do to Marley six months or a year down the road. Just when she got accustomed to me, to lose her mother all over again. Would you want that?"

Anguish wrapping her words reaffirmed his faith that Jessie's love for the child ran far more than surface deep. She worried not about what the future held for her or how to protect her secret, but how to shield the little girl whom life had abandoned.

"Forget the marriage idea. I told Vicky it wouldn't work. I want to help you though if you'll let me. I think I have a plan."

"You don't have to do this. It isn't your problem."

"The heck it ain't. You think I want that little darling growing up not ever knowing the love of a mother?"

"She has you. And your kinfolk."

"Not the same. Here's the deal. You can live with Vicky and Roy and come to the farm every morning. I'll plant sorghum. I happen to know there's a big need for sorghum. We'll use the money from harvesting to hire you one of those high-priced lawyers and clear your name." Duel tried not to look smug. While far from perfect, his plan was a good one.

"Won't hold water." She had twisted the handkerchief so tightly he was sure it would never be the same. She kept her head lowered, refusing to meet his confused look.

"I think it will work if we give it a chance."

"You saw how Victoria and Roy are stumbling all over themselves in that small house. I won't move in with them. Besides, your plan wouldn't stop gossip. We'd still be together every day. Unchaperoned."

"Well, it sure beats jumping off a cliff into the Colorado."

Jessie's face darkened. Duel wished he could take back those words. Someday he'd learn to keep his trap shut, or at least think about the words before they popped from his mouth. Before he could apologize for the slip she shot him a dubious look.

"You're taking back your offer of marriage?"

Her Wedgwood gaze further buffeted his composure. Was that roar in his ears from the river below?

"You don't have to worry. I won't pester you again."

"That's too bad, because I've changed my mind. I accept."

Chapter Seven

Jessie wore her new dress to the quiet ceremony. Standing there in the simple high-necked gray poplin, her legs shook. In fact, her body trembled from head to toe as they stood before the minister.

"Do you, Duel, take this woman, Jessie. Cleave unto her in sickness and in health, forsaking all others, so help you God?"

Duel's deep reply got lost in the whirling maze of her thoughts. Her palms grew moist. How could she vow to love and cherish a stranger she barely knew? Especially, when a few weeks before, she would have died before she ever again gave any man control over her life. What was she thinking?

You're not a wife. You're just a good-for-nothing woman. You disgust me. For that, I'm giving you to my friends. You'll pleasure them or you'll die.

Jeremiah's last words leapt through time, reminding her that she was anything but the fine woman Duel thought her to be. Even though she'd told him of her terrible crime, she couldn't help feeling she was deceiving him. He didn't know all.

She glanced sideways at the tall man beside her. The stiff white shirt he'd worn under protest seemed out of place on someone who was more at home in buckskins and rough muslin. Yet Victoria had insisted that a groom of the McClain variety should be properly dressed when he wed. The still damp ends of his hair curled over the high collar, the dark strands contrasting against the stark whiteness.

A tic in his jaw, ever apparent when irritation overcame him, marred the smoothness of his chiseled profile. Then she saw the nick just beneath his chin. The small cut reinforced her convictions. His nervousness in shaving told, far more than words, of an uncertainty that he'd chosen the right path.

He spoke of protecting and caring for her yesterday on the bluff and no doubt he meant it for he didn't speak idly. But when they came for her?

Knowing he had doubts didn't stunt the growth of her own. What gave her the idea that she could make a life with him—that she could compete with living memories of a dead woman?

"And you, Jessie, do you take this man. Cleave unto him in sickness and in health, forsaking all others, so help you God?"

The inside of her mouth became parched. She couldn't utter a single sound.

One of the children coughed. The four sat prim and proper in a row beside their mother and father on the wooden pew. Marley Rose gurgled happily in Walt McClain's lap.

"Ahem." The reverend peered at her over his horn-rimmed spectacles.

The waves of panic refused to cease. Perspiration trickled down her back. The room began to whirl like a prairie cyclone, sucking up everything in its way.

You're not a wife. You're just a good-for-nothing woman.

Jeremiah always prophesied she'd never amount to a hill of beans. Yet she now had the audacity to think otherwise.

A warm, steady hand reached for hers. The room stopped whirling. Her gaze met Duel's and his expression startled her.

His smile, the light in his eyes gave her courage.

Duel's hand tightened around hers, then he winked. She trusted him. Honor and integrity were words he lived by. Maybe love would never come, but he cared for her and that was enough.

"Would you like me to repeat the question?" the reverend asked quietly.

"No." She fell into her knight's dusky amber spell, past his good heart and into his soul. The buzz inside her head stopped. She returned his firm grip.

She wet her lips and plunged. "I do. I promise to lo . . . to cleave unto him, in sickness and in health, so help me God."

"I now proclaim you husband and wife. You may kiss the bride, Duel."

The barest brush of his lips against her cheek filled her with a happy glow.

In the rush of well-wishers, Jessie caught his glance once more. It made the sunshine much brighter.

Duel came from a long line of promise keepers. He'd said so himself.

" 'Hush little baby, don't say a word, Mama's gonna buy you a mockingbird.' "

Jessie rocked Marley to sleep in the fancy rocking chair. Upon Duel's disappearance after supper, unease had settled around her.

A man generally expected certain liberties on his wedding night. Though he'd touted their alliance as simply a business arrangement, would he change his mind? Even the ghost of a doubt was enough to twist her stomach into knots.

She smoothed the child's dark curls and smiled. Marley Rose had gotten the best of her "papa" this day. After the ceremony that made them legally a family, he'd tried everything in his power to get her to drink the canned milk he bought at the general store. Yet the girl would have none of it. It was the goat's milk or nothing. Airing more than a few damnations, he wound up having to tussle with the stubborn nanny after all.

The doorknob turned and Duel kicked the mud off his boots and removed his hat before he stepped into the room. His brief glance touched her before he looked away.

"She asleep?" He hung the hat beside the door.

"Finally."

He came closer. "Let me take her to bed."

Jessie stopped rocking. When Duel reached for the babe she trembled slightly—more from the tender care he displayed than anything else.

"You okay?" Sincerity rang in the softly spoken words.

"This is going to take some time to get used to." She held the child out and his hand grazed hers as he scooped the limp bundle into his arms.

In all the years with Jeremiah she'd never once experienced such a wonderful, warm sensation. Perhaps she was simply tired. Perhaps the crackling fire in the hearth made the room so heated. Perhaps there were worse fates than sharing a bed with this man.

Marley Rose sighed, then snuggled against his wide chest. A lump formed in her throat as she watched him amble to the sleeping area separated only by a curtain from the living area. The small bed he'd made for his little darling perched at the foot of the larger one—the one in which she'd soon find herself.

Tightness gripped her bosom as Duel tucked the blankets around the small form. A misty film covered her vision. He made a wonderful father, despite his reluctance to use the word.

Marley whimpered in her sleep. He crooned gently to soothe away her fears, then bent to kiss her forehead.

Lest he catch her watching, Jessie rose and grabbed a dishcloth. Busily putting away the supper dishes, she didn't hear his footsteps. His voice startled her when it shattered the quiet night.

"We have to talk."

Apprehension hammered in her chest as she took the chair he held for her. Was this when he told her everything had been a mistake—that he didn't need her?

"Your horse. We have to decide what to do with it."

"I don't know what you mean." The horse? What did Cinnabar do that they must arrive at a decision tonight?

"I'm trying to protect you until we can clear your name. The sorrel bears the Diamond J brand. Anyone sees the mare here, they'll start putting the pieces together."

"Oh." The blood drained from her face at the possibility.

"I know a buffalo hunter who's passing through Tranquility. He'll take the sorrel off our hands in exchange for a few staples. With his wandering ways, the man'll ensure no one'll ever find the horse."

A long sigh broke from her lips. She clasped her hands together tightly in her lap.

"I suppose we must."

"Questions about you are going to fly around town as it is. No need to add further worries to our full plate."

That Duel simply wanted to shield her against trouble brought an onrush of emotion and she blinked away the hotness. Not since she was a child had anyone protected her.

"You're right, of course. It's just that I raised Cinnabar from a foal and to. . . ."

She closed her eyes, trying to keep the tremor from her voice. Cinnabar was her baby. Duel's comforting touch on her shoulder cracked the dam of her composure. She swallowed the thickness that blocked her throat. It wouldn't help anything to make a babbling fool of herself.

"If you'd rather, I'll think of something else."

"No. It's stupid of me to try and hold on to something that would harm not only me, but you and Marley as well, Mr. McClain."

Her shoulder felt cold when he abruptly removed his hand. He straightened in his chair.

"There's something else I mean to get straight tonight. Don't call me 'mister.' A wife should call her husband by name if he asks her to. From now on you'll call me Duel."

His large hand engulfed hers. Her lips parted on a silent gasp when he brushed the tips of her fingers against his lips.

"I'll never do anything to hurt you. I'll keep you safe."

His tenderness sent waves of surprise, then a much stronger feeling of pleasure over her. She was falling head over heels into a bright light.

"And will you call me Jessie?" she asked, almost breathless.

"If you want me to." Slowly, seemingly with reluctance he released her hand. Only then did she find it easy to breathe again.

"I'd like that . . . Duel."

The chair scraped against the wood floor when he rose.

"The bed is yours. I'll make mine in the barn."

Suddenly the light around her dimmed. She should feel relief, or deliverance, or gladness. Instead a growing disappointment filled her heart. True to his promise, their joining was to be nothing more than a business arrangement.

"Duel?"

He paused at the door. "Sweet dreams, Jessie." Then he was gone.

She wanted to run after him, to pull him back. It didn't make sense to consider her feelings one minute and the next push her away. Had she completely mistaken the affection he'd shown? After all, she was merely a stand-in for the woman who filled his soul. No use kidding herself. All her new husband felt for her was pity.

Almost a week after Jessie and Duel spoke their vows, Luke McClain dismounted in front of El Paso's jail. It felt good to straighten the kinks out. Every bone ached from too long in the saddle. Bright sun glinted off his silver Texas Ranger star. He pulled his hat lower to block the rays and squinted at the sheriff sign that creaked in the slight breeze.

The message he'd gotten from Maj. John B. Jones, the commander of the Frontier Battalion, gave him a respite from an assignment that kept him one step from purgatory. Six months and still no end in sight.

Major Jones had requested he contact Sheriff Bart Daniels in El Paso, pronto. He didn't state what problem needed his attention, just to get there fast. Curious, Luke stepped into the office.

"Bart, you old desert fox. If you weren't so danged ugly I'd kiss you."

The man whirled from the potbellied stove, sloshing hot coffee onto his hand.

"Yeee doggies! Ain't that just like a Ranger to sneak up on a man." Bart dried his hand on the back of his trousers, then blew on the scalded area. "You kiss me, you whippersnapper, I'll throw your mangy carcass in the pokey an' throw away the key."

"You wouldn't do that to your dearest friend."

Luke watched the lines around Bart's eyes crinkle with mirth. The two had a long-standing friendship, and he loved bantering with the old lawman.

Bart sat the cup on his desk before he slapped Luke on the back affectionately.

"You done been without a woman too long, son. Shore don't want any man a-kissin' on me."

"I'm just so danged glad for another assignment I got carried away. Been chasing Victorio all over hell and half of Georgia and still no closer to catching the slippery Mescalero chief."

"Sit down, Luke, an' give me the lowdown. I heard him and a hundred and twenty-five warriors escaped from the reservation a while back." Bart smoothed his bushy mustache, which looked more like an array of pine needles that stuck from every angle. "Want some coffee? Just made a pot."

" 'Preciate it." Luke took a chair and propped both feet on the sheriff's desk. A grin settled on his face as he watched Bart shuffle to the stove and back.

The man handed over the cup, staring at Luke's choice of

a footrest. "Just like you Rangers. Come in here and take over."

"Aw, Bart, if I didn't give you something to gripe about now and agin, you'd think I didn't like you. Besides, you sent for me, remember?"

The man squinted from beneath bushy eyebrows that matched his mustache. "Ain't forgettin' a dad-burned thing. Ain't so old I can't turn you over my knee either." His eyes twinkled as he eased into his chair.

"Well?" Luke sipped the hot brew. Would the man ever get down to business? He had Indians to round up, outlaws to lasso, and horse thieves to corral. A Ranger's work was never done. "What's got your tail feathers ruffled?"

"Murder. Jeremiah Gates Foltry of the Diamond J got hisself shot, and eyewitnesses say his wife done the shootin'."

"You need me to arrest a woman? Don't have the heart for it, huh?" Luke pushed his hat back with a forefinger.

"Nothin' worse than a smart-assed Ranger." Bart leaned forward, propping his elbows on the desk. "I'd arrest her if I knew where in blazes she's gone. Thing is, Jessie disappeared after she pumped Foltry full of holes."

"No chance the eyewitnesses could be mistaken?" It wouldn't be the first time one of Foltry's people lied for him. Luke knew the rancher well. Couldn't say he liked him much.

"She also shot one of them when they tried to stop 'er. Pete Morgan's laid up over at the doc's if you wanna ask him some questions."

"When did this one-woman massacre take place?"

"Couple of weeks ago thereabouts. I tracked her and the sorrel she stole past Devil's Ridge before she put the slip on me at the Pecos River."

Luke had to admire a woman who could outwit old Bart. The sheriff's reputation as an expert tracker was well earned. "With the head start she could be most anywhere by now. Any idea where? Relatives who might hide her out? A lover she ran off to link up with?"

"Her mother and father live here in El Paso. Zack an'

Phoebe Sutton couldn't shed any light on where their daughter'd be going. Anything else, your guess is good as mine."

"Even the lover part?"

"I don't think so. Shoot, if Foltry even sensed another man sniffing around his wife, he'd have killed her a long time ago."

Luke sipped on the coffee, speculating. "You're not giving me much to go on here, Bart. A cold trail, no intended destination. Hell, I was having better luck with Victorio."

"Quit your bellyachin'. Thought you Rangers didn't need any help, could do most nigh anything if you set your mind to it."

Luke grunted and downed more of the fortifying coffee. "It'd be nice for once if someone handed me something easy. Bet your whittling knife ole Luke'll eventually get his man—or woman."

"The more you sit here jawin' the farther the lady's gittin'."

"Jessie Foltry may not even be alive. The desert has a way of exacting its own justice." Luke lifted his boots from the desk and rose to his full height.

"Oh, I almost forgot." Sheriff Daniels stopped him on his way to the door. "Your sister sent a telegram if you happened to come through here."

"Vicky?" It'd been a year or more since he last visited Tranquility. With his heart doing double time, he took the crisp envelope and ran his finger beneath the seal.

"Don't suppose it's anything you'd like to share with a lonely old man?" Bart squinted up at him. "You know you're like fam'ly to me."

"Well, I'll be!"

"What? What are you 'I'll being' about?"

Ignoring him, Luke finished reading the message. The news indeed thrilled him.

"Are you gonna stand there grinnin' like a 'possom or are you gonna tell me?" Bart sputtered, his nosey nature getting the best of him.

"It's Duel." Luke couldn't wipe the grin from his face. He

never passed a chance to tease the curious-minded man. "Best darn news I've heard in a coon's age."

Bart stood and put his hands on the pearl-handled six-shooters that hung from his girth. "If I hafta shoot you to find out, by God that's what I aim to do. Now, what has that brother of yours gone an' done?"

"He's got himself hitched, Mister Nosey."

"Married? Whooee! You're darn tootin' it's good news. Does Vicky say who the lucky woman is?"

"Only that he brought her home with him. So, I take it Vicky didn't know her." Luke folded the telegram and stuck it in his pocket.

"That all she says? No other news?" Bart craned his neck.

"If you ain't the beatin'est old codger I ever saw in all my born days. Time was when a man's privacy counted for something." Luke's smile stretched from ear to ear.

"I'm a thinkin' there's more. You wouldn't have wrinkled your forehead if there hadn't been."

"Christ sakes! You know, Bart, maybe I should take you with me. Maybe the reason me an' the boys can't catch Victorio is because we sit around wrinklin' our foreheads too much."

Luke dodged the empty tin cup Bart threw.

"Quit funnin' an old man. You know you're hidin' something." Bart scratched his head in frustration. "Duel passed through here a while back and looked like the devil hisself was ridin' on his back. Tore me up to see him like that. A changed man from his bounty-huntin' days. Now, there was one tough hombre. Only thing separatin' him from those killers he brought in was a heart of pure gold."

"Duel lost his reason to live when Annie and his son died."

"Great God in the morning! I wanted to ask, but you know I respect a man's privacy."

"When pigs fly! It's more like he never gave you a chance."

Bart gave a wounded sniff. "Be that as it may . . . suppose somethin' happens with another wife? Most likely be the end of poor Duel. Quit your stallin' and spill the beans. Anything else of interest in the damn letter?"

"If you have to know, Vicky says if I'd mosey back up there, I'd find another surprise waiting." The smile faded. Lord knows he needed to visit his family. Suddenly Luke was homesick. "Didn't say what in hell the surprise was."

"Well, son, guess you'd best go find out."

"I'll see where Mrs. Jessie Foltry's trail leads, and then, I might just do that." Who knows? Maybe the trail would take him within shouting distance. Nothing'd thrill his heart more than to see his brother happy again.

Chapter Eight

" 'Sweet Dreams, Jessie.' Now, couldn't I have said something a little more meaningful?"

Though the workings in a female head could be as easy to read as fresh trail in a buffalo stampede, he got the impression he'd disappointed Jessie. It wasn't a feeling he liked.

Preacher nickered gently and stuck his head over the stall, curiously watching Duel spread fresh hay in the south corner of the barn. A lantern illuminated the structure, casting a soft glow over the interior. The damp chill in the air promised the need of a fire.

"I know. A man don't need his horse telling him he's an utter fool."

After he'd made a cozy place to sleep, he unrolled his bedding and got a wool blanket for cover.

"Fine thing for a man on his wedding night."

The horse nodded his head as though in agreement. "But I have good reason. If you'd seen Jessie's face, you'd understand. For God's sake, the woman nearly crawls out of her skin every time I walk into the room."

Not that he expected anything different.

"We're not really married, you know," he continued to the watchful animal. "Not in the regular way. She's in need of a roof over her head and a reason to live. Reckon I can provide the roof, but not sure about the other part. Maybe in time."

Preacher pawed the ground. The ruckus brought the sorrel to life, causing the mare to neigh loudly. Then the goat began a chorus of blehs.

"Aunt Bessie's garter! I may as well be sleeping in Noah's ark. See what you've done? You should be ashamed of yourself."

Preacher eyed him dolefully.

Duel sat down on the straw. "That's better. Let a man get some rest."

He lowered the wick in the lantern beside him, casting the room in darkness. Instantly, the noisy animals calmed. He stretched his length onto the pallet, letting out a loud sigh.

There might come a day when he would move into the house. Not into Jessie's bed, but perhaps on the floor. Sharing the same bed would never happen, he reminded himself. Anyway, he was more partial to the hard ground and fresh air.

Then he had to consider Jessie's distrust of men. Hell, that even took into account the one she'd married today. There for a moment she'd almost bolted from the church. The panic in her eyes had made Duel wonder if they'd been like that when Jeremiah Foltry stuck the hot brand to her.

Damn! His duty now was to protect Jessie from the hangman's noose. It was the least he could do for the woman who could sing like an angel and loved a helpless little girl more than life itself.

His first order of business was taking Cinnabar to her new owner. By all that's holy, he hated asking Jessie to give up the horse who meant the world to her. It represented one more thing she would lose. *Double Damn!*

Though the day's events had taken their toll, he couldn't sleep. The strange surroundings took the blame. No moon or stars overhead. No crackling fire to disturb the quiet. No auburn-haired woman with blue eyes softly breathing nearby.

Without raising the wick on the lantern, he wandered to the door. Thin, wispy clouds cast shadows across the full moon. Light fog created a haze in the valley, adding a ghostly appearance. And lending to the haunting ambiance of the night, an owl hooted overhead in the branches of the oak tree.

Movement in the house suddenly caught his attention. Lamplight in the room outlined a feminine profile. Jessie couldn't sleep either. He wondered if she worried, if she felt safe.

Thank goodness he'd gotten the name business straightened out. A wife didn't go around calling her husband "mister." Only now he found himself in a fine kettle of fish. He was stuck with addressing her as Jessie. Somehow "ma'am" seemed safer.

What possessed him to kiss her fingertips? Not a brilliant thing to do under the circumstances. Yet it had seemed natural. The intimate holding of her long, delicate fingers had caught him unprepared. He could still taste her skin—fresh morning dew on a honeysuckle vine.

Just then, Jessie turned. Although he knew the darkness shielded him, he moved farther into the shadows. Her piercing stare out the window unnerved him. As if she could see inside his soul and found him wanting.

Lord knows he hadn't told a lie—she, Marley Rose, and he were broken people but somehow together they worked.

Neither the hazy night or the space between them could dim the brightness of Jessie's gaze through the window. If he breathed deeply enough he could almost smell the faint feminine fragrance that swirled around her. Without meaning to, he closed his eyes and inhaled.

What he was thinking could most certainly complicate his life. A man in his situation needed fortitude.

Duel straightened. Perhaps he'd just try to think of her as

his sister. Yeah, that might work. A sister. If only he could remember to remind himself.

"I pray you'll find a good home, Cinnabar." Jessie tried to remain brave as she stroked the sorrel's neck for the last time. Yet, it pained her most to realize Cinnabar would pay the ultimate price for what she'd done. She'd been there for the mare's birthing and there when ranch hands had ridden her for the first time. The branding part had been the only event in the horse's life she'd missed.

"I love you. . . ." Her voice broke. She buried her face in the rich coat away from Duel.

The gentle hand on her shoulder again came unexpectedly.

"I'm truly sorry . . . Jessie. Wish it didn't have to be this way." Duel squeezed her shoulder lightly.

The warmth and compassion that encircled her now served as a springboard for her hate. Jeremiah'd stolen her trust, he'd rendered her incapable of bearing children, and he'd taken away something wondrous—her ability to be a wife to her new husband. She'd give anything to throw herself into Duel's protective arms, relax in his embrace, and not be afraid.

"Come now." He eased her gently aside. "It's time to go. Don't worry, I'll threaten the man with his life if he ever treats Cinnabar with anything other than kindness."

She felt overwhelming gratitude. The new owner would have no choice but treat the mare well after Duel got done with him.

A tremulous sigh escaped her. Then she remembered something. The gun. She reached into the saddlebag.

"Might as well dispose of this, too, while you're at it. Don't think I need it anymore."

His amber gaze met and held hers for a long, breath-stealing moment. Then, without a word he tucked it into his waist.

Marley Rose gurgled happily in the crook of Duel's arm. Jessie reached for her.

"Pa Pa."

"Papa has to go, sweetheart." She avoided Duel's scowl by pretending to wipe a smudge from the child's face. It wouldn't hurt to encourage her. The man would have to be crazy to resist the girl's love for long.

"I told you. She'll call me Duel. I'm not her papa. Don't put ideas in the child's head." He mounted Preacher, then reached for Cinnabar's reins.

"I'm afraid she'll call you whatever she wants, no matter what you or I say."

At her gentle rebuke his tone softened. "That may be, but it'll be best to keep telling her otherwise. In time she'll understand."

Duel turned the mustang toward town. "Be back soon. I'll pick up seed while I'm there. I figure to start clearing the field today."

Jessie watched them trot to the bend in the road. "Good-bye, faithful friend."

The hurt in her chest didn't ease after they disappeared from view. She doubted it would anytime soon.

"We've got work to do, young lady."

Marley crawled on the kitchen floor while Jessie washed and dried the breakfast dishes. A pleasant little thing, the child barely made a peep unless she was hungry. Jessie glanced at the baby from time to time to make sure she wasn't trying to stick anything inappropriate in her mouth. Once she discovered Marley pulling up to a chair and standing. Jessie handed her a big wooden spoon. Marley released her hold and stood on her own, playing with the spoon.

"You're such a good girl. Walk to me. You can do it, baby." Jessie held out her hand. "Come to mama."

Big, dark eyes looked up. Marley's chubby legs wobbled unsteadily as she tried to move them. Insecurity suddenly overcame her, and the child dropped to sit on the floor.

"That's all right, darlin'. No rush. You'll do it when you're good and ready." She stooped to kiss the top of her head. "Your papa will be so proud of you."

"Pa pa."

A noise outside aroused her curiosity. Had Duel returned so soon? A quick glance out the window made her yank off her apron and smooth back a few errant tendrils. Her new sister-in-law had picked today to come visit.

"Come in, Vicky." She hid her clenched hands behind her back. "I'm afraid your brother's gone into town."

Vicky smiled broadly. "Good. Didn't come to see him anyway."

"Will you have a seat?" She hadn't expected company. Thank goodness she'd cleaned and dusted some more.

The woman offered a blue piece of crockery. "I brought some sourdough starter."

"You think of everything." Vicky had a good heart even if she was a little on the strong-minded side. Her kindness touched Jessie, reminded her of all she missed in the ways of family. "Now I can bake that bread I wanted. Thank you so much."

"Don't mention it. I promised Duel I'd bring over some of the twins' baby things." Vicky took a box she'd been balancing on a hip from under her arm. Clothing items, various and sundry, overflowed from it. Once Jessie relieved her of the burden, she curiously looked around. "Where's my cute little niece?"

Just then Marley crawled from the kitchen, no doubt lured by the sound of voices. Vicky lifted her for a hug.

"She's so precious. Her dark brown eyes make me think of melted chocolate. Makes me want another baby, but Roy says he hopes the good Lord gives us a little more time before He blesses us again. What about you?"

"Me?" The word seemed no more than a croak. Suddenly the room became stuffy. Perspiration dampened her bodice.

"You and Duel. I know it's kinda soon, but are you planning on having children?"

Jessie was grateful for Vicky's preoccupation with Marley

Rose. By the time Vicky glanced her way again, she had a smile firmly in place.

"I suppose . . . like you said, it's early yet." She began sorting through the items Vicky had brought. "You're so thoughtful to give these to Marley."

"Shoot, they weren't doing anyone any good stuck in the attic. Now were they, Sweetie Pie?" The woman cooed to Marley, who was fascinated by bonnet ribbons. "Auntie Vicky is glad she can put them to good use."

"Would you like a cup of tea or something to eat? I made some johnnycake for breakfast. Duel didn't eat before he left." He'd only come in for a cup of coffee. And though he'd played with Marley, he appeared uncomfortable in his own house. She suspected he was in a hurry to get back outdoors, and he had Cinnabar to dispose of. A sad melancholy fell over her.

"Thank you, but I wouldn't care for anything. Jessie?" Vicky's soft entreaty lifted Jessie's attention from the cracks in the hardwood floor.

"I won't even pretend to imagine myself in your shoes," the woman went on. "Married to a man you hardly know. The good Lord can verify that my bullheaded brother is not the easiest person to live with. He can sure try your patience."

Vicky paused as if collecting her thoughts. Jessie kept silent and waited.

"What I'm trying to say is welcome to the family. All of us are tickled to death. When Duel buried Annie and their son, we worried ourselves sick. We didn't think the day would ever come when, for whatever reason, he'd marry again." Vicky rose and put her arm around her. "Like Papa said, 'From our lips to God's ear.' No matter what, Jessie, you fit into our family."

"Thank you, Vicky." Tears threatened to fall. These people knew nothing about her, yet they opened their arms and hearts to her. "Your acceptance means everything to me."

How would they treat her when they discovered the truth? She shuddered to think.

"I want to throw a celebration party for you and Duel. A welcome home sort of thing for Duel and a chance for you to get acquainted with the townsfolk."

A party? Panic swept through Jessie.

"I don't think Duel—"

Vicky didn't let her finish. "Saint Paddie's Day is next week and that would be perfect."

"Shouldn't you ask him first?" Jessie managed weakly.

"Pooh on him. He'd only throw a wet blanket on it."

"I don't have anything suitable to wear." Jessie groped lamely for excuses. A wet blanket wasn't all she suspected Duel would throw. She hadn't known her new husband long, but he didn't appear the social kind . . . or one who'd cotton to unwelcome surprises.

"You're about Annie's size. Her clothes are still here. If they don't quite fit, you could alter them."

"I couldn't. It wouldn't be right to desecrate her memory. Besides, Duel hasn't given me leave to wear them. The loss is still very painful for him."

"He probably hasn't gotten around to it." Vicky waved her arm, dismissing her brother's lack of good grace. "You know menfolk. If it doesn't have anything to do with a horse, food, or whiskey, nothing else crosses their mind."

"The party's a nice gesture, but we really couldn't. Not now. Maybe later on when we get settled in."

For all the attention Vicky paid, Jessie wondered if she had a hearing problem. "No better time than the present. You need to meet the people you'll be living amongst. I won't take no for an answer."

She had to give Vicky one thing—persistence. One by one, the woman had steamrolled all of her pleas. Doom lurched in the pit of Jessie's stomach.

"Next Saturday at our place," Vicky said with a decisive nod. "We'll have a barn dance."

Chapter Nine

"She what!"

Jessie grimaced at Duel's explosion. They were seated at the kitchen table while Marley Rose played with the wooden spoon at their feet. Though the last of daylight had faded, painting the sky a dark blue, this was her first opportunity to tell him of Vicky's visit. He'd returned from town with Walt McClain in tow and began clearing and plowing the fields. She hadn't spoken to him since early morning when he'd taken Cinnabar.

"Vicky wants—"

"I know full well what that sister of mine wants—to drive me loony. A party of all things! What in hell's the matter with her?"

Fit to be tied, Duel's face had turned three shades of red and irritation flashed dangerously from his eyes. She reminded herself never to cross him.

"I tried to tell her we didn't want anything like that. I even warned her that you'd be against it. She wouldn't listen."

"You can talk to a stump and get better results. When Vicky

gets a bee in her bonnet there's no getting it out." He calmed a little now that he'd aired his lungs. "I'm not blaming you, Jess. That sister of mine is sneaky. She took advantage of my absence to lay her plans."

"What are we going to do?" she asked miserably. "Everyone will have questions. I can't reveal where I came from, what I did, and keeping silent will draw more suspicion." She twisted the hem of her apron with cold fingers.

"I'll talk to her tomorrow." Duel gentled his tone. "Don't worry. We'll sort everything out."

From the corner of her eye she watched him reach to touch her arm. The yearning for that simple bit of warmth made her pulse leap. When he pulled back his hand, the room suddenly became a dreary place.

What if he couldn't stop his sister? It would take a powerful lot of persuading to get that woman to change her mind. In fact, Jessie seriously doubted he, or anyone for that matter, could. She'd better develop an alternate plan—one that would probably contain more than a few falsehoods.

"Did the buffalo hunter take Cinnabar?" Wrenching ache for the animal's fate had stayed with her the entire day. Surely the good Lord would see fit to give the sorrel a good home. But she doubted He'd listen to any prayers from her. She'd murdered a man, broken the most sacred commandment.

"He did." Duel must have seen the worry in her face. "I warned him he'd better treat her good or he'd have me to answer to. The man seems a decent sort—just smelly."

Marley Rose grabbed her skirt, pulling on it to stand up.

"Pa pa." The girl waved the spoon and jabbered, getting their attention. "Pa pa."

"Sure sounds like she's trying to talk to you." Jessie couldn't help mentioning it, smoothing Marley's boisterous dark curls.

"Don't put words in the child's mouth, Jessie."

"For a second today I thought she was going to take her first step. She thought about it, then got scared and sat down."

"Is that so? Ain't it too early for that sort of thing?"

"I figure she's almost a year old. It's time." Jessie scooted away from the table and steadied the girl. "See if she'll walk to you."

Duel pushed his chair back and held out his hands. "Come to me, Marley. Come here, darlin'."

"Pa pa."

"I'm not your pa, darlin'. I'm Duel. Can you say Duel?" He remembered a treat he'd bought at the general store earlier and fished it out of his pocket. "Look what I've got."

Marley relaxed her grip on Jessie's finger. She put one foot out and teetered on legs of jelly.

"Come and see what Duel has for you, darlin'." He waved a red lollipop, enticing her.

The little girl took one step, then another. Halfway there, she lurched, launching herself into his waiting arms. He set her on his knee.

"She walked, Duel! Do you always use bribery to get what you want?"

His amber gaze slipped past the barrier she'd built and made itself at home somewhere in the region of her heart. The intensity of the moment made her catch her breath.

"Works every time." His slow drawl heightened the mood.

Jessie tried to tear her gaze away, but found it impossible. Something different shone in his eyes, something that hadn't been there before. He was looking at her as if seeing her for the first time—as if she were special—almost as if he thought she were pretty.

"I'll try to remember that." Her answer came out husky and broken.

"Paaaaaaa." Marley Rose fractured the moment, holding the dripping sucker to Duel's mouth.

"Oh, no. You eat it, sweetheart. I don't want that thing in my mouth."

Red sucker juice stained his lips, giving them a lush ripeness. Dangerous thoughts flitted through her mind before she could lasso them.

In self-defense, Jessie began clearing the table. If she took her time, he'd stay longer before he went to the barn.

"Will you keep Marley company until I get the dishes washed?"

He glanced up and she wished she hadn't spoken. Why did his mouth have to look so darn alluring? The man was in love with a memory. For God's sake, he couldn't bear to sleep in the house with her.

"I suppose." He tousled the top of Marley's head. "That all right with you, Two Bit?"

A smile stretched across the child's sticky face and she gurgled happily.

"We'll get out from under your feet." Duel lifted his pride and joy and made for the rocker.

By the time she finished and untied her apron, soft snores drifted from the other room. She tiptoed in.

Marley snuggled in the crook of Duel's arm, the lollipop resting on her chin. Fast asleep, the child's hand lay trustingly on his broad chest. Duel's head tipped against the back of the rocker, snores coming from his half-closed mouth.

A warm contentment waltzed through her. And keeping time on its arm floated hope. Jessie sat watching the two—a father and his child. For no matter how hard he fought it, the little girl had stolen his heart.

Thick dark lashes brushed her Texan's high cheekbones, raven's wings flush against fine granite. Honor and promise-keeping lived inside this gentle giant. Surely no knight ever worked harder in the quest for right and goodness.

Clearing the land of rocks and brush had totally exhausted him. Planting time would be gone before they knew it, thus the hurry to plow and plant the seed. Walt had done what little he could to help, regardless that his bum leg hadn't allowed for much stooping or bending.

Tomorrow she would be out there by Duel's side. After all, the crops would benefit her the most—perhaps clear her name. If she could live out her life with Duel and Marley Rose, she wouldn't ask for anything else. A lump slid into place in her throat. She wouldn't even ask for love.

Duel shifted and murmured in his sleep. Words that

sounded an awful lot like Annie. Jessie slipped from the chair and went to get Marley.

The child never stirred when Jessie took the lollipop, washed the stickiness off the girl's face, and laid her in her bed. If she'd been able to have children, she'd have wanted them to be exactly like Marley Rose.

After kissing her plump cheeks, Jessie crept back to the man in the rocking chair. Careful not to awaken him, she unfolded a blanket and draped it around him. The urge to brush a lock of hair from his forehead almost became too strong to resist. Curiously, she wondered what it felt like. But instead of giving in to temptation, she lowered the wicks on the lamps.

Her bed didn't seem nearly as cold and lonely when she crawled between the covers. Tonight she would rest better. Duel's soft snore in the next room was strangely comforting.

Duel had a hard time facing Jessie over breakfast the next morning. He'd acted like a randy stallion—unable to take his eyes off her. On top of that, he'd fallen asleep only a heartbeat or two away from her. The last thing he wanted was to cause her more anguish. It had been well past midnight when he woke and stumbled to the barn.

"Sorry I fell asleep on you last evening." He sopped a biscuit in a pool of sorghum on his plate and bit into it, avoiding her calm look. "Didn't mean to."

"It's your house, Duel. Way I see it, you can do as you darn well please in it. If anyone sleeps in the barn it should be me. No reason for you to make all the sacrifices."

Her clear gaze nearly stole his breath. With every day her bruises faded more. She grew more beautiful—and kind-hearted. She'd cut off her right arm rather than admit she couldn't stand to be in the same room with him, much less the same house. Her offer to trade places with him proved that his presence upset her. Only he wondered what had caused the becoming pink flush on her cheeks.

"The arrangements are satisfactory . . . for now." Why did

his voice have to get husky all of a sudden? And why just now did he have to remember the taste of her skin? "Better this way."

Was he mistaken or did the light just go out of her eyes? His chair scraped against the floor as he stood. Marley's sweet babbles from the other room let them know she'd awakened.

"Two Bit's up. Gotta get busy. Burning daylight," he murmured. "First I'll go threaten Vicky with her life if she goes ahead with this damn party. Pop asked me to come get him anyway."

Jessie followed him to the door where he paused to lift his hat from the nail.

"I'll have Marley fed by the time you get back. Today I'll help you in the fields."

"You don't have to." He kept his gaze fastened on his boots.

"It's my choice."

Come nightfall Duel didn't have strength left even to smile at Marley's antics. He ate a hurried supper and staggered to the barn. Lying on the straw bed, he remembered Jessie's terrified look when he gave her the news that he hadn't had any luck with Vicky. His sister was hellbent on having that damn social. Nothing he'd said put a dent in her determination. It appeared they were stuck between a rock and a hard place.

He assured Jessie they'd invent a plausible story before the event. Not that he had a clue what that would be. A muscle jerked in his jaw. He'd protect her if he had to tell every lie known to man. In some crimes there were only victims, and Jessie's case was one of them. One had merely to see the brand on her shoulder to know that much.

His lady had certainly done her share today—lifting rocks, chopping small trees, plus keeping an eye on Marley, and cooking. There had been a closeness in their combined efforts. And when she brought him lunch in the field, it reminded him of the first day they'd spent together, the day she washed his shirt in the stream. Sparked that same intimate feeling. Yes, his Jessie was remarkable.

"Spooky though how she kept popping up at my elbow when I least expected it," he muttered into the still air.

He could've done a darn sight more if he hadn't had to keep one eye on her whereabouts.

"I seem to have a hard time remembering this sisterly business. Especially when she turns those darn eyes on me." Duel plumped the hay that served as a pillow and lay back.

Pop liked her. Every other word to come out of Walt's mouth today pertained to Jessie. In fact, Duel had a devil of a time getting the man to go home.

"I'll sleep in the barn, son. Save time tomorrow. You won't even know I'm around," he'd said.

Slim chance of that. He couldn't let his father suspect their strange sleeping arrangements. It'd arouse too many whys and wherefores that he'd sooner not answer right now.

"No, Pop. With your gimp leg you need to sleep in a warm bed. Take Preacher and come back at daylight."

"But, son—"

"No buts. I insist." Not that he blamed his father one bit for finding any excuse to avoid the Austin household. Though Duel loved his sister dearly, she could drive a man to drink with her mulish disposition.

Only after he'd exhausted his supply of excuses had Walt finally given up. Yep, his father thought the sun rose and set on his new daughter-in-law and granddaughter. Duel vowed to do his level best to make sure that opinion never changed. Even if he had to rope the wind to do it. That woman and little girl deserved a whole lot more out of life than what they got. For a fact.

Sleep finally overtook him, and he felt himself drifting on a soft cloud. Damn, it felt good to relax.

The bleating of a goat sounded very far away. Strange thing to dream about. Suddenly something licked his face and his eyes flew open. He stared into white goat whiskers.

"Darn your ornery hide! Can't a man get some sleep?"

The nanny chewed calmly on his hay bed as if she hadn't a care in the entire world. "Bleh."

Thoroughly aggravated, he kicked the blanket aside and snatched the rope, the end of which dripped with goat slobber.

"You mangy critter, you chewed the rope in half!"

Wearily raising the wick of the lantern, he dragged the animal into her stall. This time he made sure she couldn't reach the tether, and reinforced the knots.

"There, maybe that'll hold you. If you get loose again, we'll have roasted goat for supper tomorrow night."

That's when he heard the whimpering sound. At first he thought it might be an owl, but the sound coming from inside the barn grew clearer.

Alert, he followed the noise, holding the light high. Could be a cougar or mountain lion. His right hand stole to his hip where the forty-five usually hung, before he remembered he'd left it on the hook inside the house. Grabbing a pitchfork, he proceeded carefully.

Huddled in a ball in the corner of Preacher's empty stall lay a dog, some kind of retriever.

"What's wrong, boy?"

Duel leaned toward him for a closer examination. The pitiful sounds coming from the animal's throat made him ache inside.

Using the most gentle tone he knew, he tried to reassure the frightened dog. "Easy now. Are you hurt?"

He knelt down and slowly stretched out his hand. Wild fright glittered in the retriever's eyes as he yelped, then retreated as far as he could.

Fear and distrust mingled with the dark shadows. From what he could see, blood matted the dog's beautiful yellow fur, and one foot dangled uselessly. Gut feeling and the red trail on the floor told him the retriever was in a bad way.

Reluctant to push further, Duel backed away and leaned against the wall within sight of the animal who watched warily.

"I'll help you, but you have to trust me, boy." The soft, soothing murmur must have worked. The retriever eased itself into a more relaxed position and became a trifle less wild-eyed.

"I won't hurt you. Only want to fix you up. Bet you're hungry, aren't you? What if I go find you some food?"

When Duel stood, the movement alarmed the animal and he again assumed a protective stance. Reminded him of Jessie.

"Hey, fellow, I'm not gonna hurt you. It'll be all right. I'm coming back, so don't go away."

He quickly crossed the clearing. Once inside the dark house, he placed one foot silently in front of the other, careful not to awaken Jessie. A chair leg suddenly caught the toe of his boot and he stumbled. *Damn!*

"Who's there?"

Chapter Ten

He froze. "It's me. Duel."

The faint scrape of a match sounded, then muted light illuminated the room. Jessie clutched the curtain partition as if it could shield her from attack. No doubt she hid her state of undress. The thought of unfettered bare skin made him uncomfortable.

From where he stood, disquiet and suspicion colored her eyes a deep indigo. He wished for a split second that he'd waited until morning.

"Sorry I woke you, Jessie. Didn't mean to scare you." He spoke to the toe of his boot, not daring to raise his gaze lest he encounter a chance peek through a thin night rail. "Go back to bed."

"Did you forget something? Are you ill?"

"Came to get some food. I found a hungry, wounded dog in the barn."

She dropped the curtain and he was shocked to find her fully dressed. Did she distrust him that much?

"A dog? Is he hurt bad?" Instant concern replaced her apparent unease.

"Afraid so. Can't tell exactly because the poor thing won't let me near him, but he's covered in blood. I just came to get some food. Thought that might calm him enough to look."

Jessie bent to pick up her shoes. "I'm coming with you."

No more than five minutes later Duel followed her swishing skirts into the barn. Jessie gasped when she entered the stall and found the shivering dog cowering in the corner.

"It's all right, fellow. We're here now." She knelt quietly. "You poor thing. Mama's here."

Duel wasn't surprised to find unshed tears turning her blue eyes into liquid pools. She recognized pain and suffering. She should. She'd certainly experienced more than her fair share of both.

"Cut off a piece of that venison for me, please."

Amazement swept over him when the retriever took the meat from her hand, then licked her fingers. And he was even more astonished when the dog let her examine him. Full of pride, Duel leaned back and watched. His lady was a miracle worker.

In the next hour Jessie hand-fed the animal, cleaned its wounds, and with his help, bound the badly cut foreleg. Now wrapped warmly in a blanket, the dog dozed.

"Do you think someone beat him?" A half-sob caught in her voice.

"Sure looks that way. If he'd fought with another animal, the gashes would've had jagged edges. These were smooth and clean."

Her chin trembled as she fought to keep control. "Why? It's so senseless."

"Who knows." His jaw clenched. He suspected the dog's condition wasn't the only reason for her emotion. "Jessie . . . keep looking forward when the pain of looking back becomes too great."

Duel yearned to hold her close, to tell her the monsters of

the world were few in number, to assure her he'd never let anyone do that to her again. The light kissed her hair, creating a breathtaking red and gold rainbow. He inhaled deeply, reminding himself of his pledge.

It didn't help. Her fresh fragrance intoxicated him. Nothing would give him greater pleasure than to cradle her in his arms. Unaware of the direction of his thoughts, Jessie shifted and their shoulders rubbed companionably. A groan slipped from his throat.

"Are you all right?"

Only the fact that the feelings yanking him inside out weren't the least bit the brotherly kind. Other than that, he reckoned he had few complaints.

"Merely yawning's all."

"Do you think we can leave him?" Worry clouded her eyes.

"You forget I'll be sleeping only a few feet away. Besides, Yellow Dog'll be just fine. He's a survivor." Just like you, he added silently as Jessie accepted his hand, letting him pull her upright.

"Guess I'll go back to bed, then." She stretched and the movement thrust her breasts outward, straining against the confining fabric.

Holy Moses! Indecent images danced in his head. How much temptation did she think one man could stand? Quickly, he turned away before he undid all the trust he'd gained.

"Marley might wake up." The sooner she left the better he'd feel. But he wanted an answer to a nagging question first. "Jessie, why do you feel the need to sleep in your clothes?"

"This and the tattered dress I wore when I left the Diamond J that night are all I have."

What a dolt, he cursed himself. A man shouldn't need reminding to provide for his wife. Womenfolk required much more than men. How could a thing like that have slipped his mind?

"The trunks are full of Annie's clothes. Guess I assumed you'd make them useful until we can afford your own."

"I'd never touch anything that wasn't mine unless you gave me leave."

"I'm telling you now. Don't know if they'll even fit, but you're welcome to use them. Just for a while. I promise. My wife won't always have to wear a dead woman's hand-me-downs."

"Thank you." Jessie started for the barn door when he stopped her.

"I appreciate what you did tonight."

Questions in her eyes revealed confusion when she faced him. She flicked her top lip with the end of her tongue, making his belly knot with a want he hadn't felt in a very long time.

"I only did what needed to be done, nothing more."

How little did she know. She'd shown him that getting to Heaven meant going through Hell and that the journey was well worth the price.

"You're quite a woman, Jessie McClain."

Before he could stop, before he could weigh the consequences, before he surely burst with need, he bent and gently kissed her forehead.

Duel headed for the fields at daybreak. He needed to get these crazy fancies out of his system. Hard, backbreaking work might cure him. A small part of him felt as if he were betraying his love for Annie, and on the opposite side of the coin, he'd vowed to cleave unto Jessie in sickness and in health, forsaking all others. That meant the dead ones as well as the living.

He sighed deeply. That sacred oath created turmoil. He had some serious thinking to do. Right now avoiding those Wedgwood blue eyes seemed the most prudent thing to do.

Yellow Dog had disappeared by the time he awakened, leaving an empty blanket behind. Perhaps the animal felt the need to move on. One thing for sure, Yellow Dog and Jessie shared a common bond. All he could do for either was let them know he cared, then back up and give them space.

Maybe in time Jessie would come to him. Or at least meet him halfway.

Tackling a large tree stump with a vengeance, he didn't know anyone was near until he heard a voice.

"Son of a gun! Why if it ain't my long lost brother after all."

He threw down the shovel and whirled. "Luke!"

Heaviness weighed on Jessie's chest as she watched Duel from the window. That he hadn't come inside for coffee gave her reason to think he was avoiding her. In the dead of night they'd shared compassion and grief . . . and tenderness. Did he regret that tenderness now?

Marley Rose tugged on her skirt, jabbering in baby talk. Jessie lifted the child and kissed her cheek. In the dead of night her Texan had offered solace and real affection. And in the light of day, all she and Duel seemed to have in common was hard work and the love of a little girl.

Almost with a will of its own, her hand rose to touch her forehead. The imprint of his breath against her skin had left a brand of its own. Same as that first night, she hadn't been prepared for the gentleness of his touch. Nor for her own response. It hadn't frightened her. Just the opposite. Strangely, her body seemed to thirst for more contact. The warmth of a touch had become something she'd forgotten in her years with Jeremiah.

While busy sorting her thoughts, she hadn't seen the horse and rider appear. Her first glance came when the man dismounted. She watched Duel turn and even from the distance, she thought she saw a smile cover his face.

Though she strained, she couldn't make out the identity of the tall figure with Duel. From the way they slapped each other on the back she knew they must be friends. Foreboding rose slowly until it strangled her with overpowering force. She didn't know the man's identity, but she knew he spelled trouble.

Just then, Walt rounded the bend in the road on Preacher.

He didn't stop at the barn, instead met the two men in the field.

The strange man grabbed the reins of his horse and the trio walked toward the house. Her pulse went into a tizzy.

"Marley, honey, you're going to have to get down and play."

"Pa pa."

"Yes, honey, your papa's coming."

The child looked at her curiously when she propped the looking glass on the window sill and smoothed her hair. A quick glance let her know the men paused at the barn to take the horses inside. She'd have a few minutes.

Despite Duel telling her to wear Annie's clothes, she hadn't had the time or inclination to go through them yet. The gray poplin would have to do for now. She smoothed what wrinkles she could and scooted to the kitchen where she donned an apron.

Duel and the stranger traded poking jabs at each other as they entered. The energy of their play filling the room reminded her of little boys' antics. Her smile died when she glimpsed the badge pinned on the stranger's chest.

A Texas Ranger!

Despair and regret sank beneath swirling black water like a giant ship scuttled by a cannonball. Too bad they didn't get to do things Duel's way. Seemed they'd run out of time. What hope did she have now of righting the wrong and clearing her name?

"Confound it, boys. Didn't I always tell you to take your wrasslin' outdoors?" Walt McClain swatted harmlessly at both men. However, the pleased look on the old man's face belied his stern words.

One thing didn't fit. Why was Duel acting so friendly to a man who could destroy their very lives? A sharp sword chopped off the head of her rosy dream. The life she'd tasted briefly vanished before her eyes.

"Sorry, Pop, you sure did." Duel gave his companion, who equaled him in height, one more jab in the ribs before he became serious. "But there's just one problem here—this isn't your house."

"Smart-assed whippersnappers. That's all an old man got for his trouble." Walt lifted his newest granddaughter and swung her in the air. Delighted squeals filled the kitchen.

Duel ignored the good-natured dressing down and met her questioning gaze. "Jessie, meet my brother, Luke. This is my wife and that little girl over yonder is Marley Rose."

"Pleasure, ma'am." Luke offered his hand.

Her mind in a tumultuous whirlwind, Jessie couldn't refuse the gesture without seeming rude. Duel's brother . . . a Texas Ranger? The man could end her charade in a heartbeat and he'd come into their home under guise of family. How much did Luke know? How much would he care if bringing her to justice split their marriage, not to mention her heart, in two?

What God has joined together let no man put asunder. The minister had so ordered. Didn't that pertain to a brother-in-law Texas Ranger?

"I wish I could say my husband's spoken of you, but that would be a lie." Jessie broke the handshake, sending Duel an accusing glare.

Luke grinned. "Most likely didn't want to own up to it, ain't that right, big brother?"

"Most likely."

"And who did you say the little lady was that Pop's got?" Luke made no secret of his curiosity.

Duel reached for Marley, who fell into his arms excitedly. "Meet Marley Rose, the apple of Pop's, mine, and Jessie's eye. The cutest little girl in the whole state of Texas."

"Whew! When you decide to change your life, you sure do it in a big way, don'cha, Duel? Vicky telegraphed news of your wedding. Didn't say anything about a daughter, though."

That explained it. Leave it to her meddling sister-in-law to send the lawman to her door. At that moment, Jessie cursed every telegraph line stretching across the West.

"Pa pa." Marley laid her head on Duel's shoulder and peeked shyly at Luke.

Dark aggravation flashed on Duel's face. "Marley Rose ain't my daughter."

"Now, I distinctly heard her call you papa."

Botheration! Luke'd certainly acquired the same bull-headed tenacity of his sister. She wondered if the McClain family harbored any more offspring. Before the day ended she'd find out. Gray would color her hair soon if these surprises kept showing up.

Sympathy for Duel's awkward tangle soothed her jumpy nerves. Jessie rescued her husband for a change.

"Please, sit down. I've made some hot coffee and homemade biscuits. Let me throw some salt pork in the skillet. I know starving men when I see them."

Walt grabbed a chair. "Don't hafta ask me twice, dearie."

That's what she liked about Walt McClain. From the start, the man's affection made her feel warm and comfortable inside. She felt especially grateful for it today.

"Me neither, ma'am." Luke followed his father's lead.

Four cups and the pot of coffee gave Jessie a place to put her nervous energy. Every time she chanced a glance in Luke's direction she found his gaze glued to her. She wondered.

"Duel, you caught yourself a mighty handsome woman. Jessie, did you say?"

Luke's slow drawl magnified her suspicions. Jessie held her breath waiting for more. The muscle in Duel's jaw clenched. She knew he was more annoyed than he let himself show.

"That's her name."

"Whoee, don't he sound as possessive as a bona fide bridegroom?" Luke winked at his father. "Wondered how Jessie managed to lasso you to the altar," he continued, "bein' how set you'd been against it."

"That the Ranger talking or my brother?"

Luke held up both hands in self-defense. "Hey, don't get upset at me. You should have known we'd all die to know the circumstances, given your past behavior. Nothing more than healthy interest is all."

"I won't abide no squabblin' at Jessie's table. You hear, boys?" Walt gave them both a baleful glower.

"Besides, if I don't take all the details back with me, ol' Bart'll skin me alive. You remember him, don'cha, Duel?"

"I remember. Nothing much to tell. I met Jessie, asked her to marry me, she said yes. End of story."

"I'm certainly glad you covered all the finer points." Sarcasm dripped from Luke's voice. "Now I can carry that back to El Paso and Sheriff Daniels can . . ."

The cup slipped from Jessie's cold hands and shattered on the floor, the same way her life was crashing around her feet. "How clumsy of me. I'll have this cleaned up in two shakes."

She met Duel's anguished concern as he knelt to help.

"I'm sorry," he mouthed silently.

"Help me," she whispered for his ears only.

"You know what's weird as hell?" Luke continued his speculation as if everyone still sat at the table. "I came this way tracking a woman named Jessie. How's that for coincidence?"

"You don't say, son." Walt's interest spurred Luke on.

"A woman named Jessie Foltry of the Diamond J ranch. She killed her husband and vamoosed. I didn't catch your previous last name, sister-in-law."

Chapter Eleven

"What the hell're you insinuating, Luke? You know damn well a question like that could get you shot in any other home. You may be my brother, but you'll respect my wife. That clear?"

The force of Duel's outburst startled Jessie. She drew to the far corner of the room. Marley Rose, who sat contentedly in her grandpa's lap, suddenly puckered up to cry.

Walt pointed a finger at his youngest son. "He's right. Luke, I won't abide no disrespect. Jessie's a right fine woman, an' a sweeter ma here to Marley Rose you couldn't find. And I'll bloody anyone's nose who says otherwise."

Proud as punch, the old man beamed at her. If the whole situation hadn't made her ill, Jessie would've hugged him.

Luke shrugged his shoulders. "Just asked a simple question."

"Then it doesn't matter. I made her a McClain and that ends the discussion."

"Appears the whole blamed mess of you are mighty defensive." Luke reached to tweak Marley's hair. "Hey there, pretty lady. Wanna come to Uncle Luke?"

The threat of violence over, Jessie bent to pick up the rest of the glass fragments. She spied the red tin can of baking powder on the shelf. It gave her an idea.

"I don't mind your question, Luke." She felt Duel's hand on her arm to stop her and knew the warning that would be in his eyes if she chose to look. She didn't—couldn't, or she would lose her courage.

"It's all right," she assured him, pretending to misunderstand. "I won't cut myself." She turned to Luke. "My name was Rumford—Jessie Rumford."

The pent-up tenseness evaporated. She reveled in her husband's tender smile.

"Satisfied, nosy brother?"

Walt and Luke helped Duel in the fields that day, leaving Jessie free to wash clothes and clean. The time provided an opportunity also to go through Annie's clothing. Though the everyday things spoke of ordinary means, a few of the items tucked away in the trunk told quite a different story. They intrigued her.

Lace and silk dresses, fine quality unmentionables, and shoes of soft kid exhibited vestiges of wealth. Perhaps Annie came from affluence. Puzzling to say the least.

A beautiful satin creation stole her breath. She held the dazzling ice blue dress against her and pirouetted before the looking glass. Tiny white flowers embellished the daring round neckline, and down each side of the flounced skirt hung garlands of more white flowers on silken cord. The swishing, bustled skirt brushed against the tops of her serviceable black shoes as she twirled amid Marley's excited squeals. With an almost reverent touch she smoothed fabric. Annie must have looked like a heavenly angel in the exquisite gown.

Her own vision in the glass faded. She could imagine Duel coming into the room and seeing Annie in the satin for the first time. His amber gaze would light possessively. . . . His taut muscles encased in sleek-fitting buckskins would alternately relax and tighten as he leisurely crossed the room. . . . He would lower his head closer and closer, until he would claim the lips of the love of his life.

A shiver ran the length of her body. As if it had burned her, she quickly folded the gown and shoved it back in the trunk where she'd found it.

Salty tears stung her eyes. Her tall Texan would protect her with his life, but he'd never love her.

When lunch came, Jessie loaded a wicker basket with fresh-baked bread, strips of venison, a jar of pickles, and a jug of apple cider. She gathered Marley and loaded both child and food into a wheelbarrow from the barn.

"Yeee doggies! It's my two favorite ladies." Walt almost tripped over his own feet in his hurry to take the basket. "You two yahoos better come on or I'll eat the whole kit 'n' kaboodle."

The nearer Duel came, the faster her pulse raced. His hat sat low on his forehead for shade, leaving her to imagine the amber lights that danced in his eyes. The feel of his lips, the warmth of his breath on her skin refused to vacate her senses. Never had anyone made her feel the way she felt now.

"I thought you might be hungry." She spoke low when he and Luke joined them.

His gaze brushed her—the base of her throat where her pulse throbbed, her chin, her hair—everywhere but into her eyes. Those he avoided. Had she embarrassed him by what she considered a "wifely" duty?

"You didn't need to go to so much trouble. Pop could've come up to the house and gotten it if you'd hollered."

"It wasn't any trouble."

"Paaaaaa." Marley Rose stretched out her arms. A silly grin covered her face when Duel took her.

"There she goes calling you pa again." Luke wiped the

sweat from his face with a handkerchief. "You never did explain the particulars, brother."

"Not anything to it." A frown deepened the crevices around Duel's mouth. "Won her in a poker game in Cactus Springs. Her father didn't want her, was determined to sell her that night if I hadn't taken her. Felt sorry for the youngun'. Didn't want to see her wind up with someone worse than me."

"You don't say? I kinda assumed she belonged to Jessie." Luke sent her a long, piercing stare.

The man's persistence hadn't dimmed even after she lied about her name. It took all of her control to be polite. "I wish that were true."

"Way I see it, brother, you're all the kin the kid's got. Why don't you just accept the fact?"

" 'Cause I'm not, that's why. Don't want her growing up under false pretenses. Marley's not my flesh and blood. I'll never give her reason to think otherwise." Duel settled down on the quilt Jessie had spread, and sat the child between his legs.

Jessie handed him a chunk of bread and watched him promptly tear off a piece for Marley. His tender care of "Two Bit," as he called her, reinforced the hope that he'd one day see his flawed logic. Being a parent wasn't about the big moment, but all the little ones that come after to fill a child's life. It was about molding and shaping, helping a child to grow and learn. Maybe someday she could convince him.

Now was not the time, however. Luke's infernal prying had set his nerves on edge. As well as her own. The younger brother either suspected something or else shared Vicky's snoopiness. At the moment she didn't care which as long as he left them alone.

Slight movement caught her attention. At the edge of the clearing appeared an animal of some sort. When it stood, she saw a bandage around its leg.

"Duel, that's the dog we doctored." She pointed toward it.

"Yep, Yellow Dog was gone when I got up. Along about mid-morning I spotted him. Stays at the edge of the field, won't come any closer. Acts as scared as he did last night."

"Poor thing. I imagine he is. Who knows what happened to him?" The animal wagged his tail as if he wanted to join them. His mournful whine carried in the breeze.

"Come on, boy. Come." She whistled for him.

"Won't do a lick of good, Jessie girl. Ain't gonna come till he gits good an' ready." Walt wiped his mouth on his sleeve.

Sure enough, the dog lay back down, his droopy head resting in the dirt. Familiar pain ran the length of her form. Yet, time could mend bones . . . and broken spirits.

There were days she barely remembered Jeremiah's rages. The days when he kept her locked in her room. The nights when he took what he wanted, knowing she'd dare not resist. At times it seemed more a horrible dream than reality.

Then there were moments when the remembering suffocated her with unbearable intensity.

"Give the dog time. It'll come around." Duel's gentle admonition invaded her thoughts.

Seated an arm's length away, she watched him caress Marley's dark locks. Her tall husband had a tenderness, a compassion that was rare. He'd trusted her, asking in return only that she be a mother for the child.

Water filled her eyes, blurring his firm jaw, sculpted cheekbones, and Roman nose. He was a proud man who'd never let her down, who was proving he'd stand by her through thick and thin. Her gaze drifted to his mouth and the deep lines on each side. The image of his lips on hers released tiny flutters in her belly. Her boldness shocked her.

Still, daydreams didn't hurt anyone. She'd never tell him he'd be an easy man to love. It would be her own little secret.

Jessie glanced away and encountered Luke's stare. A flush rose. The quizzical lift of his brow told her he'd caught her studying her husband.

At day's end, Duel dropped a bucket into the well and turned the crank to hoist it back up. The sweat and dirt covering him would have to come off before he sat down at the supper table.

Both men balked like stubborn mules, but he'd finally convinced Pop and Luke to return to Vicky's for the night.

The less his brother came around the better . . . for Jessie's sake as much as his. Pride swelled in his chest for her quick thinking earlier. Despite Luke's muttering that Rumford seemed a strange name, he'd accepted it. At least for the moment. Only Duel didn't like the way Luke kept studying her, not that he could blame him. Any man would find her easy on the eyes. He sighed. Lord knows he had his hands full with his meddlesome siblings.

That dad-blasted soiree Vicky had cooked up for Saturday would certainly test them all. Every citizen in Tranquility would have questions galore. Still, he entertained no doubts that his wife couldn't handle them. She'd become quite a trooper.

He doused his head in the bucket of water. Though his entire body needed an ice-water drenching, he settled for the upper portion. Getting Jessie out of his thoughts seemed next to impossible. Even Pop and Luke had remarked on his absent-mindedness. Fact of the matter was, the woman just didn't appear sisterly in the least. She and Vicky had nothing in common.

It was her strangely colored eyes that pulled at him. He couldn't glance at her without thinking of his mother's china. Graceful and dainty like the dishes, yet she possessed a spine of steel. Her long, elegant fingers fascinated him. A twinge of guilt shot through him; with the hard work ahead, it wouldn't take long for her soft, beautiful hands to redden and crack.

If. . . . Enough money would take her to California, Montana, or even the Alaskan Territory. Life wouldn't be any easier, but a woman could get lost in the vastness.

He'd give anything to keep her safe.

And he wished to high heaven he didn't want her so much.

A tug on his back pocket alerted him. He jerked upright.

"Bleh, bleh." The nanny had pulled the big red handkerchief from his hip pocket and calmly chewed on it.

"You good-for-nothing critter." When he yanked it away, a

loud rend brought a curse. "Now look what you did."

The handkerchief had a long tear, not counting the fact it dripped with goat spittle.

"I oughta skin you and feed your sorry carcass to the buzzards. You wait. When Marley's had her fill of your milk, I might do it."

He kicked the bucket that sat beside the well and stuffed the fabric back in his pocket. The skittering container spooked the nanny, who took off like a shot.

"Go ahead and run away, see if I care. Good riddance."

Mumbling a string of curses, Duel opened the door to the house, pausing to hang his hat on the nail just inside.

"Pa pa. Ma ma ma ma ma ma."

Marley's gleeful babbling eased the tiredness from his bones. If one could bottle the girl's spirit, it would bring a hefty fortune, he mused. He pictured himself traveling the countryside with his two ladies, hawking the elixir. For a moment he wondered about his son and how it would have been. To have heard his boy call him papa just once. . . .

"Maaaaaa." Marley tugged on his buckskinned leg, trying to stand. He bent to pick her up.

"Hey, Two Bit. Where's your mama?" Her chubby cheek was soft taffy against his lips.

"Pa pa. Ma ma."

"Duel. Can you say Duel, little darlin'?"

"Paaaa."

He turned his mouth from her prying fingers, and when he did he spied a vision in ice blue satin. Jessie stood frozen in the curtained alcove that served as a bedchamber.

Except for her auburn hair, she could have been Annie. Duel tried to swallow only to find his mouth had become stone dry.

Memories spun, encircling his head in a flurry of flashes. His wedding day . . . his beautiful bride . . . the vows . . . the breathtaking wedding gown of ice blue satin Tom Parker had insisted his daughter wear.

"I'm sorry. I only wanted to try it on, it was so pretty."

He barely heard Jessie's low murmur. The anguish came from a great distance.

"I'll take it off. It was cruel of me to upset you. It wasn't my intention, Duel. You must believe me."

Pain came in huge, gulping waves, threatening to drown him. He sat Marley Rose on the floor before whirling out the door.

Chapter Twelve

For well past the supper hour Duel sat hunched beside the grave. Despair flogged his spirit. How could he entertain thoughts of another woman when he'd failed the first so miserably?

He bore the blame for his first wife's death as surely as if he'd sent a piece of hot lead into Annie's breast. In all reality, he'd committed murder. Jessie had done no worse than he. Using a fingertip, he lovingly traced the name on the cold granite.

"Remember me always, my love," Annie had said in the final moments. "Take good care of our babe. Tell him how much his mother loved him."

She never knew the babe lived only a few short hours. Burdened with incompetence, he'd not been able to save the fragile little life Annie had entrusted to his care.

He'd waited all night for Jonas, his hired hand, to return with the doctor. He should've taken into account the man's lust for the bottle. He found Jonas in the saloon, stinking drunk. Jonas had never even told Doc Mabry that Annie needed him. Wild with fury, Duel'd knocked the man to the floor.

It was bad enough he'd let Annie down, but then he had to face her father's wrath.

"It's all your fault, McClain." Pure hate had blazed from Tom Parker's eyes. The man knew how deeply to thrust the dagger. "You killed her. My daughter would be alive if she'd never met you. I warned her of her folly in marrying a bounty hunter."

Duel never bothered to defend himself. Wasn't any use because for every word Judge Parker uttered, he damned himself ten times over.

He rested his face against the cool stone.

"Never saw a man love anyone the way Duel loved his Annie. Why the sun rose an' set in that woman's smile." Walt tipped his head sideways and gave Jessie a crooked grin. "Not sayin' he won't feel that way about you. Gotta give him time."

There was one small problem; they didn't have any time. Not if Luke put two and two together. Besides, all the hours and minutes in the world couldn't make her husband forget his true love. Jessie had pretty much ruined any chance of that happening.

"You didn't know he'd go loco over one dress, Jessie girl." Walt seemed to understand his son's disturbed frame of mind. He patted Jessie's arm, but it did little to calm her fears.

"Annie's wedding gown, of all things." The ache made it hard to breathe.

Three days had passed. In that time she'd had the briefest of contact with Duel. She could count the words he'd uttered to her on one hand. As one gone mad with grief, he rose each morning before daylight and worked until well after night set in, plowing and planting. He looked for any number of chores to prevent him from darkening the door to the house.

Fearful that he'd stop eating altogether, she took meals to the barn for him. From the way his clothes hung on his lanky frame, he'd eaten far too little of the food. Most likely he'd fed it to Yellow Dog, who continued to hang around at a distance.

"If only I had minded my own business, shown more respect for Annie's belongings. For God's sake, he looked like he'd seen a ghost."

Deep concern had lead her to confide in Walt. With the older man's help she came to understand Duel's behavior and the importance of the gown.

"None of this is your fault. That son of mine's got a barn full of good horse sense, but sometimes he forgits to use it."

"A person can't help the way he feels no more than he can stop breathing," Jessie reminded him softly. Walt opened up his arms and she leaned against him.

Last night she'd watched Duel from the window. A full moon cast eerie shadows around his silhouette. From afar she'd shared his inconsolable sorrow.

"Don't worry, he'll git his gumption back. Cain't say it'd do a whole lot of good, but I could give him a talkin' to."

"I'd rather you didn't." His father might send him running in the other direction and drive a larger wedge between them. She didn't dare risk that. "And please don't mention our conversation to him. I'd die if he found out. As it is, I worry I'm betraying him."

"This has gotta be hard for you, Jessie. It's near impossible for any woman to live in another wife's house—the constant reminders. Been better if you could have started fresh with your own doodads."

She couldn't bear to look at Annie's clothes, much less wear any except a few necessities despite Duel's blessing. Drawers, chemises, and nightgowns he'd never see. However, the two dresses she owned wouldn't last long with repeated washings.

"How was it you arrived in Tranquility without so much as an extra stitch, gal?"

Walt's question startled Jessie. She frantically groped for a suitable explanation.

I'll see you in hell before I let you leave this house, woman. Little did Jeremiah know that he'd beat her there. She hoped he found the flames to his liking.

"A fire." Another lie added to the passel she'd already told. Keeping her gaze on the tall figure out the window, she justified their usefulness. "A fire burned everything I owned. I barely escaped with my life." At least part of it was true.

Walt clucked sympathetically. "Reckon that explains the bruises and whatnots."

"I don't like to think about it." No matter how much logic she used, lying to Walt weighed heavily on her conscience. Kindhearted as the day was long, he'd quickly accepted her as a daughter. Alone in an unfamiliar town, in a farce of a marriage, she'd found a staunch ally.

From the first moment, the elder McClain's twinkling eyes and his sense of fair play had drawn her to him. Same as now when she finally met his clear gaze. Her affection for Walt was growing by leaps and bounds.

Fine way to show it though—by lying to him.

The man gave her a friendly pat. "Nosiness runs in the family, but I didn't want to ask. Figured you'd say in your own good time."

She kissed his grizzled cheek. "I appreciate that. I wondered where Duel got his quiet ways, especially after meeting Vicky and Luke. Now I know."

The main problem left was how to get Duel talking again and back into the house. Marley Rose needed him. And she so missed his company.

A light rain Saturday morning raised Duel's hopes that Vicky would call off the soiree she'd planned. No such luck.

"Your sister expects you to be there an' no excuses." Walt gave him the same stern, no nonsense stare he had used when he caught Duel smoking grape leaves behind the barn. Or the time he found Duel stealing a kiss from little Lucinda Moore.

Now, as then, the look made Duel uncomfortable. They'd

butted heads more than once, something a few trips to the woodshed cured. Pop had taught him respect in spite of his rebellion.

"You'll do right by Jessie, son." Again, that tone left the "or else" unsaid. It appeared Jessie had completely charmed his father as she did anyone who spent a minute in her company.

"Plan on it, Pop." Guilt that he'd neglected her and Marley was already eating at him. They'd not asked for anything more than a home and someone to watch over them. Of late, he'd not done much of the latter. Why had he ever thought he could?

"Don't plan—do it. The lady's been through a peck o' trouble to be by your side."

What had Jessie told his father? Not that he blamed her if she'd spilled the whole truth. He knew he'd frightened her that night he flew out of the house. Before he messed up good he'd better find out what and pronto.

"One thing I've learned, Pop, and that's to listen to you. Don't intend to stop now." Funny thing was, the older Duel got, the smarter his father became.

"Ain't so old you can pull the wool over my eyes neither."

"What're you talking about?"

"I got eyes. I saw where you been sleepin' in the barn." Walt's squinty glare accused and convicted him. "That's why you were so all-fired agin me stayin' here."

"This is my business, Pop. Stay out of it."

"Ain't right for a man an' wife to start a life that way."

He had found a whole lot of things weren't right in the world. Duel swallowed his anger. He hadn't meant for Jessie and Marley Rose to pay for his shortcomings.

A few hours later he dodged the hurt in Jessie's gaze as he helped her and Marley from the wagon. He'd tried to apologize several times on the ride to the Austin residence, but the words got stuck in his throat. Fancy that, he was more insecure in facing his wife than all the times he stared down the barrel of a forty-five in the hands of a killer. Big difference.

The only risk with the last was knowing a bullet could send him to Glory.

"Pa pa." Marley patted his shoulder as if she couldn't touch him enough.

Self-reproach for his dereliction didn't make the lump in his belly disappear. He would make up for it, he promised.

"Duel, Jessie, I'm glad to see you finally made it." Vicky waved to them from the barn door. From behind her drifted the cheerful strains of fiddle music.

"Looks like everyone in town came for this shindig." He grumbled low, casting a dispirited glance at the number of wagons and carriages packing the yard.

"I heard that." Vicky took her niece from his arms. "I have only one rule, brother."

"What's that?"

The clamoring of George and Henry for Marley's attention almost drowned out his question.

"You have to have a good time and that's an order."

He kissed Vicky's cheek. "You sound more like Pop every day."

"Jessie, you are soooo beautiful. I love your dress. Is it new?"

"You could say that."

Duel couldn't help the quick flash of pain when Jessie's blue eyes met his. He'd wondered earlier where she'd gotten the green muslin she wore. Nowhere in his recollection of Annie's wardrobe could he place the pretty floral dress.

"Come, let me introduce you to the ladies." Vicky grabbed her arm and started to pull her toward a group of goggle-eyed women.

"Just a cotton-pickin' minute, Sis." Duel stopped their progress. "I'd like to have a word with my wife first if you don't mind."

He took her aside, keeping his voice low. "We didn't discuss our story."

"If you hadn't disappeared for the last three days, we could've talked about it."

"Well, what in the devil did you tell Pop?" Duel's roughened whisper captured the circle of ladies' attention. He noticed how collectively they leaned toward them, eaten alive with curiosity. "I'm sorry. We shouldn't be doing this here."

Jessie leaned closer to whisper, her breath teasing the tendrils of hair by his ear. "My last name was Rumford. I gave your father the account that my home caught fire and everything I owned burned. It satisfied him. He said that explained my bruises."

"Good. But where did you live? They'll ask."

"Cactus Springs?"

"I suppose that's far enough removed from El Paso and easy to remember. Have you been married?" He hated reminding her, yet he must.

"No. Less story we have to keep track of. If I were widowed we'd have to invent a husband and how he died."

"Good point. Any relatives?"

"They all died in the Indian raids a few years back. What did I do, though? With no kin I'd have needed to work."

Vicky barged between them. "That's enough. You two can sweet talk later. This is a party and these women are dying to meet our newest citizen."

With that she pulled Jessie along, leaving Duel to seek other company. A sinking feeling descended all the way to his toes as he watched Jessie smile and extend her hand. As confident and capable as she appeared to be, the night wouldn't end soon enough to suit him.

He surveyed the large room, the center of which sported dancing couples, and finally located Marley Rose. George and Henry each held a hand, helping her walk. The Austin clan certainly had taken to the little girl. Watching her now, he recalled how her dark eyes had lit with joy this afternoon when she saw him. He surely needed to have his rear end kicked, he mused.

Weaving in and out of hay bales scattered about for seating, he skirted the waltzing twosomes and headed for the refreshment table. He had a sudden urge to wet his whistle.

"Would you look at that." Luke poked Duel in the ribs.

"Anyone ever tell you your habit of sneaking up on people is irritating as hell?"

"Only complaints come from the ones with a guilty conscience. You got one of those, big brother?"

"Should I, Luke?" The glare he shot his meddling sibling could have set wet kindling ablaze.

"You tell me." Luke shot back, challenging.

The wise thing to do was change the subject. Duel propped one elbow on a waist-high stack of hay. "What did you want me to look at?"

"Pop." Luke nodded toward their parent, who was hobbling around the floor with a portly lady friend. "Pretty spry on his feet for an injured old man, ain't he. Who's his partner?"

"The Widow Jones. She's harmless."

"But what about our pop? Think they might be wrinkling the sheets?" Luke made himself comfortable, copying his elder brother's lazy stance.

"Nah." Duel swung his attention from the pair and back to Luke. "Thought you'd hightailed it out of here by now, hot on the trail of that lady killer."

"Wanted to stick around for a few days, rest up, see family. Get my bearings."

The man's nonchalance didn't fool him for one second. Luke was smart as a whip. Sometimes too smart.

"Aren't you afraid you'll lose the scent?"

"Shoot, I lost Jessie Foltry's trail a long time back. By the way, don't think you ever told me where your wife's from. How much do you know about her?" Luke eyed the subject in question across the room, talking with a gaggle of females.

Duel plucked a straw from the bale on which he leaned and stuck it in the side of his mouth. "The lady killer? Or my wife?"

"Things don't change much, do they?" Luke chuckled. "Remember when Pop caught us smoking behind the barn and you told him we weren't smoking those grape leaves. Said we were pretending to be Indians and was merely testing our smellers so we could track someone who was smoking 'em."

"What I remember about that incident was Pop setting the seat of our britches on fire." Duel's grin vanished as he watched Jessie float by on Hampton Pierson's arm. Everyone knew the man's reputation with the ladies. Maybe he should rescue her. The way she laughed at something Pierson said told him she wouldn't appreciate his help. For some odd reason he felt like punching something.

"You're a lucky man, brother." Luke's gaze followed Jessie as well. "She's the prettiest woman here."

His thoughts exactly. The green print hugged her curves, accentuating her tiny waist. That Luke noticed irked him as much as the look of pleasure on Pierson's face. No man should be paying that much attention to another's wife. In fact, as far as he was concerned, everyone had gotten more than an eyeful of creamy skin. Damn her low neckline!

"She's taken, Luke." Duel made sure he didn't mistake the warning. "Find your own."

"One problem. No one here can hold a candle to her." Luke straightened from his casual pose against the stack of bales. "Since you're gonna sit here glaring all night, I think it's my turn to dance with my lovely sister-in-law."

Chapter Thirteen

"That's a mighty long face, son, for a newlywed." Walt had quietly come beside him.

Duel chewed irritably on the straw. "I should be at home, not at some damn social. Don't need to remind you that farm work is never done."

"Nothing wrong for a man to work hard." Walt slapped him on the back. "I can't say how proud I am of you."

"How come I hear a 'but' in there?" Duel asked suspiciously.

"That's 'cause there is. Right now, dancin' with that pretty wife of yours is all that should be on your mind."

Luke twirled Jessie within a few feet and Duel cast his brother a steely glare. He wasn't sure if it was the stimulating exercise or Luke's conversation that had brought the rosy blush to Jessie's cheeks, but he damn sure didn't like it.

Walt gave him a push toward her. "Quit standin' here like a three-legged mule and go cut in. Jealousy's a two-edged sword. It'll cut a man in half 'fore he can blink."

Duel shifted his weight to the other foot. "I'm not jealous, Pop."

"Well darn it, boy, you should be." Walt shook his head in disgust. "Thought I raised you to have a little more sense an' a whole lot more gumption."

So softly that he wasn't even aware he spoke at all, Duel muttered, "It's my business."

"That it is, son. Ain't meanin' no disrespect, but you got a fine woman there. I'm tickled to have her for a daughter. Jessie could teach you a thing or two if you'd listen."

True, she could. She had almost taught him to forget. Almost.

Duel spit out the straw he'd been chewing. "Guess I'll have to dance with her to shush you."

"Go on ahead, boy." Walt gave him a nudge.

Luke stopped when Duel tapped his shoulder. "Hey, big brother, the music hasn't ended yet. You wanna wait your turn?"

Duel shot a cursory glance to Jessie's hand resting lightly on Luke's arm before he met her gaze. If the sparkle in her eyes got any brighter he'd surely go blind. His mood soured worse than curdled milk.

"You up to bloodshed?"

Luke returned his glare but quickly relinquished his hold.

Duel put his hand on her waist. "Shall we, Mrs. McClain?"

With a mischievous blue twinkle she matched his formality. "I'd be delighted, Mr. McClain."

Luke's loud groan reached them as they swept away.

The rise and fall of Jessie's bosom lured Duel's attention. If he bent her just the right way he could probably steal a peek of her luscious full breast, for the swell began a tad above the square neckline. The tantalizing thought caused him to miss a step.

"I'm rusty as the devil."

"I hadn't noticed." She smiled up at him, and he was struck by the brilliance of her pearly teeth.

How come he hadn't paid attention to that before? Or the way she filled out her clothes much more than Annie had? Jessie's rounded curves seemed formed for his body.

"Duel?"

"What, Jess?" He pulled his attention from the gently heaving swells and found her sooty-lashed gaze equally fascinating. Concern glistened in their depths.

"I'm glad for this chance to apologize for my untoward behavior. I've wanted to a thousand times since that night, but you haven't come to the house." She lowered her gaze to a spot on his chest. "I'd die before I intentionally hurt you."

The top of her auburn head tickled his lips, the scent of rainwater-fresh hair reeled his senses.

"The apology isn't yours to make." He hated how deeply he'd wounded her and it stung. "I've acted an . . . begging your pardon for my vulgar language . . . like an ass the last few days."

"Let's forget it and go on, shall we?"

"Only one thing more. I was wrong. I shouldn't have forced Annie's things on you. You deserve your own. Like I said, I've been an ass." He took long strides, sweeping her around the dirt floor in three-four time. "Hope Luke didn't pester you with too many questions."

"A few. Your brother's quite a likable fellow."

"Yeah. But keep a healthy regard for him. He's cunning as a snake."

"I did volunteer that I'd made a living as a seamstress."

A low admiring whistle came from his lips. "One thing about it, Jess, you've got a head on your shoulders." And, a very pretty one at that, he might add.

"You don't think he knows, do you?"

"We're safe—for now." Duel tightened his hold, drawing her closer than necessary. He'd do his darndest to make sure she stayed that way.

"I'd be a ninny to count on that lasting. Have you heard the talk buzzing around the room?"

"Some. The murder appears to be the topic." He concentrated on weaving through the maze of dancers, intent on pushing unpleasant things to the back of his mind for the night.

"Speculation is rampant on where Jessie Foltry is. I can't name the number of times people remarked on the similarity of my name and my sudden arrival in Tranquility." Her voice caught.

Duel felt the same band strangling his chest. He held her tighter to him. "Shhh, quit worrying. Let's enjoy the moment."

He wanted to give her more reassurance that she had nothing to fear. "Tomorrow is soon enough to fret. It's only idle gossip."

"So far." Her whisper sent shivers up his spine.

"Shush. None of that. I want only pleasant thoughts while we're here." Pleasant things, like the weight of her breasts thrusting against his chest.

"I missed you, Duel." Jessie's voice became thick with emotion. "I thought you were going to stay mad at me forever."

"You did nothing. I merely had some things to sort out."

"Marley Rose missed you, too. The slightest noise sent her scurrying for the door. It nearly broke her heart when her papa didn't come through it."

"I intend to remedy that. Can't have my two best girls getting long faces."

He thought it odd for Jessie to stumble. Thus far she had followed every step perfectly. He tried to see her face, but the top of her head shielded her features. Silence stretched for a long minute. The dog seemed a harmless subject.

"Yellow Dog is still hanging around." He swung her around, enjoying the feel of her in his arms. "Funny thing. I go to feed him and find someone's beat me to it."

"I didn't know you were feeding him too." Her laughter tinkled merrily. "Guess he won't go hungry."

"Reckon not. In light of all the attention, sooner or later he's bound to become friendly, Jess."

"Only when the animal's ready to trust again will he let us get close." Shadows instantly darkened her mood.

Mister, you ever been so scared, you think the next second is going to be your last? You're looking in the face of the devil and wondering how on earth you can keep him from taking your soul? She'd stood poised on the edge of a cliff when she spoke those words. In spite of all that had happened since then, she hadn't moved that far from the edge.

"Forgive me. I asked you to think of nothing unpleasant."

"Duel, I'm not a fragile egg. Quit apologizing. I won't break," she murmured quietly and allowed her head to rest in the hollow of his throat. "What I did stands between us just as surely as does your former wife."

Damn!

Maybe she was right. For some reason though, recalling Annie's face lately took a lot more effort. Each time he tried, it was Jessie he saw.

They twirled silently amid other couples. The weight of her head on his chest aroused a fierce protectiveness and the touch of her hand on his shoulder made the skin sizzle beneath his shirt.

"Marley's loving this opportunity to play with other children," Jessie said at last. "It's good for her."

He tried to divert his attention from the feel of her skirts swirling, grazing, caressing his legs. He attempted to focus on the direction she nodded, to block the intimate touching, to prevent certain images from entering his mind. He failed.

The devil take him. She'd imbedded herself inside him. A ragged breath only served to inhale her fragrance. Yet it intoxicated rather than calmed.

At that moment she moved, affording him the view he'd hoped for. The neckline gaped slightly, allowing a peek of one lush mound—all the way to the brown edge of a nipple. His body responded with need that he'd denied far too long.

"Jess . . . my throat . . . I need some cider."

"Me, too. I think I've danced every dance. My feet aren't used to this."

Aunt Bessie's garter! If he didn't get some fresh air right away, his embarrassment would be public knowledge. He hurried her toward his father.

"See, son, that wasn't so bad. You're still walking."

Barely—and with a decided limp. If his father only knew. "Jess, you wait here with Pop and Luke and I'll get us some refreshment."

Without waiting for a reply, he hurried for the nearest door, only to be stopped by Vicky.

"Not running out on the party, are you? Looks like Jessie's having a good time, and the children are keeping Marley Rose occupied."

"Can't a man get some fresh air without a bunch of questions?" He wasn't running anywhere except for the cover of darkness. He ran exasperated fingers through his hair. "I think I see Roy calling you, Sis."

When she turned to look, he quickly scooted for freedom. Damp night air hit his face, cooling the sweat that soaked his underarms.

Pop had been right about one thing. Jessie was something. Not even Annie had brought the strange excitement he experienced now. His love for Annie had been serene and steady. Not at all like this rolling, dipping sensation of riding a wild bronc.

The door swung out and Luke joined him. "Anything wrong, big brother? Looks like you took a fever or something."

What he felt could certainly describe a fever. Only he didn't know how a man could get one simply from looking at his wife.

"Tarnation, Luke. Is it a crime for a man to get a breath of air and cool off?"

"Jessie can sure do that to a man. Hey, you reckon God put people on this earth merely to torment a man?"

"What people?" Duel wasn't sure where Luke was going.

"Women people. If she wasn't married to you—"

"But she is and don't forget it." The warning exploded before he thought twice. Duel shifted uncomfortably under Luke's long stare.

"I hate to keep repeating myself, but you're the luckiest man alive, Duel."

The silence lasted for all of two seconds before Luke spoke again. "Remember when Pop caught you behind ol' man McDougal's store stealing a kiss from Lucinda Moore?"

Funny Luke should bring that up because that's exactly the way he felt now. Only it hadn't been a kiss, but a glimpse of his wife's breast he'd stolen.

"Yep, he accused me of having manure for brains. In fact, told me so often I got to believing it."

"Left an impression on me, too. Manure for brains is what you've got all right, leaving Jessie at the mercy of the likes of Hampton Pierson." Luke chuckled as if quite pleased with himself. "I came to tell you the man's moonin' over her."

"The hell you say!" A fine thread of ire wound through his blood. No doubt Pierson was ogling down Jessie's dress. The ire turned to anger.

Sure enough, he found an animated Hampton talking with Jessie. He made a beeline for the refreshment table for two cups of cherry cider before interrupting.

"Here you are, darlin'." He ignored her startled look at the uncharacteristic endearment as he handed the drink to her. "Sorry I got delayed."

Jessie's uneasy glance between them, coupled with tension he could slice with a knife, made him curse the day Vicky arrived at her grand plan for this shindig. He glared at his opponent.

"Mr. Pierson was kind enough to—" she began.

"I was just telling your wife it's a good thing she wore green," Hampton interrupted. "Saint Patrick's Day and all. You haven't been away so long you've forgotten the tradition about pinching those who don't wear green, have you, Duel?"

Anyone who dared pinch his wife would get some broken fingers and that wouldn't be all. He returned the man's cool challenge with an icy fix. Then a slight jostle, as if entirely by accident, sent red cider down the front of Hampton's starched, white shirt. The man sputtered and fumed.

"Sorry there, Pierson." He didn't bother to hide his smile. "Looks like you'll have to go clean yourself off."

"If you'll excuse me, Mrs. McClain." Hampton could barely control his temper. Stiffly tipping his head, he turned.

"And when you come back, find yourself someone else to talk with, Pierson. My wife will be occupied for the remainder of the evening." Duel felt satisfied with the events.

"You did that on purpose." Jessie's wide eyes held puzzlement as she gasped. "You should be ashamed."

"Me? What did I do?"

Luke strolled over, chuckling. "Was I mistaken or did Pierson have a red stain down the front of his shirt? He came by me so fast I barely got a glimpse."

"Seems someone thought he looked better that way." Jessie returned Duel's smile and the warmth of it reawakened the embers he'd doused with cold night air.

"How about we head for home, Jess? I've had all the excitement I can stand for one night." That was putting it mildly.

"Whoa, Preacher." He pulled to a stop at the front door and jumped down from the wagon seat.

Clouds rolled across the moon as he relieved Jessie of her sleeping burden before lending her a hand down. She'd been very quiet on the ride home and he wondered if she was angry. His experience with womenfolk had taught him he'd know sooner or later. He supposed he might've overreacted just a bit. But he wasn't sorry.

Inside the house, he kissed Marley and put her to bed.

"Guess I'll take Preacher to the barn and turn in for the night." He kept his hands busy twirling his hat and his eyes on the door.

"Could you stay for a moment?"

The fleeting glance he cast in her direction showed worry shimmering behind her distant gaze.

"I suppose." He took the chair opposite from her. "Shoot."

"It might not be anything, but then again . . . tonight a woman by the name of Charlotte Brown said she knew some Rumfords in Pecos County. She asked if they were any relation."

"Strange coincidence. Rumford is not an everyday name."

"That's what I thought when I spied the baking powder can and picked it. Why didn't I choose Smith or Jones?"

"Charlotte Brown, you say? Don't think I know her."

"She was an elderly woman well past her prime. Chattered a mile a minute. Could it be she was merely pretending so she'd have something to talk to me about?"

"Possible. Still, if someone like Luke started nosing around, it could upset the applecart." Knowing his brother's penchant for meddling, he wouldn't put it past him. "Don't worry about it. I'm sure it was nothing. I think all in all the affair went smoothly."

Except for the agitation her dress caused. She looked so beautiful, a vision in green. Across from her now, seeing her slender neck sloping down to meet her ample bosom, he felt overheated again. The mysterious green dress.

"Tell me something."

Jessie waited expectantly for him to continue.

"I've wondered all evening where you got the dress you're wearing. Mind me asking?"

She smoothed the sprigged print. "I took apart several of your wife's dresses and fashioned one that you'd never seen. I added lace from one, cord from another and rearranged the neckline." Jessie bit her lip nervously. "Are you mad?"

Madly attracted could describe his mood. "Not even a little bit. I told you to do what you will with them. It's most becoming on you."

That she would go to such lengths to avoid reawakening memories touched him deeply. It also meant she must care for him some to go out of her way to spare his feelings.

Relief swept her features. "Thank you, Duel."

He rose to go before he did something he shouldn't—like taking her in his arms, and kissing those lush, pink lips.

"Jess?" He paused with one hand on the knob. "You made me a very proud man tonight. I'm glad you're my wife."

Chapter Fourteen

Jessie went to sleep with a smile on her face. And she awoke floating on light, fluffy clouds.

For someone to have pride in her and show it came as a surprise. It'd been so long since anyone appreciated her, she'd forgotten the last time.

"I'm glad you're my wife," Duel had said.

She hugged herself. Her new husband continually caught her off guard. At the dance he'd looked at her with something more than admiration. His special treatment made her feel like a princess. And his jealousy over Hampton Pierson's attention shocked, but pleased her. Her smile grew and a giggle erupted.

Marley Rose gave her a strange look.

"Your papa likes me."

"Pa pa."

Grabbing the girl's hands tightly, she swung her around in a circle. Gleeful laughter filled the little house.

"Maybe not as much as Annie. It's not love, but he feels something." Her heart near to bursting, she lifted Marley and kissed her cheeks. Then, she brushed aside the black curls and whispered in the child's ear. "I like your papa too."

Marley clapped her little hands excitedly as if approving the shared secret. Her laughter charged the air when Duel opened the door.

"Appears my two girls are happy today. Could hear you clear to the barn."

"Paaaa." Marley reached for her hero.

"Hey, Two Bit, what's got you in such a good mood?" He kissed her rosy cheek before admonishing, "I told you it's not Papa. I'm Duel."

The way the gentle giant of a man held the fragile girl caused Jessie's stomach to flip-flop. He was strong, tough when he had to be, yet good and kind—to children and dogs. And her. Jeremiah had lacked all those qualities.

"I'll teach you, woman, to run away from me. The only question you'll ask from now on when I say jump is how high. Because I own you." Jeremiah had spat those words in her face after bringing her back the first time she'd tried to escape.

"I hate you! You'll never break me, never." She'd vowed that even when Jeremiah came at her with the glowing metal rod.

Anger mottled Jeremiah's face when it came within an inch of hers. *"I'll show you what you get for fighting me."*

The smell had been worse than the pain, for once the stench of burning flesh entered a body's nostrils, nothing could erase it. The odor lodged in her brain. Now, the slightest malodorous scent sent her reeling back to that fateful day.

Despite her vow that he'd not break her spirit, she'd had to reach deep inside afterward for the will to continue her fight.

She shook her head to get rid of Jeremiah's memory. It took several minutes to slow her heartbeat.

"Ma." Marley pointed to Jessie.

Saints be praised the girl couldn't talk, she thought, or she'd be telling Duel their secret.

"Yes, darlin'. That's your mama. I suppose you can call Jess anything your little heart desires."

When would he realize Marley had him wrapped around her finger? And how come it was all right for the girl to call her mama and not him papa? Not that she minded. She couldn't love Marley more if she was her own.

Smells of baking biscuits drifted from the kitchen. "Oh dear!"

Duel and Marley followed on her heels.

"Sure does smell good, Jess. Reckon I could eat a horse, or one nanny goat. How about you, Two Bit?" Duel sat her in a chair and reached for a pair of coffee cups.

No one could understand Marley's jabber, but that didn't stop her from giving them an earful. Jessie supposed she was sharing her thoughts on the subject.

The sourdough biscuits had baked a nice golden brown, thank goodness. She transferred them to a plate and set them on the table.

"Jess?"

Duel touched her arm lightly. He looked like he'd swallowed a mouthful of cod-liver oil when he reached into his pocket and fished something out. She waited expectantly.

"Pop slipped this in my hand last night. It belonged to my mother and I want you to have it." A glitter of gold came from the ring he held out.

"Your mother's?" Sudden emotion choked her airway. The mist in her eyes wasn't from the smoke that came back down the flue and into the room. "I don't . . . are you sure?"

"Pop's idea. And it wasn't anything that Annie ever wore. Tom Parker bought her wedding ring. Said this little gold band wasn't good enough for his daughter."

Jessie held out her hand and let him slip it on her third finger. "It's absolutely beautiful! A perfect fit."

She held up her hand, admiring it from every angle.

"Now, when we meet up with Hampton Pierson again, he'll have no question that you're taken."

Did she still detect a note of jealousy in his voice? A thrill stole into heart. To give her such a precious gift had to mean he cared for her.

"I'll treasure it always." She blinked hard. "No one has ever been this good to me."

If he looked like he'd swallowed cod-liver oil before, now he had the appearance of its effects—shifting on first one foot, then the other. She supposed her making a to-do over the ring embarrassed him.

"Sit down and eat those biscuits while they're hot. Put some food in your belly before you start work."

While he poured sorghum over the buttered delicacies, she gazed at the ring. Maybe her fuss hadn't flustered him, maybe it had been the duty and honor part that had done it. After all, his pop had been the one who told him to give it to her. He hadn't said it was his idea. Maybe he simply felt obligated. It would be better if she didn't attach too much meaning to the gesture.

Jessie gazed at her finger one more time.

In the next few days life settled into a routine of sorts. She helped Duel and Walt plant the sorghum, and spring rains gave the crop a nice start. True to his word, Duel spent more time with Marley Rose. And her. But when bedtime came, he headed for the barn.

Toward the end of the week, Vicky and the twins came to visit, bringing news that Luke had gone on his way. Jessie breathed much easier.

"Said he had an idea about Jessie Foltry's whereabouts."

"What kind of idea? Did he say?" Though caution colored Jessie's question, it came from between stiff lips.

"Muttered something about Cactus Springs and Pecos." Vicky absently watched Becky and Betsy playing peekaboo with Marley. "Wonder what kind of woman would kill her husband in cold blood?"

Hands of doom tightened around Jessie's throat. She hoped her face hadn't become as pasty white as it felt.

You disgust me. You're worthless, can't even bear a man a child to carry on the Foltry name. Tonight I'm giving you to my friends. Maybe you can show them your gratitude.

Jeremiah's threat filled her head, taking her back to that last evening when she'd finished it once and for all.

"One never knows what goes on between a husband and wife, Vicky. Could be that Foltry wasn't the kind of man everyone thought."

"A spat don't give a woman the right to take his life. Shoot, if that was the case, I'd have shot Roy a long time ago."

"I never had the chance to properly thank you for the party you gave for us." Jessie changed the subject before she lost her composure. "Duel and I had a wonderful time."

Compliments were a surefire bet to change Vicky's course. The woman glowed.

"Gladys Stanton is having a quilting bee at her house next week and asked me to invite you. Course we do more gossipin' than actual sewing—especially Charlotte Brown."

It didn't sound like her cup of tea. Especially with the Brown woman in attendance. Jessie could only imagine the questions the nosey women would put to her.

"Thank you, Vicky. I—"

In true Vicky fashion, her sister-in-law didn't wait for her to finish the sentence but babbled on. "Before I forget. The ladies are organizing a women's suffrage meeting for Tuesday of next week at six o'clock in the church. I might have already told you. I've spread the word to so many I can't remember."

Jessie gave her a fleeting smile, not bothering to reply. She recognized a head wind when she saw one and Vicky wasn't slowing down for anything.

"Can you believe it? Wyoming gave women the right to vote eleven years ago and so far no other state has followed their example. The Fifteenth Amendment even gives black men the vote, but not us women. Shameful, that's what it is."

"Yes, I agree," Jessie slipped in when Vicky paused to catch her breath. Oppression remained despite the rapid advances of the law. What chance would she stand in a court of law that sanctioned a husband's abusive treatment of his wife? Clearing herself of the murder charge seemed hopeless. A married woman had no rights—not even the right to her own body.

The glint of gold on her finger kept her mind occupied while Vicky prattled on. When they found out who she was and what she'd done, who among Tranquility's female ranks would stand with her? Would the esteemed Susan B. Anthony or Lucy Stone stand beside her? She doubted it.

Duel stomped dirt off his feet outside before he opened the door. He gave the visitor a suspicious scowl.

"Hope you're not trying to rope my wife into anything, Sis."

Now, as each time before, he filled the room with his presence. Jessie tried to still her quickening pulse. Sun-drenched and tanned, he encompassed her with a vital intensity she couldn't explain. His unleashed power awed her in the way lightning streaking across a stormy sky did. Beautiful . . . and dangerous only in a heartbreaking sense.

"Who, me?" Innocence flashed across Vicky's pretty face.

"You're not fooling me. Remember, I know you."

"Oh, Duel, we're just having harmless woman talk." She rose and smoothed her flowered calico dress. "I do declare, look at the time. I've got to get home and fix supper."

"No need to rush off on my account." Safe behind Vicky's back, Duel winked at her. Dangerous and filled with devilment.

"I would dearly love to stay and chat, but duty calls. Come, girls, your father'll think we deserted him."

Betsy put down Marley's rag doll. "We go, Mama? See George an' Henwy?"

"Tell your cousin good-bye." The woman reached for each girl's hand.

"We play tomannow," Becky explained seriously.

Vicky turned to Jessie. "Remember, Tuesday of next week, six o'clock at the church."

Duel waited until the door closed after his sibling. "What the hell was that about?"

"Women's suffrage meeting." She watched him roll his eyes.

"You going?"

"No. That's a volatile subject and bound to draw attention. I should try to keep to myself. Be as unobtrusive as possible."

How she'd accomplish that he didn't know. Afternoon sunlight through the window pane caught her hair, transforming the auburn strands into a golden, fiery halo. Unobtrusive? He didn't think anyone would dare use that word to describe his Jess. If so, they needed spectacles.

"Did you need my help with something?"

"Came in to see what that sister of mine had cooked up now. Afraid I learned a long time ago not to trust her too far."

"Vicky brought news that Luke left town."

"That shouldn't put that wrinkle on your forehead. Seems you'd be glad to hear the news."

"He's blazing a trail for Cactus Springs and Pecos. Said he might stumble across Jessie Foltry's trail by backtracking."

"Damnation!"

Heavy, pounding rains drove Duel into the house, much to Jessie's delight. A slow, lazy fire in the hearth, rumbling thunder, the clatter on the tin roof, and the soft click of knitting needles gave her a sense of tranquil belonging. The three of them were a family.

Marley Rose teetered unsteadily as she released her hold on Jessie's skirt and attempted to walk unaided to Duel, who sat staring into the low flames in the fireplace. No doubt he was lost in days past when he sat with Annie on such a day as this. Perhaps they'd planned their lives, dreamed of children on a rainy afternoon like this.

She yearned to smooth back the lock of hair that had fallen forward, and banish the wrinkle in his brow. And tell him her only desire lay in sharing a small corner of his life. She'd never ask for more than that.

The happy little girl had almost reached him when she suddenly bobbled and fell. Her head struck the floor.

As she began to whimper, Duel lifted her into his lap. "There, Two Bit, it's all right." He kissed the red lump on her forehead tenderly. "I've got you."

She sniffled loudly and smiled away the hurt. "Pa pa."

"No, baby, I'm Duel, not your papa."

"Pa pa." Tiny fingers patted him as she snuggled into his chest.

Jessie's heart swelled watching the two of them, and she lost count of the stitches. The crocheted cap for Marley would end up looking like a sock if she didn't keep her mind on her knitting.

"Never mind, I love you anyway, darlin'." His breath stirred the dark hair on top of the dark little head. "Someday you'll understand why I can't be your papa."

"She doesn't care about the whys and why-nots, Duel." She spoke low, glancing up from her task. "You fill a need in her life, and she loves you for that."

"It wouldn't be right to let her believe a lie."

"You can straighten her out when she gets old enough to understand. I can't see what harm can come from giving in." She couldn't help pointing out. "Besides, you don't seem to be making any headway in changing her mind."

Just then a knock sounded on the door. With the rainfall and thus no work, Walt hadn't dropped by. She didn't think Vicky would get out in the deluge unless something had happened. Fear rose from the pit of her stomach. Perhaps this was the moment they'd been dreading. Her day of reckoning. Duel's questioning scowl didn't help as he sat Marley in Jessie's lap and moved to open it.

"I'm s-sorry, mister, I c-come in?" A woman's voice, her teeth chattering from the cold, drifted past Duel's large frame.

"Who is it, Duel?" Jessie rose to stand beside her husband.

"P-please, I come see my b-baby."

Chapter Fifteen

"Please, come in by the fire." Jessie urged the half-frozen stranger inside. Whatever the woman meant about wanting to see her baby would have to wait until she warmed herself. Still, the puzzling request triggered no small shock.

Water formed in puddles around the woman's feet. Rain had plastered her hair as well as her clothing to her body. She stood transfixed, her dark eyes never leaving Marley Rose.

"Duel, will you get a blanket to warm this poor woman?"

He returned a second later and Jessie helped spread it around the stranger's shoulders.

"My baby. *Dios mío,* my baby."

Jessie wasn't sure the wetness on the woman's face was from the rain. Icy fingers of foreboding closed around her heart.

"Kindly explain yourself, ma'am. Who are you?" Duel's gruff tone finally broke the woman's trance.

"Maria." Her gaze fixed once again on Marley. "Marley Rose's *madre.*"

The only noise in the room was Duel's heavy breathing. He sounded as if someone had suckerpunched him in the belly. Jessie clutched her chest to quiet the pain radiating from deep inside. It spread through her veins until the ache became like a fireball. It couldn't be. She refused to think how empty their world would be without Marley Rose.

"What proof do you have?" Duel's features hardened into the piece of granite from which his face could have been chiseled. "You expect to waltz in here, lay claim to the child, and we'll turn her over just because you know her name? Not in a million years, lady."

"Please, senor. I only want to see her." Maria's hands trembled as she clutched the blanket tighter.

"The man who wagered Marley Rose in that poker game told me her mother was dead, that she had no one." A tic in his jaw twitched. "You telling me he lied?"

Raw hurt sprang from the hoarse question. If he lost another child, Jessie feared he'd slip back into his shell never to return. Marley Rose had plugged the gaping hole from which his spirit seeped.

"Will Gentry take what he want. He take me. Marley Rose come nine months later."

"Why did Will Gentry tell my husband you were dead?" Jessie felt compelled to try and make sense of it all.

Maria dropped wearily on the floor before the hearth. "Gentry steal Marley. I follow. I see the evil he do." Though water from the wet strands streamed down her face, Maria didn't attempt to brush it away.

"Why didn't you try to stop him?" Anger tinged Duel's question.

"I only one woman. No law in Cactus Springs."

Even if there were, Jessie suspected Maria wasn't strong enough to stand against Will Gentry. Men like him and Jeremiah made their own laws and dared anyone to stop them.

"I follow you. I watch. I see good people. Good home. I see much love."

Sympathy for Maria swept through Jessie. The woman had

been a victim, her plight no better than Jessie's. She knelt beside Maria.

"Would you like to hold your little girl?"

Tears trickled down Maria's cheeks as Marley Rose held out her arms.

"Maaaa."

Mother and child came together and Jessie's heart broke from the bittersweet image. Maria's love for Marley shone in the tender way she pressed her daughter to her bosom.

Through the blur Jessie glanced up at Duel. Agony ravaged his features and his amber eyes were suspiciously damp. He spun and grabbed his hat. The door slammed behind him as he stalked heedlessly into the rain.

She knew his destination. Without going to the window she knew he'd seek solace on the hill. This couldn't happen to him again. Not now. Not when he'd opened his heart and allowed a little dark-haired girl to climb inside. And what about her own hurt?

"I'll make some coffee to warm you, Maria." She stumbled to the kitchen before the sobs tore from her throat.

Duel returned much later to find Maria playing with Marley Rose as if nothing was amiss. The sight reopened old wounds that twisted his gut inside out. He'd sat on the hill in the driving rain until he became frozen from the cold.

"I was worried about you, Duel." Jessie lifted his sopping wet hat and hung it on the nail, then she draped a blanket around his shoulders.

He barely felt the hand drawing him to the fire. He'd need more than the flames of a blazing hearth to melt the glacier that had formed in his chest. He doubted anything could thaw his chill.

"You'll be lucky if you don't catch your death."

Death would be a welcome relief if it would stop the grief that raged inside.

"It'll be all right." Jessie's comforting murmur sounded far away, as she brushed dripping tendrils from his forehead.

He glanced up to see Jessie bustling toward the kitchen.

"Senor, I give thanks for taking good care of Marley."

Maria's soft accent drew his attention to the one place he'd tried to avoid since entering. Now that the woman didn't look like a drowned rat, he noticed how much she and Marley favored each other. Same black hair and eyes. Same shy smile. Marley Rose was an exact copy of her pretty mother.

"Wasn't hard. She's a special little girl." Even though he sympathized with Maria, he couldn't disguise the stony hardness of his tone. Surely as Gentry had ripped Marley Rose from Maria's arms, she meant to do the same to him and Jessie.

"Drink this hot coffee." Jessie eased a tin mug into his hands. "After you get it down, you need to change into some dry clothes. Don't want you getting sick."

"Papa." Marley pulled on his leg. "Papa."

A mouthful of buttermilk couldn't have made his stomach churn more. The child didn't understand she was reaching into his heart and pulling it out by the roots. She didn't know how big a crater she'd leave.

"Hey, Two Bit." He pulled her into his lap and kissed the top of her curls. He missed her already, and she hadn't even left.

"The rain's stopping." Jessie spoke softly from the window. Duel thought he heard a catch in her breath.

"Guess you'll be going soon, Maria." He supposed he should offer her a place to stay for the night, but that'd make Marley's leaving more unbearable.

"I leave soon." Misery painted Maria's quiet statement. It puzzled him. She had what she came for.

"Jess, better get Two Bit's things together." He raised Marley in the air and playfully nuzzled her stomach. She giggled and grabbed handfuls of hair. "Ow. You still know how to get even."

It took a full minute to get loose from her grasp. He settled her out of reach from anything tender. "Appears you're going on a journey, darlin'."

"Senor, you mistake."

"What?"

"I give you Marley Rose. I no give her good life. She be safe here from Will Gentry. He no find her. He very mean."

"But—"

"She stay here. You and lady nice people. You give her good life."

"Why did you come so far to leave empty-handed?" The disbelief on Jessie's face had to match his own.

"I hide. I watch. I see much love here. Now, I go back to family. I know Gentry not hurt her."

"You sure you can live with this, Maria?" he asked.

"I sure." Maria rose. "Rain stops. I go now."

With a tightness squeezing his chest, Duel handed Marley Rose to Maria for one last good-bye. He realized the agony the woman must feel. Couldn't be any easier than the day he nailed Annie and his son's coffin lid shut.

"*Vaya con Dios, niña.*" Maria hugged her daughter tightly, then gave her to Jessie.

"Don't worry, we'll keep her safe." Duel put his arm around Jessie's waist.

He buried his face in the short dark curls. Oh God, he thought he'd lost his baby. It'd been too close for comfort.

The woman paused at the door and turned. Duel would remember her stricken face long as he lived. "I ask two things."

"Name them."

"Tell Marley Rose her *madre* love her." Maria wiped away her tears and lifted her chin defiantly. "And if Will Gentry come, you kill him."

The kitchen door opened and Duel watched his two ladies step out. Laughing, Jessie swung Marley around in a circle before she set the child on her feet and reached back inside for a basket.

"That Jessie's a sight." Walt had caught him watching her again. "Picked a handsome one, son."

"Yep, she sure is." Try as he might, Duel couldn't keep from admiring the gentle sway of her hips as she carried the basket of laundry to the clothesline. He'd seen few woman with a walk like hers—loose, easy, and full of promise.

"Your mother's ring looks pretty on her hand."

"Yep." Talking to his father about Jessie made him uncomfortable.

"Hard for a feller to keep his mind on his work when she's within eyeshot."

Absently, Duel chopped at a clump of weeds. "Yep."

"Cotton-pickin', boy! Watch what you're doin'. Came within a hair of choppin' my foot."

"If you hadn't moved your darn foot and put it right in the way, I wouldn't have scared you, Pop."

"You're gettin' meaner'n a rattlesnake, son."

But Duel wasn't listening. He had other things to occupy him. His heart seemed to float as he gazed at the two people who made his world. A smile curved his lips as Marley Rose toddled after Jessie as fast as her chubby legs could go. A week had passed since Maria appeared at their door. Though he felt guilty, and he appreciated how great a sacrifice the woman had made, he thanked the good Lord every day for letting him keep the child.

At that moment Jessie bent over the basket. The sight of her skirted bottom stuck in the air caused a swift intake of air.

"What's the matter, son? You feelin' poorly?"

If Walt only knew. Poorly didn't begin to describe the way he felt. Jessie affected him in ways no other woman had. When she turned those Wedgwood blues on him and smiled in the special way that only she could, his toes curled right up in his boots. Yet she resisted his efforts to get closer.

"I'm fine, Pop." Long as Jess didn't bend over again. Or smile at him. Or flash her sooty-lashed eyes his way. Come to think of it, he'd not been fine since she'd ridden into his camp that night.

"Still sleepin' in the barn, I take it." Walt stuck both hands inside the bib of his overalls, making his chest puff out.

"That's my affair, doesn't concern you if I am."

"Was that Jessie's idea or yours?"

"The nosey bug bite you or something?" Duel felt guilty at his snappish reply. His father merely worried. He leaned on the hoe. "It was my idea, Pop. There are unusual circumstances."

"She has feelings for you, son. I've seen how she looks at you when you're not payin' attention."

"I think you're wrong about that." Dead wrong. Being made to wear a man's brand like a steer would sour any woman against menfolk.

"Learned a long time ago, if it walks like a duck, and quacks like a duck, it's a duck. Yep, she's got feelings."

He wished Walt was right, wished with all his heart and soul. Nothing would please him more than holding her in his arms, whispering sweet nothings in her ear.

"Maybe she needs a little persuading," Walt continued.

"What do you mean?"

"Court her proper like. Pick her some posies. Buy her some of them fancy chocolates. I hafta draw you a picture?"

Perhaps his father had something there. He marshaled his thoughts into a neat, straight row. Perhaps courting her would change her view, let her see him in a different light. It'd be worth risking his feelings for such an outcome.

"Surefire way to a woman's heart all righty."

Some women, but would the same hold true for Jess? The wind lifted the hem of her skirt, revealing a trim ankle. Then a sudden gust blew the skirt higher until it exposed the white fabric of her pantaloons and a flash of curved leg. Duel swallowed a big wad of spit and choked.

"What's the trouble, boy? Swallow your tongue?" Walt peered at him through narrowed slits.

The fit of coughing prevented him from replying. It took several minutes to regain control.

"Sure actin' strange today, son, if I do say so."

Strange wasn't all. A man should be able to look at his wife without making a fool of himself.

"Do you mind keeping your opinions to yourself, Pop?" He applied the hoe vigorously to a thistle patch.

Walt softly murmured something about "It's a duck." Then he touched Duel's arm. "Look."

Duel turned and what he saw raised alarm. Yellow Dog had circled the edge of the field and now crept toward Marley Rose. The bandage on his leg had evidently managed to come off. Either that or the animal had chewed it off. More likely the latter.

"The dog seems friendly enough. You don't suppose he'd bite the girl, do ya?" Walt voiced Duel's exact thoughts.

First instinct told him to shout a warning, get Jessie's attention. On second thought, that might scare the wounded retriever into doing the unthinkable.

Yellow Dog was so large, Marley so small. One bite could kill the child. His stomach churned. He felt ill. Before he remembered he'd left his forty-five slung over Preacher's stall in the barn, he reached for it and came up empty.

Spying a hefty rock, he picked it up. He didn't know if he could hit the animal from that distance, but he meant to try.

"Well, I'll be a horned toad!"

"What?" Duel's attention quickly swung back to the scene.

Yellow Dog had dropped to the ground and was crawling across the bare dirt on his belly.

"Boobie! Boobie!" Marley Rose waddled excitedly to him, holding out her arms.

By now, Jessie saw the dog and watched, poised to react if needed. Animal and child met. Yellow Dog's head drooped shyly, then he flicked his tongue and licked Marley's hand.

The rock made a soft thud when it dropped to Duel's feet.

Chapter Sixteen

When Duel came in for supper that night he held a surprise behind his back. Sweat lined his palms.

"Papa." Marley Rose hugged his legs exuberantly.

"Hey, Two Bit." He knelt and gave her a one-armed squeeze. She pursed her tiny lips expectantly for his kiss, which he gave. Much as Marley's welcome warmed him, his mind was on other things tonight. He was relieved when, the greeting satisfied, the girl resumed her play.

A searching glance found that "other" thing in the kitchen. Jessie bustled between the table she'd just set to the cookstove. And when she bent to lift bread from the oven, his mouth became dry as a creek bed in a drought.

Her shapely hips would fit his hands nicely. In fact, they seemed made for that exact purpose. His hand tightened around the posies still hidden by his backside. In what he hoped was a casual stroll, although it felt more like a lope, he moved toward her.

"Evenin', Jess."

"Duel . . . I thought Marley Rose had kept you occupied at

the door." Her breathless answer raised his brow. He couldn't imagine the reason for her short-windedness.

"Have a nice day?" The room seemed extraordinarily hot.

"The usual." Jessie brushed back a tendril of hair that had slipped from the ribbon at the nape of her neck. "Supper's almost ready. Venison stew and hot bread."

A streak of flour on the end of her nose and across her cheek drove him wild. He reached to wipe it off.

He sniffed. "What's that I smell?"

"Sweet-potato pie."

"My favorite." Duel brought the flowers forward with a flourish. "For you, Jess."

A pink blush spread prettily across her cheeks. "Oh, Duel." She buried her nose in the bouquet of bluebonnets, Indian paintbrush, and pink wine-cups. Then she promptly sneezed.

"Bless you." Everyone sneezed from time to time, he thought.

Again she sneezed as she reached for a glass and filled it with water. "Aaachoo."

Perhaps posies weren't such a grand idea? "Bless you again."

"I'm sorry. I'm . . ." Another sneeze completed her sentence.

"Mama—pwetty." Marley Rose clapped her hands, showing her appreciation for the colorful blossoms. Duel lifted her into her chair.

"Yes, sweetie, very . . ." Jessie set them in the center of the table just as another sneeze erupted. She hurriedly reached into her apron pocket for a handkerchief.

Duel stood helplessly. He'd committed another blunder. "Jess?"

Blowing her nose, Jessie gave him a big smile. "The flowers are beautiful. It's so thoughtful." She slipped the handkerchief back into her pocket.

In between sneezes, she brought the pot of stew and bread to the table.

"Sit down, Duel." She sent him an expectant look as she

took her place beside Marley Rose. She reached for the knife and loaf of bread.

"Are the posies doing this to you?"

"Good heavens, no." She smothered her mouth when another sneeze overtook her.

"Appears that way." He filled Marley's plate with a good helping of thick, mouth-watering stew, cutting the meat into tiny pieces for her. "There you go, Two Bit. Eat up."

Jessie handed him a slice of bread and put one on Marley's plate before she sneezed again.

He reached for the offending flowers. "I'll throw them outside."

"You'll do no such thing!" Jessie snatched them. Water sloshed down the front of her apron as she clutched the flowers to her bosom. "It's the nicest present anyone ever gave me."

Duel had trouble believing that a bunch of limp wildflowers that brought fits of sneezing numbered at the top of Jessie's list of best gifts. He had trouble, too, with the sparkling jewels her blue eyes had become. The forced swallow wasn't from the big bite of stew he'd taken.

"I saw Yellow Dog come up to Marley Rose today." Changing the subject might help the situation.

"I wasn't sure what the dog was up to, but I knew he'd not harm Marley." Jessie put the bouquet back on the table out of his long reach.

"Wish I'd shared your faith. Nearly gave Pop and me a heart attack."

"You worry too much, Duel. Where's your trust?"

"Right here." He covered her hand with his and could barely contain his joy when she gave him a brilliant smile.

Patience, he reminded himself, encouraged by her actions. One bunch of posies did not a courtship make. Time to change tactics. Next time he'd make darn sure his gift wouldn't cause any ill effects.

* * *

Saturday found Jessie in town for some shopping. Engrossed in perusing the array of piece goods, she scarcely heard the bell over the door of Tranquility's only mercantile store. She moved on to a row of bonnets.

"Mrs. McClain, how nice to see you again." Hampton Pierson made a beeline for her.

Jessie groaned inwardly and replaced on the shelf the lace and flowered bonnet she'd been admiring. Her pleasant day in town had just turned gloomy. So much for the leisurely shopping she and Duel had indulged in after leaving Marley Rose at the Austin house to play with her cousins.

"Afternoon, Mr. Pierson." She searched the store for her husband. Last time she saw him he'd been haggling with Mr. Dexter over the price of cartridges for his gun.

Hampton leaned against a counter cluttered with jars of pickles, licorice, and gum drops. "That divine creation would look mighty handsome on you, ma'am. Perfect match for your lovely eyes."

"I'm merely passing time while waiting for my husband." She prayed he'd leave before Duel saw him. Funny that she'd not noticed the night of Vicky's party how the man waved his conceited good looks under her nose. "It's much too expensive and besides I've no place to wear a bonnet that fancy."

"I'd be honored to purchase it for you, Jessie. Consider it a token of my—"

"Consider this, you womanizer." Duel stepped from behind a stack of wool blankets and slammed his fist into Hampton's jaw, catapulting the man to the floor.

"Duel!" Horrified, Jessie pressed her hand to her mouth.

"The lady's my wife, Pierson." He drew back again, aiming to take another swing, but Jessie caught his arm.

"Please, Duel."

"It'll pay you to remember that."

"I do declare, McClain."

Hampton rose to a sitting position and dabbed at his bloodied nose. She didn't know how the man could be so calm.

He dusted the dirt from his impeccable white shirt, meeting Duel's glare with bland humor.

"You misunderstand my intentions—"

"Your intentions are perfectly clear. Stay away from her if you know what's good for you."

Pure venom laced Duel's warning. Despite the warm, sunny rays streaming through the smudged window, Jessie couldn't prevent the shiver that raced through her.

I own you, Jessie. You'll never be free of me. You wear the Diamond J brand now. Everyone will know you belong to me.

Jeremiah's hate appeared without warning, accompanied by the putrid smell of seared flesh. Nausea rose up into her throat. Would the day ever come when she would no longer be considered a man's property? Had she merely traded one intolerable situation for another?

The glare she sent Duel could have withered the most hardy fruit on the vine. Then she spun on her heels and hurried from the establishment.

"Jess?"

She paid no heed to his call. Nor did she stop when he fell into step beside her. They passed the wagon where Preacher eyed them and passed the church where they spoke their vows.

Finally, Duel took her arm. They stopped under the shade of an elm tree at the edge of town.

"Jess, I'd apologize if I knew what the hell I was apologizing for. What did I do now to get your dander up?"

With hands on her hips, she faced him.

"Duel McClain, get one thing clear. I am not anyone's property—not yours, not Jeremiah's—no one's." Her voice broke. "I wear one man's brand for all eternity, I'll not wear another's."

"Oh, Jess, that's not what I'm about. Don't you know by now I'd never do a thing to hurt you? Or let anyone else?"

"Not all brands are visible, but they're burned on just the same." When she needed a firm, loud voice to drive her point home, her voice betrayed her. The words came out in a raspy whisper.

Jessie didn't resist when he pulled her into his arms. Her face pressed against his broad chest, she marveled at the wild, furious beating of his heart. It was the kind of panic that came when a person was scared and running like the devil.

"I was only protecting you, Jess," he murmured into her hair, "protecting you against the Jeremiahs and the Hampton Piersons of this world. Don't you see?"

"Protecting is one thing. Obsessing is something else altogether."

"I don't want to own you. You're not a slave. Sure I told him you were my wife 'cause you are and I'm not about to share you with any other man. I want you, all right?"

Her own heart began a frenzied drum beat. Warm, safe, protected, she let her body melt against his strength.

"I thank the good Lord each morning that He saw fit to put two beautiful ladies in my care." He lightly touched the curve of her back. "When I think of my life before . . ."

A shudder ran the length of his muscular form, reminding Jessie of how Yellow Dog felt that night she bound his wounds.

A beautiful lady? No one had ever made the mistake of using those words to describe her.

What makes you think you deserve a new dress? Jeremiah had pitched a shapeless sack at her when she'd asked him for a length of material to sew one. *You think new clothes will make you pretty? Who put that idea in your head? Look at your hair, your scrawny frame. You're ugly and don't forget it.* She never had. She never would.

The man had raised his fist and laughed when she cowered into a frightened ball. After that she'd never asked her husband for another thing, merely dreamt of freedom.

Even though Duel looked at her sometimes like she was special. Even though he'd picked her wildflowers. And even though he'd just knocked a man on his backside, that didn't put her in the "beautiful" category.

"Mr. Pierson's a pest, I admit, and certainly preens like a peacock around town, but he's harmless." Jessie shifted her feet and Duel released his hold, allowing her to draw away.

"The nerve of Pierson buying my wife a bonnet—or anything else for that matter! But I did fly off the handle a little." He had the grace to look sheepish.

"That's calling a jackass a mule." Jessie smiled, recalling the shocked expression on Hampton's face when he saw Duel. She guessed he hadn't heard her say she was waiting for her husband. "I could've dealt with the situation if you'd given me the chance."

"Someone has to teach Pierson a little respect."

His gruff tone hid a big heart.

"And that lot fell to you?"

"If need be." He lifted a lock of her hair and tucked it behind her ear. "It has nothing to do with owning you. And I'm not doubting your ability to take care of Hampton." He took a deep breath. "Certain obligations come with the marriage territory. Things such as duty and honor . . . and respecting your spouse."

"Then it's some chivalrous notion? Nothing remotely connected with men's proprietary rights?" Why was her stomach turning somersaults, her breathing fast and heavy?

He leaned close, never considering what his nearness did to her. Never realizing the turmoil he caused. She briefly wondered if his heart still raced as it had when she laid her head against it.

"Not even a smidgen."

"Afternoon, Duel. Mrs. McClain." Charlotte Brown strolled by, twirling a parasol above her head to block the sun's rays, and smiling.

Duel smiled and tipped his hat. "Nice day, Mrs. Brown."

He waited until the nosy woman moved on. "The privilege of keeping you safe makes me feel special. Remember that day on the cliff?"

"How could I ever forget? I live with that moment."

"I promised to not let anything happen to you. A McClain

promise. By all that's holy, I mean to keep my word."

Charlie Maxfield, with Jane by his side, rode past. Both strained their eyes to see what was happening beneath the elm tree. A cloud of dust caused by their surrey covered Duel and Jessie.

"Damn! Word must already have spread. Looks like everyone in the county's come to ogle us." He waved his arms furiously to fan away the grit.

"Surely they can't have heard about you and Hampton Pierson this fast?"

"You haven't lived in Tranquility before." When he bent his head, his lips brushed her ear, making tingles scamper down her neck.

He stood much too close. Jessie swayed. His arm lent support for her buckling legs. The naughty tingles reached her knees as his breath fluttered inside her ear.

"But, sweetheart, never in a million years will I apologize for knocking Pierson on his rear."

She felt feverish from the warmth of his nearness, the unexpected endearment, the amber lights dancing in his eyes, and his tender smile that smoothed the rough edges of his chiseled features. Not in this lifetime had she known a man like Duel McClain.

"Confound it, Jess. I just can't think of you as my sister."

Barely had the strangled declaration slipped from his lips when he dipped his head and captured her mouth with his.

Chapter Seventeen

The heady scent of shaving soap and bay rum swirled in the mild breeze. Added to the unexpected heat of Duel's kiss, Jessie had to concentrate on her breathing to keep from swooning. The wild heaving of her breasts told her she came dangerously near to such a fate. In all her years she had never felt so weak and feverish.

Duel's mouth, indeed every inch of the man, vibrated with life and sizzle.

A sense of decorum somewhere in the back of her head ranted that this behavior was inappropriate for broad daylight. Yet she didn't want the kiss to end. When he released her and took a step back, the afternoon sky, the blades of tall saw grass swam around her. She clutched to him for support while her skin continued to burn with a strange heat his touch had brought.

As she blinked and fought to catch her breath, she noticed two women, slack-jawed, staring at them. "Oh Duel . . ." Mortification set in.

"Damnation! Can't a man kiss his wife without everyone in

the whole darn town gawking?" Duel berated the pair. Still, the smile never left his face.

"Come, Jess." He offered his arm. "I didn't finish my business with Mr. Dexter."

"Suppose we run into Hampton Pierson?" A silent prayer pitter-pattered across her mind.

"Kinda hope we do. Wouldn't mind dusting the floor with the seat of his britches again."

Her startled gasp brought his quick assurance. "Just funnin' you, Jess. I promise to behave."

Pray tell he kept his word. She couldn't imagine anything more unseemly than having two grown men fighting over her. And yet a flush made her bodice stick to her skin. She'd never had a champion such as her tall Texan before. The taste of him lingered on her lips like rich, succulent berries.

Mr. Dexter had just finished tacking a handbill to the front of the store when they returned. He greeted them with a sly grin.

"Just missed Hampton if you came back to finish the job, Duel. Most excitement we've had around here since Jane Sims spent the night with Charlie Maxfield and he had to make an honest woman of her." The man chortled, slapping his thigh.

"Not lookin' for Pierson. Reckon I got my point across." A twinkle glistened in Duel's eyes when he glanced down. "What's that you're hammering up, Dexter?"

"Marshal Cobb from over New Braunfels way brought this several weeks ago and asked me to post it. Bein' as how we have no sheriff, he left it with me. Got lost under a shipment of bedding."

Jessie felt Duel's muscles clench beneath her hand, which she'd casually looped through the crook of his arm. Then she saw the source and went rigid.

A reward for the capture of Jessie Foltry!

The sizable sum promised for her capture stunned her. Five hundred dollars would guarantee plenty of attention. At least there was no picture.

"Sure is a shame your wife has to share her name with a woman like that." Dexter shook his head. "Plumb strange."

Panic crushed her chest and she choked on her ragged breath. Her husband's calm gaze did little to settle her terror. Nothing would. *She had a price on her head.*

"Shoot, Dexter. It's a common name. I'm willing to bet there's at least a couple of hundred in the state of Texas."

His cool reply amazed her.

When the shop owner opened the door for them to enter, Duel gave her a gentle hug. She forced a calmness she didn't feel and stepped with him over the threshold.

Luke McClain hooked his boot heel over the brass rail of the Firewater Saloon. Cactus Springs didn't have that much to offer. About what he'd expect in a one-horse town. Firewater appeared the best of the drinking establishments that lined the dusty street. That was, if he'd been there for that. He wasn't.

"Your pleasure, mister?" The barkeep's thin, wispy mustache drooped well below his chin on each side and wiggled when he talked. Thick muttonchop sideburns jutting to his jaw gave the man a comical appearance.

"Your best rotgut." He surveyed the room. Half empty, the Firewater's possibility for information seemed limited to the barkeep, two saloon girls, and a handful of rowdy cowboys.

His mentor, Maj. John B. Jones, had taught him the value of saloons. "No better place to get the lay of the land, son."

Staring at the poor choices, Luke didn't hold a whole lot of hope for success here. Yet one never knew.

The barkeep slid the small glass across the bar. "That'll be two bits."

"Business slow?" He flipped a coin onto the counter before downing the fiery liquid in one gulp.

"For this time of day. Things start jumpin' about dark." Barkeep polished a glass with a dishrag. "Haven't seen you around these parts."

"Nope." The glass made a thump when he set it down, then pushed it across with two fingers. "Another."

Silently, the man refilled it and pocketed a second coin. "What kind of business bring you to Cactus Springs?"

"Depends." Luke cradled the drink between his thumb and forefinger. "Know a family from here by the name of Rumford?"

"Cain't say's I do."

"Might've had a fire and burned 'em out? Woman went by the name of Jessie?"

"Nope." The man's mustache twitched as if a cork on the end of a fishing pole. He picked up a box and toted it through a doorway.

A scantily clad woman sidled up beside Luke and propped her elbows on the bar. Her cherry red lips curved enticingly.

"Howdy, ma'am." Luke tipped his hat.

"Whew, better watch out, cowboy, or I'll take you home with me. Went my whole life an' nary heard 'ma'am' at all. Now you make the second time in five months." Her blond locks brushed his arm as she leaned forward to give him an unrestrained view of her charms.

"Bet I know who the first was," Luke muttered quietly. There wasn't another man in Texas more polite than his older brother.

"Buy a woman a drink, mister?" The woman boldly stroked his arm. He returned her smile.

"Be obliged if you'd join me, ma'am."

"Name's Ellie." She reached across the bar for a glass, then poured a generous portion from a tall, amber bottle.

"Luke." He eyed the liquid in his still full glass. He had gulped the first one to prove his manhood. Never hurt in a strange town. Sorta put folks in the right frame of mind. But now he had better slow down. A cool head couldn't stand too much libation.

"Well, Luke, I do like that name." Ellie swigged her drink. "Tell me, are you in a hurry?"

"Don't reckon I am." He understood her implication and

he might have taken her up on it had the circumstances been different. However, he had other things more pressing on his mind. "Lived in Cactus Springs long?"

"Pert near all my life." She eased the red strip of fabric off one shoulder, then let the tips of her painted fingernails slide across her bare skin.

"Ever hear the name Jessie Rumford?" He casually reached and refilled her glass. *Please let her say yes.* He didn't like the burning in his gut. His brother's wife couldn't be a cold-blooded husband-killer.

"No, ain't familiar." Her answer shot his hopes to hell.

Ellie squinted at him suddenly. "You couldn't be kin to a man who came through here an' won Will Gentry's kid in a poker game, could you?"

"My brother."

"Well, I'll be a saint from the Pearly Gates!" Ellie certainly couldn't lay claim to that distinction by any stretch of the imagination. "Goodness, that was one handsome man. Mannerly, too."

"Duel McClain. Don't suppose you saw a woman with him?"

"He was alone. That is till he got saddled with the kid." Ellie tipped the glass and let the liquid slide down her throat. A thin trail dribbled from the corner of her mouth. She wiped it with the back of her hand. "I helped him find necessities for the babe. Didn't know beans about takin' care o' her."

"Duel's got the hang of it now, I reckon." With Jessie's help, he added silently. He shuddered to think what would happen to his brother if his new wife turned out to be a murderer. Losing one had almost destroyed him. What would losing a second do to his state of mind?

The woman sent him a suspicious stare. "Why do you keep askin' about this woman? What do you want with her?"

Luke pulled a badge from his shirt pocket. The silver etchings caught the dim saloon light.

"Texas Ranger, ma'am. Just doing my job's all." Rotten job it'd turn out to be if he had to arrest his sister-in-law. Duel would never forgive him, not in a thousand years. Hell, he might not even forgive himself. Jessie McClain had cast a spell over them all.

Satin ribbons hung from the bonnet in Jessie's hands, the same bonnet she'd admired in Dexter's store. Stricken with a loss for words, she met Duel's expectant stare.

"Well, aren't you gonna put it on?" He shifted Marley Rose from one arm to the other. The girl kicked her feet excitedly and reached for the hat.

"I wish you hadn't spent hard-earned money this way. Tell me it didn't have anything to do with Hampton Pierson."

If he bought the hat to prove something, the giving of it would lose meaning. Duel didn't have to give her a new bonnet to prove he was the better man. She already knew that. But if he gave it because he wanted her to be the prettiest woman in Tranquility, she'd cherish it for the rest of her days.

"Jess." The low timbre as he murmured her name made tingles two-step up her spine. "I'd never spend a cent in trying to outdo Pierson 'cause the man knows more than I'll ever know about courting a woman."

"You're courting me?" The wonder of it filled her heart. His free hand touched her cheek softly. Damn that hot moistness that formed behind her eyes.

"No law against it that I know of. I bought this bonnet because it was made for you. I fancied you wearing it to church on Sunday and being the envy of all the womenfolk there."

The work-roughened skin on his finger chafed as he wiped the tear that slipped from the corner of her eye, but to her it felt like velvet.

A blush rose. He'd picked her posies and taken her breath away with a lacy blue bonnet.

Her husband was courting her.

"Now that you know all the whys an' why nots, put the darn thing on, Jess."

She could barely contain the joy as she slipped it on her head and tied the ribbons. The beveled mirror reflected a rosy-cheeked, passable-looking woman. But that wasn't her main focus. The man standing behind stole her thoughts.

Someday she'd tell him how much she loved him. Maybe. If she could find a tiny space in his heart to squeeze into. That was all she asked. It wasn't much.

Marley clapped her hands. "Oooooh, Mama pwetty!"

Golden glints turned Duel's hazel eyes to amber. Unflinchingly, he met her stare in the glass.

"Yes, darlin', your mama is indeed pretty."

Rattled by his declaration, Jessie quickly untied and removed the hat before she made a fool of herself. "Better see to supper. Time enough wasted."

Dusk had transformed the sky into a pinkish purple. Jessie admired the muted colors through the kitchen window, comparing them to how she felt inside—all soft and warm and peaceful.

"Two Bit, how about you and me going to feed the animals while your ma sets the table?" Duel, with Marley in tow, followed her into the kitchen.

"Boobie?" The girl pointed through the window. "Papa, Boobie?"

"Now, darlin', you know I want you to call me Duel." He kissed her forehead. "And for the life of me I don't know why you stuck "Boobie" on Yellow Dog."

A smile lifted the corners of Jessie's mouth as she watched the two keepers of her heart.

Yes, pinkish purple. That described her to a tee.

Marley kept them entertained long after supper with her mixture of simple words and childish blather. The girl evidently was filling Jessie in on her exciting adventures with her papa. Only she had no idea what the child babbled. Amid the strange harangue Marley threw in "boobie" and "cheeba."

"What is she saying, Duel?" she asked when her fits of laughter eased. "Sounds like 'cheeba.' "

"Beats me. Could be what she named the goat, I reckon.

Seems I recollect I first heard it right after that nanny butted me in the rear."

"Why 'Cheeba'?" Suspicion underscored her next question. "You didn't use any foul language, did you?"

From everything she'd heard, children latched on to swear words faster than anything else.

"I did call the critter a she-demon." He thought a minute before adding, "Yep, had to bite my tongue, but I'm positive that's all I said."

"She-demon. Cheeba. Kinda alike if you use a little imagination." Jessie chuckled. Marley Rose sure came up with some colorful names for things.

"Two Bit took a shine to that nanny. The ornery thing stood there and let Marley climb on her back. Still have trouble believing it."

"Cheeba, Mama. Pwetty, Cheeba . . . pwetty Boobie."

Marley scooted out of Jessie's lap and waddled to Duel who lifted her up. She rubbed her eyes to stay awake.

"Yes, sweetheart. Appears you've found some friends."

"That's another thing." Duel scratched his head in thought. "The way Yellow Dog has taken up with her. I can't get within arm's length of him before he runs like a scared rabbit, yet the animal comes right up to Two Bit and licks her hand. Did it again tonight. I was getting Preacher some feed and next thing I knew there he was letting her crawl all over him."

"Animals sense a kinship with children for some reason. Guess it's their innocence." Or perhaps they sense little ones haven't developed a reason to hate yet. Hate spawns cruelty. Jessie knew from experience about that.

Duel yawned, stretching his arms above his head. Marley poked her elbows in his stomach to look up at him.

"Papa sweepy?"

"Darlin', I'm Duel," he reminded her patiently. "Duel."

Marley nodded her little head, setting her black curls jiggling. A serious expression darkened her eyes. "Papa. Papa sweepy?"

"Damn! Our child does have a stubborn streak, doesn't she?"

Their child. The sound of that smacked of permanence. How permanent could a life in hiding be? When the next sound could be the scratch of a stiff rope around her neck.

Jessie wondered if he realized what he'd just said. Or the implication that he'd accepted his fate? Someday he'd break down on the papa business. Merely a matter of time. One thing about it, Marley's persistence didn't show any sign of abating.

"Isn't it your bedtime, little girl?" He tweaked her nose. "I see Sandman jumping in those eyes." Duel stood her on the floor. "Go let your Mama get you ready for bed."

"Come, sweetheart, let's find your nightgown."

Marley slipped her hand inside Jessie's, then she looked back at Duel. "Papa come?"

"I'll come kiss you goodnight in a minute."

All too soon they'd bedded Marley down for the night. Jessie's favorite time of the day, between supper and bedtime, had come to an end.

He lifted his hat from the nail and twisted it around and around. "Suppose I'd better head for the barn."

For the space of several heartbeats he stared at her. It was if he wanted to say something, but the words wouldn't come. She wished for courage to speak her thoughts—to tell him how she felt—that she'd changed her mind.

"Duel, I didn't thank you properly for the bonnet." She drifted across the room. "I've never seen a more lovely hat."

Those weren't the words she wanted to say. That his kiss stole her breath and melted her insides—that his courting art touched her in places no one ever had—that she loved being his wife. Those were things she couldn't tell him.

"I'm proud you like it, Jess."

He held her spellbound in his gaze. Time stood still while the smell of all that was Duel circled her head. An honest smell of a good man who was willing to work his fingers to the bone for a woman in trouble.

Before she could back out, she stood on tiptoe to kiss his deeply lined cheek.

"Thank you so much for all you've done." Her voice came out husky and soft.

"Shoot, we can do better than that." He swept her up and lowered his head.

A current surged through her when his full, sensual lips met hers. And when her mouth parted softly in surprise, his tongue dipped inside.

"Oh, my," she managed after he let her go. At that moment she was more than pinkish purple. Red-hot and sizzling fitted her better. When she came to her senses, she realized she'd shamefully flung her arms around his neck. Hastily, she dropped them.

"I'm not apologizing for that, Jess." Determination lodged in his stare.

"Not asking you to." She felt equally determined.

"You're a beautiful woman and . . ." He left the rest unsaid as he reached for the knob.

"Please," she touched his arm. "Don't go to the barn."

Chapter Eighteen

Don't go to the barn. Her request had lingered like a double helping of sweet-potato pie long after he made his way out the door.

"You can sleep in the house tonight," she'd urged.

"I can't bed down knowing you're only a few feet away, Jess. Don't trust myself." He tried to explain all the while her wild honey taste clung to the inside of his mouth. The kiss had drained every last shred of resistance. "You'd be a fool to trust me."

"I don't understand what it would hurt, Duel." The agony in her tone had matched the tightening in his belly.

Didn't she realize her mere presence sent unbearable torture through his body? Being close to her did a damn sight more than hurt.

"When I move into the house, it'll be into your bed, madam." He hadn't meant to be so blunt. Must've been the kiss that made him so reckless. "You and I both know you're not ready."

Warm sunny rays drenched Duel as he knelt in the field

and grabbed a handful of soil. Around him a sea of small, tender shoots poked their heads from the rich black dirt.

The sorghum should make a bumper crop. That is if insects or hail didn't get it before harvest. Then he would hightail it to Austin and get the best darn lawyer money could buy.

Correction. He'd have to settle for second best. The finest in the whole state of Texas was Tom Parker. More than likely time hadn't dimmed Parker's hatred. After all, the retired judge blamed Duel for the loss of his only daughter. He seriously doubted Parker would give him the time of day even if he did swallow his pride and seek the man out.

"I'll find a good lawyer, Jess," he muttered into the wind. "We'll clear your name. We have to—for Marley's sake. And mine." He added the last quietly as if afraid to speak too loudly.

Duel crumbled a dirt clod between his fingers and watched it scatter in the wind. Though her trust had grown by leaps and bounds from their first meeting, Jessie still had moments when she'd drawn back as if expecting blows. He'd made progress but it wasn't fast enough to suit him.

"I'll just have to be patient." Tell that to the burning need that wound past his groin clear down to his toenails. He wanted Jessie more than he'd ever wanted any other woman.

"Son, that's what I keep tellin' folks. Patience."

The gravelly drawl came from directly behind. Deep in thought, Duel hadn't heard his father's approach.

"Morning, Pop." He rose to stand at eye level. "What brings you out so early?"

Walt snorted. "This ain't early. Already milked Roy's two cows, gathered a basket of eggs, an' arm wrestled Saint Peter."

A chuckle erupted at the image of his father trying to harness Vicky and Roy's Saint Peter. The white mule fought the bit harder than any animal he'd ever known. Contrary as the day was long.

"Took a while, huh?"

"Longer'n it'd take to tussle with the devil an' handcuff

him." Walt put both hands inside the bib of his overalls, hooking his thumbs on the outside rim.

"You came all this way to complain?"

"Came to get some of Jessie's vittles. Like her cookin' a whole lot better'n your sister's."

That wouldn't take much, being as how Vicky burned everything she put on a stove. Couldn't even boil water.

Walt squinted against the sun. "Ain't it about breakfast time, son? Don't tell me I missed it."

Just then Jessie stuck her head through the open kitchen window. "Breakfast is ready, Duel." She noticed Walt and smiled prettily. "Morning, Walt. Come on in. I've made plenty."

"Much obliged, Jessie." Walt lowered his voice to a loud whisper. "How's the courtin' going?"

"Prefer to call it becoming familiar. And, if you must know, it's going better'n expected."

"That's my boy." The man slapped Duel on the back. "Chip off the old block. It'll be worth all the effort. That woman's the salt of the earth."

They washed up at the well and minutes later sat down before flapjacks, fried eggs, and sausage.

"Saw a ring around the moon last night." Walt piled a heap of flapjacks on his plate and drowned them with thick sorghum.

"Don't say." Duel looked up from his task of fixing Marley Rose's plate. "Think it means rain?"

"Darn tootin'. Never knowed it not to." The man chewed on a large bite and winked at Marley. "Ain't that so, Angel?"

"G'anpa." The child offered a handful of flapjack to her idol. Syrup oozed from between her fingers and ran down her arm.

"No thanks, Angel. You eat it. Got me a whole plate over here." Walt shoved another forkful in his mouth. "Mmmm. Best darn flapjacks a man ever ate, Jessie."

"How's Vicky? I've been so busy of late that I haven't had time to visit." Jessie passed Walt the plate of sausage.

"That girl's got more irons in the fire than the blacksmith in Sherman's army."

Duel laughed. "Always did, Pop. That's because she's so blasted nosey. Wants to know everything that's going on."

"Just like Luke. I swear those two took after your mama. Wonder if Luke's found that woman yet." Walt stuffed his mouth with sausage and chewed thoughtfully. "Son, did you notice the handbill over at Dexter's store?"

"I saw it."

"Gave me the chills alrighty. Murderin' her husband. Wish that woman didn't wear the same name as *our* Jessie."

The sunshine streaming through the open kitchen window suddenly lost its warmth. Jessie shivered. If wishes were gold, she'd be the richest woman in the territory. Not a day went by that someone didn't remark about her name. She felt the noose tightening around her neck and almost choked on her food. They'd come for her sooner or later. God help her that it would be later. A sparkle on her hand released a deluge of pain. The ring Duel had placed on her finger. She twisted the keepsake nervously and prayed for one more month, a week, one more day of peace and happiness.

Then she met her husband's steady gaze. It told her that he'd stand beside her. No matter what came, he'd be there. Even if he couldn't stand to sleep in the same house where he made love to Annie. Before she realized his intention, he reached for her hand. A reassuring squeeze renewed her flagging hope.

"The scuttlebutt in town says you an' Hampton had a slight disagreement. Folks say Hampton ended up on his butt," Walt gave Marley and Jessie a guilty look and amended, "I mean his rear end."

Duel released her hand. A low rumble in his throat preceded his reply. "Got what he deserved. Reckon he'll mend his ways from here on out and leave my wife alone."

True to Walt's prediction, the rains came. The thunder and lightning bounced off the hilltops and shook the farmhouse in the lush valley like a giant angrily shaking its toy.

Marley Rose wailed in terror. Her little fists kept a death grip on Jessie's dress. Jessie hugged her close and watched Duel through the window. The storm scared her too. She wished he'd come inside. But he'd been determined the rain wouldn't stop him from checking on things outdoors.

"It's all right, sweetie." She smoothed the hair back from the girl's tear-stained face. "I won't let anything hurt you. This big, bad storm will pass. Shhh, you're safe and sound."

Even as she tried to calm Marley's fears, a jagged streak of electricity darted to the ground. It struck a tree a few yards from where Duel stood.

A scream burst from her throat before she could stop it. Outside, force from the lightning knocked Duel to the ground.

"Oh, God!" Her blood turned to ice. She frantically wiped beads of moisture from the pane. If he wasn't dead, he needed help.

"Please let him be all right."

Heedless of Marley's terrified wails, heedless of the pouring rain and dangerous lightning, she put the child down and ran to Duel's side.

By the time she reached him, he groaned and tried to rise to his feet. With all the strength she could muster, Jessie helped him stand.

"Are you hurt?" she screamed to be heard over the rumbling and crashing.

He appeared dazed and disoriented. "Don't think so."

Jessie gripped his arm and tried to direct him to the house with him resisting every step. Then she noticed yellow and red flames licking from the roof of the barn.

"Lightning's hit the barn!"

He followed her gestures, the enormity of the crisis finally sinking into his confused brain. "Preacher!"

Thick smoke swam up her nostrils, stinging her eyes, when Duel swung open the barn door.

"I'll get Preacher. You get the goat," he said.

She tried, but her lungs burned. Coughing overtook her, making it impossible to see her surroundings.

Duel reappeared, shoving a wet cloth over her mouth and nose. "Hold this. It'll help."

Feeling more than seeing her way, Jessie groped through the gloom. Though midday had barely passed, heavy clouds coupled with dense smoke made the goat's whereabouts a guessing game. She'd inched along several feet when a chorus of 'blehs' met her ears.

"I'm coming," she called, her voice little more than a rasp through the cloth.

Had she made it all this way to be doomed to a fiery end? Her burning, watering vision could barely discern the animal's shape. The cloth that had helped keep smoke from her mouth fell as she struggled to untie Marley's Cheeba. She lost precious minutes when the stubborn knots refused to yield.

When at last the rope came free, Cheeba bolted for the exit, leaving Jessie to follow blindly, gasping, and choking.

Blessed rain and fresh gulps of air welcomed her through the portal. She'd made it. Exhausted, limp, and coughing, she lay on the soaked ground for what seemed an eternity before she tried to locate Duel.

"Duel, where are you?" Haze still blocked her vision, distorting the world around her. "Duel!"

There was no answer. No sight of him. Alarm swept over her in towering waves.

"Please answer me, Duel." Her voice shook.

Fearing the worst, she got to her feet. Much as the fire and smoke terrified her, she'd go back in if it came to that. She'd enter the mouth of a dragon to save the man who'd stolen her heart.

Before she'd taken two steps, he stumbled from the structure. He was leading preacher, and Yellow Dog lay draped across his arms. Duel's soot-blackened face was a sight to behold.

Joy that he had survived made her giddy.

"Thank the heavens above! You made it." She hurried to

relieve him of his burden. But she'd no more than claimed the dog's weight when Duel collapsed, lying prone in the mud.

"Duel!"

Careful as she could, she laid the limp retriever beside the man. She didn't know if Yellow Dog was alive or dead, but Duel became her first concern.

"Speak to me." Quick as she could, she turned him over and brushed mud from his blackened face.

Instead of a roaring, wild creature, the storm now had become a passive lamb. Light rain romanced the gentle land, kissing the treetops and tender shoots in the field.

Mindless of her own soaked-to-the-bone state, Jessie lifted Duel's head onto her lap and smoothed wet locks of hair off his forehead.

"Duel, please talk to me. I can't imagine what life would be like without you. I've never before known anyone as honorable and kind as you. Don't leave me."

His eyelids fluttered, but didn't open. For this giant of a man, her knight who could turn darkness into day, his lethargic condition shocked her. Usually a vital man, Duel now showed a vulnerability she didn't like.

With her fingertips, she traced his full, pleasure-giving mouth. Then almost as if against her own volition, she bent and placed her lips on his.

Nothing mattered—not the rain, not the burning barn behind her, not even Marley's cries from the house. In that moment, in that sphere of time and space, only she and Duel existed. He tasted of smoke and desire. Fire and ice.

Suddenly he began to wheeze and cough, his eyes staring into hers. Jessie released her pent-up breath.

"Preacher. Gotta get Preacher out." He rasped, jerking to his feet.

"You already have." She pointed to the horse who snorted and nodded his head as if to say, "I'm just fine."

"Dog?" His quick glance located Yellow Dog, who by this time had recovered sufficiently to raise his head. Soft whimpers stole from the animal's throat. He knelt. "Thought you was a goner for sure, boy."

"Did the dog get trapped in the barn?" Yellow Dog's soulful eyes spoke clearly of his pain. She joined Duel by his side.

"Yeah. That was what took me so long. A beam fell, trapping him and Preacher." The dog didn't resist when Duel painstakingly felt his legs, then his whole body. "No broken bones. Could have some bleeding inside, can't tell."

Yellow Dog licked Jessie's hand with his velvet tongue, but kept wary eyes on Duel.

"Will you carry him into the house?" she asked. "I want him out of the rain tonight."

"Two Bit'll love that."

She followed his gaze to the blazing structure that seemed destined to ashes. "Nothing you can do. At least we saved the animals."

The dog didn't resist when Duel lifted him. That fact alone revealed the depth of Yellow Dog's misery.

Jessie grabbed the goat's tether, intending to lead her to a spot beside the house that offered some shelter.

"Oh no, you don't. I'll not have that ornery beast in my house. No siree." His black scowl left no room for compromise. "I'm not Noah and that house yonder ain't a blasted ark. Next thing I know, you'll be having Preacher in for tea an' crumpets."

"Not entirely what I had in mind, Duel." A giggle slipped out at the visual image of the horse sitting at her kitchen table sipping a cup of tea while the goat butted Duel every time he bent over. "The poor thing's dripping wet. I'm going to put her against the house under the eaves. Unless you object to that?"

Marley fussed over her Boobie like a mother hen. An old rug served as a bed, and nothing would satisfy the little girl until she had tucked a blanket over the animal.

Dry now, albeit a bit under the weather with some nasty chills that came and went, Jessie felt unusually happy. More than she had a right to. A cloud of doom, heavy and dark, hung over her head. Trouble on a fast horse was racing toward her. Until it arrived though, she'd allow herself to enjoy the moment of tranquility. Darkness had fallen, putting the events of the day on a page of the past. Tomorrow would begin a fresh page. Who knew what it would bring?

At the moment she had a sweet, darling child to watch over. Her wandering gaze brushed past Marley, who sat beside Yellow Dog with one tiny hand resting on his back, to Duel, who dozed peacefully in the chair. And she had the best husband any woman could want, for however long time allowed her.

The dim glow of the lamps softened Duel's chiseled features. She'd come close to losing him today. So close her stomach turned somersaults when she remembered.

His head rested against the high chair back, long legs stretched out in front of him. He belonged to her. They shared the same name.

A stirring wound through her, beginning as a lazy stream. She loved this man, her knight who appeared from nowhere on the Texas Plains. Admired his honesty and forthrightness. The focal point of her attention shifted to the way his hair curled possessively around the high neck of his rough chambray shirt as if to gloat its privilege.

When she let her gaze roam freely down his muscular legs, a heat radiated from within her. A different heat from that of a quick and searing brand, this kind attached, melding itself to her soul. In that instant she realized, no matter how hard she tried, she could never separate herself from it.

Her breathing quickened at the swift revelation.

She loved him.

Didn't much matter if he returned the favor. She suspected he'd never feel toward her—or any woman—the way he'd worshiped his Annie. Yet she accepted and lived with that knowledge.

Sudden light-headedness came that had nothing to do with

her emotional well-being. This nauseous, sick whirling told Jessie she'd caught something.

"Papa, papa." Marley had gotten tired of watching the sleeping dog and now demanded Duel's attention. "Boobie, Papa."

Sleep-glazed eyes squinted at the girl. "Ain't it past your bedtime, Two Bit?"

Jessie suppressed a grin. He'd not corrected Marley's "papa." Her gaze met his half-raised eyebrow innocently. The full import of the day's events hadn't sunk in yet. Most likely he hadn't given any thought to the night.

"Yes, it is." She held out her hand, fighting the chills that shook her. "Little girl, your bed is calling."

Instead of the obedience Marley had shown in the past, she jerked away. "Boobie. Mine Boobie."

Duel lifted the distraught child into his lap. "Yellow Dog—Boobie—will be right here. Go to bed like a good girl. Maybe he'll feel like playing with you tomorrow. Okay?"

Marley's wide, dark eyes darted from Duel to the animal as if to digest what he'd said. "Cheeba?"

"Shoot fire! Yes, Cheeba too." He ruffled her dark curls with affection.

"Choot! Choot!"

"Huh-oh. Duel, you're going to have to watch what you say. She picks up everything."

Amid a chorus of 'choots' Jessie carried her to bed.

"Guess I'll head for the . . ." A bright flush stained Duel's neck and traveled still higher. "Just this minute realized I don't have a barn to go to. I've no place—"

Chapter Nineteen

A noise startled Duel, awakening him from a light sleep.

"Ohhh. Stop." Thrashing sounds came from behind the curtained bedroom. "Please!"

The words shot through the durable fabric clear and crisp.

He threw back the blanket that covered him and rose from the pallet on the floor. Stealing quietly on the balls of his bare feet, he peeked around the corner of the limp partition.

Moans gurgled deep from Jessie's throat as she tossed wildly, fighting the bedcovers.

"Don't!"

Her agonized cries cut him to the quick. Clearly she struggled to escape from something—or someone. He could hazard a guess.

"I'm no animal. Don't do this."

Duel moved swiftly to capture her flailing arms. He sat on the narrow space beside her.

"Jess, it's me. Wake up, Jess." He gathered her to his chest, trying to calm the herd of wild horses that seemed intent on leaping through his rib cage. "I'm here."

"Don't leave me." Her plea ripped apart his earlier good intentions.

When I move into the house, it'll be into your bed, madam.

That's what he'd vowed. And he'd meant every word. Now, thanks to the fire, he had no choice but to sleep in the house. Still, that didn't mean he'd take advantage of the unfortunate situation. He couldn't. Wouldn't. Gently, he eased away.

"Don't go. Please." Jessie repeated, gripping his bare arm. Her touch reminded him that save for buckskins covering his lower extremities, he was naked.

Only an executioner with a heart of stone could've refused that plaintive entreaty.

"I'll never leave you, darlin'." He hadn't meant the "darlin' " part to slip out. It just had. If she hadn't heard it, maybe he could take it back. When he smoothed back her hair, his fingers brushed her fevered skin.

"You're sick, Jess. Why didn't you say anything?"

She smothered another low moan with the back of her hand. Her uncontrollable shivers reminded him of a sapling in the middle of a Texas twister.

Duel released her. "I'll be right back. Need to get more quilts for you and replenish the wood in the fire."

"No. Please stay with me." Jessie clawed the empty air.

A thin sliver of moonlight pierced the windowpane and spilled across the bed. In the dimness, her face projected impenetrable fear.

He hastened to reassure her. "I'll be right back, Jess. You're freezing."

Forgoing stoking the fire, he grabbed some extra quilts, stubbing his toe on a chair leg in his haste to return. He swallowed a whole string of curses.

"See, here I am." Limping painfully, he spread the thick cover over her. He wished to high heaven he could ease the wild terror on her face.

"You won't hurt me?" She gripped the quilts tightly around her neck.

Damn! The last thing in the world he wanted was to cause

Jessie pain and grief. Unsure of what he should do next, he shifted his weight as he stood beside the bed.

"You should know by now I'll never hurt you. A McClain promise. Remember?"

"Duel?" As if only now recognizing him, suddenly Jessie stretched out her hand. "Will you hold me, Duel? For a little while. Until I fall asleep?"

Air gushed from his chest in one fell swoop. Blindsided by a quick right to the belly felt more like it. Hold her? His buckskins grew tight with a deep, steadfast longing. He ached to slip his hands beneath her gown, to caress the silky skin he knew he'd find.

Then holding her would not be enough.

Indecision wound its way through him, an ivy seeking sunlight and truth. Thing was, he didn't trust himself to keep his emotions under lock and key. This "becoming familiar" business had taken him into dangerous territory. Still, he couldn't turn a deaf ear. What sort of man could—except perhaps Jeremiah Gates Foltry?

That decided it. If Jessie asked him to jump over the moon he'd bust a gut trying. It was little enough to ask after the hell that man had put her through.

"Just try to get rid of me, Mrs. McClain." The ropes beneath the mattress protested when Duel settled comfortably with his back against the high mahogany headboard. Another gift from Judge Parker. Must have cost the man a small fortune, yet he insisted on only the best for his daughter. Things a sodbuster could never afford.

Jessie slept then while he kept watch. He'd not let dreams, monsters, or illness befall her if he could help it.

A contented sigh broke from Jessie's lips as he pulled her against him. With the cover tucked snugly around her, she let her head rest next to his heart. In that moment his throbbing toe was totally forgotten.

Dawn neared when she awoke. Her startled gaze took in his presence, but she didn't recoil. "What?"

"You woke last night, fevered and with chills. Do you remember?"

"I dreamt I begged you to not leave me. That wasn't a dream, was it?"

Duel shook his head.

"Oh dear. I suppose you sat like this all night? I'm sorry."

"I'm not. You feel better now?" He relished the soft tickle of her hair against his bare skin.

"Yes." A few seconds later she turned to look up at him. "Duel, are you happy?"

The question caught him off guard, for he'd been neck deep in fancy—fancyin' her breath, wispy and light on his body, fancyin' the feel of her beneath him, fancyin' what it would be like to make love to his new wife. His eyes popped open.

"I'm happy as a man has a right to be, I reckon." He met her stare honestly. "Are you, Jess?"

She lowered her gaze as if embarrassed. "It's this business arrangement of ours that bothers me."

A rock tumbled and lodged in the pit of his stomach. Was she wanting out of their marriage?

"Are you disappointed in me? Have I done something to upset you?" Except for one small detail, they seemed to have it running smoothly, he thought. A swarm of doubt twisted and turned inside him. He choked for fear that he'd lose her before he had a chance to show her how wonderful life could be.

"This business arrangement," she repeated again. "Is there any way you suppose we could change it?"

Change it? What in the name of Jehosafat was she talking about?

Jessie bit her lip and continued. "I find it . . . unacceptable."

If she was trying to tell him she wanted out of the marriage he'd make her spell it out. "How so?"

"I'd like a real marriage, not just one in name only. Are

you . . . can you bear the thought of me as your wife? Just a little?"

A real marriage? Until this very moment he considered the likelihood of that happening as nothing short of a miracle. Had the lightning flash earlier injured his brain?

"You want a real marriage?" He spoke the words slowly as if they needed time to sink in.

"Not a pretend one." She allowed a quick glance. Probably to judge his reaction to her shocking words. "I'm tired of pretending. I'd like to wake up every morning with you beside me."

"Are you ready for that, Jess? Do you know what you're asking?"

"I've never been more ready. That is, if you think—"

Bless her. This woman he married was the most sensitive, caring, simply delectable person he'd ever known. He savored the thought as if it were an unexpected taste of honey.

"Darlin', I've already squared the past." He stroked her cheek much as a sculptor would mold and shape the features of his love. "I'll never forget Annie, but I've made a whole new life. We're a family—you, me, and Marley Rose."

He gently traced her lips with his fingertips before he lowered his mouth to capture hers.

Bedcovers fell away when she put her arms around his neck.

The place he tread upon was holy. A place he'd never been before, and he gave of himself one tiny morsel at a time.

From her lips his kisses trailed to her slender throat, pausing at the rapid pulse at its base. There he pressed his mouth reverently. The gentle rhythm of her heartbeat seemed the only sound in the universe.

If love had a sound, surely this would be it. The quick beating of two hearts in tune with unheard music.

He inched farther, torturing his body with agonizing patience. Slow and easy, clearing her gown from the path as he went.

Tasting, touching, caressing.

Hardened nipples tempted. He laved her ample mounds with his tongue, suckling on the nibs until she mewed and moaned.

Silver moonlight bathed her body with iridescent rays. He sucked in his breath. Jessie was more beautiful than he ever dared imagine. The best thing of all was he didn't have to steal peeks. She lay exposed for his eyes only, and he drank his fill.

Pausing for a second to remove his buckskins, he had to ask one more time. "Are you sure about this, Jess?"

"Yes. I'm sure."

Her answer came as a silky thread spun by the most diligent spider. Had they created a web of fragile strands or could it withstand a stiff breeze? They'd soon find out. Beside him, a shudder ran the length of her body when he took her in his arms.

"I won't hurt you. Anytime you want to stop, just say the word." He spoke the vow into the soft cloud of her hair.

He didn't expect an answer. None came. Only a tender sigh as she melted against him.

Though he longed to obey his needs and rush to the beckoning goal, he proceeded slowly and with great caution.

Tracing tiny circles on her bare shoulder, he acquainted her with a sensuous light touch. Down her arm, across her stomach, up the middle between her breasts, and then her throat. Growing bolder, he slipped his fingers over her creamy shoulder and down her back.

Gently on her back side, he moved in small, swirling arcs. Her skin was smooth, soft as a baby's bottom. Suddenly, he encountered a patch of rough, crinkled flesh. Chunks of ice formed in his veins as he froze. The brand.

Jessie moaned as if in pain, hiding her face among the wispy curls on his chest.

"I'm sorry. Does it still hurt?" Sick remorse made his belly twist and buck, trying to relieve him of his supper.

Tears sparkled in Jessie's eyes when she met his troubled gaze. "It's healed. It's just that I almost forgot for a little while."

She pulled the bedcovers up to hide her nakedness. Duel cursed his clumsy blunder. He had ruined the tender mood. He rose and pulled on his buckskins.

Outside, a thin, wispy scarf draped over the moon. The cloud momentarily blanked the silvery rays, making him locate the buttons of his breeches by touch alone.

Behind him a delicate swish echoed in the quiet alcove and he envisioned the muslin gown settling over Jessie's bare breasts just as the wispy cloud had hid the moon—teasing, tantalizing.

A groan rose to his throat before he could stifle it. No amount of clothing could hide what his eyes and his heart had seen this night. His memory had forever captured Jessie's exquisitely rounded curves, her sweet spirit. Covering his mouth, he hastily muffled the groan.

"Duel, I'm sorry. I truly am." She reached out to stop him when he started to leave.

The simple gesture spoke of her despair. That she would fault herself for his stumble bathed his soul in wonder.

"You don't owe me anything, Jess." The small hand resting on his arm released ripples of warmth. He covered it with his free one. "It's my place to make the amends."

"I'd like you to stay. Please?"

Duel sat on the edge of the bed facing her. Auburn tendrils framed her face, spilling onto her bosom. Reminded him of a beautiful angel. If she knew how much he wanted her, how hotly the river of desire ran in his blood, she'd chase him from the house and bolt the doors.

When he started to speak she placed her fingertips on his lips. "Don't talk yet."

Misery crawled into the far corners of his heart as he waited for her to gather her thoughts. Moonlight turned her blue eyes a silvery gray. She'd never looked more precious to him—or more aggrieved.

"I thought I could do it. Thought that what Jeremiah did to me didn't matter. I intended to carry through." Her musical voice lowered to almost a whisper. "I wanted you, not as a wife dutifully lets her husband, but in every way a woman desires a man."

"You don't have to explain, Jess." He knew about that desire, for it seeped into his every pore. Oh God, sweet torture.

"But I do." She wet her dry lips. "If you'll give me more time . . ."

"I'll let you have all the time you want." The delicate curve of her cheek beckoned and Duel couldn't resist. He caressed, exploring her smooth features. Darn her mouth for looking so kissable.

"I'm not going anywhere, lady," he murmured. "Not even if you invite that blasted goat into our parlor."

She rewarded his attempt at lighthearted humor with a skittish smile.

"Thank you."

"We'll just take it one small step at a time. No need to build up a head of steam right off." Now why had he uttered those words? Anyone with any sense knew you couldn't control a head of steam—it darn well spewed when and where it wanted.

If gaining her trust didn't mean so darn much, he'd forgo capping the pressure that'd built inside him and throw caution to the wind.

"Then will you understand when I tell you I want you to share my bed, but not my body yet?"

Inside, every fiber resisted the notion. It would be nigh impossible to lie beside Jessie and try to keep his manly needs in check. After all, a man could be exposed to only so much temptation. Outwardly, he kept his doubts cloaked in what he hoped was his best poker face.

"If that's your wish, I'll respect it."

But how, he didn't know. Lord, help him. Somehow, someway he'd find the strength.

Jessie threw back the quilts for him to climb in beside her.

Chapter Twenty

What was that saying—"Fools rush in where angels fear to tread"?

The thought snaked through his mind, offering little reassurance as Duel slid in next to Jessie. His leg touched hers and he jerked as though he'd come in contact with one of the deadlier vipers. He sure hoped the good Lord'd take pity on this fool.

His head sank into the goose-down pillow. He hadn't slept on a regular bed in such a long while. The fluffy softness surprised him.

Jessie laid her head on his chest and his arm encircled her as if it were the most natural thing in the world.

"Thank you, Duel." Her voice was low.

"For what?"

"Not hurting me. Not forcing me. Not laughing at this."

"Your needs are just as important as mine, Jess." More, the way he figured it.

"I keep forgetting that you're different."

"I'll try to make sure you never regret hitching up with this poor dirt farmer."

She shifted and in the dim light he returned her pointed gaze. "I want you to look at it. If we remove the mystery of it from between us perhaps that will help."

Duel knew what 'it' meant. She was right. The thing stood like an impenetrable wall, reminding him of her pain and suffering, and her of the awful deed she'd done. Still, it looked bad enough from a distance. He really didn't care for a close-up view.

"Light the lamp, Duel." Jessie sat up, and he had no choice.

Sulfur lingered in the air moments after he struck the match. Adjusting the wick to a low flame so as not to awaken the child, he stared out the window while she slipped the gown off her left shoulder. Rain had extinguished the fire, but the charred timbers of the barn stood outlined by the midnight sky.

"You can turn around." Her light touch felt good on his shirtless back. Too good.

"We don't have to do this."

"I know, but I want to get everything in the open where we can deal with it."

Smart move. Wasn't that the same advice his father had given him in regards to telling Annie about his bounty hunting?

"Lay your cards on the table, son," Walt had urged. "Feller can't see where he stands till he knows the hand he's drawn."

Duel didn't know if it'd work now like it did then. He sure hoped for a miracle—and the courage to not let his lady down. He took a deep breath. Whatever it took to keep Jessie's faith in him from crumbling he'd do. He clenched his jaw tight.

Still, nothing prepared him for the nearness. If he'd been standing, his legs would've buckled. A scarred ridge of skin rose in the shape of a diamond, with the letter 'J' nothing more than an elevated hard welt. The red, puckered skin around it had drawn back as if it'd tried to fend off the atrocity by shrinking. The taste of bile soured on his tongue. He couldn't bear the thought of Jessie's torment.

"Touch it, Duel. This is what I killed a man for. This is why I'll swing from a rope."

Not if he could help it. He'd fight any man who attempted to hurt her again. At that moment he'd never hated another human being as much as he despised Jeremiah Foltry. His hand balled in a fist as rage swept him down a mighty waterfall. He tumbled end over end, shutting his eyes against an unknown man's taunting face, of the devil he imagined Foltry to resemble.

Jessie took his fist and gently uncurled the bent fingers, then her breath fluttered against him as she kissed his palm.

When Duel opened his eyes he discovered they'd filled with tears. In the last four years he'd found little reason for them. He blinked hard. The tears weren't for him, but for his brave, strong woman—his wife.

Taking her face between his hands, he raised her gaze to him. Love, deep and sure, replaced the rage. He'd found a priceless jewel. His lips found hers and he tasted his fill of the woman of his dreams.

Nothing could tarnish the contented smile on Jessie's face the following morning. Regarding her image in the looking glass, she slipped on the new bonnet. Jittery hands reflected the turmoil inside as she tied the silk ribbon in a pretty bow. Every part of her body felt electrically charged.

Marley tugged on her skirt. "Pwetty? Mine pwetty?"

Jessie lifted the pint-sized child who made her feel almost whole again. The toddler reminded her of what could never be. The time had come to tell Duel her secret and risk losing him in the bargain. Would he change his mind about wanting half a woman? Soon, she promised. He deserved to know. She only hoped she hadn't kept her silence too long.

What was that he said to her that night in the barn? Something about keep looking forward when the pain of looking back is too great. How could she? Stuck in no-man's land, looking forward held as much pain for her as what she'd left behind.

Adjusting the fabric rosebuds around the girl's soft collar, Jessie gave her a gentle hug. "Yes, sweetheart, Marley Rose is the prettiest little girl in the county."

A low growl came from inches away where Duel struggled to attach a stiff collar to his collarless shirt. Each time he almost managed to get the elastic fastener buttoned in back, it sprang free and shot across the room.

Frustrated, he yanked off the offending article of clothing. "I'm not wearing this contraption. If I can't go to church like I am, then, by Heaven, I'm not going."

"Sweetheart, you'll have to get down while I fix your . . ." She avoided his stern look. "Duel's shirt."

Marley toddled off calling, "Boobie. Boobie."

"Thank goodness Yellow Dog wanted out this morning." Jessie took the rigid neck accessory from him. Talking about last night was out of the question. "I'll do it for you. Turn around."

He complied with her request. "I suppose the poor animal had his fill of coddling. Glad to see him up and around."

With his height she had to stretch to bring the stiff fabric across the front to the back. In so doing, she leaned into him, her breasts grazing his solid back. He jerked as though she'd gouged him with a needle.

Her smile deepened. They still had a way to go before they'd be comfortable in each other's company, but in her estimation they had passed a major hurdle last evening. How glorious to awaken beside her husband.

Not even the blackened timbers of the barn dampened her spirits. Bright sunlight splashed the field of sorghum, the meadow of wildflowers, and the grave atop the hill.

"Hold still. I won't bite, you know." She raised his collar-length hair and slipped the cumbersome piece beneath. The coffee brown strands teased, doing a mating dance with her fingers.

Duel's soft answer challenged her imagination. "No ma'am, I reckon you don't bite. But you sure as heck make me wish I was one of them biscuits you make so well."

"A biscuit?" The task finished, she twisted around to stare. "Why on earth a biscuit?"

"I love to watch you savoring each bite like it was the best morsel you ever tasted. The way you lick your lips with the tip of your tongue, your pleased expression drives me crazy."

Duel drew her so close she could hear the pounding of his heart. Or was that her own? She didn't care. Those worries vanished the second his mouth touched hers. When her lips parted, he explored inside, leaving the taste of wanting on her tongue. And when the kiss ended, if she'd ever truly doubted it, she knew he'd romanced and won her soul.

"I want to satisfy you in every way, to know I'm the cause of that special smile on your face." He tweaked the ribbon beneath her chin and winked. "Someday I will."

Jessie hummed a quiet tune all the way from the farm into town. If she hadn't had Marley Rose on her lap, she probably would've floated right off the buggy seat.

Little did Duel know he'd fulfilled another pledge—that he could claim sole responsibility for her radiant beam.

Few people roamed Tranquility's main street. They passed the barber shop, the stables, and the saloon on the way to the church at the end. A man, a woman, and a precious little girl. Not connected in all the traditional ways, they were a family nevertheless.

All of a sudden the window of Dexter's General Store caught her eye. The dress looked exactly like the one—no it couldn't be. She swivelled in the seat to get a better view.

"Duel, isn't that Annie's—?"

He wouldn't meet her stare. "Yep."

"But what—?"

"Traded it." He flicked the reins and chucked softly to Preacher. "Wasn't doing us any good so I traded it along with a gallon of goat milk for your fancy bonnet."

For a moment Jessie imagined the wind played tricks on

her. She couldn't have heard right. Both were hard to conceive. Duel giving up a prized possession of the one he loved and wrestling with the goat he hated for a gallon of milk. It boggled her mind.

Yet that explained how he bought the hat without a cent in his pocket. Though she'd wondered, she hadn't dared to ask. A fragile thing, a man's pride.

She tried to swallow, but a lump of regret blocked the passage. He'd sacrificed so much to give her a beautiful gift. And she'd not had the decency to share an important secret. Not a good way to repay a man's kindness.

Marley Rose babbled, pointing excitedly to every dog, cat, and bird they passed. For someone so young, the child took absolute enjoyment from every living creature. Sadness pervaded Jessie's thoughts. Marley's mother was missing these moments.

Preacher pulled into the churchyard. Duel maneuvered the buggy between a group of others. The little church would see a full crowd this day.

Already several women craned their necks to get a better look at Duel and Jessie, who'd come only once before. She straightened the blue satin ribbon beneath her chin, inhaled deeply, and handed Marley Rose to Duel.

"Appears we're a novelty of sorts." Jessie accepted her husband's hand and stepped down.

" 'Twould appear." His intent gaze burned a path to her heart, pushing aside everything until only sunlight and rainbows remained.

Her breath held suspended for several moments when his lips twitched. He wanted to kiss her. But please, not right now. Not in front of the church and in full view of anyone who cared to watch, especially the busybodies who continued to stare. It would mortify her.

"Papa. Mine Papa." Marley Rose patted Duel's chest. The cute antic broke the spell.

Laughter bubbled forth as Jessie stepped toward the open

church doors. "She's become mighty possessive, husband dear."

"Because you encourage her, wife dear." Duel took her arm and nodded politely to the women who whispered like magpies behind their hands.

Seemed he'd gotten a mite possessive in the bargain. Just for show, she reminded herself. Still, the pleasant sensation of her skirts swishing against his legs made her buoyant. Not even the gossiping old biddies could smother her cheery day.

"How good to see you, Duel, Mrs. McClain." The reverend shook their hands as if he were vigorously priming a pump. "Right pretty day, don't you think?"

"Beautiful." Duel's eyes held hers.

Jessie didn't know if he spoke of the weather or something entirely different—her blue bonnet perhaps. Strange flutters whipped into a frenzy in her stomach.

"Reverend, I've heard nothing but praise for your work from Tranquility's townfolk," she said.

Vicky waved anxiously and, with Roy and the twins in tow, hurried toward them. "Jessie, I love your bonnet. It's absolutely divine. I'm pea green with jealousy."

"Thank you." She cast Duel a swift glance. "A gift from Duel."

"My, aren't we special." Vicky nudged Duel with her elbow. "Very nice, brother. See, Roy. Why don't you ever buy me anything like that?"

"Never have anything left over, darlin'. We have six mouths to feed to their three. Takes all I can scrounge up for necessities. Besides, what adornment does a beautiful rose need?" Roy's eyes twinkled like two stars. Clearly, he loved sparring with Vicky. Jessie respected any man who could hold his own with the strong-minded woman.

Walt ambled up with his uneven gait. "Heard you had a bit of bad luck, son. Terrible about the barn."

"News sure travels fast, Pop."

"G'anpa!" Marley almost jumped from Duel's arms.

"Hey there, Angel girl." Walt hugged the child, then had

trouble releasing her grip from his neck. Seeing her determination to hold on, he took her from Duel.

"This is the first I've heard of it. What happened?" Roy asked.

"Lightnin' struck it. Burned nigh to the ground."

Hampton Pierson strolled through the door and paused, glancing around the room. Huh-oh, trouble. Frantic dismay released an army of chills up her spine. The man seemed bent on meandering their direction.

"Reverend will start the service soon." Vicky urged the twins forward to the McClain pew.

Jessie breathed a sigh of relief, but before she could follow suit, Hampton gained her attention. Now a few feet away, he nodded and grinned.

"Coming, Duel?" She quickly reached for Marley Rose.

Fire and brimstone reigned that fateful Sunday. Reverend Dinsmore spoke of sin and all things that were an abomination before God. Guilt lay heavy on Jessie's soul. No sin in the entire world was greater than taking a life.

You won't kill me! You don't have it in you. Never have, never will. You're too scared. See how you're shaking.

Jeremiah had laughed in her face. Then she pulled the trigger. He jerked as he lay there. Disbelief replaced his cold cockiness. She'd squeezed the trigger again, then again.

The lace handkerchief in her palm resembled a limp wad of tissue paper by the time she forced the memory into submission.

Remorse swept through her veins for what Jeremiah had forced her to do. No matter what, she couldn't go back.

Seated beside her on the wooden bench, Duel's thigh rested easily against hers. Through the layers of petticoats and skirt, she could feel his warmth and firm muscle. Her loving gaze moved to his chiseled profile. Strong and steadfast.

Lord help her, even if it were within her power to rewrite the past, she wouldn't. For if the events hadn't played out the way they did, she'd never have known how real love could be.

An angry glare marked Duel's face. His eyes had narrowed to jagged shards of glass, and a tic in his jaw made the only movement among the rigid peaks and valleys of his features.

Jessie followed the path of his fury.

Hampton Pierson. She should've guessed.

The man relaxed in a pew ahead and a little to the right. Both men eagle-eyed each other with a menacing glower. She should have known this would happen. And over a stupid bonnet.

Reverend Dinsmore closed his sermon with the Lord's Prayer, then dismissed the congregation.

Somehow, she had to steer Duel past Hampton without his creating a scene. The task seemed unlikely. Dare she enlist her sister-in-law's help?

"Vicky, I think Hampton Pierson's trying to get your attention."

"Wonder what he wants?" Vicky set sail for the hapless victim. Jessie collected herself.

The woman was still talking a blue streak when they reached the door and she dared look back.

"Nice sermon, Reverend." Duel extended his hand.

"Heard about the barn, son. The good Lord giveth, and He taketh away."

"For a fact. The main thing is the animals were spared."

She barely heard the conversation. Hampton had escaped and was almost upon them. Now wasn't the time to exchange pleasantries. Oh no, too late.

"Mrs. McClain, I wanted to say what a breath of fresh air you bring to our paltry little town."

"Thank you, Mr. Pierson. If you'll excuse me, I need to have a word with Mrs. Brown over there."

Duel captured her arm and she didn't need to see his face to know a black storm brewed. They progressed down the steps and had gone not more than a few feet when Hampton brushed past.

Suddenly, Jessie had to stifle laughter. White chalk covered the seat of the Lothario's black breeches.

"Hey, Pierson," Duel drawled after him. "Got something on your behind. Think you'd better go change before you try to sweet talk a man's lady."

Chapter Twenty-one

The pink dawn had faded into light blue when wagon after wagon load of people and supplies poured onto the farm Monday morning.

"What's going on, Duel?" Jessie peered over his shoulder out the window.

"Reckon it's a barn raising." He hurried out to meet the early arrivals.

She barely had time to speculate on their good fortune before she was hurrying to the door. Vicky burst in, her arms overflowing. Behind her trailed George, Henry, and the twins, each carrying more.

"Mornin', Jessie. Brought a ham from the smokehouse and turnips and squash from the root cellar."

"My goodness. You've certainly brought enough."

Vicky stared as though Jessie'd sprouted horns. "There will be lots of hungry men to feed."

"Mama, can we go play now? Can we, huh?" George asked.

Henry's eyes sparkled. "Can we, Mama?"

"In a minute, boys. I'm talking to your Aunt Jessie. Don't

interrupt." Since both hands were full, the woman blew a sprig of hair from her face.

"Maybe you need to sit down for a minute, Vicky. You must have been up since midnight."

"I don't have time for that. We have to get organized."

Oh dear. That sounded ominous when her sister-in-law said it. She braced for a trying day, though her heart swelled with gratitude. The thoughtful efforts of the townsfolk touched her. Jeremiah would never have allowed anyone on his ranch. But due to the kindness of neighbors she barely knew, they would now recover from the storm.

Charlotte Brown and Gladys Stanton made it to the door. They, too, had arms laden with food, which they unloaded in the kitchen at Vicky's capable direction.

"Boys, I want you to stay out of the men's way out there." Vicky gave a stern warning. Apparently she'd had to deal with boys being boys in times past. George and Henry were just little men waiting to grow up.

"Cain't we even watch?" George's disappointment reflected in both boys' faces.

Sadness whispered in the back of Jessie's mind. If Duel's son had lived he'd no doubt be trailing in his father's footsteps. From what she could figure, he'd be almost a year older than Betsy and Becky, who were adorable three-year-olds.

Guilt trampled down her happiness. Having a son was special to a man. Duel would never have that—not with her. Would he hate her when she told him?

"No. And watch out for your sisters," Vicky added.

"Aw shoot, do we hafta?" Henry kicked the floor with the toe of his shoe.

"Jessie, how about Marley going out with the children? They'll keep an eye on her."

"I'm sure Marley'd love it." Misgivings made her wish she'd said no. Considering the little darling's penchant for putting things in her mouth, she needed close supervision.

Against her better judgment, she watched helplessly. Flanked by the twins, and shepherded by George and Henry,

Marley toddled happily. Jessie prayed she worried for nothing.

"She'll be fine, Jessie." Her sister-in-law's assertion did little to reassure her. "Now, we have work to do. Those men'll build up a hearty appetite before you know it."

In no time at all, Jessie had forgotten her worry. Pots lined the top of the wood-burning stove and more were moved to a fire they'd built outdoors. Many of the women she'd never met, since they came from distant farms. She couldn't keep her gaze from straying to Jane Maxfield, whose swollen stomach looked ready to burst.

Envy swept over her as she stirred a cake batter. The way Jane's hands rested protectively on her belly, the glow on the woman's face, all made Jessie wish for the impossible. She poured the thick mixture into pans and sighed. The joy of impending motherhood she could only imagine.

You don't deserve a child. I'll teach you to bite the hand that feeds you. Then Jeremiah had kicked her stomach until the newly begun life inside spilled out onto the floor—her punishment for another escape attempt.

Jessie struggled to push the horrible memory back into the locked box where she kept it. Even in death, the man strove to torment her. Sliding the cake into the oven, she moved to a bulging bowl of soft dough and took pleasure in punching her fist into it. Then she glanced anxiously out the window and relaxed only after she located Marley Rose.

When the noon hour arrived, they'd fixed enough food to feed an army. Duel set up makeshift tables under the ash and chokecherry trees, while the ladies filled them with mouth-watering dishes, cakes, pies, and bread.

"There you are, sweetheart." Jessie lifted Marley, her cheerfulness fading at the ring of dirt around the child's mouth. She ran her finger lightly over the small teeth and found grit. "You've been eating dirt. Shame, shame."

"Mama?" Marley opened her hand, proudly showing a crushed flower. "Pwetty."

Duel met them at the well. "Figured she'd need her face washed."

"Our daughter's been eating dirt, Duel."

"It's not the end of the world, Jess. It won't kill her or anything." A strand of hair had pulled loose from the twisted knot at the nape of her neck, and he pushed it back from her face.

His touch released a swarm of butterflies in her stomach. He made her feel every inch a woman. From across a room or from the far side of a field of sorghum she was conscious of his every breath. She knew no man besides Duel who'd sleep beside his wife without forcing his attentions on her. That fact alone made her love him more.

Suddenly Duel stiffened. Jessie followed his gaze to find Hampton Pierson boldly watching. The man stood apart from the others who'd gathered beneath the trees to eat.

"I didn't know he came." Unease cut a path, creating havoc with her mind.

"Wish he'd stayed away, but the man's determined to be a thorn in my side."

Jessie brushed his arm with a light caress. "Don't let him goad you into anything foolish. Not over me."

When he switched his aggravated regard to her, she added quietly, "It's you I want, Duel McClain."

Through the open kitchen window, Jessie could hear the children calling, "Red rover, red rover, let Henwy come over."

Elbow-deep in sudsy dishwater, she smiled. It wouldn't be long before Marley Rose would join in. The girl had turned into a regular chatterbox and signs indicated it could only get worse.

"Wasn't that bad about Evelyn Butler dying an' leavin' those little children?" Charlotte Brown asked during a moment of quiet.

The dishtowel in Vicky's hand whipped the air as she vigorously dried the rinsed dishes. "I'll say. Wonder what'll happen to those kids now? You suppose they'll put 'em in an orphanage?"

Jessie pulled her attention from the window. "I don't believe I heard about this. Who was Evelyn Butler?"

"She lived about two miles out of town. Died of the fever." Jane's brow wrinkled in concentration. "I believe her husband got killed in a cattle stampede two years ago. Abel Butler worked off and on for Jesse Chisholm."

"Abel stayed home long enough to get Evelyn in the family way, then he'd hit the trail again," Charlotte said.

Vicky gave the group of women her best disapproving scowl. "Poor thing."

"How many children did she leave?" Jessie could imagine the little things' fear, the horrible feeling of abandonment.

"Three. Two boys and a girl," Charlotte supplied. "I'd take them in if I weren't so old. As it is, I just can't." The woman shrugged her shoulders.

Jane chewed her bottom lip. "Charlie and I might take one of them, but all three would be a huge burden on us."

"Seems a shame to split up a family. Without a mother or father, they don't have anyone but each other," Vicky said.

Jessie's heart was breaking. "Do they have other kin?"

"Disease, Indians, and accidents pretty much wiped them out." Gladys Stanton joined the conversation at last. "I heard tell of a grandmother over in the next county, but folks say she's in poor health and up in years."

"What are the children's ages?" Jessie heard herself asking.

Vicky eyed her with curiosity. "Are you thinking of adding them to yours and Duel's brood?"

She clamped a lid on her thoughts, yet she heard herself reply. "Could be. I'd hate to see them doled out like pieces of fruit to this one and that. Or worse, to live out their childhood in the cold confines of an awful orphanage."

"The boys are two and four. The girl is three." Charlotte gave her a strange look as well.

Hope spread. Duel could have his sons. She would have another daughter, and playmates for Marley Rose. Perhaps the revelation she must share with her beloved would lose its sting if she could replace it with other children.

Perhaps?

Later, she sat with the women in the coolness of the chokecherry trees. Laughing children played their games, almost drowning out the sawing and hammering in the background.

"Ring around the rosy, pocket full of posies." Small voices blended with the melee. The younger children, Marley included, held hands and formed a circle while the older ones enjoyed Blindman's Bluff and Ante Over.

Jessie's attention wandered to the newly raised barn that neared completion. Squinting against the bright sunlight, she searched for the familiar form that helped paint her world pinkish purple. Through narrowed lids she spotted him on the roof, and her calm pulse became a fast-moving stream. As she watched, he took a sheet of tin from a man on a ladder, laid it over the beams, and nailed it down. Duel's tremendous strength locked the tin in place with a mere two strokes of the hammer.

The power of the man didn't begin and end with the physical. His patient restraint during the nighttime hours bespoke strong character from deep inside. And honor few men could equal.

The front door slammed and Vicky marched from the house. "Jessie, Henry knocked over the lamp in the sitting room and broke the globe. I'll go to Dexter's tomorrow and get you another."

"No rush. I'm sure he didn't intend to do it." She had discovered a few things about little boys since becoming part of the McClain clan. "Do I need to sweep up the glass?"

Vicky shook her head. "That's part of his punishment. I told him he couldn't come back out until he cleaned it up."

"No harm done." She couldn't hold Henry at fault for his boyish exuberance.

When she looked for Marley again, the girl had disappeared from the laughing band of children. Jumping to her feet, she scanned the area. Suddenly she spied her quarry and the wild stampede inside slowed down to an organized trot. Marley's little legs hurried to catch her "Boobie," who stood cautiously apart from the loud goings-on.

Jessie sprinted for the child. By the time she came close, Marley had chased the dog farther into the trees until they were completely hidden from view.

"Marley Rose, come here this instant." She circled a thicket, getting her skirt entangled in a bramble bush. "Marley Rose, come to Mama."

"You lose your girl?"

The voice startled Jessie. Whirling, she faced none other than Hampton Pierson. Alone, separated from help, her panic rose. Though the dapper man had never given her cause for alarm, a leer twisted his usually pleasing features and turned her blood to ice water.

"My daughter wandered off." From years of practice, she adopted an unruffled demeanor, offering a fleeting smile. "What are you doing out here, Mr. Pierson?"

"I followed you. Been trying to find a way to get you alone all day, my dearest." The man stepped closer. His loud, rapid breathing filled the air between them.

"I'm sorry, Mr. Pierson, but I really cannot allow you to use such an endearment." She prayed her low but stern rebuke would dissuade him. "I'm a happily married woman. This isn't proper."

"Your comeliness has smitten me. I'm unable to think of anything but my darling Jessie." Desire set Hampton's eyes ablaze.

She tried to portray a calm she didn't feel. "I could use your help in finding Marley Rose. I'm worried she'll get hurt." Truth be known, that scared her worse than Hampton. She jerked her skirt free of the thorny branches and edged toward a clear path.

"No hurry." He blocked her escape with his body. "We'll find her later. First, I'd like to kiss your ruby lips."

Jessie's hand stung when it connected with his cheek. Her fear forgotten, she was plain mad now.

"Oh, I love a woman with spirit." Her resistance merely inflamed him. Hampton pulled her against his chest.

"Then you'll love this, you womanizing jackass!" Before she could stop it, her knee rose with force into his crotch. And when he doubled over in pain, she hit him with her fist.

At that moment, Yellow Dog bounded from the green growth snarling, attacking the man's leg. Marley Rose toddled behind calling, "Boobie. Mine Boobie."

Jessie scooped up the wayward child and started for the house.

"Call him off. For God's sake, please." Hampton had lost all his bluster. The man kicked and fought to release the dog's hold on his limb. Still, Yellow Dog clung tenaciously.

"You promise you won't force your attentions on me in the future?" Despite the shaking that had reduced her knees to rice pudding, she basked in a satisfied glow.

"I promise, hope to die, stick a needle in my eye," the wild-eyed man ranted, his face awash with pain. "Now, please. I beg of you."

"Down, Yellow Dog. Come." She snapped her fingers and whistled. The dog immediately trotted to her side and stared up at her, his tongue lolling out the side of his mouth. Jessie could have sworn she detected a lopsided grin on the animal's face. Not that a retriever could do that. Still, he looked mighty pleased with his work.

More swishing of limbs alerted Jessie to other danger. She clenched Marley to her bosom. Only this time it was Duel who came forth.

"Papa." Marley Rose tried to jump from her arms.

"You all right, Jess?" Grim lines marred his chiseled features. He shifted his gaze from the man on the ground to her.

"I'm fine." She wondered how long he'd been there and how much of the scene he'd witnessed. "Mr. Pierson, on the other hand, has learned a valuable lesson."

"Sorry you don't need my help. It would be pure pleasure." Duel put a gentle hand on her elbow. "Seems you took care of the suck-egg mule all by yourself."

His admiring scrutiny almost did her in.

"I don't think Mr. Pierson will present any more problems." She whistled softly. "Come, Yellow Dog, let's go home."

Duel turned for one last parting shot. "Consider yourself lucky, Pierson, that my wife dealt with you before I did. Now get off my land and don't ever set foot near my wife again."

Chapter Twenty-two

"Git your caboose in here, son. You look worse'n a treed polecat." Bart Daniels waved Luke into the inner sanctum of the his office.

"Shoot! I feel worse than that, Bart." Luke swept an inch of dust off the only available chair and dropped onto it. "Don't you ever do any cleaning?"

"Folks o' El Paso don't pay me to traipse around here in one of those frilly white pinnyfores carryin' a mop bucket." The sheriff's mustache bristled like porcupine quills.

Luke grinned at the image. "Hold onto your galluses, old man. Too early in the day to get riled up. Besides, you don't have the figure for a pinafore."

He dodged the pencil thrown at him.

"Always hafta be a smart-ass. One in ever crowd." Bart leaned back in his chair and propped his elbows behind his head. "Feelin' worse'n a lowdown polecat, huh? Now why do you suppose that is? If'n I was a bettin' man, I'd say it's concerning the Missus Foltry."

A deep sigh escaped. "Remind me not to play poker with

you." Luke fidgeted in his chair. "Got any coffee handy?"

"Reckon I do." The man cocked his head to the side and glared at him through one eye. "If'n you think the pot's clean enough to suit you."

"Dang it, you old coot! Guess I'm paying for my earlier comments." He watched Bart shuffle to the potbellied stove for the soot-blackened pot. He reckoned there was a lot still to come he'd wind up paying for. Like when he arrested his new sister-in-law.

Ain't nothing easy when duty and fam'ly's involved. That had become the McClain family mantra. Luke had first heard his grandfather say it, then his father.

Lord, they'd spoken the truth. Duty. Family loyalty. Which fork in the road would he take? And at what cost?

"You gonna tell me why you're here, or am I gonna hafta drag it out of you?" Bart passed him a steaming cup of black liquid.

"With your smeller you should have been a coon dog." Luke sipped on the brew, playing the game he loved.

"You know, Luke, if you wasn't so durn likable, I think I'd just shoot ya for bein' such an annoyance."

"Didn't know you loved me so much." He followed Bart to his chair and watched him sit down in a huff. "I'm thinking Duel's new wife is Jessie Foltry. Leastwise, that's what my gut tells me."

"What? Why would Duel marry a husband-killer?"

Luke wiped his eyes. He'd asked himself the same questions. "Hell, I don't know. Maybe she didn't level with him. Maybe she did and he doesn't care. Maybe I'll sprout wings and join a band of angels."

"The likelihood of that happening is slim."

"So's the chance Duel's wife ain't Jessie Foltry."

"Great God in the mornin'! I can see why your tail's a dragging."

"That ain't the half of it. I found the woman to be everything Duel needs and then some. Shoot fire, Bart, I ain't sure I didn't fall in love with her." Luke wearily pushed his hat onto the back of his head. "Called herself Jessie Rumford before she took to wearing the McClain name. Got the face of an angel with a disposition to match. And she's wrapped Pop and Duel around her little finger."

Bart hooked both thumbs in his galluses and reared back. "You're sure she's the same woman?"

He related the fact he'd found no Rumfords in Cactus Springs, and the ones in Pecos County'd never heard tell of her. "I came back here to ask Jessie's parents some questions."

Bart ran his fingers through the thin wisps of hair that remained. "Her father died two weeks ago. Reckon worry kilt ol' Zack Sutton. You can talk with Phoebe, though I doubt she'll be much help."

"Worth a try. Think I'll mosey over there." Luke sat his cup on the only corner of Bart's desk that wasn't buried beneath a ton of paper.

Phoebe Sutton answered the door with fire in her eyes and a rifle in her hand. "State your business."

Luke lifted his hat politely. "Texas Ranger, ma'am. Don't want any trouble."

"Trouble's what you'll be getting if you don't get off my porch."

He ignored the threat. "I came to talk to you about your daughter."

"Don't know where she is. Ain't seen hide nor hair of her." Phoebe raised the rifle to her shoulder.

"Hold it, ma'am. I just came to talk." Hell, he'd hate to hafta shoot the old woman in self-defense. Wouldn't look good on his record.

The long-barreled weapon wavered slightly. "Make it quick. Don't have all day."

"I think I know Jessie's whereabouts."

"Then why haven't you arrested her if you know?"

"Want to make sure first. If it's the same one, she's married to my brother, Duel McClain."

Phoebe let the rifle drop to her side. "Is she all right? I worry about her, you know. She's my baby."

"How well did you know Jeremiah Foltry?"

"Hated the man's guts. A shifty-eyed weasel. Jessie changed after she married him." The woman clucked between her teeth. "Had a bad feeling. Zack claimed Jeremiah beat 'er. She never came around us what she wasn't covered with bruises."

"You or your husband ever ask her where she got them?"

"Shore. Jessie, she tried to make light of 'em. Made all kinds of excuses." Phoebe stood her rifle beside the door frame and motioned to the chairs on the porch. "Care to sit a spell?"

"Be nice, ma'am." Luke wondered at the change that had come over Phoebe. The woman had gone from hostile to a virtual jabber box. More than likely, she ached to hear about her daughter.

"It had to be hard on you when she shot Jeremiah and disappeared that way." He settled onto a hard wooden chair.

"If she shot him, he durn sure deserved it. I raised my girl up in the faith." Phoebe pursed her lips as if daring him to say different, and perched stiffly on a rocking chair. "You know, a woman can only take so much."

"That's a fact, ma'am." Luke was beginning to get a clear picture of Foltry, and every new shred of information made him despise the man more. He didn't like the direction this investigation had taken. Didn't like it one dad-gum bit.

"Jeremiah was pure evil. About a year ago he stopped her from having any contact with us." A faraway look came into her eyes. She rocked slowly. "Jessie sent us a note telling us not to worry, that ever'thing was fine, but said she wouldn't be able to see us for a while."

"If you don't mind my asking, who delivered the note?"

"Not Jeremiah, if that's what you're thinkin'. A woman who worked there brought it. Had a sneaking suspicion Jeremiah didn't even know Jessie sent it."

"Only doubts?"

A tear inched down her cheek. "We knew Jessie lived in a

bad, bad situation. Not a blasted thing we could do about it."

Luke felt sorry for the lonely woman. More and more Jessie appeared to be a victim, not the cold-blooded killer they'd led him to believe. Still, his job was to bring the woman in, not judge or convict her. Would Duel understand that? Pain knifed through his belly.

"Tell me, Ranger, is she happy and well? What does she look like?"

For the next half hour, Luke described Jessie's life with Duel in Tranquility, the McClain family, the farm.

"Tranquility. I like that," she said, then she pierced him with a pointed stare. "Your brother. Is he an honorable man?"

"The best, ma'am." But, what about him? How could he put his sister-in-law in jail for defending herself? What kind of man did that make him? Somehow honor soured in his stomach.

"Pwetty. Pwetty, Mama." Marley's voice sounded strange.

"What sweetheart? What's pretty?" Jessie turned from her thoughts of how best to tell Duel her secret and the little detail of adding the orphaned Butler kids to their family. And how to tell him she loved him so very, very much.

She gasped. Blood dripped from the child's hands and mouth.

"Marley!" She managed to reach the girl as she collapsed to the floor. So much blood. What? How?

When she lifted the precious bundle, a piece of glass fell from Marley's clutched fist and clinked onto the floor.

"Oh, my baby. What have you done?" The words ripped from her raw throat. Marley's eyes fluttered. She was so limp. Sickening terror welled from deep inside Jessie.

Shock made her knees wobble and she barely made it to a chair. With Marley on her lap, she ran her finger inside the girl's mouth and encountered tiny fragments of glass.

"Jess, what happened?" Duel came from outside. "Did Two Bit have an accident?"

"I don't know." Her frightened voice sounded far away. "I looked up and she was standing in the doorway with blood dripping everywhere."

"What the hell?" He bolted to her side, his ashen face reflecting his own horror.

Dear God, if something should happen to the love of his life, she'd never forgive herself. Why hadn't she kept a more watchful eye on Marley?

"A piece of glass fell from her hand. Just now when I felt inside her mouth, I found more of the same."

"Do you think she was eating it? And where in tarnation would she get glass?"

"We'll worry about that later, Duel. Right now saving her is all I care about."

"I'll go for the doctor." He started for the door, then abruptly turned. "No. Not this time. I won't make that mistake again. We'll take her to him."

Without being told, Jessie knew he referred to Annie. This couldn't be happening to him again. They had to save Marley Rose. She couldn't die.

"It's glass all right." Doc Mabry held up a blood-soaked piece of cotton. Bits of glass glittered from it. The man peered over his glasses. "Know where she got it?"

Miserable and guilt ridden, Jessie could only shake her head.

"My wife found her like this, Doc."

"Don't know how much she ingested?"

"If we knew that, we'd tell you," Duel snapped.

Jessie laid her hand on his arm. "The doctor's trying to help. He'll take care of our daughter." He has to, she added silently.

Torture darkened his amber eyes as they met hers. He drew her to him and they tightly clung to each other for comfort.

"It'll be all right, Duel. Marley's a tough little girl."

"She's so small." His lips bothered the hair at her temple and when his voice broke, she felt a cold fist closing over her heart. "She trusted us to care for her. Maria trusted us, claimed she was better off with us. Ha!"

"I know." Misery prevented her from saying more.

Doc Mabry raised from his bent stance over the child. "I've done all I can. The rest is in the good Lord's hands. Take her home, cook some potatoes, mash them up and roll them around a ball of cotton."

The man paused to let that sink in. Then his stern stare over the glasses perched on the end of his nose made her swallow dryly. "Here comes the hard part. You'll have to force her to swallow them. However, if you make them small enough, they should slide down easily. The glass fragments'll stick to the cotton and she'll pass them through."

"You sure this'll work, Doc?" Duel sounded unsure.

"It should. Course, we don't know how much she swallowed."

"What if we can't get the potato balls down her?" Jessie could only imagine the difficulty they would have.

"It'll help if you massage her windpipe. But you must use whatever means necessary to get her to swallow them. Even if you have to force them down her throat."

Jessie's long glance swept the still, fragile form. "How long will she be unconscious?"

"I hope only a day or two, though I really can't say. It's not up to me." Doc put his shiny instruments away. "If I were you I'd pray."

"There, it took both of us but we got some down her." Duel couldn't have been more tired than if he'd been in the saddle for a solid month. A lingering glance at his companion indicated a similar haggard appearance. Although he'd tried to relieve her mind, he knew Jessie blamed herself.

"Was it enough to help? I can't see any change." Her voice trembled. She smoothed Marley's dark curls and choked back a sob. "I'll never forgive myself if something—"

"It's not. Marley Rose will be awake before you know it,

chattering about Boobie and Cheeba." He held Jessie to him tightly.

He loved Jess in a deeply satisfying way. It didn't surprise him that she had succumbed to emotion. He'd never known a woman with more grit and courage than Jessie. A faint-hearted woman couldn't have survived all those years with a monster.

Forcing a lighter tone, she remarked, "It'll be daylight soon."

Faint rays filtered through the window. "Yeah, I'll have to feed the animals."

"What would you like for breakfast?"

"Not hungry. Just coffee."

"I don't think I could get anything down either."

The weight of her head resting on his shoulder lent a companionable closeness. Neither had slept a wink all night.

His attention lit on an oddly bare lamp beside the chair. Strange that the globe was missing.

"Jess, did something happen to the lamp globe?"

She raised to look and suddenly clasped her hand over her mouth. "The globe! Yesterday Vicky told me Henry had broken one. When I asked if they needed help sweeping it up, she said Henry was taking care of it."

A few seconds later he watched her kneel to look beneath the chair.

"I found it."

"Damnation! Pushed it under the chair instead of sweeping it up. That's a kid for you."

"Evidently enough stuck out to draw Marley's attention and she crawled under after it. I remember her saying that something was pretty. Why didn't I check to see if Henry picked it up? Why didn't I?"

"Not your fault, Jess."

"Tell that to Marley Rose's mother."

He understood her anger. Hell, he'd carried enough self-recrimination around for the last four years to know. Still, it hadn't done a lick of good except make him a bitter man.

It'd taken a little girl and a branded woman to give him a reason to live.

He'd never known that something so small could make him feel that important. Or that he could get so gloriously happy over a simple grin. The tightness in his chest hurt. He felt a sob begin somewhere in the region of his heart.

What of Jessie? He watched her bustle about sweeping up every last sliver of glass. By the time she finished, the floor'd be clean enough to eat off of.

Her redemption hinged on the same little girl and a field of sun-ripened sorghum. God, he wished he could make it mature faster. One thing he'd learned growing up with his brother: Once Luke sank his teeth in something he didn't turn loose until he got what he wanted. He'd be back, no doubt about it. But would he give the sorghum time to ripen?

Lying in his arms, Marley moved her hand, opening and closing it.

"Jess! She moved."

Chapter Twenty-three

"She seems some better, doesn't she, Duel?"

His gut clenched. Two Bit did seem to show signs of improvement. Still, he hoped they weren't grasping at empty air. The mind did strange things to a person.

He rubbed Jessie's shoulders and felt unusual peace when she leaned into him. The lamp's glow brought forth golden red glints in her hair. Deep lines around her mouth told of extreme weariness when she met his eyes. God, how he loved his woman.

"Come to bed, Jess. Sitting there watching her isn't going to make her get well faster. You haven't left Two Bit's side since she took ill."

Jessie's sigh filled the space. "I keep thinking she'll awaken and need me."

"If you don't take care of yourself, you'll be no good to her when she does wake up."

Vicky and Pop had hovered all day, and though Jessie didn't mind their helping in other areas, she'd refused their offer to sit with Marley. Remorse ate at Vicky for the unfortunate accident. But Jessie's guilt did more than eat, it consumed.

"Come and lie down for a while. We can hear her if she wakes up."

Resigned, Jessie nodded and stood. "Guess you're right."

She remained fully clothed as she stretched out on the bed. He lowered the wick on the lamp until it barely flickered, then turned to leave the curtained alcove.

"Don't go. Please."

How could he refuse the beckoning of an angel? He glanced at the empty space next to her. No more than he could stop breathing.

"Lie beside me."

Thunderation! Didn't she know the trouble she invited? He was already embarrassed by the bulge in his trousers, which thankfully the dim light hid. But lying close to her, she would feel proof of his desire.

"I need you, Duel."

Truth to tell, he needed her as badly or worse. He hated to think of a time when she wouldn't be by his side. Fighting back that horrible thought, he removed his boots.

Seconds later, Jessie's pliant curves molded into the spoon shape of his body. His arms came around her. Back against chest, her rounded behind fit into his groin as if it'd been sculpted specifically for it.

A groan rose, which he quickly repressed. *Get your mind on other things, McClain, or you'll scare the daylights out of her.*

He thought about planting, harvesting, about the moon and the stars which he could see through the window. Other things beside the smell of vanilla and spice.

Desperate to clear his mind, he inhaled deeply, only to suck a silky strand into his mouth. Jesus! He could think of nothing except the way she made him feel. Despite his intense efforts his body refused to obey the commands.

Closing his eyes, he tried to recite the books of the Old Testament. Genesis, Exodus, Leviticus, Numbers.

Jessie rolled over to face him, her blue eyes shining in the muted light.

Confound it, what came after Numbers? He started again. Genesis, Exodus—

"Duel?"

There went his focus. "Yes, Jess?"

Her hand brushed his swollen member, and he gasped at the unexpected pleasure. Lord, help him.

"Would you kiss me?" Her throaty whisper heaped more fuel onto the already blazing fire.

The mute fairy got his tongue. All the reasons why he oughtn't grant her request vanished in the night air.

She tasted of honey and wild berries—the flavor of sultry, summer days. Excruciating desire flowed through him like hot oil. He needed her as a drowning man needed a life raft. At this point, were the reverend to ask him, he couldn't swear Genesis was even a book in the Bible. Jessie had become his genesis, his beginning. She was the origin of all things pleasurable and good.

"I don't know that I can stop this time, darlin'." He murmured the words against her lips, trying to warn her without separating himself from her lush mouth. "I'm merely a man, not a saint."

Leaning back from him, she touched his lips with her fingers. "Don't talk. I choose to be your wife in every way. This time there'll be no turning back."

Afraid to hope she meant to keep her word, Duel didn't resist when she unbuttoned his shirt. Nor did he stop her when she pushed her hand inside to caress the fine hairs on his chest.

Between hungry kisses and heated strokes, they shed their clothes. The pile beside the bed grew until they had no more left to add.

From the tips of her dainty toes to her auburn crowning glory, Duel stroked, kissing every inch. A light brush here, a forceful flit there, he gave his lady pleasure, and in turn, stole a piece of her to tuck inside his heart. Just in case.

Jessie's airy caresses greatly disturbed his quest for control. Her fingertips flirted with his neck, back, and buttocks, threatening to cast him over the brink.

"Ahhh. You drive me insane, lady." He nibbled on a delicately formed ear, then left a trail of kisses down her throat.

The urge to plunge into her, to satisfy his primal needs almost overpowered him. Still, he recognized and respected the fears lodged deep within her and stifled his body's craving.

When at last her raspy breathing matched his own, Duel rolled over and pulled her on top. He tried to ignore her pointed breasts thrusting into his chest.

"It's up to you, darlin'. If you want me, here I am. You have control of whatever happens."

Moonlight cupped her beautiful breasts, traced her lush curves. He almost burst with need to be inside her. The wild thought crossed his mind that if she turned away from him now, he would surely die of longing.

Honest passion danced across her features and he could have sworn tears sparkled in her eyes.

"Thank you, my dearest."

With unhurried movements she lay upon him, her pliant shape molding against his hard muscle.

Lazily, her mouth came to his in a lingering kiss.

And when he strove to continue, she pushed herself above him and teasingly dipped her head until the ends of her hair brushed his chest. Then with deliberate torment, she dragged the strands across his nipples, down his belly, and . . . Oh my.

Each silky tress skimmed over and around his inflamed member, each individual strand paying homage to the tumult they were creating.

Matthew, Mark, Luke and John!

Just as he reached the last of his fortitude, she gently took his thickness and guided it into her velvet softness. Moist heat closed around him.

She eased down upon him, and when she started to move

her hips, tight, pulsating waves carried him to the land of milk and honey.

Later, lying with her head on his chest, Jessie smiled. A blanket of blissful calm spread through her. The experience she'd just savored couldn't have happened to her.

Not after the years of nothing but sheer horror at the mere thought of intimacy with a man. Not after she'd betrayed Duel's trust in her. She didn't deserve such happiness.

Nagging guilt dimmed her glow. He gave her strength and she'd repaid him by hiding a terrible secret.

The steady beat of Duel's heart gave her courage to do what she must do. Even if he hated her for it.

"Duel, are you asleep?"

"Just tryin' to catch my breath. You, dear lady, are something else." His admiring tone added to her shame.

"I have something to tell you—something I should have told you from the start."

He drew small circles on her bare shoulder. "Can it wait till morning? If it's waited this long . . ."

She sat up and covered herself with the sheet. "It's important."

"Well, in that case." He shifted until he leaned against the headboard. "Shoot."

Now that she had his attention, she lost courage. What words did a woman use to destroy a man's dream of a son of his own?

"You have to understand about the night I shot Jeremiah and what drove me to it."

"Jess darlin', no one in their right mind would blame you for what you did. I sure don't."

"They're coming, Duel. Sure as the stars are twinkling in the sky, they're coming to take me away."

"They'll have to get through me first, and that includes Luke too. I'll fight every last one of them."

She lovingly traced the deep crease by his mouth. "You can't stop them. Hush now, I have to tell you my secret."

"Don't know why. I already know everything I need to about you," he grumbled, and took her hand. Opening it, he rested his palm against hers, fingers touching fingers.

"About a month before I ki . . . before that night, Jeremiah kicked my stomach until he killed the life inside me. There was so much bleeding. I couldn't stop it."

Those scenes ran through her mind as if they'd just happened. "I lost my baby."

"Jess, I'm so sorry. For your sake, don't do this. The bastard! I wish . . . I wish . . . Oh God!" Duel slammed his fist into his pillow.

"The assault permanently damaged me. A doctor told me I'll never have children, not ever. My anger festered until I couldn't take it anymore." She covered her face with her hands unable to look at her tall, noble Texan.

"Don't, Jess."

"I have to. You deserve to know what you've gotten." She took a deep breath. "Jeremiah came into my room that night, pulled me downstairs where several of his friends waited."

Her voice shook recounting the vivid memory. "He shouted that I was of no use to him since I couldn't bear children."

"His own damn fault, the sorry-assed bastard!" Maybe the pain in his voice came from grief that he'd hitched his dream to half a woman, or maybe from anger. Six of one, half a dozen of the other. Didn't make any difference. He wouldn't want her after this.

"Anyway, he told his friends to take me and do what they wanted. They laughed. I snatched the pistol out of Jeremiah's holster and . . . and—"

Duel held her so tightly she could hardly breathe, as if by doing that he could prevent the nightmare from consuming her.

"Shhhh. Don't think about it. He's not worth wasting a pennyweight of thought over." He cradled her face between his hands, forcing her to look at him. "I have you now and you're safe."

She didn't want to see his stricken look and know that she'd caused it.

"Open your eyes, darlin'." His gentle tone could have tamed the wildest, meanest maverick.

She wiped her tears and braced herself. Yet strangely, the amber lights held nothing frightening. What shone forth, poets had expressed for centuries in sonnets of love and adoration.

"I feel unworthy to have you." This time the tremble appeared in his deep voice.

"You want me? After everything I've told you?" She prayed for a miracle.

"Jess, you're not an animal to be turned out or sold." Duel kissed her soundly.

"You're not disappointed? I know how much you want a son."

"Darlin', I promised to stand by you in sickness and in health, for better or worse, until death do us part. I didn't vow to do all that just till I changed my mind. Besides, what you told me only makes me love you more."

Unless her hearing had suddenly gone bad, he'd just declared his love for her.

"You love me? For real?"

"Is that so hard to believe? After my jealous rage over Hampton Pierson's attentions and me pawing you every time you came close to me? Of course, I love you."

"But Annie?"

"That part of my life is over. I loved her once. That was then, this is now. I see that. You're my wife and I'm damn proud for you to wear my name." Peering at her sternly, his gruff addition erased all doubt. "One more thing. I wed you because I wanted you, lady, not because of any thoughts about offspring."

"Thank you." The words came out no louder than a whisper. Her gratitude ran deep, making the simple statement seem inadequate for what she felt.

"Don't have to thank me. I haven't done anything. Just wish

I could bring Foltry from the dead and horsewhip the son of a bitch." He tenderly pressed his lips to her open palm. "What you had to suffer . . . God, help me . . . no woman should ever have to go through."

A languid peace wound its way through Jessie. Their second lovemaking session had left her totally exhausted, but in a good way.

Snoring softly beside her, his arms holding her safe, Duel exhibited the same contentment. The harsh lines on his features seemed softer, meshing with his sensitive inner spirit.

He'd shown uncommon compassion for her this night. Despite the driving urges she knew he battled, he'd respected her mental fears and let her go at her own pace.

Overwhelmed by his thoughtfulness, she caressed his cheek. How she loved this man, her knight of the Texas Plains. His tender lovemaking made her feel more than a fairytale princess in a storybook. The toasty flush inside made her the most beautiful woman in the world.

And tomorrow they'd discuss the Butler children.

Chapter Twenty-four

Henry hid his tear-stained face in his mother's skirt, ashamed, too afraid to come out.

Vicky pushed him toward Duel and Jessie. "Apologize this instant or your father's taking you to the woodshed."

The boy stared glumly at his shoeless bare toes. His mother prodded, this time in a softer tone. "Go on, son."

"I'm sorry," he mumbled.

"Louder, Henry."

Jessie's sympathy went out to the little boy. "It's all right. He doesn't have to do this."

"Yes, he does." A determined scowl marred Vicky's attractive features.

Henry sniffled, wiping his nose on his shirtsleeve before he raised his head. "I'm sorry, Uncle Duel an' Aunt Jessie. I didn't mean to make Marley nearly die."

"We know you didn't, Henry." Duel mussed the top of his nephew's already tousled head.

"Will she get well?" The boy sniffled loudly again, a tremble in his little voice.

Jessie caught Duel's anguished gaze. She meant her reassurance for both. "Yes, honey. She will. I know she will."

Confidence sprang from merely saying the words. To her husband her eyes vowed their little girl would come back to them. Duel reached for her hand and squeezed.

"Vicky," he turned to his sister. "Would you mind watching Two Bit for just a little while?"

"Be happy to, brother. Henry an' me'll stay for a while."

Curiosity teased as Duel led her by the hand into the bright sunshine. "Where are you taking me?"

"A place you've never been." His arm settled comfortably around her waist. "About time you met someone."

Halfway up the hill, Jessie realized he headed for the lonely grave at the top. That he wanted to break down the barrier between them made her heart jubilant. After the deeply satisfying night of lovemaking that still brought a flush when she thought of it, she felt humbled and more proud of Duel.

Not even in the beginning had Jeremiah spared a moment to consider her emotional or physical distress. He'd plunged into her with a savage intensity, daring her to protest.

She cast a sidelong glance at Duel. Though he was a mystery at times, she couldn't imagine him treating her with anything less than respect. The common bond they shared required she repay him in kind.

"I wouldn't want to intrude. . . ."

"You'll never do that, darlin'. Don't waste a second thinking such nonsense. I want you in every part of my life."

A slight breeze greeted them when they topped the gentle incline. An awe came over her that was hard to explain. Jessie felt as if she'd entered a church.

Duel squeezed her waist. Hatless, his coffee brown hair ruffled in the wind. His proud jaw and noble carriage still reminded her of a great Apache warrior. She melted with love for this giant of a man.

"Annie, I want you to meet Jessie." His deep voice quavered with emotion, giving the sole indication of his deep sentiment. "This lady's my life now. I love her with my heart and soul."

The flower-strewn resting place blurred as Jessie blinked. Then her gaze sought Duel's and she spoke softly. "Annie, thank you for giving me this wonderful man. I'll take very good care of him." She took a deep breath. "You see, I love him too."

His head lowered, his firm mouth descending, teasing, touching hers. The moment became a timeless time, the lonely hilltop a placeless place where dreams and reality collided.

Forever after she'd always remember a sun-dappled morning when proof of Duel's love became etched on the stone tablet of her soul.

She'd never dreamed her life would overflow with such a bounty of goodness and love. The dizzying whirl in her head made her feel as if she stood poised on a high precipice while balanced on one leg. How long would her luck last? And, how could she keep it from ripping her heart out when it ended?

They stood arm in arm, her head snug in the curve of his shoulder. Silence did have a sound. It was the solemn whispers of two hearts embracing, becoming one.

Then Duel knelt for a reassurance before they turned to go. "Somehow, I knew you'd approve of her, Annie. Now you don't have to worry about me anymore."

Marley Rose slipped in and out of her deep sleep. At the present, the limp form rested in Jessie's lap while she fed her more of the potatoey cotton balls.

The main problem lay in getting them to go down. Jessie found herself trying to swallow for her.

Duel had moved two kitchen chairs beside Marley's bed where they could hold her more easily when feeding her. Now, he set the bowl on the floor and took one of the little hands.

"Come on, sweetheart. Swallow for Mama." She massaged the small throat and finally found success.

Since she followed the doctor's instructions to the letter, Marley had choked only once. It had terrified her. Luckily, Duel showed an aptitude for getting things unstuck.

"What's that noise?" he asked suddenly.

Jessie wiped her little darling's mouth and cocked her head. "I don't hear anything except your father snoring in the chair."

Vicky and Henry had long since gone home. Walt, however, had camped in the sitting room. Marley's situation broke his heart. She'd never seen the man so worried. He worshiped his newest granddaughter.

"No, it's something else." Duel dropped Marley's hand and went to investigate.

A few minutes later he returned. Sharp clicks on the wooden floor captured her attention, and she looked up in astonishment. Yellow Dog padded along by Duel's side.

"I found him scratching on the front door and whining. Almost broke the darn thing down."

The whimpering animal sniffed Marley's feet, licked her hand, then jumped onto the empty place beside Jessie as if the chair had been put there specifically for him.

"Hey there, Boobie." Jessie scratched his ears. "Duel, he's come to check on Marley Rose. He senses something bad's happened to her."

"Nothing like being booted out of the way by an overgrown mutt." Though he grumbled, he wore a pleased look. "Guess he'll be wanting to sleep with us too."

"The poor thing's worried. Animals are very loyal to the ones they love."

"That's all well and good, but if he thinks he's gonna take my place, he's got another thing coming."

Yellow Dog chuffed and eyed him balefully.

"Seems he's issued you a challenge." Jessie placed Marley back in her bed and tucked a light blanket around her.

Despite Duel's growl, he smoothed the dog's head. "And

I'm drawing the line when that mangy goat starts head-buttin' the door to come in."

The heaviness squeezing Jessie's heart seemed to lessen. Her smile felt warmer than it had for days. Surely the angel of death would stay away, seeing the love that surrounded the special little girl.

"I think her color's better, don't you?"

"Marley's better, you say?" Walt asked. Evidently Yellow Dog's arrival had wakened the man. He ambled to the bed. "Don't seem as peaked as she did."

"Pop, that might not mean anything."

"Shoot fire, son, we gotta have hope." Walt patted Yellow Dog's thick coat. The man appeared to think nothing strange about the animal's perch beside Marley. As if it were an everyday occurrence.

"Walt, now that you've had a nap, would you mind sitting with her for a spell?" Jessie asked. "We've some chores to attend."

"Be glad to, honey." Walt beamed with pride that they found him useful. "Take as long as you need. Ol' Yeller and me'll have a nice conversation."

Knowing the man she loved as a father would watch for any change, Jessie bustled around the kitchen while Duel got caught up outdoors. A sweet-potato pie for supper might lift everyone's spirits. Besides, doing nice things for Duel made her feel more worthy of his love.

When she slipped the pie into the oven, she caught sight of him, hoe in hand, chopping weeds in the sorghum field. The wavy stalks, full of spiked florets, reached almost to his waist. Briefly, she wondered how long till harvest.

"Please, let it hurry," she murmured quietly. An ominous feeling overcame her that perhaps time grew short.

With the supper meal cooking, she washed some necessities outside on the rub board. Busy slipping the clothespins over the tops of Marley's clean diapers, she felt a presence behind her and whirled.

"I never get tired of watching you." Duel's slow drawl sent a rush of heat through her veins.

Breathless anticipation made Jessie tongue-tied. She fumbled with the clothespins in her apron pocket and regarded the source of her problem.

"Won't get any work done that way, Mr. McClain."

"Not work I'm thinking about." The twinkle in his eyes reminded her of a naughty little boy. He shifted the sprig of grass that hung from his mouth. "Most surely it's not chores on my mind at the moment."

He sauntered closer until she could feel his gentle breath on her cheek.

"Your father . . . we can't."

"Pop's occupied."

"Do you have no shame? It's the middle of the day."

Jessie felt the hammering in his chest when he drew her into his arms. Her resistance melted in a puddle at her feet. She slipped her arms around his neck.

"Was thinking we could initiate the new barn." The blade of grass fell from his mouth. The next second she was swimming in a sea of passion, drowning with desire.

"Ahem. Indecent, that's what it is, brother." The lazy accent came from behind, throwing cold water on their rising excitement.

"Luke!"

Indescribable fear shot through Jessie. The man would've returned for only one reason. Duel's muscles tensed, tightening the hold on her waist.

She forced back the bitter taste that rose in her throat and smiled. "You've come a long way, Luke. Duel's forgotten his manners. Climb down and stay to supper."

The younger McClain grabbed the saddle horn and slid to the ground. "I'm here on business."

Instead of releasing her, Duel drew her closer, clearly intent on physically protecting her. Thank heavens his pistol hung from the nail beside the front door, or she was certain he'd put a bullet in his brother. A mist blocked her vision.

She'd known from the start her time had been limited.

Why now? The sorrow inside her screamed. Not when her darling Marley Rose lay at death's door. Not now when she'd found the greatest love she'd ever known.

Raw thickness made Duel's voice unrecognizable. "What the hell kind of business is that, Luke?"

Luke's gazed narrowed, piercing her heart. "On behalf of the state of Texas, I'm here to arrest Jessie Foltry for the murder of her husband."

Chapter Twenty-five

Numbing cold invaded, blocking the warm sunshine. Jessie's entire body shook as if someone had submerged her in a tub of ice water.

Duel took his hands from her, removing the only warmth left. Then he pushed her behind him and widened his defiant stance. "Her name's Jessie McClain. Can't let you do this, Luke."

"Darn it, Duel! I was afraid of this." Luke's arms rested at his sides where he could easily draw his weapon if push came to shove.

She couldn't have two brothers killing each other over her. Resolute, despite her watery legs, she pushed Duel aside.

"Stop it. I'll not have bloodshed on my account." She faced her beloved. "It's over, Duel. Luke has to take me back."

"Sorry, Jessie." Luke released pent-up tension in a big swoosh of air. "I was hating like hell to have to do this. For what it's worth, I think Foltry had it coming."

"You're damned right the man deserved it. That and more," Duel exploded. "Ain't no cause to lock a woman up."

Luke ignored his brother's outburst. "I spoke with your mother, Jessie She's worried sick about you."

"Mama?" Jessie pictured the frail woman who had taught her decency in all things. Too bad she'd failed. She supposed she'd disappointed her mother and her father.

"Yeah, Phoebe and I had a nice long talk. She's a special kind of woman, Jessie. Felt real bad for her." Luke touched her arm gently. "Have some terrible news."

"You don't know any other kind, do you, Luke?"

Jessie knew Duel's rudeness sprang from hurt. He blamed himself that he hadn't delivered the one promise that meant so much to them both.

"I come from a long line of promise-keepers," he'd bragged just after she'd met him. It seemed ages ago.

"What news do you bring, Luke?" She dreaded to imagine. Didn't know how much more she could stomach.

"Your father died about three weeks ago. Your ma said it was his heart. Went in his sleep."

She sagged against Duel, unable to stand.

"I'm sorry," Luke murmured.

No tears came. A wall of heavy sadness kept them at bay. She felt Duel lift and carry her to the bench by the well. She felt the cool water slide down her throat. She heard the pain in his voice, but it all seemed to be happening to a stranger, not to her.

"Jess darlin', can you hear me?" Duel patted her face gently.

His kiss brought her back to reality. The warmth of his love encircled her, driving the ice from her blood. Her Texan had that way about him—to always know the right thing to do.

A few yards away, Luke waited patiently, still in the same spot they'd left him. Jessie sympathized with him. The younger McClain was a good, decent man. Duty-bound, some folks called it. She couldn't fault a man for that.

Right now, Luke hated the job they handed him. She could see it in his eyes, his dejected stance. No use making things more difficult than they were.

"Duel, I've got to go. You know I have no choice." She pulled away from him and went to Luke. "I'll pack some things. If that's allowed?"

"Sure, Jessie. But, I was thinking. It's kinda late in the day to be starting out." Luke kicked a dirt clod with the toe of his boot. "Tomorrow's soon enough."

"In that case, stay for supper. Your Pop's in the house."

Luke shifted his attention to Duel, who'd followed Jessie from the well. The proud man waited for an invite from his brother.

"You're always welcome to sit at my table, Luke. Despite everything else you're fam'ly." Duel clapped him solidly on the back.

"Can't pass up an opportunity to spoil my new little niece, now can I?"

Worry tightened the knot in Jessie's stomach. "Marley Rose is sick. She might not make it."

"My little angel hasn't taken a turn for the worse, so why do I feel like I'm attending a wake? Why all the long faces?" Walt asked, putting down his coffee cup with a bang.

His fork frozen in mid-air, Duel fixed the root of the problem with a stare. "Luke, why don't you explain to Pop the reason we're in a devil of a mood?"

Deafening quiet met his question. Finally, his younger brother lifted his eyes from his plate.

For a long moment Luke watched Jessie push her food aside, not bothering to taste it. "I don't think this is the time, Pop. After supper we'll talk about it."

The table shook under the impact of Walt's fist. "By Josie, we'll talk about it now, or I'll know the reason why."

Her face white as a newly hatched eggshell, Jessie covered her mouth with her hand. The sparkling tears in her eyes broke Duel's heart in a million tiny pieces. He would sell his soul to buy her freedom. If not her freedom, just a little more sand in the hourglass. The grains of sand dropped much too quickly. The sorghum wasn't ready. Two Bit clung to life by a thread. Without Jess to give their daughter courage to fight, who knew?

Most of all, he wasn't ready to give her up. Loving her had been the easy part. Letting her go would rip out his guts, his sanity, and everything else in between.

"Luke's taking me back to El Paso come morning." Her voice quivered, but she held her head high, her jaw firm. He'd never been so proud. What would he and Marley do without her strength to lean on?

"Takin' you back? What in tarnation for?"

Luke withered a smidge under his father's icy stare. But, when he spoke, he was defiant. "I'm sorry it has to be this way, Pop. Lord knows I'd rather be chasing horse thieves or Indians. But I have a job to do, laws to uphold, whether it sets well with folks or not. I hafta look at myself in the mirror."

"Don't try to sell me on law work and quit the double talk. Tell me straight out like a man."

"All right." Luke took a deep breath. "I'm arresting Jessie Foltry for the murder of her husband. She'll stand trial in El Paso."

Walt jumped to his feet, knocking over his chair. He paid no attention to the clatter. "You're not takin' her anywhere less'n you go through me to do it."

"Pop, I don't want any trouble. Just doin' my job."

The elder McClain's voice shook with anger. "Tell that to that sweet angel lyin' in there. Jessie an' Duel are all the hope that precious thing has. You take Jessie away and you'll be stealin' her will to survive. No sir, I won't let you."

Walt stalked from the room. The front door slammed shut behind him, leaving a heavy silence at the table.

Jessie touched Luke's hand. "Go talk to him. He lashed out like that because he's hurting. Worry puts words in people's mouths they wouldn't say otherwise."

It amazed Duel that Jessie could show tenderness to the man who wanted to subject her to a humiliating trial and maybe worse. Yet, that quality endeared her to him more.

She accepted her fate and met it head-on. For better or worse. The ache in his chest pounded harder.

"Come on, Luke. Let's go talk to Pop." He pressed a quick kiss on her lips. "I'll be right back. We've plans to make, lady."

They located their father in the barn, leaning against Preacher's stall. Duel hadn't seen his father cry since they'd buried Lily McClain. For him to do so now revealed the depth of his misery.

"Pop, it'll work out. Marley Rose will be up and around before you can shake a stick. And Jessie? She's a strong woman. I'll see she gets a good lawyer."

Walt wiped his nose on a faded red hankie. "I don't care what anyone says, I'm proud to have Jessie McClain as a daughter. A heart as kind an' pure as hers cain't have blood on her hands."

"She did it, Pop. It's true." God, how he wished he could change that.

Luke touched Walt's shoulder in sympathy. "I fought with myself all the way here, whether to turn in my badge and forget what I know or do my duty to the state of Texas. Unfortunately for us, duty won out. For what it's worth, Jeremiah Foltry was a mean, rotten son of a bitch. But it doesn't change the fact Jessie shot him to death."

Duel flinched under his father's piercing stare.

"How long've you known about this? I could've helped you if you'd seen fit to confide in an old man."

"Not at first. I knew something was eating her, but didn't know what." Memories of that day on the cliff heaped on more guilt. He'd promised to protect her. Fine promise that turned out to be. "Jessie told me the day I asked her to marry me."

"Sounds like my girl. She has honor and 'tegrity. Could see it right off."

A long sigh came from Luke as he kicked the goat's milk pail, sending it skittering across the dirt floor. "Dad-burn it, Pop. I can't take her away from her sick child."

"It won't hurt any to wait a few days, will it, son? Jessie's not going anywhere."

Unseen hands seemed to be strangling Duel. He gasped for air. "What's a couple of weeks more or less? Give the sorghum time to ripen."

"What's the sorghum got to do with anything?" Walt asked suspiciously.

"I planned to use the money from harvest to hire Jessie a lawyer." He shot an accusing glare toward Luke. "We'd hoped to hire someone to clear Jessie's name before the law showed up on our doorstep. Seems we merely ran out of time."

"Your ma an' me always raised you to do the right thing, Luke. I believe you'll do that now."

Duel watched his brother march to the barn door where he stood staring toward the farmhouse.

"Don' worry, son." Walt bent to pluck a hay stem from Preacher's feed trough and stuck it in his mouth, leaving half dangling out. "You can lead a mule to water, but you can't make him drink. An important thing to remember. But in this case, I think the mule's gonna drink."

"Hope you're right." Marley's life, their future depended on it.

Minutes later, Luke threw up his hands and walked back. "How long till that crop's ready, Duel?"

"Won't get near as much for feed as we'd get letting the heads mature. Rumor has it they're paying a dollar a bushel at the sugar mill. Don't know the price for feed. I reckon we could start cutting next week."

"I'll probably lose my badge over this, but I'll hold off till Marley Rose gets well. No longer."

"Shout Hallelujah!" Walt danced a jig.

Overcome with gratitude, Duel stretched out his hand. "Thanks, Luke. You don't know what this means to us."

He'd managed to add a few more grains to that hourglass.

"I think I do." And for the first time since arriving, Luke smiled.

* * *

"Your brother's truly a caring man, Duel." Jessie lay in his arms. While the thundercloud hanging over them hadn't disappeared, she felt grateful for the short reprieve.

"At least Two Bit'll have her mama for a few more days. That's the important thing."

"You think Luke and your father will be comfortable in the barn?"

"They will if that darn goat'll leave 'em be. If it weren't for Two Bit, I'd have skinned and cooked the pesky thing before now."

Jessie smiled, knowing his threats never posed a danger to Marley's Cheeba. The small flicker of light from the lamp beside the bed allowed her to memorize every feature of her beloved's face. Each moment of their time together now seemed more precious.

Beneath the covers, his gentle touch moved to her naked thigh. She willed herself to think of nothing beyond this night, to enjoy the strange heat his caresses left on her skin. Where his hands went, glorious excitement followed.

"I should be ashamed to take enjoyment in our lovemaking, but I'm not. It's the most 'right' thing I've done my whole life."

"You talk too much, woman," he said with a growl, his kisses smothering further conversation.

Womanly passion burned its way into the core of her being. Musky wetness spread between her legs, between her breasts. Emptiness inside cried out, yearning for him to fill it.

When he did, the completeness of it rocked her soul. She savored every ripple, every crashing wave that washed away her pain. If she tried hard, perhaps she could store it up for the times when loneliness would be her sole companion. A cold jail cell would be a long way from the warmth of Duel's arms.

The gallop beneath the soft mat of chest hair slowed to a fast trot. Jessie buried her face in the dark brown wisps and gripped him fiercely to her.

"There's so much we need to discuss—"

"Shhhhh. Tomorrow's soon enough for that, darlin'. Let's enjoy the here and now."

With wild abandon, she met his sensuous mouth halfway and felt desire rise swiftly once again. She'd never grow complacent as so many wives did if fate gave her the chance to live out her life with this Texan. Each second shared with him would be Heaven on earth.

"If things don't go well, if they sentence me to—"

"You're not gonna hang! Don't say it, don't even think it."

"I have to tell you this. You've given me the will to fight. Without you beside me, I'd have crumpled long before now." She reveled in the luxurious texture of his hair. "Thank you, my husband."

In one smooth move, Duel rolled over and brought her atop him. His amber gaze pulled her inside to the secret place no one had ever gone. She glimpsed the thick scars that had shaped him into the noble man he'd become. He allowed her to see not only his faith, but his insecurities as well.

"No matter what happens . . ." He spoke softly and with such tenderness. "No matter what, I love you, Jessie McClain."

Chapter Twenty-six

Marley Rose steadily improved, much to everyone's relief. Only one thing ruined Jessie's joy. It meant they'd leave soon.

During the week of waiting, Luke joined Duel and their father in the fields. From sunup to sundown they sliced the stalks with sharp sickles and tied them into bundles. The stack on the wagon, which they rolled into the barn come nightfall, grew higher.

On this day, Roy, George, and Henry had come to help. Jessie stood with Vicky in the shade of a tree watching. Ever since they'd broken the news of her impending journey to Roy and Vicky, Jessie felt awkward in their company, unsure where they stood in the matter. Even now, an uncomfortable silence stretched. A sidelong glance at the woman gave Jessie no clues as to her state of mind.

Vicky finally broke her uncharacteristic lull. "Thank goodness we didn't get the hordes of grasshoppers that we had in 'seventy-four. Those pests wiped out every bit of wheat, sorghum, and corn that year."

"Yes, we're lucky." Too bad her good fortune didn't apply

to other areas. Asleep in her arms, Marley Rose stirred. The bloom in the child's cheeks measured Jessie's remaining time in Tranquility.

A short distance away, Duel stopped for a drink of water from the bucket she'd taken them. Sweat dripped from his face. Her own temperature rose when he shot her his famous grin before he emptied the bucket over his head. That opened an opportunity to be near him, for the men would definitely need more.

"Jessie?"

Her name softly spoken drew her attention back to Vicky. The woman placed a hand on her shoulder.

"I knew when you first came that something bad had happened to you. All those bruises, your busted lip. I knew someone had beaten you within an inch of your life." Vicky stopped. Jessie waited, not knowing where her sister-in-law was headed.

"Though I've driven Roy to wit's end, he's never once laid a hand to me in anger, so I can't profess to know what it's like." She went on. "It's a terrible thing for a woman. Guess what I'm tryin' to say is I can't blame you for what you did. Who knows? Had I been in your shoes I probably would've shot the man too."

Jessie turned to face Vicky. She was surprised to find tears in the woman's eyes. The afternoon heat seemed tepid in contrast to the warm hug her sister-in-law gave her.

"You don't know how much that means to me." Jessie swallowed, counting her blessings that fate led her in the right direction. The McClains had hearts as big as the Texas sky.

"Six months ago I didn't even know you. Now, I can't imagine our family without you." Vicky's voice broke. "You've given my brother reason to live again. He loves you with every breath he takes. Shoot, I love you like a sister."

Their hugging awoke Marley Rose. She stared at them with big, round eyes.

"Vicky, will you—"

"You don't even have to ask." The woman interrupted in

true Vicky fashion. "I'll watch over this precious little girl till you get back. An' don't think for a moment I'm gonna let her forget her mama."

Till she got back. That bit of optimism broke the tiny thread holding her emotions together. Despite her resolve to be strong, Jessie broke under the strain. She sobbed against Vicky's shoulder.

"If things happen that prevent my returning, I'll always remember you. You're a saint, Vicky. Thank you."

The noise of a team of horses pulling a wagon suddenly shattered the quiet afternoon. Jessie dried her eyes and watched as the horses trotted past them straight to the field. The driver seemed familiar, yet the quick glimpse didn't allow for recognition. A huge contraption sat in the bed of the wagon.

"It's Hampton Pierson," Vicky said.

"Oh dear." Jessie's stomach swirled in alarm. She transferred Marley to Vicky's arms, then hurried to stop Duel from doing something regrettable.

Within earshot, she winced. Steel punctuated Duel's clipped warning. "Pierson, I warned you to keep off my property. You're not wanted—"

"Hear me out, McClain." Hampton climbed down, unbothered by Duel's drawn fists.

Breathing hard from her sprint, Jessie reached his side and held his arm tightly.

"Two seconds. And you better talk fast."

"You have good reason to hate my guts, McClain. I've been a fool and I wouldn't blame you if you knocked me into the next county." Sincerity rang in Hampton's statement. Although he clearly didn't relish this meeting, he stood his ground. Jessie admired the dapper man for that.

"Then why the devil are you here?" The question rumbled in Duel's throat like muffled thunder.

"Want a chance to do what's right's all. I realized I've acted a complete idiot. I apologize, ma'am, for my disrespect." He lifted his hat toward Jessie.

"Thank you, Mr. Pierson." Her grip on Duel's arm loosened. "I accept your apology."

"Brought my McCormick Reaper. Don't know what your hurry is in cuttin' your sorghum. I do know this—you wouldn't harvest this early without good reason. Wanna do the right thing by you, neighbor to neighbor."

Still Duel hesitated. Of all the McClains, Duel forgave least easily. She called it fierce mule-headedness.

"Come on, son," Walt urged. "You can shave off two weeks usin' the reaper. Ain't that more important than your danged pride?"

Within the hour, the men had the reaper unloaded. From her vantage point through the kitchen window, Jessie watched the horses pull the innovative marvel through the stalks of sorghum.

A festive spirit of sorts pervaded that night over supper. Egged on by her grandpa's teasing, Marley Rose jabbered nonstop from her seat at the table. Duel seemed lighter of heart than she'd seen him since Luke's sudden reappearance.

That is, until his brother made an announcement. "Marley Rose has recovered. We'll leave tomorrow, Jessie."

Jessie's fork clattered noisily onto her plate. A cold quiet slammed into her chest. Duel almost choked on a mouthful of food.

"Damn! Can't you give us a few more days?"

"Sorry, Duel. Wish I could. Way I figure it, now that you have the reaper, you'll have time to sell the wheat and get that lawyer by the time we make it to El Paso." Luke looked as miserable as she felt. The war inside him still raged. No reason to make it harder on him.

"Duel, it's time." She placed her hand atop her beloved's on the table where it had fallen. "We knew we didn't have forever. I'm ready to get it over with and accept the consequences."

"That's the spirit, girl." Walt wiped his mouth with his handkerchief. The action took longer than needed. Jessie suspected he hid the tremble of his lip she'd glimpsed. The man had certainly won her admiration and respect.

"Don't expect me to like it," Duel grumbled at his brother. "Ever since we were kids you've always busted a gut to try to best me."

A red flush spread over Luke's face. "It's not about who's toughest, or oldest . . . or best."

"Don't do this, Duel." Jessie hurried to keep the peace. A rift like this could split a family down the middle. She refused to be the cause of such a calamity. "Luke has a sworn duty to uphold the laws. We can't interfere with that."

"Boys, listen to her. Long ago your grandpa said if a storm cloud's a hangin' over your head, it's better to let it go ahead an' rain. Storm'll be over with that much quicker."

Jessie gathered her hope, which had fallen somewhere in the vicinity of her feet. "Your father's right. The sooner I put this behind me the sooner I can get back here and we can get on with our lives."

At least she prayed for that outcome. She stilled the ugly whispers in the back of her mind. The ones that knew it would take a miracle.

Morning dawned before sleep came. Jessie lay soaking up all the sights and sounds she might not witness again. She couldn't waste one second of her precious time to the unconscious.

Duel mumbled and rolled over to face her. Every line, every feature of his face she sketched on the canvas of her memory. Careful not to awaken him, she reached out to trace the outline of the generous mouth that fit hers so well.

"It's not too late," he'd whispered in the darkness. "We'll saddle Preacher. By daylight we could be far away from here."

She'd stared at him long and hard, desperately wanting to go with him. "I don't know if you want that kind of life, but I can't live looking over my shoulder, wondering when someone will find me. Surely you want better for Marley Rose."

He'd held her tenderly. "I hate it when you're right. Running is no kind of life. We'll do this the proper way."

"Not that you don't tempt me, my dearest." She'd cloaked her despair in soul-stirring kisses. That had led to lovemaking that made all their previous times seem like virginal courting.

Now radiance through the window cast a golden hue across his tanned face. It would tear her heart out when she left the farm and the people she loved.

"Rest well, my glorious knight." She kissed him softly and climbed from his side. A lot remained for her to do before she rode from the man who had given her self-worth.

His rough chambray shirt lay on the floor where Duel had flung it in his haste. Lifting it, she hugged it to her face and breathed the fragrance of her love. One more item to relegate to memory.

Yet the action was her undoing. A sob rose as she slipped her arms into sleeves that swallowed her and pulled the fabric around her naked bosom.

Duel awakened and reached out for her. She fell into his embrace. "Caught you trying to steal my clothes."

"If that makes me a thief, I'm not sorry." She snuggled tightly against him, thankful that destiny led her to his campfire that night. At least she could meet her fate having known true love. "I'm trying to be strong. It's so hard."

"You can be strong later." Light kisses trailed across her eyelids, her nose and mouth. "Right now, you don't have to be anything except my wife."

Delightful tingles leapfrogged up her spine as he burrowed past the clothing to her heaving breasts. Eagerly, he cajoled the rosy tips to attention and seduced each between his lips.

Marley Rose stirred restlessly, reminding Jessie of other obligations.

"We shouldn't do this now." She made a feeble effort to nudge him away but found she lacked both the heart and the will to deny him the treat he'd found. Faint, mewling noises came from her throat as waves of pleasure ebbed and flowed. Already a thin layer of moisture covered her skin.

Had she found her voice, protesting would've been the last thing on her mind. A few tugs and the shirt fell to the floor.

She arched and pulled him even closer, reveling in the rich texture of his hair. She'd never known such a man or this kind of love. Life didn't play fair. And it certainly had no sense of humor. It seemed strange to give her this great gift if she couldn't keep it.

Duel shifted and she took advantage, reaching between them. His hardness throbbed against her palm in rhythm with his heartbeat.

"You're playing with fire, Jess. Know it?" The tortured whisper came from above as he stretched his length on hers.

She returned his steady gaze and guided him to the wet opening. Oh yes, she certainly hoped so.

"My love, my Jess." He exhaled sharply as he slipped inside.

Jessie marveled at his control. The agonizing, slow descent must aid a man in savoring every moment. Yet she found herself impatient. She wanted, no welcomed, the freedom of wild, unrestrained mating, to feel his fullness to the depth of her being. It seemed the only way to quiet this insatiable craving.

Or to make the memory so vivid it would carry her into eternity. . . .

She wrapped her legs around his bare backside. Every sensual thought and desire exploded when he filled her in a rush.

Don't think, don't move, don't breathe. Simply float. This must be what it feels like to die. Incredibly happy and free. No pain, only joy. Wave after wave crashed until she lay limp, trying to slow the mad heaving of her chest.

A light, feathery touch brushed her lips. She opened her eyes. His sorrow-filled gaze burned into her soul.

"Duel?"

"We've but barely begun this love of ours." He put his cheek to hers. "How can I let Luke take you from me?"

"The choice isn't yours to make."

"Damn! Not sure I can. It hurts to breathe."

"We both knew I couldn't stay from the start." She pulled from his grasp. "We have to get dressed now. It's time."

And if she didn't, she might accept his foolish notion that running would solve all their problems because each breath caused excruciating pain beyond any she'd ever known.

He sighed. "Ahhh darlin', I reckon that's the way of things. But I hate like hell to let you go."

Luke sat astride his horse, holding the reins of a mare he'd borrowed from Roy for Jessie's use. The day had turned cloudy and cool, a fitting accompaniment for Duel's mood. No sunshine or rainbows this day.

Standing beside him with tears sparkling in her eyes, Vicky held Marley Rose. Horrible pain clogged his airway, his chest hurt with wanting as Jessie kissed the child who called her "Mama."

"Be good, little one. Mind your Aunt Vicky. I'll be back before you know it."

He knew the great cost of her composure. Jessie wouldn't break down until she was out of range.

"Mama? Mine Mama!" With a sixth sense that children sometimes had, Marley seemed to know impending tragedy. The child grabbed Jessie's neck in a furious grip.

"Take her in the house, Vicky. Don't let her see me leave." Finally, she pried the little fingers loose. Spinning, she buried her face in Duel's shoulder.

"Don't worry, darlin'." He smoothed the silky auburn length that she'd simply tied back with a ribbon. The hairstyle made her appear more an innocent young maid rather than a wanted criminal. "We'll take good care of Two Bit and I'll see you soon as I finish here and get you a lawyer. It won't be more'n two weeks. I promise."

Though she refused to let herself cry, her body trembled like a slender reed in a stiff gale. He held her close for one last time while he shot his brother a stabbing glare.

"I'll hold you responsible if anything happens to her, little brother." The promise came stiffly, his voice thick.

Luke met his threatening gaze calmly. "It won't," he answered shortly, then, "For what it's worth, I hate—"

"Spare me your apology." With watery vision, he looked down at Jess, found her lips, and drank deeply.

"Duel, thank you for showing me what real love is," she breathed after he released her. "I never would've known."

"I'll be with you, darlin'." His hand shook as he laid it over her heart. "In here. When you're scared and alone, just close your eyes and listen. I'll be there."

The horse must've moved, because her foot missed the stirrup and she stumbled. Or the blame could've lain with the moisture glimmering in her eyes. Either way, Duel lifted her up, his hands lingering on her soft curves, loathe to turn her loose. Afraid if he did, he might never see her again. The thought of that made his blood run cold.

"It's gonna work out, Jess." Just how he didn't know. If Tom Parker refused to hear him out, their chances were slim to none. It would take the skills of such a man to clear his lady's name. Still, he couldn't let Jessie sense his doubts. "I know in my heart."

"I love you, Duel."

Her quivering bottom lip shattered his stoic determination. Only Luke's nudge in his mount's ribs saved Duel from pulling her down and daring his lawman brother to stop him.

Before the horses made two steps, the sudden flash of her wrapped in his shirt that morning prodded his memory. Both of their scents, the naked flesh of each had married within the folds of this very clothing.

"Wait! I forgot something."

Chapter Twenty-seven

Luke reined to a stop. "What now?"

Duel ignored his brother's impatience and jerked the shirt off his back, almost ripping the buttons in his haste.

"Take this with you." He stuffed the item into Jessie's saddlebags. "Since I can't go with you, I'm sending the next best thing—a piece of me to keep. When you're scared . . ."

His sudden action poked a hole in the dam of her brave front. Tears streaming down her cheeks prevented her from replying. She touched her fingers to her lips, then leaned down to lay them on his.

Yellow Dog whined pitifully until they vanished from sight. Wave upon wave of sorrow crashed over him. His knees buckled under the weight. Feeling more helpless than he had in a long while, he stared blindly until the last particle of dust settled back to the ground. Emptiness surrounded him. No falling grains of sand to break the silence. The hourglass had run dry.

Just when he reached his lowest point, a wet tongue licked his fingers, dragging his attention from the deserted road. He looked down. Yellow Dog nuzzled the hand that hung limply by Duel's side.

"Hey, boy." The animal's affection came unexpected, yet it brought strange comfort. That Yellow Dog had overcome his fear of him at that moment seemed remarkable.

He fell to his knees and stroked the soft fur. "She'll be back, I promise."

How he'd deliver on that, he hadn't the foggiest notion. With nothing but bruised faith and hope in his heart, he turned to the fields.

"Gotta get busy, boy. Time's a wasting."

Yellow Dog trotted dutifully by his side as he harnessed the team of horses Hampton Pierson had left overnight for the McCormick Reaper.

Working night and day, Duel had finished cutting the grain in four days. He paid no attention to his aching bones or the need for sleep. Aware solely of the minutes clicking inside his head, he'd driven himself relentlessly.

Now, with barely two hundred dollars in his pocket, he shifted Marley Rose to his left arm. He'd stood outside the Travis Hotel for what seemed an eternity.

Waiting.

The man he'd come to Austin to see hadn't passed in or out. He supposed that some, most assuredly including the man for whom he waited, would call him chicken. Facing Tom Parker would take all his backbone and then some, for the man had a sharp tongue. Fire and brimstone took on new meaning when the retired judge spoke his mind.

"Papa?" Marley Rose patted the back of his neck as if sympathizing.

Perhaps the child gave willingly of the love and comfort she herself sorely needed. It broke his heart to hear her crying in her sleep, calling for her mama.

That's why he didn't correct her on the name she insisted on calling him. Sudden events had knocked her secure world awry. Sure as the sun rose, the little darlin' grieved for the only mother she remembered.

"Don't worry, Two Bit. I can do this for Jessie's sake."

"Mama?"

"Yes, little darlin'. For your mama."

A low growl rumbled deep in the throat of the animal beside him, reminding him of Yellow Dog's presence. Strangest thing. When he mounted Preacher and rode off from the farm with Marley Rose in his lap, the dog had trotted right alongside. He'd expected that after a mile or two the animal would turn back. But he hadn't. After a full day of it, he knew Yellow Dog meant to accompany him. The poor thing had walked beside them the entire distance.

Needless to say, it thrilled Marley to have her 'Boobie' come along. The child kept up a stream of conversation to the dog in her own special language, which he seemed to understand. Mixed with an occasional growl, the dog yipped back at her.

Now, several passersby eyed them curiously, giving the animal a wide berth.

"Easy, boy." Duel knelt and rubbed Yellow Dog's head. "Ain't gonna get us what we need with you threatening to latch on to someone by the neck." He stared deep into the soulful brown eyes. "You hafta stay out here. The sign on the hotel says no dogs allowed."

Yellow Dog whined and licked his hand. "And no biting, understand?"

Duel stood, took a deep breath, and pushed through the hotel doors.

Following the clerk's directions, he quickly found Room 201. Duel rapped, and listened intently for sounds on the other side. He heard nothing, no footsteps approaching, merely silence. That's why he jumped when the door abruptly opened. He faced the man who blamed him for his daughter's death.

"You!" Tom Parker spat the word as if it had left a bitter taste on his tongue. Parker had aged, and the cane on which the man leaned heavily added a frailty that Duel had never noticed. "I have nothing to say to you, Duel McClain."

Before the judge could slam the door in his face, Duel quickly stuck out his foot, blocking it.

"Give me one minute, sir. Then, if you still want me to leave, you'll never hear from me again." The hurried speech left him short of breath. Fear that the man would refuse to listen ate a hole in his gut.

Not bothering to reply, Tom Parker hesitated, then motioned them inside with a quick nod.

The plush quarters seemed appropriate for the man who wore luxury like a second layer of skin. A carpeted sitting room with soft leather chairs greeted him. And beyond through a doorway, a gigantic canopied bed awaited.

The judge stiffly pointed to a chair, which Duel gratefully took before he lost his nerve and bolted. Parker sat opposite him, leaning his cane—a polished stick of brown wood topped with a gold handle—against the chair.

The man's hawkish gaze pierced Duel's thick armor. Ill at ease, he held Marley Rose on his lap and tried to curtail her squirming. Now that he had the judge's attention, he didn't know where to begin. What did one say to a man who despised the ground you walked on?

"Why did you come, knowing the way I feel?"

"An extreme matter of a personal nature." He took a deep breath and plunged. "I've come to hire your services, sir."

"How dare you! After everything that's happened, I'm stunned that you have the gall to ask for my help—in any matter." Parker's eyes flashed. "My opinion of you hasn't changed."

A tic developed in Duel's jaw as he tried to swallow his anger. "Didn't reckon it had. But I need some lawyering and I came for the best. You're the finest in Texas."

Marley Rose slid from Duel's lap to the thick carpet where she stretched out. The smile on her face told him she enjoyed the softness. A far cry from the minimal comforts of the farm house. Sharp guilt stabbed his conscience.

"You must've been out in the sun too long. Won't do it. Not for any good-for-nothing gunslinger, not for anything—"

"It's not for me, sir. It's for this little girl." His jaw ached from the tense clenching of his teeth. "No matter what you think of me, can't you at least have mercy on a child's misery?"

Marley sat up, evidently sensing the two men were discussing her. Her round brown eyes stared from one to the other.

"She yours?"

"Not in the normal way, but I suppose you'd say she belongs to me. Leastwise, I'm caring for her."

"More than you did for your wife and son."

Duel glared at the man whose hate ran deeper than the Colorado.

"Sir, can't we carry on a conversation for two minutes without you bringing up the past? Doesn't change anything to keep harping on it."

"Might be a long time ago to you, McClain, but for me it happened only yesterday." The man answered tersely.

"Papa?" Marley Rose held out her hand to Duel.

"Not 'Papa'. Duel, darlin'." He reminded her gently in light of the scared look pasted on her face. "Judge, refuse me all you want, but Marley Rose has no one in the world 'cept me and Jess. Her father wagered her in a poker game, and her mother didn't want to fight hard enough to keep her. Now she's been stripped from the arms of the woman she calls 'mama.' You tell me how much this child has to give up before she's even reached her second birthday."

"Not my affair. Can't cure all the ills of the world."

"No, but you can darn sure give an innocent woman a fighting chance," he spat back.

"Leave it to you to be hooked up with a nefarious woman. You married to her?"

"Jessie's the finest woman I know! I take offense to you speaking of her in that tone of voice. And yes, she's my wife." He clenched his fist tight. His restraint came with a price, for he longed to knock Tom Parker from his sanctimonious high horse.

"Mine Mama." Marley Rose puckered her lip to cry.

He lifted her to his lap. "It's all right, Two Bit. We'll find another lawyer for your mama. There's more than one in this town."

Instead of Marley snuggling in the security of his arms, she pushed away and walked the short distance to peer up at the judge.

Duel's heart ached for the child's confusion. She didn't understand the harsh words, but she surely must feel the strained atmosphere. Right now he feared for what Parker might say, or do, to her. The man seemed hell bent on destroying his life.

The way he saw it he'd made two mistakes—one in wasting time coming to Austin, the other in thinking he could convince his former father-in-law to help him. Both seemed a lost cause. Two hundred dollars couldn't touch the services of the more flamboyant but capable lawyers. Even so, he'd beg if it came to that. He couldn't live with himself if he let Jess down.

Rising to his full height, he hoped to scoop the girl up before she caught Parker's wrath.

"I made a mistake in coming here. A bigger one in thinking you cared more about justice than you did about revenge. We'll be going, Judge."

In stunned silence, Duel watched Marley crawl into the man's lap. What surprised him more was that Judge Parker didn't rebuff her or reach out to stop the child.

Once in the man's lap, Marley Rose laid her small hand on his chest and declared, "Mine G'anpa."

At first Tom Parker stared at her as if she was some hideous creature from a nightmare. Then slowly, a rare smile broke, transforming the deep wrinkles into lines of laughter.

"What's your hurry, son? Sit down."

* * *

Bleak gray walls stared back at Jessie. She wanted to cry, the pain was so intense. Before her legs buckled, she sank rigidly to the horsehair mattress stretched upon a wooden frame.

"I'm sorry, Jessie," Luke had declared more than once on the way to El Paso.

She knew he meant it, for she had seen the battle waging in him. Doing his duty hadn't come easy this time around.

"I love being a Ranger, you know. Helping in the fight to civilize this state." The stars overhead had been extra bright that night. They matched the sparkle in Luke's eyes when he talked of his great love of law work.

Jessie reckoned his signing on with the Texas Rangers was a lot like a man receiving a calling from God to preach. Luke's commitment was no less sacred.

The agony in the younger McClain's voice echoed her own searing pain. "Dad-blasted! Even though I know in my heart you had good reason for what you did, I have to bring you in. There has to be a trial. That's the way of it."

"I know," she answered softly, laying her hand over his. "You have no choice. I don't hold you to blame."

"But I didn't particularly wanna be the one to destroy my own brother. We might have our disagreements now and again, but I love Duel."

She didn't take it amiss that he worried more about hurting his brother than he did about her. It should be this way.

"I can see that, Luke. You're family despite everything."

"You betcha." He stretched out on his bedroll and put his hand beneath his head. "Don't think Duel shares that opinion."

"He's scared. Can't see how all this is going to come out." Neither did she. A cold stiffness had spread upward from the soles of her feet to form an icy tomb around her heart.

Luke turned his head slightly to her then. Compassion and goodness had shown in his face. "You're some kind of woman, Jessie, and I'm proud to have you for a sister-in-law. I'll help you all I can. You can depend on that."

* * *

They rode into El Paso two weeks to the day after leaving Tranquility. In that time Jessie sought to prepare herself.

"I apologize fer the 'commodations, Miz Foltry . . . um, I mean, Miz McClain." Bart Daniels chewed on the stubby end of a cigar.

The loud click of the lock might as well have signaled the closing to the gates of Hell for all the comfort it gave Jessie.

No need to wonder anymore what that place was like because she was there. Bleak didn't begin to tell the story.

Though she'd never had reason to speak directly to Sheriff Daniels, she'd seen him around El Paso in those rare instances when Jeremiah had brought her to town. Folks had extolled Daniels' uncommon fairness in matters pertaining to his job.

Yet Jessie got the impression the quality didn't end with his duties, it extended directly to the man. He would be someone to have on your side.

The strangling in her throat prevented her from answering. The open metal bars offered no privacy. She felt as exposed and violated as she had when Jeremiah took his liberties.

"Ain't no place fer a lady, Luke." Bart shook his head sadly. "No siree. Gives me a case of sour stomach."

"Luke?" She couldn't stop the quiver in her voice. "I hate to . . . I know a person in my circumstances doesn't have the right to ask for favors." The words stumbled over her tongue. "But would you—"

"Don't worry, Jessie. I'll be right here till Duel comes." Luke's gentle assurance capped the nausea that had risen. "Ain't going nowhere. Damn sure ain't no one gonna take you."

"Thanks, Luke." The upheaval in her stomach didn't leave. She needed one more favor. "Another thing—please visit my mother and ask her to stay away."

"I don't understand. Your mother would be someone to talk to, to draw comfort from in your time of need."

"I'm too ashamed. One way or another, I'll soon be gone.

My mother has to live here with her friends and acquaintances. It's better this way, Luke."

"All right. Now, try and get some sleep. Duel will nail my hide to the wall if you have dark circles under your eyes when he comes."

Her frightened gaze followed him to the chair in front of the sheriff's desk, watched him prop it lazily back against the wall with two legs off the floor. Somehow she felt safer and not nearly so lost. She twisted the gold band on her finger and thought of the night Duel had given the precious ring to her.

What were he and Marley Rose doing? How long would it be until she saw them again?

"Now, tell me what crime they've charged this little one's mama with." Judge Parker jiggled Marley Rose on his knee.

Duel cleared his throat. "Murder, sir."

"The Devil you say!"

"There are some who would say it was justified." He took the two hundred dollars from his pocket. "Not saying it'll be easy, Judge. That's why I'm paying for your services."

Tom Parker didn't reach for the stack of bills Duel laid on the low table in the center of the room. In fact, the man didn't even acknowledge their presence.

"Who'd she send to glory?"

Duel didn't hesitate. "Her husband, sir."

One thing he learned a long time ago about Parker. The man valued the truth, the whole truth, and nothing but. He dealt with cold, hard facts no matter how ugly.

"Sam Hill!" The judge swung his attention to Duel and he found himself sweating under the riveting fix. "You think she deserves my help? I'm a lawyer, not a magician."

Biting back the sharp retort on the edge of his tongue, Duel kept his anger in check. The diamond brand surrounded by angry, puckered skin lunged from memory like a ferocious cat.

Hell yes! And, she deserved a protector, even if that came in the shape of a reformed bounty hunter.

"Wouldn't trust her life with anyone else but you, Judge. Despite our differences I know you to be a fair and honest man." Emotion suddenly took his voice and the rest came out nothing louder than a whisper. "I love her with all my heart and soul. Jess gave me reason to live when I wanted to die."

A pained expression swept across Tom Parker's face. "Then, son, guess we'd better cut to the chase. Tell me everything and don't leave out a single detail."

Chapter Twenty-eight

"Hey, girlie!" a voice called through the high, barred window in Jessie's cell.

She flattened against the wall, clutching Duel's shirt to her heaving bosom. Ugly taunting outside raised her fear several notches. She prayed Luke and Sheriff Daniels would get back soon. Both lawmen had lit out after a young boy brought news of a shooting in one of El Paso's many saloons.

"Come over to the window, Miz Foltry. Ain't gonna hurt you none. Jus' wanna talk."

That sinister voice was familiar. She couldn't swear, but it sounded like Pete Morgan, Jeremiah's closest friend. The one she'd turned the pistol on when the man tried to grab her that fateful night.

Whatever this mob's intentions, she knew it didn't bode well for her. From the blackness, arms shot through the bars, grasping at air. She pressed into the cell wall. She hoped the square window measured too small for a man's girth. For if they did remove the bars somehow . . . God help her.

Her chest hammered with sheer terror, and Jeremiah's

sneering words echoed in her head. *You're nothing to me. With a snap of my fingers I can squash you like a bug. And the beauty of it is that no one can stop me.*

"Keep looking forward," she whispered Duel's words.

Uncontrollable tremors shook her. *Please let Luke and the sheriff return before things reach a more critical stage.*

Holding Duel's shirt to her face, she breathed his fragrance. The smell of him enveloped her. She tried to imagine the feel of his arms around her. Behind tightly clenched eyes, she pulled his face into view. The proud, chiseled features of her beloved.

"I'll be with you, darlin'. In your heart. When you're scared and alone, just close your eyes and listen. I'll be there." Those parting words comforted her now.

As she stood remembering, an unfamiliar noise came. Her eyes flew open. A wad of spit glistened on the floor a few feet away.

While she speculated on the origin, another wet glob slingshotted, landing near the first. Raucous laughter brought out her anger. These scum were of Jeremiah's ilk, taking pleasure in tormenting helpless beings. *Hurry, Luke,* she prayed.

"Do you men have a license for loitering?" Luke's soft twang from beyond the window brought immeasurable relief.

"Don't need no license."

"You do now." A deadly warning lurked behind Luke's reply.

"One Ranger against the six o' us? Gonna arrest us all?"

Then she heard the sheriff's familiar gravel. "I'm thinkin' we can handle the job, Morgan. Now, break up the party or I'll arrest the lot of you fer not only loiterin' but spittin' on public property."

"Jus' paying your jailbird a call, Sheriff. No harm in that. After all, the slut deserves it for killin' Jeremiah."

The wall outside shook violently as something slammed against it. Jessie could only imagine the cause. However, the grunt that followed and Luke's terse threat confirmed her suspicions.

"I ever hear you use that word again, you're a dead man, mister."

"Jus' calling a spade a spade's all."

A split second later, the grunt turned uglier. Sounds of misery underscored the guttural noises.

"If I catch you spitting into her cell again, I'll rip off your arms and feed 'em to the mangy curs that roam the streets. You got that?"

"You silver-tongued devil, Luke." Jessie could hear, rather than see, the broad grin that must cover Sheriff Daniel's face. "Stole the words right outta my mouth. Now, boys, that goes for any of you yahoos who come within ten feet of my jail."

Grumbling followed, but the group seemed to take the advice to heart. Shuffling footsteps moved away from her window. She collapsed onto the narrow cot.

However, one man shot parting words that made her freeze. "I'll get the rest o' this town together an' we'll be back. Only next time it'll be to hang the murderin' witch."

"Better get you an army 'cause you'll need it. The woman will have a fair trial or my name's not Luke McClain."

Oh, God. They meant to take her out of jail and string her up like a piece of meat. No one could keep her safe. Luke and the sheriff couldn't hold off the entire town.

A few moments passed before Luke and the sheriff came inside. Sheriff Daniels' normally placid complexion had turned two shades of red.

"Spittin' in my jail. Threatening to lynch my prisoner. Great day in the morning!"

Luke didn't break his stride until he had the iron door unlocked. Concern cast a pall on his young features.

"You all right, Jessie?"

She nodded, not trusting her voice. Panic rippled as though over rigid bumps of a washboard. Each thud had reaffirmed the possibility that she might not live to see her husband and little girl again. Nothing assured her tomorrow's sunrise would come.

He held out his arms. "Come here."

She flew into the haven. He wasn't Duel, but he was family and his touch comforted.

"I'm not gonna let anything happen to you, Jessie. You believe that I'm not gonna let that mob in here, don't you?"

"Yes," she whispered.

Yet deep inside doubts bubbled like fermented yeast. He'd do his best to keep her from harm, that was a given. After all he came from the same strong cloth as her husband.

But could two good men stop an enraged mob bent on revenge?

"The circuit judge'll be here in three days, Jessie. Wonder what in the devil's keeping Duel."

Her stomach lurched. If Luke worried . . .

"Do you suppose he had trouble?"

"I know my brother and he'd be here unless he hit a snag."

Duel hadn't deserted her. He wouldn't. He'd promised to come. Still, a small voice nagged. *Why should he waste good money on a losing cause? They'll hang you in the end anyway.*

"I talked to your ma like I promised."

Luke's unease was plain to see. He'd clearly opposed her wishes.

"Did you make her understand?"

"Aw, Jessie, it made her cry. I almost bawled myself. Me a grown man. Don't ever ask me to do anything like that again."

"I won't," she murmured through stiff lips.

She'd arrived at the decision after much soul-searching. A selfish part of her cried for her mother's embrace. If she could just feel the warmth of her mother's touch one more time . . . But her head told her to spare Phoebe Sutton the townsfolk's retribution.

Bart Daniels kicked on the door to the jail for Luke to let him in. Since hearing rumors of a forming lynch mob, they kept the door locked.

"A durn turtle's slow, Luke. Jessie's food'll be colder than kraut."

"Sit steady in the boat, you old coot." Luke slid the bolt. "And what in the heck would you know about kraut?"

Bart's porcupine mustache bristled. "More'n you. For your information, my ma was a full-blood German. Pay attention sometime and you might learn a thing or two."

"Peas n' taters! Always spouting about something. Let me have Jessie's food. After that walk, you most likely need to sit down and rest your bones a spell."

"Ain't a dad-burned thing wrong with me. An' I'm not too old to whip some of that sass outta you either."

The affectionate banter between the two men lifted Jessie temporarily from the doldrums. Her affection for Luke grew. He saw the old sheriff's value and respected the man.

Luke's deep caring for her welfare went beyond mere words. For instance, he'd rigged some blankets around her cell that she could pull shut when she wanted privacy. Duel and Luke shared more than simply a last name.

Then, when you threw the sheriff onto the pile, the odds in her favor grew. She harbored no doubt. Sheriff Daniels and Luke would lay their lives on the line to keep her safe. For the first time since she'd arrived in El Paso, she didn't tremble inside. She accepted the warm plate of food.

"Thank you, Luke."

The man returned her fleeting smile and winked. "Don't worry about Duel. He'll come soon."

"Yes, you're absolutely right." She lifted the blue checkered cloth that covered the plate. The red beans and cornbread smelled good, only she wasn't hungry. Her appetite had vanished when she left Tranquility.

"Think we have a mess of trouble, Luke." Bart peeked through the curtained front window.

Light from burning flares first entered the jailhouse as dancing shadows, twisting on the walls. Jessie stared at the kaleidoscope of color in fascination. The red glares became as bright as the midnight sun, while a loud babble outside grew to a roar.

"Reckon how many?" Luke jerked rifles off a rack on the wall and began shoving cartridges into them.

"Can't say."

"What's happening?" Fear put the sharp tone in her voice.

"Probably some liquored-up folks spoiling for a fight. Don't worry, we'll handle it, Jess."

"Open up, Sheriff. Got half the town out here. We want the woman."

"Over my dead body, you law-breakin' varmints." Bart broke a corner glass pane and propped the rifle barrel on the wood. "All of you go home 'fore someone gits hurt."

"Through you or over you, makes no never mind to us. We mean to see justice done." The determined answer echoed through her cell. Like the fingers of death, they reached inside and closed around her throat, making it hard to breathe.

No one had to tell her justice meant swinging from the end of a rope. The blood drained from her face. She moved to crouch on the floor against the wall. Lucky for her she did, for a rock hurtled into the space she'd just occupied. This came from the barred window in her cell.

They had the jail surrounded!

"Jessie Foltry, you're a murderin' tramp!"

"Yeah, we'll make you pay for what you done."

"Burn in Hell, Jessie Foltry."

The threats continued with no sign of abating. This angry mob had become inflamed.

From amid the chaos, shots rang out. Bullets whizzed past the lawmen's heads. Breaking glass flew. Jessie stuck her fingers in her ears and watched in horror as Luke and Bart returned fire. Thank goodness both still stood after the initial skirmish.

"Let's burn 'em out!" shouted a voice during a momentary lull.

"You boys burn the jail and you'll have every Texas Ranger in the state riding down here!" Luke didn't budge from his lookout. He kept his rifle aimed and Jessie knew he'd not give her up without a fierce fight. Not because she'd married his brother, but because he lived and breathed duty and honor.

"I'd pay a mind to him if'n I was you. Wanna step into a den of rat'lers you just go right on ahead and light that fire."

Silence met the sheriff's warning. Perhaps he'd gotten through to them. She prayed.

"The citizens of this town have the right to defend it against murderin' harlots. All we want is justice. Bible says an eye for an eye."

So much for hoping they'd seen reason. These men seemed determined to administer their brand of revenge. The weight on her chest grew heavier until it threatened to choke her.

"You'll get your justice," Luke shot back. "This woman is gonna get a fair trial. That's the law."

"Only two o' you agin' fifty o' us," a voice called.

"Good enough odds if you ask me!" The sudden deep timbre released a swirl of excitement in her. She'd never forget that voice if she lived to be a hundred. "Besides, me and this Schofield are thinking of evening things a bit."

Could it be true? Maybe she'd only imagined it.

"Duel, that you?" Luke called.

"Yeah, brother, it's me."

The air Jessie had kept at bay expelled in a rush. He was here. He'd come! Her promise-keeper hadn't forsaken her.

Yet now that he'd arrived, would the mob kill him? After all, he stood out there among them.

"That woman in there that you're so all fired anxious to string up is my wife. I'll kill any man here who tries to do her harm."

Dead silence ensued. Then Jessie listened to the loud murmurs.

"That's Duel McClain!"

"I heard tell o' his skill with a forty-five."

"Me, too. Ain't fool enough to go up agin' him."

"I ain't aiming to git myself killed."

From the sound of it, the mob was dispersing. She'd known of Duel's bounty-hunting past, but she never dreamed he'd forged such a formidable reputation. Simply his name alone put the fear of God into this unruly group. This was a different side of the kind, compassionate man she'd grown to love.

Time stood still as she waited for the first glimpse of her beloved. Evidently, he wanted to make sure the crowd scattered before he let down his guard and came inside.

Anxious, she smoothed back her hair and shook the wrinkles from her skirt. She must look a sight.

Sheriff Daniels unbolted the door. Luke stepped outside to greet his brother.

Suddenly, the click of paws on the wooden floor drew her attention downward.

"Yellow Dog!"

Before she could gather her composure, Duel's large frame filled the doorway. Her throat constricted and tears filled her eyes. She didn't remember him being so tanned. Or quite so tall. Or quite so dangerous. No wonder he'd sent the crowd home. He was a vision of power and tenderness all wrapped up in one.

He had come.

Chapter Twenty-nine

A telltale wetness in his lady's blue eyes captured Duel's attention first. The sparkling orbs glistened, beacons of light from a colorless face.

His inadequacy as protector of the one he loved rolled around in his belly like a gut full of buckshot. He should've taken her and Marley Rose so far away no one, not even Luke, could've found them. High up in the Rocky Mountains lurked many hiding places.

But he hadn't. The heavy bars between them told more than words that he'd let her down. He removed his hat and twirled it between his hands.

Do you, Duel, promise to protect, to cherish her, to keep Jessie in sickness and in health, as long as ye both shall live, so help you God?

Damn! He'd broken every vow he'd made when they stood before the preacher. How could a man claim to cherish his wife if he hadn't protected her? And the sickness and health part—right now she didn't appear too healthy.

When his gaze traveled past her face, he noticed how frail,

almost gaunt she'd become. Her clothes hung on her frame, her once lush curves no longer rounded. He'd failed her in every way that mattered. Now, she couldn't help but see the mistake she'd made in taking up with a man like him. Guilt forced away his scrutiny until the toes of his boots slid into focus.

"You came!" Jessie's breathless declaration stirred his remorse until it became a frothy foam. "I was worried, afraid something had happened."

"Or that I changed my mind?" There, he might as well say what she already thought. He stopped the hat-twirling and held the worn Stetson in a steel grip. Her tone told him what he knew he'd find written on her face if he dared look up.

"But you didn't."

From the corner of his eye, he watched her hands slide from the iron bars that separated them. His jaw clenched.

"Nope."

"You're not that kind."

Hope fluttered on bruised, battered wings. Maybe Jessie wasn't disappointed in him after all. Maybe she didn't regret claiming his name. Maybe she could find a reason to return the love he felt for her. Suddenly, the toes of his boots held about as much attraction as a tree full of hoot owls.

He searched for the right words to tell her how he felt. In the silence, a whine drew her attention again to Yellow Dog. She knelt and rubbed his head. "Hey, boy. I didn't expect to see you here. Duel?"

"The fool wouldn't stay behind. Walked all the way to Austin. Guess he's come to trust me. At least he tolerates my rough ways." Duel's shyness left. "Or maybe he hungered for your tender touch . . . like me."

Jessie reached for his hand. Palm to palm they stood. The heat from her gaze drove away any remaining doubts. He pitched his hat toward a spindly chair, ringing it on the sharp wood that rose from the high back.

She ran her tongue slowly across pearly white teeth. "I've missed you, sodbuster."

The steady beat of his heart picked up the pace. Without taking his gaze from her face, he hollered, "Bart, open this door so I can kiss my wife."

"Orders, orders, orders, that's all I git around here." Bart pushed aside the rifle he'd been cleaning and stood, his arthritic bones creaking. "A body would think I ain't anything more'n a lackey."

The jangle of keys mingled with Bart's grumbling.

When the cell door swung open, Duel scooped Jessie into his arms. "I've waited too long for this, Mrs. McClain."

Then, he kissed her forehead, her eyes, and her nose before he settled his mouth firmly on her lips and sampled his fill. His topsy-turvy world righted on its axis for one brief moment. He was with his lady.

Her breath came in excited gasps when he released her at last. "I've lived in fear that you wouldn't get here in time. That they'd hang me before I got a chance to see you again."

"And deprive the world of the best sweet-potato pie maker I ever saw? I gave my word I'd come and a McClain never goes back on his word." *Except the one about protecting*. He felt the shiver that coursed through her.

"Those men seem bent on keeping me from reaching trial."

"Hush, darlin'." He held her tight, his chin resting on the top of her head. "I'm here now. No one is gonna hurt you. No lynch mob for sure."

They stood as one until her trembling stopped.

"I love you, Jess. Don't ever forget that." The pounding against his chest, where her breasts were becoming familiar with his shirt, aroused a desire so strong he almost forgot where he was. He wanted to take her to the nearest bed, kiss away every problem that worried her.

"I won't forget. No more than I can lose sight of how much I love you." Her husky reply made tracks up his spine.

"Hey, Jessie, look who I've got." Luke ducked through the door with Marley Rose riding on his shoulders, oblivious to the scene he'd interrupted.

"Mama, mine Mama!" The excited child put a stranglehold

on Luke's head and dug one leg into his collarbone as she tried to climb down from her perch.

"Whoa, Peanut." Luke turned in a circle in his attempt to disentangle himself. Yellow Dog added to the melee, barking and nipping at his heels. "Duel, help me. I've crossed the trail of mountain lions, cougars, and some of the meanest desperados in the territory, but this little girl puts 'em all to shame."

"Marley Rose! You didn't tell me our daughter came with you."

Duel accepted her look of reproach with good grace. The sound of that 'our daughter' part turned his insides to hot wax. The buckshot that'd rolled in his belly earlier melted from the warmth. Mercy, he'd lie down in a tub full of hot wax any day if it would bring that bright flush to her cheeks.

Grinning, he followed on her heels. "I didn't get around to it yet. Had a few other little incidentals on my mind."

Luke yelled again as Marley bounced up and down, grabbing two handfuls of hair.

Leaning back in his chair at his desk, Bart howled with laughter until tears ran down his face.

"Ain't a dad-blasted thing funny, you old coot. You could offer me a hand, you know." Luke grunted in pain as he plucked Marley's fingers from his right eye.

"This is the darn-tootinest sight I've seen in all my born days." Bart wiped his face on his shirtsleeve.

Stretching over Jessie's head, Duel lifted Marley from his brother's shoulders. "I could've warned you about putting Two Bit up there. I learned the hard way."

"Lord have mercy!" Luke rubbed his afflicted eye, then the reddened skin on his neck. "That child is dangerous."

Marley snuggled in welcoming arms. "Mine Mama," she said, patting Jessie's cheek while glaring at Luke as if daring him to object. Which he didn't because he was busy nursing his wounds.

Duel cleared his throat, suddenly overcome by the sight of the two people who filled his world. Their joy in being together again filled the room. The girl had missed the comfort of her mama's caress. More than that, Two Bit missed her cooking, 'cause she'd eaten very little of what he'd stirred up.

The excitement over for the moment, Yellow Dog sat on his haunches, his tongue lolling from the side of his mouth. Duel wasn't surprised that the animal's watchful eyes never left his beloved family.

Tom Parker ambled inside, doffing a handsome black derby when he passed through the door. His cane thudded on the planks as he joined the party.

Duel brought his former father-in-law forward.

"Jess, this is Tom Parker, retired judge and the best darn lawyer in the whole state of Texas." He basked in the light of hope that shimmered in her eyes. "Just like I said."

Jessie grasped Parker's extended hand tightly as though it was a life raft. "Judge, meet Jessie, my wife and this little angel's mama."

Marley Rose pointed to the silver-haired man. "G'anpa." Then, she patted Jessie's cheek again, her voice soft with love. "Mine Mama."

This time Luke coughed, clearing the way for speech. Duel could see the emotion in his brother's face. "Judge Parker, Duel forgot his introducing manners. Don't rightly know if you remember me. I'm his brother, Luke, and the codger wearing the silver star over there is Sheriff Bart Daniels."

"Wouldn't have recognized you, son. Last time I saw you, you were wet behind the ears." The man accepted Luke's grip.

"Not much has changed, Parker," Bart said, sauntering over. "Still's wet, though I tried to teach him ever'thing I know."

"Now, look here, you old goat." Luke waved a finger beneath Bart's nose. "I've got more sense than you can shake a stick at."

"Depends on if you're usin' a puny stick or a hickory limb," Bart returned, not letting Luke get one up on him.

"How about an olive branch, boys?" Duel shoved his way

between the squabbling twosome. "We have some business to get to."

"Mister Parker," Jessie ignored the ruckus. "I'm pleased to meet you. You were Annie's father?"

"None other."

Through narrowed eyes, Duel watched the former judge size up his lady. Whether Parker accepted Jessie or not remained to be seen. But one thing for sure, he'd best not hurt her.

Jessie touched his arm lightly. Then, with deep sincerity spilling from her face, she spoke from her heart. "I've got some awfully big shoes to fill, sir. Not in a million years can I measure up to the special kind of woman Annie was. Heaven forbid if I try to replace her, that's not what I want. I'll do my best to keep her memory alive. I only hope to never bring shame to the McClain name."

Judge Parker looked astounded. Whatever picture of Jessie he'd formed in his mind, Duel could tell this hadn't been it.

"I thank you for your honesty, madam. I wasn't prepared to like you."

The man's brutal frankness didn't put a dent in Jessie's smile. "I'm sure you miss your daughter terribly."

"For a fact." A soft swoosh of air left the man's mouth. "For a fact," he repeated sorrowfully.

"Did my husband mention what you've gotten yourself into, Mr. Parker?"

"The main parts. Tomorrow will be soon enough to fill in the gaps." He stared wistfully at Marley Rose resting her head on Jessie's bosom. For a moment Duel could've sworn he saw a mist clouding the man's eyes. "That's a fine girl you've got there, Miss Jessie. She's mighty lucky to have a mother who loves her so much."

Parker turned to Luke. "Now, son, show me to the nearest hotel. These weary bones need a soft bed."

"Yes, sir."

Before Tom Parker turned away, he winked at Jessie. "Don't worry about a thing, madam. The cavalry's here."

"Duel, you coming?" Luke asked.

"Not yet. Be along in a while." He hadn't come all this way to sleep.

Since his hands were pretty well tied in regard to breaking Jess out of jail, making sure she got a fair trial was one promise he meant to uphold. Come hell or high water.

"G'anpa?" Marley pointed after the men.

"Duel, how come she's calling Mr. Parker 'grandpa?' Seems to me he'd take offense to it, considering he lost his daughter and all."

"Strange thing. When I went to the judge's hotel room in Austin, he nearly threw me out. The man still hates my guts. After getting a full dose of his hostility, I started to leave. Two Bit refused. She climbed up in his lap and declared right then and there that Parker was her grandpa."

Jessie squeezed the girl to her. "One small thing from our special little package made such a difference. I could tell how much the title pleases Judge Parker."

"Proud as a kid with a new pair of shoes all right."

"The bond they've forged seems every bit as strong as the one she has with your own father."

"Sure seems like it."

"Does this mean you've cleared the past between you two?"

"Let's say we've reached a truce for the time being." A shaky truce at that. Whatever he had to agree on to get the judge's help in freeing his Jess, he'd do in a heartbeat. Even if that meant standing on his head in the middle of Main Street.

Marley raised her head and yawned big.

"She's sleepy, Duel. Why don't you take her over to the hotel?"

The air backed up in his lungs. Admitting his shortfalls came hard. "Can't. Gave Parker every cent I have."

"Then where are you and Marley going to sleep?"

"Wasn't thinking much on anything other than getting here. Guess we can always stretch a bedroll under the stars." The thought of separating from Jess again, even for the length of a night, made him ill. Precious little time might remain. "Or in the jail doorway."

"She's just a baby, Duel!"

"Two Bit hasn't complained yet." Still, guilt that he couldn't provide better accommodations brought back the buckshot in his belly. What kind of man dragged his child on such a journey with no thought to her comfort? For once, he wished for Tom Parker's wealth.

"She can sleep here with me if Sheriff Daniels agrees."

Jessie's quiet calm did little to ease his conscience. Behind iron bars wasn't any place for a child—or his wife.

Never had he felt so inept. That he'd not had any choice in the matter didn't hold water with him. He watched Jessie smooth back the dark curls on their daughter's head. Opportunity had been there. He'd simply chosen the wrong paths when the choices presented themselves. His problem appeared to be not seeing far enough down the road.

Noise and bluster announced Luke's return. "Big Brother, Judge Parker said to tell you there's a room waiting for you and Peanut over at the hotel."

Dad-gum it, the man'd done it again! Just like when Parker bought Annie that fancy wedding dress, and the bed, and countless other things he couldn't provide for her. Now, Parker was doing the same with Two Bit, rubbing Duel's nose in his lack of funds.

His jaw jutted out stubbornly. "Don't need it. Already—"

Jessie's firm grip on his arm stopped him.

"Duel, let the judge do this. Don't let pride stand between your child and a soft bed. She's so tired. Please?"

How could he refuse her request? Staring down into her upturned face, his heart melted. He wanted to make love to his wife until she begged for mercy. Then he'd take delight in knowing he caused the rapid pulse in the luscious hollow of her throat.

"Sure, Luke." He took the dozing girl from Jessie's arms. "I'll go put her to bed. A little rest won't hurt anyone."

The parting left him feeling as if he'd eaten raw cactus, needles and all. He lowered his head and kissed his wife soundly. Something to carry with him through the long, lonely night.

"I'll be back at dawn. Luke assures me the rabble-rousers have settled down—at least for now." He knelt to the dog's level. "Boy, it's your job to guard our lady. Don't let anyone hurt her."

Yellow Dog snarled, a rumble coming from deep inside as if to say he'd protect Jessie with his life if necessary.

"Good boy." Standing, he touched his wife's cheek with his knuckle. "You'll be safe, darlin'. I promise."

Chapter Thirty

Duel lowered Two Bit to the middle of the big bed. The child didn't move a muscle, even when he tugged to remove her shoes. Only after he got them off did he realize he'd forgotten to put on her socks before he'd stuck the blasted things on her feet that morning. Her heels were raw where the shoes had rubbed her tender skin.

He reached into his saddlebags for some salve and dabbed it on the sores.

Fine parent he made. She needed a mother. Not just any mother, she needed Jess. Earlier, seeing the two of them reunited, his heart had swelled. Now, all he had to do was make sure the two of them stayed that way.

A painful lump in his chest kept air from reaching his lungs. He felt as though he stood on one side of a huge chasm with Jess on the opposite rim, and there was no way across it.

He stood staring at Marley for some time. He couldn't remember the last time the child had slept so sound or looked so peaceful. Not since her mama had ridden away from the farm.

Though the bed beckoned his weary body, he knew sleep would not come. A quick stroll over to the saloon he'd spied across the street could relax his taut muscles. He might even find Luke over there and wheedle a drink out of him.

One last glance at Two Bit assured him she'd not miss him. But to ease his peace of mind, he informed Judge Parker, who occupied the adjacent room.

"Would you mind keeping an ear open for Marley? I gotta unwind. Be across the street. Won't take more'n a few minutes," he told Parker.

Though the retired judge gave him a curious look, he nodded. "I understand, McClain."

The man's pleasantry took Duel aback. He had become accustomed to Parker's spiteful tongue. This sudden bend toward congeniality required a similar return.

"I suppose I owe you thanks for arranging a bed for Two Bit. It's plain you fancy her a great deal."

"Sam Hill, you mule head! You're the one who paid for it."

Weariness washed over him anew. The late hour had befuddled his brain. What the devil was Parker talking about?

"Judge," he began, trying to stifle his growing impatience. "I gave you all the money I had in the world."

"And I'm giving it back." Leaning heavily on his gleaming cane, Parker pressed a sack into his hand.

Astonished, he stared at the bag. Without opening it, he knew it held the remainder of the two hundred.

"Why?"

"I wasn't sure I'd take this case. Indeed, I wanted to for all the wrong reasons. Until I met Miss Jessie."

"You were taking it merely to stick a knife in my back?" The man hadn't meant to help at all. Parker had intended to send Jessie to the gallows as revenge for Annie.

Parker rubbed his wrinkled face. "I'm not proud of my intentions. I wanted you to hurt. Not just some, but a lot. I wanted to settle the score for you ruining my daughter's life."

"And your feelings for Marley Rose?" Had the love the little girl gave so freely merely provided Parker with the means to destroy them all? The muscles in his jaw tightened. "Was that an act?"

"I worship that child. Getting to know her is the best thing that ever could have happened." Light shone from Parker's gunmetal gray eyes. "She brought happiness again to my life when everything inside had died."

"You said meeting Jessie changed your mind?"

"I saw how much she loves Marley Rose—and you. Also, I can't envision that warm, compassionate woman as a cold-blooded killer. Horrendous circumstances had to have forced her hand."

"Let me get this straight. You're still going to take Jessie's case, but you don't want my money?" Might as well clear up all the loose ends.

"The relationship with my granddaughter is payment enough. I thank you for that, McClain."

Words didn't come easy to Duel. He guessed in Parker's own way, his acceptance of Jessie and Marley Rose was an apology of sorts. It seemed the man wanted to bury the hatchet after all these years. A big man would accept it. Could he be a big man?

Duel bit back a lifetime of hateful words he'd stored up for Parker. It wouldn't accomplish anything to use them now. A small child's unfettered love had brought about a miracle he'd never thought to see.

The deadman's hand that had given Two Bit to him had not dug him a grave on Boothill but brought happiness beyond compare. If he hadn't camped outside Cactus Springs to put some space between the girl and her reprobate father, he might never have found Jessie. Now, it appeared the tyke had single-handedly glued together his broken relationship with Annie's father. Everything fell into place after Marley Rose came into his life. He'd finally made the right choices.

Duel had learned something about survival and a little about love. He'd traveled a far distance from that night. Regardless of the overwhelming hurdles facing him in the upcoming trial, he didn't view his cup as half empty, but as half full. And, when Jess became a free woman, the darn thing would flow over the top. Knowing all this made him a big man.

"I would've walked to the ends of the earth to keep Annie and my son alive. In loving her I only brought her death. I'm truly sorry, Judge."

Parker placed a heavy hand on his shoulder. "Do me a favor. Can you call me Tom?"

Opposite the Imperial Hotel, in the White Elephant Saloon, Duel poured a shot of whiskey down his gullet. Thoughts of the day ran rampant in his head. He'd made peace with Tom Parker, and he was with his love at last, for better or worse, for richer or poorer.

Till death do you part.

Damn! The words chilled his blood. If, Heaven forbid, the worst should happen, they might as well hang him right alongside his wife, for he wouldn't want to go on living.

Jess had shown him a body can survive anything if the will is strong enough. Because of her he had learned a man can find love and satisfaction again. Even after he'd buried all hope of it six feet under. But, Hellfire! He couldn't—wouldn't—a second time. That asked too much from him.

"Hey, ain't you that McClain feller? The one that's married to that murderin' husband-killer?"

The fighting words pierced his thoughts. The hair on the back of his neck stood on end. While Duel glanced around to find the source, one hand moved to the Schofield in his holster.

Though he wanted to recoil from the one-eyed jackal, he forced a deadly calm. For Jess and Two Bit's sake he'd walk away from this fight. He slowly set the whiskey glass on the top of the bar and turned to leave.

"You bein' impolite ain't you, mister? I asked you a question?" The man now blocked his way.

Up close, the black eye patch lent an evil touch to the sneering face. Though he'd never seen the man before, Duel recognized the type. Mean as a rattler and spoiling for a fight.

"Step aside." His hand poised over the smooth handle of the forty-five.

Duel knew he'd spoken in a quiet tone, so it amazed him when the room became deadly still. Conversations ceased, the piano player stopped the music. All eyes focused on him.

"Or what? You gonna shoot me for asking something the whole town's itchin' to know?"

"I'm not looking for trouble. Just want some peace and quiet." His gaze scanned the curious faces of the crowd. They all appeared angry and sullen.

"Now that's too bad. All the good folks in this town want is justice."

"By lynching, I suppose."

"If we hafta. Jeremiah Foltry was a friend. Mebbe that slut of a wife of his was keeping your bed warm the whole time she carried the Foltry name. And that brat of yours."

Duel felt the heat rising. An ache to silence the man's loud insinuations became overpowering. "Leave the child out of this."

"Seems to me she didn't waste any time in marryin' up with you. Mebbe you helped her plan on doin' poor Jeremiah in."

"If you have proof of that, why don't you take it to the sheriff?"

"I reckon that kid cain't be hers. Know fer a fact that Jeremiah fixed her good where she cain't—"

Rage enveloped him. Before Duel could stop, his doubled fist slammed into the one-eyed jackal's face. The man sprawled backward onto the floor. Satisfaction settled over him at the sight of the unconscious form.

While the crowd gaped in astonishment, Duel pushed through the doors into the night.

Given Jeremiah's friends that he'd met so far, he had an even greater respect for Jessie and her endurance through eight years of hell.

* * *

Jessie woke the next morning much happier than she'd been since leaving Tranquility. Though the three of them might be considered misfits in anyone else's book, Duel, Marley Rose, and she were a family. And they were together come what may to the bitter end.

Luke and Sheriff Daniels both snored fitfully on cots tucked against the furthermost wall. The younger McClain gripped the pistol that lay across his chest.

Yellow Dog raised his head when she stirred, and gave her a sorrowful stare. The dog seemed to know that trouble followed and there was nothing he could do about it.

"Hey, fella." She stroked the soft golden coat through the bars. "You're part of our little family too. A misfit like the rest of us."

A sudden knock at the door brought the animal to his feet with a threatening growl. Luke's boots hit the floor as he jumped to attention. The startled look on the man's face made her laugh softly. Yet Sheriff Daniels slept on, completely oblivious to the disturbance.

"Luke, open up." Duel pounded as if pursued by demons.

It took Luke a good minute or so to get the sleep from his eyes and locate the keys. Jessie watched it all with amusement. Why they'd bothered to lock the door escaped her. After last night's ruckus, most of the panes in the front window had been shot out. Should anyone want in, they had only to crawl through the opening.

"Grandma was slow, but she was old." Duel greeted his brother cheerfully. "Gonna sleep your life away?"

"Cain't a man get some rest?" Luke ran his fingers through his hair and stumbled to the washbasin. "Better yet, can you come back at a decent hour, brother?"

"Where I come from, Luke, six o'clock is a decent hour." Duel's gaze met Jessie's and she melted inside with wanting. "Besides, wasn't you I came to kiss. The lady I traveled half way across the state to be with, and whom I intend to kiss when you get that blasted cell open, is awake."

Blubbering in the remains of yesterday's water, Luke wiped

his face. Then he pitched the last of the contents on Bart Daniels' prone form. "Wake up, old man."

"Jiminy crickets, Duel!" Wet from his head to his waist, Bart rubbed his bristly mustache. "Fine way for a lawman to git woke up. Anyone ever tell you to respect your elders?"

"I didn't do that, Bart. Blame Luke."

While they waited on Luke to mosey over with the keys, Duel caressed Jessie's cheek through the bars. "Have a good night, milady?"

Warm, languid ripples stirred her imagination. Thinking of lying with him in a field of clover, or in their bed in Tranquility, made her feel as if she'd been dipped in smooth, rich molasses. Her legs threatened to give way while her mouth filled with longing for his taste. A good night? She could describe every minute they were together as simply fantastic.

"Exceptional, now that you and Marley Rose are here."

"Why the devil do you hafta keep the cell locked anyway, Luke. Surely you see by now Jess isn't gonna try to escape."

Jessie loved the husky gravel in Duel's voice, knowing that his deep caring put it there. He loved her. He still wanted her and she ached for him. His chiseled jaw looked more square today, more determined to see the right of things. Muscles flexed beneath her touch. Her knight was strong and tough.

"You got manure for brains, Duel? In case a mob gets through us, they cain't get to her that easy. Precautionary measure's all." Luke explained as if he were talking to a child. "By the way, where's Peanut this mornin'?"

"Having breakfast with Parker. She'll be along soon. Why? You thinking of giving her a ride on your shoulders?"

"Lord help a sinner! Ain't never doing that again."

The door squeaked when it swung open at last. Duel swept Jessie into his arms, kissing her long and hard.

"I've missed you, darlin'." He breathed heavily against her ear, causing tingles to sashay down her body.

"It's only been a few hours," she reminded him.

"One second away from you is too long. I can't wait to get you back home where you belong."

A heavy anvil dropped, squashing her rising passion. "If things go in our favor."

"Don't say 'if.' It's 'when.' I'll not give up. Not ever. Tom Parker's the best there is. He likes you, you know."

"He's awfully sad, but he's nice. I felt a kinship with him right off. I'm glad Marley thinks of him as her grandpa."

"Those two are close, that's a fact. We had a long chat last night. Jess, he gave back the two hundred dollars I gave him."

"He's not going to take my case?" Panic ricocheted off all her hopes and dreams.

"Slow down. Tom Parker's gonna defend you. He's gonna do it for free." Duel raised her hand to his mouth and kissed first the palm, then the back. "Seems you made quite an impression on the man, my dear."

"For free?" The magnitude of the gift overwhelmed her. No one had ever done anything for her for free before. Except for Duel taking her in, of course. But that didn't count because in the beginning, their relationship had been purely a business arrangement—she took care of Marley Rose in exchange for marriage, a roof over her head, and a place to hide.

"Yep." His wide grin reminded her of George or Henry.

"I take it you talked about other things besides me. You seem rather light-hearted this fine morn, Mr. McClain." She lovingly brushed a lock of hair off his forehead.

"Yep. Talked about forgiveness. The judge asked me to call him Tom."

"Guess that clinches it then. Anyone who wants you to use his first name considers you a friend. Pure and simple." She fell into the deep amber lights of his eyes. "What I want to find out is do you finally forgive yourself for what happened?"

He looked away, unable to face her. "Their deaths were my fault. Always will be. Time ain't gonna change that."

The demons of the past continued to haunt him. Until he forgave himself for the tragedy, they would always walk in his shadow. She hoped one day he'd see that a man wasn't liable for things he had no control over.

Tom Parker chose that moment to appear with Marley Rose.

"Mama," Marley clamored, toddling across the uneven floor to her side.

"How about a big hug, little lady?"

The girl ran into Jessie's outstretched arms with her mouth puckered for a kiss.

"Mine Mama," she informed Duel in Marley Rose fashion.

"You got some of that loving left for me?" he asked her.

Marley kept a grip on Jessie's dress while she leaned out, her lips resembling a catfish's. The loud smack drew Luke's attention.

"Hey, Peanut. Don't be giving away all my kisses now."

Defiance glistened in her brown eyes. "Mine Papa."

"Darn it, I know he's your papa. What's that have to do with anything?"

"Watch it, Luke. I'll sit her on your shoulders."

"If it's all the same to you, I'll just watch from over here." Luke grabbed the blackened coffee pot and hurried outside for water, ignoring Duel's laughter.

"Papa?" Marley pulled on his arm impatiently.

"Yes, I'm your papa. What do you want, Two Bit?"

Jessie's heart almost burst with joy. He'd finally accepted that he was the girl's father. Praise be!

"Boobie." She pointed to Yellow Dog.

"Sure is, darlin'."

"Cheeba?" This time Marley shrugged her shoulders and turned her hands up.

"Cheeba's at home. You'll see her in a few days."

Satisfied, the girl scooted from Jessie's arms and sat down by Yellow Dog's side.

"Duel, you let her call you papa. No more fuss about it?"

"Guess that's the way of it, Jess. Reckon I am."

Suddenly, a man burst through the door waving a piece of paper.

"Sheriff, the circuit judge'll be arrivin' this afternoon on the stage."

"Oh no." A fit of nausea swept over her. That meant her trial would be tomorrow. They hadn't had time to prepare.

Chapter Thirty-one

"It's time to get down to business, Miss Jessie. I need to know the details about the night Jeremiah Foltry lost his life."

The horrifying scenes that she'd tried to forget came tumbling back.

I'll make you sorry you were ever born! Jeremiah had told her that often enough. The man had always made her feel cheap and used and—yes, sorry for the day she'd drawn her first breath.

Jessie glanced from the stern, no-nonsense face of Tom Parker to her husband's rock-solid profile. Duel squeezed her hand, letting her know he meant to stay by her side, through the thick and the thin of it.

Yes, she'd been sorry for being born until she met her tall Texan. He'd shown her a compassion and love she'd never known before. Still, in the dead of night her fears of being unworthy of her good fortune came calling.

"It's all right, Jess. I know it's hard, but Tom has to know so he can defend you."

She took a deep, steadying breath and over the course of

the next two hours, painted a picture of her purgatory—except about the brand. The pain of that ordeal prevented the telling.

They were concluding the session when Phoebe Sutton marched into the jail and up to Sheriff Daniels. Jessie's heart slammed against her ribs.

"I came to see my daughter and I won't take 'no' for an answer," Mrs. Sutton declared.

"Yes, ma'am. I wouldn't dare," Bart mumbled.

Why had Phoebe persisted despite her request? Didn't she know it'd accomplish nothing good? Knots tightened in Jessie's stomach. She struggled to turn her attention back to the judge and their discussion of her chances.

Tom Parker rose. "Well, madam, I'll be truthful with you." Her hand got lost somewhere between the two of his. "It isn't going to be the easiest case I ever fought."

Her tongue worked in a suddenly dry mouth.

"Do you think we stand a chance, Jud . . . Tom?" Duel's voice wavered a trifle. Not so much that she should've noticed. Still, in the months of living by his side, she'd grown accustomed to his moods and each variation in his tone.

"Course we do, son. We have right on our side." He dropped her hand and lifted his derby off the back of the chair. "Get a good night's sleep and I'll see you tomorrow, Miss Jessie. Try not to worry."

Phoebe Sutton stood silent, waiting for Parker to take his leave. Narrow, pursed lips gave the woman who'd given birth to her a stern demeanor. Dread filled Jessie, for her mother appeared forbidding. Had she come to chastise?

Duel cast Jessie a questioning look. She slipped her arm around his as much for support as to send a message.

"Mama, I'd like you to meet my husband. Duel, this is Phoebe Sutton, my mother."

"Oh, Jessie. Forgive me, but I had to come." Phoebe's unforgiving frown crumbled. She threw her arms around her daughter, a sob welling up.

Jessie released her grip on Duel and held her mother close.

For a full minute she bit back the tears that threatened, savoring the warm embrace for which she'd yearned one last time. Words refused to take form.

After several heartbeats, they drew apart. Only then did Jessie trust her voice. "When I sent Luke to convey my wishes, it wasn't for selfish reasons. Please understand. I wanted you to stay away for your own good, Mama. The good folks of El Paso can be petty and mean. Never would I want to cause you suffering on my account."

Phoebe touched her cheek ever so gently. "You're my flesh an' blood. When you hurt, I hurt. I don't give a hoot what anyone thinks of me."

Childish giggling drew their attention. Luke stepped into the jail with Marley Rose in tow. Not taking any chances, this time the small girl walked by his side, holding her uncle's hand.

Marley hurried on her chubby legs. "Mama. See?"

"What is it, darlin'?" Jessie swung her up into her arms.

"See?" Marley held forth a handful of gum drops.

"I see. Uncle Luke bought you candy."

"Wuncle Wuke." The girl nodded. She popped an orange morsel into her mouth, then pushed a green one toward Jessie.

"Mama, eat."

Proud to see Marley sharing instead of calling everything 'mine,' Jessie allowed the small fingers to push the treat inside her mouth. "Ummmmmm. Good."

Chewing on the candy, Jessie realized she hadn't introduced Marley to her mother. "Mama, meet my daughter, Marley Rose."

The glare Phoebe cast toward Luke could've withered a fence post. "You didn't see fit to mention that I have a granddaughter."

"Cotton pickin'! Knew there was something my pea brain skipped. Pardon my mistake, Mrs. Sutton."

Over the top of Marley's head, Jessie caught Duel's loving

gaze. The look told her how much he enjoyed the entire scene.

"Two Bit, this is your Grandma Sutton."

The child stopped poking the sweets into her mouth and gave Phoebe a large brown stare. "G'anma?"

"Yes dear, your grandma." With a tightness in her chest, she watched Marley reach for the woman.

Phoebe held her stiffly at first, apparently unaccustomed to the strange feeling.

But Marley wriggled until she found a comfortable place, put her small arms around the woman's neck and announced, "Mine G'anma."

That did the trick. Phoebe softened and kissed Marley, sticky gum drops and all.

Darkness had settled over the town when Duel insisted on staying the night with her. Phoebe had taken Marley under her wing to give the two of them time to be alone. Her mother's caring touched Jessie.

No one had to voice the fear painted in the deep purple twilight. This might be the last time she'd spend with her beloved for, true to the telegram, Judge Warner had arrived on the noon stage.

Tom Parker had called Warner a hard but fair man. Though known by reputation only, the circuit judge aroused a certain disquiet in Parker's demeanor.

The underlying pall Jessie sensed earlier descended upon her.

"That night . . ." She stared at her hands. When she raised her head she met his gaze with steady determination. "All those months ago, when I rode into your camp. I've never regretted it." Jessie leaned into the circle of her husband's arms, enjoying the smell of his nearness. "I only wish our time hadn't been so short."

"Don't say that, Jess. We have to hope for the best. I won't let you give up, not now."

She twisted around until she could peer into the familiar

face that occupied her dreams. "You, my dear sodbuster, taught me how to love and gave my life meaning. You took away the ugliness and made me smile again. When we were apart and I wondered if I'd ever see you again, I thought I'd surely die from the pain."

Duel's eyes blazed with amber heat. "I know. Me too. But it won't happen again. I'm gonna make sure you spend the next forty years lying next to me in our bed. That's just at night. In the day, you'll make me sweet-potato pies and practice on being a mother."

"You sound like we'll have more than Marley Rose. I told you I'm unable to bear children."

"I'm not forgetting. I've been meaning to talk to you about something. Pop told me about a passel of kids who lost their parents. They need a home real bad. I was thinking we might offer for 'em when we get this behind us."

Jessie stared at him in amazement. How strange that they both had the same idea.

"Duel, the Butler children! Vicky told me about them and before I could speak to you, Luke appeared on our doorstep. Would you truly take the children to raise?"

"Yep. Would take a lot of hard work, but I reckon neither of us shy away from that."

"You'll have two sons," she said, remembering that there had been two boys and one girl. "And Marley will have a sister."

Their sweet little girl who never complained, who took whatever happened in stride, would be tickled pink.

"The more the merrier, I always say."

"Did I tell you today how much I love you?"

A smile sneaked across his face like a naughty child coming out of hiding. Her chest swelled with the magnitude of her good fortune. If only it'd last a little bit longer.

"Yep, but my lady can never tell me too often." He swooped down and captured her mouth.

His kiss carried her to dizzying heights where the thin air made breathing darn near impossible.

If they hadn't been in her cell, with Luke and Sheriff Daniels trying to keep their eyes on other things, she had no doubt where their passion would've led. As it was, circumstances shackled his wanton desires.

Unlike Jeremiah, Duel would move heaven and earth to preserve her dignity. Unlike Jeremiah, her Texan had compassion and kindness for all living things. And, unlike Jeremiah, her knight—on a black horse called Preacher—would never hurt her. Indeed, he loved her more than life itself.

How unfair that she should find this completeness in her life last instead of first—before Jeremiah Foltry had ruined her chances for bearing children. Strange that she'd had to go through the worst to get to the best.

"Duel, when I was a little girl, I used to throw rocks in the Rio Grande and watch the ripples spread. It's like that now. With each widening ring, my life is encompassing more and better things. From a small wave, which was you, I now have Marley Rose, all of your family, my mother and Tom Parker, and if we're lucky, three more children. I feel truly blessed."

"No, darlin', I've been favored since the first time I saw you. Think the word is moonstruck."

There went that warm molasses, turning her bones to jelly again.

Soft pink rays of dawn woke Duel the next morning. His arm and neck ached. Sometime in the wee hours, he had finally dozed off with Jessie asleep in the hollow of his shoulder. And with the blankets firmly drawn across the metal bars, they were in their own small world.

The fresh smell of vanilla and spice flooded his senses. Strange. It'd been so long since she'd baked, yet the aromas still lingered in Jessie's hair and on her skin.

When he inhaled, silky tendrils playfully teased his lips. She looked so peaceful lying on his chest. Heaviness grew until it consumed every corner of his heart.

Dear God, he'd gladly take her place if they'd let him. A

delicate, sensitive woman like her seemed ill equipped to fight for her life.

Jess had said last evening that he'd taught her to love and given her life meaning. Small in comparison to what he'd learned from her.

Damnation! He wished he'd had enough foresight to have seen the toll this trial had taken on her. Wished he had faith that wrongs would get righted. Wished he was good at waiting.

Shoot, he reckoned putting a hole in a wanted man's forehead at four hundred feet—four hundred yards with a rifle—was the only skill he had. He sure wasn't good at much else.

The greatest fear of all, the one that made him break out in a cold sweat each time it entered his head, was that Jess would stop loving him. Heaven help him if that ever came to pass.

She stirred. The panic in her blue gaze as it caught his slammed a fist into his gut. For two cents he'd bust her out of this jail and light out for parts unknown.

The thought vanished as soon as it appeared, for he knew she'd not allow it. Still, her obvious terror did things to him he didn't like.

"Why didn't you wake me? I don't want to spend the precious little time we have sleeping."

"You needed the peace you could find only in your dreams. Besides, I enjoyed watching you sleep." He tucked a strand of auburn silk behind her ear and let his hand glide down the long column of her neck. "You're so beautiful. I'm awfully glad we became familiar, 'cause I'm in love with you, Mrs. McClain."

Wetness turned her eyes a watery blue. "I feel unworthy."

"I keep remembering how patient you were with me. It took me way too long to put my demons to rest."

"At least they're gone now. We have each other and our love to make sure they don't return."

"The rest of our lives, darlin'."

"That may not be long enough. Strange that my fate depends on a handful of citizens and a judge." Her hand shook as she pushed back a lock of wayward hair. "I'm scared, Duel. Real scared."

"I'll be right beside you. I'm putting my money on Tom Parker to straighten out this mess."

"I have a favor to ask."

"Anything for you, darlin'. Want me to lasso the moon, shoot Judge Warner, or something a tad more dangerous?"

She brushed aside his attempt at lighthearted banter. "If my punishment is hanging, promise me you'll take Marley Rose and leave. Right away."

His gut twisted worse than a bucking bronc. The picture of her twitching at the end of a rope, of her lovely neck snapping at the sudden fall, released a rush of cold sweat.

"It's not gonna happen, Jess." Not even if he had to lay the whole town to waste. He'd never let them have his beautiful Jess, who'd already suffered more than any human should.

"Promise, Duel." Her voice took on a sharp edge he'd not heard before.

"All right. But, I'm telling you, it's not gonna come to that."

"Good to have a plan—just in case." Her bottom lip trembled, and she held it between her teeth to still it.

Chapter Thirty-two

Jessie figured everyone in town must've turned out to witness her trial. The White Elephant Saloon had probably never held so many at one given time. Luke and Sheriff Daniel's headaches in getting her from the jail to the defendant's table increased by the minute. Hands reached out to touch, grab or pinch the scandalous woman who saw fit to put a tragic end to her husband's life. It was strange, she thought, to worry about a few bruises when she had much more at stake.

"This court is now in session." Judge Warner banged his gavel to quiet the noisy chatter. "When I point to you, come forward and sit in the jury box. I'll not have any shirkers, either."

Amid laughter and rude comments he filled the twelve vacant chairs. Then he turned his attention to Jessie. His concentrated peer made her heart sink into the dirt floor of the saloon. Tom Parker's assurance that the man gave fair and impartial treatment appeared in error, for he seemed to have already determined her guilt.

Yellow Dog, who lay beside her feet, raised his eyes as if

offering sympathy. Her nerves on edge, she allowed flitting glances around the saloon—the place in which others would determine whether she lived or died.

It astounded her that they'd use such a inappropriate establishment to hold a trial. It didn't appear seemly for any proceedings other than the serving of spirits to thirsty, lusty men. She tried to avert her gaze from the mural where a naked woman perched in full view. The mirrors surrounding it purely served to magnify the outrageous portrait.

"Do you understand the charges against you, Mrs. Foltry?" The monocle in the man's right eye reflected light from the kerosene lamps sitting on the long bar and along each wall.

Jessie tried to swallow, but the spit hung in her parched throat. She barely managed to nod her head.

Tom Parker placed his hand over hers and spoke. "Miss Jessie's name is McClain now, Your Honor."

"Crime was committed under the Foltry name. For the duration of this trial the court'll refer to her as Jessie Foltry. So ruled." He banged the gavel to emphasize the point.

Separated from her by a double length of rope, Duel stood a few feet behind her. When she sought his support, his loving gaze calmed her rising panic. She shakily returned his smile.

Tom Parker stood. "Your Honor, out of regard for the defendant and the womenfolk in the room, and in deference to the severity of the business of this court, I respectfully request the ahh . . . painting above the bar be removed until these proceedings are over."

Judge Warner scowled at the second interruption before he lifted a glowing cigar stub from the ashtray and stuck it in his mouth. The man inhaled deeply, then blew out a puff of smoke.

"So ruled. Sheriff, take down the obstruction."

Bart Daniels motioned for Luke and several other men to do the judge's bidding. Several minutes later the monstrosity rested on the floor out of Jessie's sight.

"This court won't abide any further interruptions, Mr. Parker," the judge warned, removing the gold-rimmed monocle and wiping it with a handkerchief.

"I understand, Your Honor."

Jessie wondered at the unruffled calmness Tom Parker projected. Her life hung by a thread, and the stern man with the gavel controlled the scissors that could snip that thread without warning.

Judge Warner propped the piece of glass back over his eye. "Now, Mrs. Foltry, stand up and tell the court how you plead."

Shaky knees prevented Jessie from rising. Only after Tom Parker helped her did she make it to her feet.

"Guilty, sir." Her voice quaked.

"Damn right, she's guilty. Murdered Jeremiah in cold blood!" The loud snarl came from behind her. She couldn't bring herself to turn around. She didn't want to see from whence the hate came. The man most likely was one of the mob who'd appeared at the jail. It gave her an uneasy feeling to have them so close.

"You'll refer to me as Your Honor, madam. Not sir." That the judge chastised her instead of the man who spouted his opinions increased her wariness of a stacked deck.

"Yes, Your High . . . Your Honor." Good Heavens, she almost messed up again. There were so many rules. And the imperious man did act like some king.

"It's all right, Miss Jessie," Parker whispered beside her ear. "You're doing fine."

She wasn't so sure. The prosecuting lawyer gave her a satisfied leer and straightened his leather vest as he stood. The man's protruding teeth gave him the appearance of a donkey.

"Since the defendant admitted she did murder poor Jeremiah, why waste the court's time? Let's take her out an' hang her now. Save the taxpayers money."

The angry tone aroused Yellow Dog. He growled in warning.

"You're out of order, Mr. Langtree. Trial's over when I say it's over an' not a second sooner."

Deflated by the dressing down, Robert Langtree sank back into his seat.

"Present your first witness, Counsel," Judge Warner ordered.

"Doc Willoughby." Mr. Langtree announced loudly, as if everyone in the room suffered of deafness.

"Don't hafta shout, Counselor. Doc Willoughby, take the stand."

Jessie watched the short, balding man as he swore to tell the truth, the whole truth, and nothing but the truth and settled his girth in the seat. He met her gaze, giving her a kind smile.

"Doc, tell the court about bein' called to the Diamond J."

"I had many occasions to visit the Foltry homestead. Mostly I came on account of Mrs. Foltry needed doctorin'."

Langtree glared. "I was referin' to that night in February when Jeremiah got killed, not any other."

"You didn't specify. Like I said, I fixed up Mrs. Foltry most times." The doctor's anger flared. Jessie could see the man's loyalty lay with her, and her chest swelled with warmth. He'd been a dear friend.

"Jeremiah Foltry—tell us about him."

"Well, Pedro Sanchez burst into my office after dark and said to come quick, that Foltry and Pete Morgan had been shot. I gathered my bag and rode out to the ranch with him."

"Was Mrs. Foltry there when you arrived?"

"Didn't see her. Only Jeremiah lying in a pool of blood. Knew right off he was dead. Took a bullet outta Morgan, then got Sanchez and Evers to lift Foltry into the wagon to haul him back to town."

"Evers? That's Josh Evers?"

"Yep."

"Anyone else out there except Pete Morgan, Pedro Sanchez, an' Josh Evers?"

"Didn't see no one else."

"Did you determine what killed Jeremiah?"

"Gunshot."

Laughter filled the room. Langtree flushed a bright red.

"What kind of weapon?"

"Took a forty-five slug outta Foltry's chest. Guessing that's vhat might've caused the big hole. Purely an educated uess."

Again the crowd tittered.

"Quiet, or I'll have you removed," the judge banged his avel loudly. Then he turned to the inept counselor. "Any nore questions, Mr. Langtree?"

"No, Your Honor."

Doc Willoughby looked relieved and started to rise.

"One moment, Doc." Tom Parker unhurriedly rose to his eet.

"Go ahead, Mr. Parker." Warner swivelled the cigar to the ther side of his mouth. The action made the monocle fall nto his chest. He grabbed it and leaned back.

"Tell the court about the other occasions you were summoned to the Diamond J."

"I often went to treat Mrs. Foltry after Jeremiah beat her. Vanted me to patch 'er up so's he could have another shot t killing her. Mean as a snake, that Jeremiah."

"Objection, Your Honor!" Langtree pounded his fist on the able in front of him. Spit flew from his overcrowded mouth. This testimony's irrelevant. Jeremiah Foltry's not on trial nere."

"Your Honor," Tom Parker answered as if speaking to a hild. "The events leading up to the crime are not only perinent, but necessary to establish the defendant's state of nind."

"Overruled, Mr. Langtree. Sit down. You may proceed, Mr. 'arker, but stick to the facts."

"Now, going back to the week before the shooting, did you ay a call to the ranch?"

Misery engulfed Jessie. Her shame was about to become ommon knowledge. She couldn't bear for the entire town o hear the sordid details of her life, worse yet for those facts to sully the McClain name. Even if the doing of it would save her.

Before the doctor could answer, a commotion erupted behind her. Upon turning, she saw the entire McClain clan filing into the saloon.

They'd come all this way for her. Walt, Vicky, and Roy had come to show support for a woman they barely knew. It touched her deeply. Yet here she was about to bring dishonor to their name. Soon they'd hear the events that had led to her sinful crime.

"Yes, I went to see Mrs. Foltry a few days before that fateful night."

"Before we get to that, Doc, let's go back to a month before Jeremiah died. Can you tell us why Foltry called you?"

"He'd beaten and kicked his pregnant wife in the stomach causing her to lose her baby. She hemorrhaged badly. Almost lost Mrs. Foltry."

Horrified gasps traveled through the onlookers.

Tom Parker paced up and down in front of the twelve jurors. As a whole they sat stone-faced. Their cold, emotionless faces sent chills racing up her spine.

"How did you know the blame was Foltry's?"

"The man bragged about it. Claimed the child wasn't his and that he meant to get rid of it."

"So he wanted you to save his wife. A man who'd murdered an innocent babe."

"Reckon so. Don't rightly know why. Cain't count the times he beat her within an inch of her life, then called me."

Jessie dropped her head. She couldn't bear to look at anyone, not even Duel who had already heard the awful facts.

"And each time you patched her up. Yet you never told the sheriff."

"It wouldn't do much good. Most folks shy clear of those kind of squabbles. Besides, ain't no law against a man beatin' his wife. Although there should be," Willoughby added.

"I object to this line of questioning, Your Honor. Don't see what Counsel is tryin' to prove. That Jeremiah slapped his wife around ain't the issue here. Like Doc said, ain't no law against a man hittin' his wife."

Langtree's objection simply reinforced what Jessie already knew. No one cared a fig what a man did to a woman. The double standard concerned no one except other wives in the same situation. She would see no justice in this room.

"Your Honor, I'm trying to establish the fact that my client acted in self-defense against a deranged man," Parker argued.

"Overruled." The force of the gavel hitting the table startled Yellow Dog, making him whimper. She calmed him with a touch, alarmed by the tremors beneath the layer of fur.

"Continue, Counselor."

"Thank you, Your Honor." Tom's serene smile must surely have irritated Mr. Langtree. "Doc Willoughby, you did nothing to help Miss Jessie?"

Doc Willoughby stared at the floor and mumbled, "No."

"Wonder why it was that Miss Jessie never went to your office in town. Why was it you always had to travel out there?"

"Foltry kept her prisoner. Wouldn't let her off the ranch."

"He tell you that?"

"Yes."

"Did Miss Jessie ever ask you to help her escape?"

"Once. She begged me."

"Let me get this straight. Jeremiah Foltry called you numerous times to assist in the treatment of his wife. You knew she was being held prisoner, yet did nothing to help her."

"I'm not proud of it. I wish I'd had the courage." The kindly doctor wiped his eyes. "I truly wish I had."

"Ever treat her for broken bones?"

"Many times."

"Burns?"

"Yes."

"Dislocated limbs?"

Unable to answer, Doc Willoughby nodded his head.

"Now, days before the shooting occurred, you went out there again. This time was different, wasn't it?"

"Foltry wanted me to examine his wife. He wanted to know

if she'd be able to get in the family way." Willoughby wiped the sweat from his forehead.

Jessie held her breath, willing the man to keep silent. It was one thing for Duel to know the damaged goods he'd gotten, but quite another for the entire town to hear about it.

"And what did you find, Doc?" Tom Parker asked gently.

Please don't tell. She put her hands over her ears to block the sound.

"I saw where someone had repeatedly jabbed a sharp instrument into her womb, rendering her unable to ever bear children."

The quiet inside made her shiver. So silent. So still. It reminded her of a calm before a huge storm. A quiet so silent it hurt to breathe. Oh, dear God the pain.

"You know who was responsible?"

"I accused Jeremiah. The man laughed and said it served her right. Called her names and bragged he'd fixed her good."

Duel hated the deadly silence that swept over the packed crowd. Pop, Vicky, and Roy gave him silent encouragement. Their loyalty meant Jessie had become someone special to them.

Then his gaze found his beloved. He could see the strain, the fright lining her delicate features. Judge Warner had denied his request to sit by her side. Yet that was where he should be. Though he stood mere feet away, it seemed more like miles.

An ache inside his chest, as crushing as a mighty locomotive, grew until it threatened to explode.

Duel wanted to swoop her up and shoot any man who dared to stop him. Wanted to carry her far up in the hills where no one could ever hurt her again. Wanted to love her until she forgot the horrors that filled her dreams.

Helpless, he clenched his hands until the short fingernails drove into his palms. He never felt the pain.

Damnation!

He surveyed the makeshift courtroom. Surely these folks

could see that she'd been pushed to the brink, been justified in defending herself. Doc Willoughby move slowly through the throng. The man seemed to have aged twenty years since taking the stand.

Against a far wall stood the one-eyed jackal who'd challenged him the night he arrived. The man caught his gaze and sneered. This had to be either the Evers guy or Pete Morgan. He guessed the latter. The jackal had claimed to be a friend of Foltry. Judging by the man's friends, Foltry's mean streak—the one the doc had described—didn't surprise Duel.

That the man ever laid a hand on his sweet Jess filled him with unspeakable rage. The taste filling his mouth was as rank as a broth from the devil's dinner table.

Chapter Thirty-three

Sheriff Daniels took the chair next. When he allowed a quick glance Jessie's way, it was as apologetic as the doc's. It was clear to Duel where the lawman's sympathy lay.

"Now, Sheriff, is it against the law for a man to lay a hand on his wife to keep her in line?"

"As the law reads, I can't legally arrest a man for that. But if I'd knowed—"

"Just answer the question yes or no, Sheriff."

Bart twisted uncomfortably. "No, it's not against the law."

"And is it a crime for a woman to shoot her husband dead?"

"Robert, you know good an' well it is."

"Then we're all agreed that Miz Jessie Foltry is the one on trial here."

"Plain as the nose on your face."

Langtree pointed his finger at Jessie. "Is it a fact that Miz Foltry, with malice aforethought, shot her husband, left him in a pool of blood, and ran from the law to avoid facing what she'd done?"

"That's her confession."

"Is it indeed a fact, yes or no?"

"Yes."

"Thank you, that'll be all, Sheriff."

Duel listened intently as Tom Parker got his turn. In his opinion, Bart had damaged their case. Yet, by the time Tom got finished, he'd let Bart state as a matter of record that no matter the limitations of the law, the man found other ways of dealing with wife-beating. It wasn't tolerated when he knew of it. No man had the rights that Jeremiah took.

Phoebe Sutton interrupted Duel's concentration with a tug on his sleeve. The woman held Marley Rose in her arms.

"Mr. McClain, I want you to tell Mister Parker that I aim to tell that judge what a rotten, evil man Jeremiah Foltry was. I want to help my daughter."

"Thank you, Mrs. Sutton. I'll pass that along first chance I get." He also meant to find out why Parker didn't ask the doc about the brand on Jessie's shoulder. It occurred to him that Jess might not've mentioned it. He'd seen firsthand her fierce privateness.

Two Bit climbed into the crook of his arm. She seemed unusually quiet, as if she sensed the trouble her mama was in. Her dark curls pressed against his chest.

Protectively, he wrapped his arms around her. Through narrowed eyes he watched Luke being sworn in. God help his brother if he made things worse for Jess.

"Ranger McClain." Langtree still spoke as if he could drive home his points through sheer volume alone. "After months of endless searching, you arrested Miz Foltry and brought her back, ain't that right?"

"Yes."

"You found her after she weaseled her way into your family, ain't that true?"

Before Luke could answer, Parker jumped angrily to his feet. "I object to the derogatory terms and tone of voice Counsel is using, Your Honor. This trial can be carried on in a decent, respectful manner. Besides, I can't see what these questions have to do with Foltry's murder."

"I'm provin' to the court to what lengths Miz Foltry went to avoid detection. Merely pointin' out the bare truth, Your Honor. If Mr. Parker can't handle the facts . . ."

"Mr. Langtree, try to refrain from such tactics. We'll have no name callin' here."

The prosecutor shifted his weight from one side to the other. "The defendant is your sister-in-law, ain't that true?"

"Yes."

"She married your brother a few weeks after she committed this awful atrocity. By her actions, changing her name, taking on another husband an' child, didn't she seek to establish a new identity to avoid arrest?"

The truth in Langtree's accusation hit too close to home. Only Duel alone knew, and he'd cut out his tongue before he admitted a word of it.

An angry flush engulfed Luke's face. "No, cotton pickin'! Jessie married my brother because she deserved some kindness. Because she needed to know that there were decent people in the world. Lord knows she'd never gotten anything but grief from Foltry. Or this town for that matter."

Amen. And she deserved to have the child that had been denied her. He knew how it felt to have a babe snatched away.

"Did she put up a fuss when you placed her under arrest?"

"No. She came willingly."

Langtree marched to stand before the twelve jurors.

"To sum it up, Jessie Foltry shot her husband in cold blood, shot Pete Morgan when he tried to stop her, rode off in the dead of night to meet up with Duel McClain, an' got herself married to him to further cover her tracks. Ranger McClain, I'd say your brother's a lucky man to still be breathin'."

The insinuation released a stream of molten fury. The man made it sound like Jess had planned every move beforehand and even more subtly, that he'd helped her. He stepped toward the witness box and Langtree. But Tom Parker stopped him.

"You're only going to make things worse," Parker mumbled.

Duel owned that it might, but he'd sure like to wring that Langtree's neck. However, he moved back to his spot.

"My brother was lucky, but not in the sense you suggested. He's mighty lucky to find a fine woman like Jessie. I only hope to find one like her someday."

Luke's outburst brought down the judge's gavel. "Your comments are uncalled for, Ranger."

So were Langtree's lies, but the judge couldn't see that. Duel longed to tell them all how wrong they were about his Jess.

Thank goodness Langtree finished and now it was Tom's turn. "Ranger, in all the months Miss Jessie lived in Tranquility, did she have access to any number of weapons—knives, guns?"

"Yes."

"And she never once gave in to this killer instinct my esteemed colleague suggested. Never even threatened anyone?"

A thin smile formed when Duel remembered Jess's encounter with Hampton Pierson that day in the woods. No call for them to know about that. He'd seen what happened when anyone backed her into a corner.

"As far as I know, Jessie never shot or threatened anyone."

"Thank you, Ranger. You can step down."

"Your Honor, I call Pete Morgan," Langtree bellowed.

Duel's jaw clenched as he followed the one-eyed jackal to the front. So he'd been right. A turbulence boiled inside him.

From where he was, he could see the color drain from Jess. She slumped lifeless in her chair. He prayed Morgan wouldn't favor her with a full-face view, for she seemed paralyzed with enough fear already. He prayed the man would be struck down by lightning when he opened his mouth.

Langtree sent Jessie a smug I've-got-you-now smirk that made Duel feel like grabbing the man by the throat.

"Pete, you were there that night when Miz Foltry began her terrible rampage. Tell us what transpired."

"Transpired?"

"You know. Tell us what happened."

"Poor Jeremiah. He never lifted a finger to hurt that woman o' his. Always tried to shield her from harm an' from townsfolk learning the real truth—that she was tetched in the head. That's why he never allowed Miz Foltry to go to town. If'n he kept her locked up, it was fer her own damn good."

Shocked gasps echoed throughout the saloon.

Forget wishing for lightning. If it hadn't come after that cock-and-bull story, it wasn't coming. He'd known from the start the one-eyed jackal would spread lies. Only nothing had prepared him for these whoppers.

Nor had it Jess. Her mouth hung open in disbelief and he could see a red flush creeping up her neck.

"Go ahead, Pete, what happened?"

"Jeremiah, me, an' Josh was jawin' at the foot o' the stairs. Miz Foltry came down, yellin' like a banshee. Well, I knowed right off the woman had fallen off her rocker. Had a wild look about her. Spooked me real good." Morgan shifted in the seat and wiped spittle from his mouth.

"What next?" Langtree prodded.

"She grabbed Jeremiah's forty-five afore he knowed what was happenin'. Then she shot him point-blank in the chest. Well, I tried to wrestle the weapon out o' her hand and she shot me too. Only thing I saw after that was a flash o' her sweet little ankles as she ran out the door."

Langtree wore a cat-that-ate-the-canary expression as he took his place at the prosecuting table. Duel had never known such anger, not even at the Good Lord when He took his Annie. This was like a boiling cauldron, consuming his every thought.

If the sheriff hadn't confiscated his six-shooter at the door, he'd surely have shot Morgan and Langtree and anyone else who cared to try to stop him. In all the years he bounty-hunted he had never taken pleasure in killing a man, but he would these two jackals.

Tom Parker stalked up and down in front of Morgan for a

long minute before he stopped and stared at him. The crowd became eerily quiet.

"In your opinion, Mr. Morgan, my client is loony. You arrive at this professional deduction because you're medically qualified?"

"I seen plenty o' cows 'n horses with the walleye," Morgan blustered. "I know a crazy woman when I see one, an' that woman is sure 'nuff crazy."

"You stated Jeremiah Foltry never laid a hand toward his wife. Mr. Morgan, how do you account for her broken bones, bruises, and assorted other maladies?"

"Clumsy. Pure an' simple. The woman was always fallin' an' hurtin' herself."

"What were you doing at the ranch that night, Morgan? Isn't it true Jeremiah Foltry told you and Evers that he was giving you Miss Jessie because she'd outlived her usefulness to him? Isn't that true? Remember, you took an oath to tell the truth."

"Well, part of it might be."

"Which part?"

"Jeremiah was tired o' her. Weren't no use to a fam'ly man. Couldn't begat him a brat. Not sayin' he ever was of a mind to want one. Don' know nuthin' about that. Firsthand, I know he had to keep 'er locked up or she'd run off. Josh 'n me, we earned the right to give her a poke after ever'thing we did fer him."

"What services did you render for Foltry?"

"You know. Things to keep folks in line, including his wife, an' making 'em pay when they stepped over."

"You punished Miss Jessie when she tried to leave?"

Morgan gave Tom Parker a belligerent stare. "Didn't break no laws. Only did what Jeremiah told us. That woman's still alive, ain't she? An' Jeremiah's cold in the ground."

"What sort of things did he ask you to do?"

"Scaring people mostly. Said once that a healthy dose o' fear is all the weapon a man needs." Morgan sneered and wiped his mouth again with the back of his hand.

"So, Jeremiah was tired of his wife, considered her a hindrance. Yet he bore the blame for her condition. Seems to me he meant to be shed of her one way or another. Either by killing her or giving her to you and Evers to share."

"I ain't sayin' he did nothin' wrong."

"You don't have to, Mr. Morgan. The facts speak for themselves. I'd say Miss Jessie is more sane than the lot of you."

Parker started back to his seat, apparently finished with Morgan. He stopped, pulled a watch from a fob pocket by the gold chain, and turned to Judge Warner. "The noon hour is approaching, Your Honor. I propose we adjourn for lunch."

"I'm going to overlook your high-handed ways, Mr. Parker. I'm the judge in this here court and don't you forget it."

Tom's smile could've melted butter. "My apologies, Judge."

"Court's adjourned till one o'clock. Sheriff, take the defendant back to the jail." The gavel signaled an end.

Duel, along with his family, Jessie's mother, and Yellow Dog, paraded after Sheriff Daniels with his charge. As soon as the jail door closed behind them, he handed Two Bit to Walt and pulled Jess against him. The fact that he could make the pulse throb in the hollow of her throat gave him immense satisfaction.

"Would that I could spare you this humiliation. I'd take your place in a heartbeat."

"I know." Her body trembled in his arms.

"I'd like to get my hands on that lying sack of manure," Vicky interrupted. "Tryin' to make people believe you're crazy. I just wish I had as much gumption as you, Jessie. When I think of all those years in that man's—"

"Honey, why don't you an' me take a walk to that hotel I saw down the street an' get some food to bring back to these folks," Roy broke in when his wife paused for air.

Jessie turned with gratitude. "Thank you for coming all this way, Vicky. You and Roy don't know what your support means to me. And Walt." She kissed Pop's cheek. "I love you like my own father."

"Do me a favor, Jessie girl. Can you call me Pop?" The

McClain patriarch shot Phoebe a quick glance. "That is, if it meets with your approval, lovely madam."

"Don't know why it wouldn't." Phoebe smoothed her hair into the severe bun at the nape of her neck and smiled.

Why indeed. Duel caught the flash of interest between the pair. Jessie's mother just might be the thing Pop needed. Maybe? The man had to be lonely since his Lily of the Valley passed on. Walt'd used that endearment for Duel's mother as long as he could remember.

"All right, Pop." Jessie gave Walt a sweet smile that told Duel how pleased his father's request had made her.

He liked the sound of the word on her tongue.

"Shoot, we couldn't let you go through this horrible trial without family by your side. So we got Gladys Stanton to stay with the children and we came lickety-split."

"Come on, Vicky. Food, remember?" Roy prodded her toward the door.

"G'anpa. Boobie?" Marley scooted down. Then, taking Walt's hand, she pulled him toward her favorite playmate. "Boobie."

"Hold up there, little angel. I'm comin'."

The clickety-clack of a cane on the sidewalk outside came seconds before Tom Parker pushed his way inside. Duel quickly pulled him apart from the others.

"Tom, how are our chances?"

"Too early to tell. Truth be known I'm a little concerned about the jury. A trifle too passive, if you ask me. Can't tell what they're thinking. Could go either way."

"Do you think they believed Morgan?"

"Be fools if they did. Son, we're not done yet. I just hope Miss Jessie can hold up."

Duel followed Tom's gaze. Jessie stared out into space, completely unaware of the commotion around her, lost in her own inner turmoil.

Doc Willoughby's testimony sounded in his ears. *"Saw where someone had repeatedly jabbed a sharp instrument into her womb, rendering her unable to ever bear children."*

Horror washed over him now as it had earlier. He thought back to when she rode into his camp all bloody and afraid. Recalled how she shrank from his touch, wincing as if he'd struck her. They'd traveled a far piece from that. Now she flourished under his attention.

"Don't worry about Jess. She's made of pretty strong stuff. Has to be or she'd not have survived that hell."

"The lady's made an impression on me. I'll do everything I can to see she goes free. Nothing short of that will do."

"Jess is something, all right. Mrs. Sutton wants to tell what she knows about Foltry."

"That's good. I hadn't decided whether to put her up there or not."

"One thing more. When you questioned Doc Willoughby, why didn't you ask him about the Diamond J brand on Jessie's shoulder?"

Shock rippled across Tom's features.

Chapter Thirty-four

Tom called Phoebe as his first witness when it came his turn. The woman's voice shook and she dabbed her eyes with a serviceable handkerchief.

"My girl is not mad, nor has she ever shown any sign to be. She grew up with a respect for all livin' creatures. But she changed when she married Jeremiah Foltry."

"Changed how, Mrs. Sutton?"

"For one thing, Mr. Sutton and I didn't see her much. When we did, I noticed she never smiled anymore an' she never came around us what she weren't covered with bruises. Jessie had a sadness deep inside her that seemed to eat at her soul. I knew something bad was wrong. We'd always been so close." A pitiful sob escaped from Phoebe. She buried her face in the kerchief, unable to continue.

Jessie ached for her mother. She shouldn't have put her through this. The blame sat squarely on her own shoulders. It was no way for a daughter to repay the woman who'd brought her into the world.

"I'm sorry, Mrs. Sutton. This is terribly hard on you."

"I raised my girl in the faith an' she wouldn't have shot the man less'n he durn sure deserved it."

Parker walked toward his seat, then he whirled. "One more thing. You received a note from Miss Jessie, didn't you?"

"About a year ago, I reckon. It said for us not to worry if she didn't see us for awhile, but that ever'thing was fine."

"You knew 'everything' wasn't fine, didn't you?"

"Mr. Sutton and I knew Jessie lived in a terrible situation and there weren't a blasted thing we could do about it. That's what killed my Zack—a broken heart."

"Thank you, Mrs. Sutton." Tom turned to the judge. "I call Mrs. Jessie Foltry McClain to the stand."

Oh, no. She couldn't get up there. She couldn't sit in that chair facing all these people and tell them what Jeremiah did to her and what she did back. Jessie shook her head vehemently.

"Please," she whispered.

"Come, Miss Jessie." Mr. Parker gently took her arm.

Moving against her will, she let the man lead her to the ill-fated seat at the front of the room. Her legs gave way and she collapsed into it.

"Do you swear to tell the truth, the whole truth so help you God?"

Her hand shook where it lay on the Bible.

She didn't know if the word would come out or if it would stick in her throat. She opened her mouth.

"Yes," she managed with downcast eyes.

"I know this is very painful for you and I'm indeed sorry." Tom Parker took her hand in his and it gave her strength. "How long were you married to Jeremiah Gates Foltry?"

"Eight years, give or take a few months."

"Do you suffer from fits of insanity as Morgan claims?"

"I'm very sure I have my right mind, Mr. Parker."

"Now that we've got that cleared up, did Jeremiah ever have occasion to strike you?"

"Yes."

"Break your bones?"

"Yes." *Dear God, did she have to relive every detail?*

"Burn you?"

Jessie could only nod her head. These were things she'd spent the last eight months trying to forget.

"Tell the court what kind of man Jeremiah was."

"He threw terrible temper fits. He did things, awful things. Seems the more he hurt people and animals, the more pleasure he took from it."

"What did you do to bring on this kind of rage?"

A life free of Jeremiah had been all she'd ever wanted and it was that very thing that made him so angry.

"I tried to run away." The words came softly, pulled from her mouth by an unseen hand.

"How many times?"

"I lost count after fifteen. It became like a game to him. He'd leave a way open to me on purpose, then get Morgan and Evers to chase me down and bring me back."

"We heard testimony that you conceived a child. Was Jeremiah the babe's father?"

"Yes!" The answer exploded before she could stop it.

"But he denied it?"

"Although he never had reason to think otherwise, he claimed the child wasn't by him. I swear on the Holy Bible that I never laid with any other man until I married Duel McClain."

"So he viciously killed it."

"Jeremiah said even if it was, he didn't want his seed growing in my body. Said I wasn't fit. He kicked my belly, then slammed my head against the floor. When I came to I was alone. I couldn't get up. The pain in my stomach made it impossible." She wiped her eyes, trying to rid her head of the memories, trying to stop the quiver in her voice.

"Blood soaked my dress and the floor. A broken broom handle lay beside me. I knew he'd violated me with the jagged end because blood stained it also." There, she'd told the part she hadn't even shared with her tall Texan. The slate was clean.

She twisted the plain gold wedding band Duel had placed on her finger. Now he knew how broken she was. For a moment she wondered if he'd have given her the treasured gift if he'd known everything.

"Your Honor, I have a highly unusual request. I'd like to ask Miss Jessie to turn around and slip her bodice off her left shoulder."

"I object, Your Honor!" Langtree bounded from his chair, his buck teeth seeming to pop from his mouth. "This ain't a bawdy house. What are you tryin' to pull, Parker? Big city lawyer come in here an' try to push your way around, treat us like yokels."

Tom Parker ignored the flustered opposing counsel. "I beg the court's indulgence, Your Honor. I seek to prove the depth of Jeremiah Foltry's degradation. I have the right to prove my client suffered undue provocation and that she was entirely justified in the steps she took to protect her life. This is substantiated by the callous murder of his own child."

Judge Warner leaned forward, a frown on his face. "You're not trying to give this court a song and dance, are you, Mr. Parker? I wouldn't take kindly to such behavior."

"I assure you, Your Honor, I have only pure intentions. I feel it's in the best interests of my client. After all, she's on trial for her life. She's entitled to show all the facts."

"Surely you ain't gonna buy that hogwash, Judge." Langtree became extremely agitated. "It's not gonna work, Parker."

Jessie felt the sting of mortification. Undress in front of this crowd of people to show the world her mark of shame? How did he even know about it? Duel was the only person she'd told. Silently she begged the judge to refuse.

"I'm going to allow you some leeway, Mr. Parker. But, I'm warning you. This better not be your attempt to dramatize these proceedings or I'll see you disbarred."

"Thank you, Your Honor." He turned back to Jessie. "I realize you loathe doing this thing I ask, but please know I wouldn't request it if there were any other way."

Under Tom Parker's sympathetic touch, Jessie turned her back to everyone. The buttons stubbornly refused to go through the holes as she became all thumbs.

"Please don't make me do this," she whispered, deeply humiliated. "Please."

"I wish there was another way, Miss Jessie. I truly do."

Finally the buttons came free and she draped the layers of material, chemise and all, baring her left shoulder.

"Oh, my God!" slipped from Tom Parker's mouth.

Audible cries of anguish sped rampant through the saloon. The shame she bore lay open for all eyes. Her cheeks stung. Breaking, she hid her face in her hands.

As the shock died, absolute quiet took its place. The only sound was Tom Parker clearing his throat of some mysterious obstruction. Jessie's furtive glance found him wiping his eyes.

His soft words had great effect. "People of this court, ladies and gentlemen, I offer the most damaging proof of Jeremiah Foltry's fury. Sickening though it is, I believe words alone could not do the horrible deed justice. Branded like an animal so no one would doubt that she was his property. I ask you, is this fair and just treatment of a husband against his wife?"

Gently, Parker tugged the fabric up to once again hide the monstrous Diamond J. Jessie made herself decent. When she turned around she was surprised to see Duel.

He held forth his arms. Mindless of the people who watched, she fell into his embrace and the comfort he offered.

This Texan was her shelter, her savior, her love for all time.

"Hush, darlin', I'm right here beside you." He held her trembling body tight.

"Mister McClain, this is not allowed. You can't—"

"The hell I can't, Judge. This woman's my wife. I mean to be by her side through the rest of these here doin's. I have an obligation." His tone brooked no dispute. The jut of his jaw underlined his determination.

"Son, take the empty chair at my table." Tom Parker tried

to soothe the savage beast in his former son-in-law. "I have a few more questions, then she can sit beside you."

Jessie felt cold and alone when Duel released his hold and stalked to Mister Parker's table. She knew he didn't like it, but he respected Tom Parker.

"Now, Miss Jessie, how did you get the brand?"

"I tried to run away. Morgan and Evers caught me. When we got back to the ranch, they held me down while Jeremiah seared me with the hot brand. He did it to remind me what would happen if I continued to try to escape."

"One more thing and we'll be finished, my dear." She liked the genuine fondness in his tone, trusted the flicker of faith she saw in his eyes. "What happened the night Jeremiah died?"

"He told me that I was worthless. He didn't want me anymore so he was giving me to Morgan and Evers to use as they wished. He struck me across the face several times, then pushed me toward them." She tried to still the quiver in her voice, struggled to hold up her head with pride. She almost succeeded. "He treated me like a discarded piece of meat. I wasn't going to let him hurt me anymore. Not Jeremiah. Not anyone."

"You became enraged?" Parker probed the old wound.

"I knew if I didn't do something, one of the three of them would kill me before the night was over." She took a deep breath. "I grabbed Jeremiah's pistol from his holster. I aimed it at his chest and I pulled the trigger. I don't remember much else until I rode into Duel McClain's camp."

Silence met the end of her testimony. Langtree sat unmoving. In light of the overwhelming evidence, he waived asking her any questions, for which Jessie was supremely grateful.

"Thank you, madam." Then, Tom Parker took her hand and helped her back to her seat beside Duel.

"Mr. Langtree, do you have anything to say as we conclude this trial?"

"Yes, Judge. Despite the sympathy of this court, Jessie Foltry did willfully murder her husband. The law states that murder is murder no matter the circumstances and she should be punished to the full extent of such law."

"Mr. Parker, any argument?"

"Judge, gentlemen of the jury, the first amendment of the Constitution of the United States gives everyone the inalienable right to life, liberty, and the pursuit of happiness. It doesn't say everyone but Jessie Foltry McClain. It says every citizen has the right to keep their own life and to be free of oppression. Jeremiah Foltry tried to take that from her. He meant to do so once he'd totally destroyed her body and soul."

Parker turned to his client and pointed. "But though he did torture and maim her body, Jeremiah Foltry could not destroy his wife's spirit. That was one thing he could not touch and it filled him with horrible rage. No matter what punishment he devised, she continued to seek escape.

"Miss Jessie hated the taking of his life. It went against everything inside her. However, to save herself, she did what any man or woman here would've done. She has to live with her actions, which is punishment enough. I leave it in your hands. God have mercy on your souls."

"It'll be over soon, sweetheart." Duel placed his arm protectively around her shoulders.

"Jury members, proceed into the next room and decide the guilt or innocence of Mrs. Foltry." The gavel soundly struck the table.

Through a misty blur Jessie watched the somber-eyed men file out the door. They held her life in their hands. From the expression on their faces they appeared to have already decided her fate. None glanced in her direction and the steely coldness emanating from them chilled her.

"They reached a decision before they even left the room." She clutched Duel's hand. "Remember your promise to leave and take Marley Rose. Remember?"

"Jess, don't give up now." He caressed her cheek with a knuckle. She leaned against his strength. "They'll do the right thing. What do you think, Tom?"

"Unless I miss my guess, Miss Jessie, you'll soon have your name cleared. You did real good." The man laid his big hand on her shoulder. "You make me mighty proud."

"Amen to that, Tom," Luke added, deeply moved.

The entire McClain clan stood protectively around, shielding her from the town's misguided cruelty. Holding Marley, Phoebe entered the circle they enlarged to accommodate her.

Thickness blocked her ability to speak. For all those years she'd stood alone with no one to lean on. Now generosity and love surrounded her. Indeed she'd been blessed.

Suddenly the jury was filing back into the room.

"Oh, no, Duel. They can't have decided this quick, they just left a few minutes ago."

She'd known the men had made up their minds before they went behind closed doors. It could mean only one thing.

Chapter Thirty-five

Jessie's fear rose in stifling waves. "Mr. Parker?"

The man patted her hand. "Now don't get in a stew. It doesn't necessarily mean anything bad."

She stared at the twelve men, most of whom wouldn't meet her gaze. One man did however, and she wondered at his black eye. Couldn't remember it being there before. Had they fought?

Judge Warner turned to the head juror. "Have you reached a verdict?"

"We have, Your Honor."

"What say you?"

"If it please this court, by a unanimous decision, we think the defendant has been punished enough by Jeremiah Foltry. Not guilty, Your Honor."

"What?" In his agitation, Langtree sprayed everyone who was near.

Jessie couldn't believe she'd heard right. Had they truly given her freedom?

With a whoop and a holler, Duel lifted her up and spun

around in a circle. Walt hugged Phoebe while Vicky, Roy, and Luke grinned from ear to ear.

Judge Warner's gavel quieted their celebration. "Order in this court!"

Shaking with excitement, Jessie sank to her chair. Duel stood behind with his hands never leaving her.

"The jury has declared you free, Mrs. Foltry. May I say in all my years as a judge that I have never heard the equal of abuse such as you portrayed. It shook my faith in humanity. Let us all hope we have learned something today. You may go, and may peace be with you."

"You ready to go home, Mrs. McClain?" Duel turned to his love, his shining light.

"Papa, home? Cheeba?" Two Bit spoke up from Jessie's lap. Her Boobie perched like a sentinel by the child's side.

They sat in a handsome surrey he'd purchased for the trip back to Tranquility. The fringed top shaded them from the hot Texas sun.

"You weren't exactly the McClain lady I meant, but yes, darlin', we're going home."

The girl twisted to see the seat behind, pointing as she chanted. "G'anpa, G'anma, G'anpa. Mine."

Musical laughter bubbling from his Jess's mouth topped the happiness inside. As he'd known earlier, his cup indeed overflowed.

They'd talked Phoebe into moving to Tranquility with them. And Tom Parker? The man had tied his horse to the back of the surrey beside Preacher and announced he'd tag along for the ride.

Now, Phoebe sat between Tom and Walt, proud as could be with the two gentlemen's attentions. As different and mismatched as they each were, they were still family. All brought together by one little runt of a girl.

"Duel, are you ready to make it official?"

Jessie's question caught him off guard. Engrossed in his thoughts, he'd lost the thread of the conversation.

"What's that, Jess?"

"Will you truly make Marley Rose a McClain?"

"Son," Tom joined from behind. "I've been meaning to bring up that very thing. You need to have the child's name changed soon to protect you from someone taking her away. I can handle the paperwork if you'd like."

Two Bit a McClain? Yeah, he liked the sound of that. And the way Jessie beamed at him, blinding him with her beauty.

"Marley Rose McClain. Has a ring to it. We'll do it."

"Thank you."

He felt as though she'd dropped a sack full of gold in his lap. Getting ready to go home had taken a few days. He and Jess had used the time to renew their wedding vows. They'd completed one vow a night while they lay in each other's arms. So far they'd gotten through love and honor, but hadn't quite made it to obey yet. Somehow passion always overtook them before they reached that vow. Darn it. He had a feeling that one would never be within his grasp.

The glance he cast his beloved's way spoke of all that was in his heart. His auburn-haired wife read the message and sent back a similar one of her own. No dots and dashes, just love. They were going home.

"Wagons, ho!" He raised his arm and let it drop to the northeast, signaling Roy and Vicky to follow in their wagon.

The smell of lumber and paint wafted in the breeze. Duel leaned against the pitchfork he'd used to put a fresh bed of hay in Preacher's stall. He stood in the doorway of the barn looking over the newly constructed addition to the farmhouse and the separate dwelling for Pop that sat a little apart.

Thanks to Tom Parker's generosity before he departed for Austin, they had added three extra rooms and a large porch to accommodate the family's expansion.

"Want my grandchildren to have room to grow," Tom had explained. "And a place for me to stay when I visit, which I plan on doing very often."

In the space between the two dwellings, Jess had planted

a winter garden. Turnip tops, onions, and hardy squash plants added greenery to the black soil. Jess showed potential for growing things.

His gaze found Phoebe dozing in the rocking chair on the shaded porch. He couldn't help the grin that made itself at home. Jessie's mother had settled right in as if she'd always been there, and she seemed to spend a powerful heap o' time at Pop's little cabin. Wouldn't surprise him if wedding bells didn't chime in the air soon.

"Papa, look." Four children, all stair steps, chased Marley's Cheeba, trying to wrestle the goat down to put a rope around her neck.

Yellow Dog, who refused to answer to anything other than Boobie, danced under their feet, yipping as if this was his last day on earth and he had to make sure he filled it to the brim.

Funny thing. For a man who'd been so dead set against changing his ways, his life had taken amazing turns. Two sons, two daughters, and a wife who thought he could lasso the moon—how lucky could a man get?

He knew there was a part of Jessie that ached for a child of her own, though it could never be. Sometimes in church he caught her staring at someone's new babe and it brought a lump to his throat. He'd spent many nights convincing her that it didn't matter to him. And he planned on doing a heck of a lot more. But the pain went mighty deep. It would take a powerful amount of loving to completely heal his wife.

Suddenly he had a profound thought. Perhaps Annie'd had to die so he could rescue Jessie. Perhaps things played out the way they were meant to, and nothing could've changed them. His chest tightened. Perhaps he needed Jess and the children as much as they needed him.

In that instant he found the total peace that he'd fought tooth and nail against. He accepted the fact that a man can't always protect the ones he loves. He had to have faith and do the best he could. Jess'd taught him that.

A wagon turned off the road. He breathed easy. His Jess had returned from her errands in town.

"Whoa, there." She pulled the team he'd bought in El Paso to a stop in front of the barn.

Late afternoon sunlight bouncing off her hair made it shimmer. A contented smile graced her kissable lips. His breath got stuck somewhere between his lungs and his mouth. She was a beauty.

A king surveying his kingdom couldn't have been happier than he was at that moment. A queen, heirs galore, a castle, a plot of land, it couldn't get much better.

Jess climbed from the seat, then reached into the back and lifted a picnic basket. A picnic at this time of day? It'd be dark in a little more than an hour.

"Need some help, darlin'?" He wondered why his voice had turned so husky. Always seemed to when she was near.

"No, I've got it."

The way she carried the basket made him wonder if it was filled with eggs. He eyed her as she gingerly set it on a barrel. Then she came into his embrace, fitting snugly in the circle. She put her arms around his neck.

"I need a kiss, dirt farmer. Know where I could find a man who'd oblige a lady?"

"Reckon you're looking at him, ma'am. I do a lot more than oblige. I guarantee complete satisfaction."

"I do declare."

She tilted her head, welcoming his mouth. He did oblige.

"Duel," she murmured beneath his lips.

Moments later, she drew back, her blue eyes staring into his. "Do you think we can fit one more?"

"One more what? What're you talking about, Jess?"

She grabbed his hand, pulled him to the picnic basket, and opened the lid carefully. A baby no bigger than a minute lay sleeping on a soft blanket.

"One more child."

"Aunt Bessie's garter!" The surprise had him at a loss. "You leave for a few hours and come lugging another babe home. Jesus, Jess. Don't tell me you found it sitting at the side of the road."

"No, silly. Doc Mabry delivered her yesterday but he lost her mother, a young, scared girl who had no one. Doc did what he could, but she died anyway. And now this wee one needs a family. Can we keep her, Duel?"

The flush on her face, the sparkle in those eyes drove a hard bargain. She didn't know it yet, but he'd never be able to deny her anything. His heart and soul was in her hands.

Tenderly, he touched the babe's downy soft cheek.

"Suppose one more won't make much difference. What are you thinkin' of naming the little thing?"

"How about Lily?"

Her suggestion they name the girl after his mother made his chest swell. Perfect. Pop would have another Lily of the Valley and they'd have another daughter to love and care for.

"Good choice, darlin'." As an afterthought, he added, "From now on, would you at least warn me when we're adding to our family? Don't know if we can take in all the unwanted leftovers in the world."

"Oh, I don't know." She lifted the tiny bundle and hugged her to her breast. "I figure we can stop after ten."

Duel rolled his eyes.

Reckless Embrace

MADELINE BAKER

Some folks say they are just two kids who should never have met—a girl from the wrong side of town and a half-breed determined to make his mark on the world. Their families fought on opposite sides at the Little Big Horn; there can be no future for them.

But when Black Owl looks at Joey, he sees the most beautiful girl in the world. And when she presses her lips to his, she is finding her way home. In each other's arms, they find a safe haven from a world where hatred and ugliness can only be conquered by the deep, abiding power of courageous love.

[illegible]
P.O. Box 6640 ___5080-3
Wayne, PA 19087-8640 **$6.99 US/$8.99 CAN**

Please add $2.50 for shipping and handling for the first book and $.75 for each additional book. NY and PA residents, add appropriate sales tax. No cash, stamps, or CODs. Canadian orders require $5.00 for shipping and handling and must be paid in U.S. dollars. Prices and availability subject to change. **Payment must accompany all orders.**

Name: ____________________

Address: ____________________

City: ____________ State: ________ Zip: ________

E-mail: ____________________

I have enclosed $________ in payment for the checked book(s).

For more information on these books, check out our website at www.dorchesterpub.com.

____ *Please send me a free catalog.*

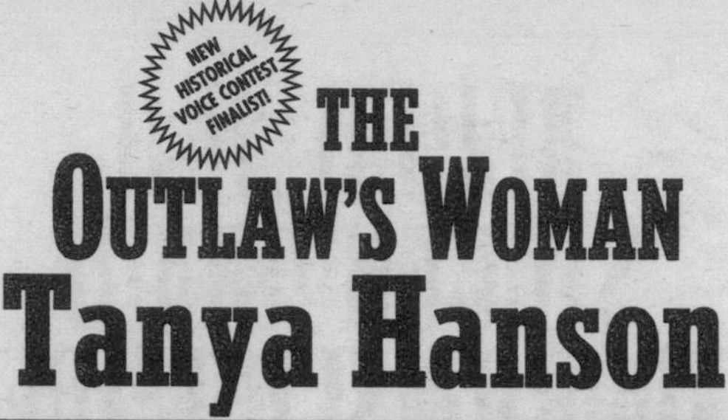

Dena Clayter carries a secret. In the midst of a blizzard, the young widow harbored an outlaw. She fed and nursed the injured fugitive, frightened not of the man but of the longings he incited. She yearned for his touch, the comfort of his arms, his lips against hers, and their passion flared hot enough to burn away all her inhibitions.

Now Dena is racing across the West to try to save him from the hangman's noose. For more than just his life hangs in the balance—Dena's own future and that of their baby stands in jeopardy. And the expectant mother has to know if a bond conceived in winter darkness will be revealed as love in the light of spring.

Dorchester Publishing Co., Inc.
P.O. Box 6640 __5106-0
Wayne, PA 19087-8640 $5.99 US/$7.99 CAN

Please add $2.50 for shipping and handling for the first book and $.75 for each additional book. NY and PA residents, add appropriate sales tax. No cash, stamps, or CODs. Canadian orders require $5.00 for shipping and handling and must be paid in U.S. dollars. Prices and availability subject to change. **Payment must accompany all orders.**

Name: ______________________________

Address: ______________________________

City: ______________ State: ________ Zip: ________

E-mail: ______________________________

I have enclosed $__________ in payment for the checked book(s).

For more information on these books, check out our website at www.dorchesterpub.com.

____ Please send me a free catalog.

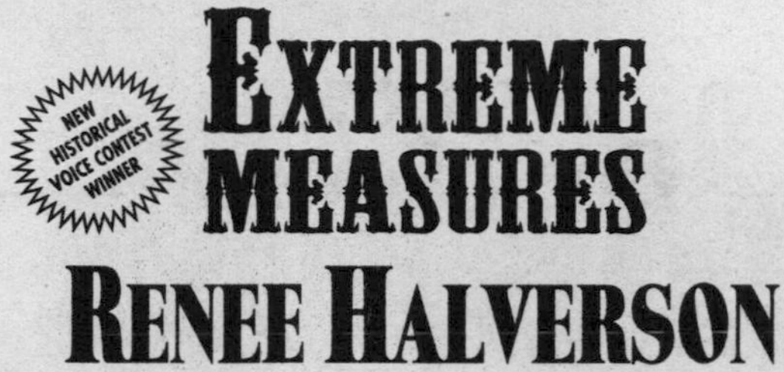

RENEE HALVERSON

If André DuBois were a betting man, he would lay odds that the woman in red is robbing his dealers blind. He can tell the beauty's smile disguises a quick mind and even quicker fingers. To catch her in the act, he deals himself into the game, never guessing he might lose his heart in the process.

Faith O'Malley depends on her wits to succeed at cards, and experience tells her the ante has just been raised. The new gambler's good looks are distracting enough, but his intelligent eyes promise trouble. Still, Faith will risk everything—her reputation, her virtue—to save the innocent people depending on her. It won't be until later that she'll stop to learn what she's won.

Dorchester Publishing Co., Inc.
P.O. Box 6640 __5062-5
Wayne, PA 19087-8640 $5.99 US/$7.99 CAN

Please add $2.50 for shipping and handling for the first book and $.75 for each additional book. NY and PA residents, add appropriate sales tax. No cash, stamps, or CODs. Canadian orders require $5.00 for shipping and handling and must be paid in U.S. dollars. Prices and availability subject to change. **Payment must accompany all orders.**

Name: ____

Address: ____

City: ____________________ State: __________ Zip: ____________

E-mail: ____

I have enclosed $__________ in payment for the checked book(s).

For more information on these books, check out our website at www.dorchesterpub.com.

____ *Please send me a free catalog.*

ATTENTION BOOK LOVERS!

Can't get enough of your favorite **ROMANCE**?

Call **1-800-481-9191** to:

* order books,
* receive a **FREE** catalog,
* join our book clubs to **SAVE 20%!**

Open Mon.-Fri. 10 AM-9 PM EST

Visit **www.dorchesterpub.com**
for special offers and inside
information on the authors you love.

We accept Visa, MasterCard or Discover®